RED DRAGON

RED DRAGON

E.A. STARK

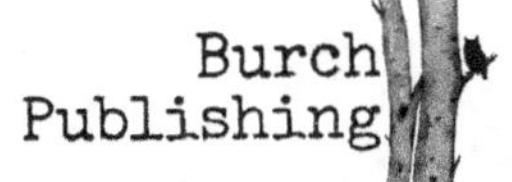

COPYRIGHT

DEDICATION

For Abi, Burton, and Shane, and all the lives that have crossed their paths.

May their journey remind us that every step we take is part of a greater design.

Love, loss, chance meetings, and inexplicable turns are never random.

They are the threads that weave us into who we are meant to become.

Fate is not always kind, nor is it always clear.

But it has a way of leading us exactly where we belong.

RED DRAGON

THE ABI ACARDI SERIES

THE
ABI ACARDI
SERIES

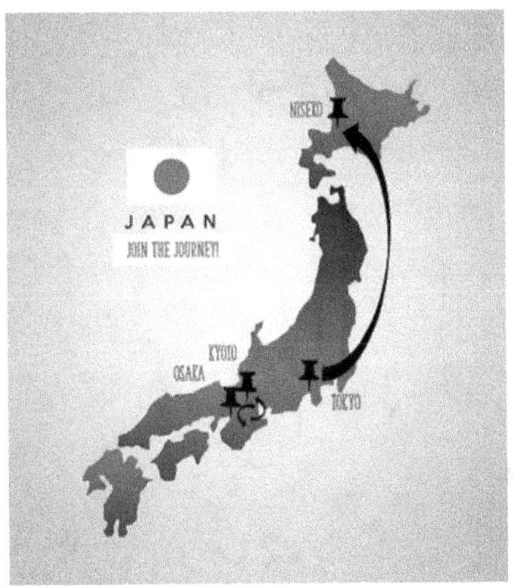

THIS BOOK IS MORE THAN A STORY—IT'S A JOURNEY.

Close your eyes for a moment and imagine the neon lights of Tokyo glowing against the night sky, the quiet beauty of Kyoto's ancient temples, the lively streets of Osaka filled with the scent of sizzling takoyaki, and the snow-covered peaks of Niseko whispering adventure.

Now, open your maps. At the start of every chapter, you'll find a location. Type it into Google Maps, switch to Street View, and journey down the same paths as Abi Acardi.

See what she sees. Feel the pulse of the cities. Discover the hidden gems tucked between modern skyscrapers and centuries-old shrines. From bustling train stations to narrow alleyways, secret gardens to glowing cityscapes—let Japan unfold before you. Follow Abi's footsteps, and who knows?

Maybe one day, you will find yourself standing in the very places she once did.

PROLOGUE

They waited in the shadows for it to arrive. An anonymous link—no name, no trace. Just a message on screens illuminated in the darkness.

IF YOU ARE WORTHY... YOU WILL FOLLOW.

Across Japan, these words sparked a fire in some. In high-rises and alley dens, cafés, and park benches, they leaned forward, caught by the pull of something they didn't fully understand. But the draw of acceptance was alluring.

Then came the voice. Distorted. Haunting. Laced with authority.

"You are here to serve my wishes."

There was no image. No face. Only the words—weaving directly into their minds.

"But you must compete for that honor."

The screen strobed black and white as a symbol ignited, bold and hypnotic. A Red Dragon flickered like neon.

"This is not a game. It is a test."

Challenged, some froze. Others grinned.

"The right to wear the mark is not given. It is earned."

They knew the rumors. A symbol seared into skin, whispered in secret. Proof of something few dared speak aloud.

"Many of you will fail..."

The screen shifted to concrete walls. Water, dripping into puddles on the floor. A single light bulb suspended over a blindfolded and bound figure sitting in a chair. Breath too quick, gasping, the jarring clip captured the terror for those watching. But before they could question it, the screen darkened and a shot rang out, followed by an eerie silence.

In red, the words misted across the screen.

THIS IS THE PRICE FOR FAILURE...

A map appeared. Kyoto, Osaka, and Tokyo were clearly marked. No explanation. No instructions. Just coordinates glowing with a list of tasks. Then, the final words:

THE HUNT BEGINS NOW.

| 1 |

Malibu House

Sitting at her desk, peering out over the ocean, Abi looked at the stack of unopened mail she'd brought with her. One in particular stood out from the rest. Afraid to open it, she slid it a few inches away, still not ready to know what direction her life would take.

"Come on, Abs. You said you'd open it on your Birthday. Today is the day. Stop procrastinating," she mumbled to herself. Getting up from the chair, she walked about the room with palms sweating. "Just open it. Everything will be fine."

Taking a seat again, she ripped open the corner edge and ran her finger down the seam. Tightly closing her eyes, she took out the paper inside and held it in front of her before unfolding the letter. With one eye creeping open, she read, "Dear Ms. Abigail Acardi, I am delighted to inform you that the Committee on Admissions has admitted you to the Class of 2029 under the Early Action Program. Please accept my personal congratulations on your outstanding achievements."

Heart pounding a mile a minute, Abi froze and found it hard to catch her breath as she slowly lowered the letter to the desk, her hands trembling.

"I actually got in..." she whispered, her voice breaking under the weight of disbelief and pride. Tears welled up and spilled over, painting her cheeks. Out the window, she marveled at the clouds in the sky. A small smile tugged at her lips as the magnitude of the moment washed over her. "I did it, Mom," she whispered. "I got into Harvard."

A commotion downstairs broke her away from the news. Standing to take one last peek in the mirror, Abi smiled, feeling a sense of accomplishment.

Happy to finally wear the stunning silver dress that had been hanging in her closet all this time, she loved how it elegantly hugged her body and accentuated every curve. Clasping her diamond bracelet around her wrist to match the necklace and earrings Burton had bought her, she was nervous for the evening to begin. Never having attended anything like this before, her hands slightly shook as she opened the door and left her room.

Descending the stairs, she found Burton escorting a man with a briefcase toward the front door.

"Thanks for your help on this, Brad. Appreciate it." Burton shook the man's hand.

"I'll be in touch when it gets done."

"Great."

The second the guy left, Burton closed the door behind him. He immediately gravitated to her as she walked in his direction.

"Who was that?" Abi asked as Burton could not stop staring.

"My lawyer."

"Everything okay?" she asked.

"All good." Not elaborating, he said with bright eyes, "Wow, you look beautiful."

"Thank you. It's my Mother's," she blushed, taking note of his designer suit. "You look pretty nice yourself."

"It's your special day. I had to dress for the celebration." He approached with open arms. Hugging her and kissing her forehead, he said, "Happy Birthday, Abs."

She beamed. "Thank you so much."

Scanning the main floor, she got her first glimpse of all the floral arrangements and the evergreen trees twinkling with pretty white lights to celebrate the holiday season.

"Do you like it?" He escorted her toward the living and dining rooms as Abi took it all in. "I thought flowers were the way to go."

In amazement, she replied, "It's so lovely." Captivated by the calming atmosphere, she quickly became immersed in the aromatic scent of roses and lilies. "I don't know what to say."

The festive seasonal greenery, embellished with an array of white flowers, featured pillar candles glistening inside glass cylinders along a silver runner. Abi walked down one side of the long table, feeling a mix of emotions.

Burton stood at the end of the dining table set for twenty guests. "You only turn eighteen once. We needed to do something big."

She sent a smile his way.

"How are you holding up, all things considered?" he asked.

"Doing my best to keep it together." She lowered her head. "It's the first Birthday without Mom. Guess there will be a lot of firsts like that this year..."

Admiring the matching china, hinting at how many courses there would be, the crystal sparkled in the light. Each place setting had a fancy napkin and a boxed bonbonniere for each guest.

Double-checking his lists, Martin rounded the corner with his iPad in hand. "Ah, Miss Abi! Happy Birthday, my dear. You look lovely."

"Thank you, Martin," she said as Burton stood by proudly.

The regal gentleman scanned the main floor as Rosa appeared to make a few last-minute adjustments to the table.

In seconds, the tiny woman's face lit up. "Happy Birthday, Miss Abi!" Excited, she offered open arms as Abi fell into them.

"Thank you so much."

As Rosa went about her duties, Martin turned. "So, Miss?" he asked, scanning the room. "Are we ready for your celebratory dinner this evening?"

"Absolutely. Everything looks wonderful. More than I could ever imagine."

"I am glad you like it. Turning eighteen is the beginning of adulthood. Hopefully, this evening will start you off on the right foot."

"I hope so, too," she gushed, her hands clasped together whimsically. "I've never had a party like this before."

Burton placed his hand on the small of her back. "Well, after everything that's happened the past couple of months, you deserve it."

Tearing up, she hugged him. "Thank you for everything you've done for me." Out of the corner of her eye, Abi spotted Sara descending the stairs. Quickly moving a safe distance from Burton, she stayed mindful of the girl's feelings.

Her actions did not go unnoticed.

Dressed formally in black, Sara joined in. "Happy Birthday," she said, thankful they'd somewhat made amends a few weeks back.

"Thank you," Abi replied with a smile. "Appreciate that very much."

Reaching out to her, Abi hugged the girl and watched Burton's reaction. He seemed relieved they were now getting along.

Stepping toward Martin, Burton whispered something in the man's ear.

"We'll be back in a moment," her famous friend announced as they walked into the office, leaving the girls behind.

To avoid a silence developing between them, Sara said, "The house looks so nice. They did a great job."

"Yes, it's beautiful."

"Are you excited for your friends to arrive?"

"Very much so. Not long now. Everyone should be here shortly."

Martin emerged from the office and thankfully walked back to them. "Excuse me, Miss Abi."

"Yes."

He corralled her with one arm. "Can you walk with me a moment?"

Unsure what was up, she replied, "Sure." Turning to Sara, she said respectfully, "Excuse me a second."

"No problem. I will go and see how Anton and Rosa are doing."

Curious as the two walked toward Burton's office, Sara stared at them, wondering what was happening.

Guiding the birthday girl to the glass pocket doors, the regal gentleman said, "Master B would like to have a word."

"Alright."

The man slid the pocket doors open.

Burton waved her inside. "Come in. I want to discuss something with you before your guests arrive."

Making sure they weren't disturbed, Martin closed the doors and stood watch with his back to them.

"Have a seat," B said, walking around the desk. Sitting on the edge of it, he rested his hands on his lap. "I know you've had a difficult few months and hope living with me has been, well, let's say, standable."

She tilted her head. "If it weren't for you fighting the court order, I would have had to return home and live with my Dad. I'm so grateful. I wouldn't have survived all of this without you."

"So..." Burton slid a box across the desk and placed it before her. "As of today, having turned eighteen, you can legally make your own decisions. With that said, I wanted to give you my gift. Please keep this just between us if that's okay."

Peering at the box, she loved the white, patterned paper and silver bow. "You didn't need to get me anything."

"Why's that?" he chuckled, getting up to sit on the edge of the desk close to her.

"Because you've given me so much already..." She lowered her head.

"Hey..." he said sympathetically, placing his hand on her shoulder. "I'm happy I was here to help you."

She nodded. "Well, you don't know how much this means."

Hoping to steer away from having a heavy conversation on such a happy occasion, he said, "So? Are you going to open it?"

Abi took the box and untied the pretty ribbon before lifting off the lid. Inside, she peeled back the tissue paper and found a leather book embossed with her initials. Taking it out, she opened it to find a page outlining the specifics of a bank account in her name.

Speechless, she tilted her head upward, hands shaking. "Burton, I... I can't accept this."

"Sure you can," he replied casually. "Let me explain why." He grabbed a bouquet of red roses in a crystal vase with a pretty ribbon wrapped around the stems. Holding it, he added, "While thinking about what to get you for your Birthday, I could have bought you something like a car, a Jacob and Co. watch, or a piece from Harry Winston, but knowing you, this is the more practical gift, believe it or not. See, as of September, you will be attending university. Because your Father has withdrawn financial support, I've given you this money so that you can attend the school of your choice without worrying about tuition, housing, and other living expenses. It is in trust, so Martin, as your legal guardian, will help you manage it until you turn twenty-one, even though I highly doubt you will need his assistance – but he is there if you need him." He did not elaborate on why they'd set it up this way.

"What about you? Can't I talk to you about it?"

"Of course you can," he said lightheartedly. "We can discuss it any time you'd like."

Standing, she smiled with arms open.

He did the same.

Hugging him, she said, "I don't know what to say. Thank you," and kissed him on the cheek.

Taken by surprise, his chin dropped for a moment, a subtle but telling gesture that softened the intensity of his presence. "These are for you, too. I thought they would brighten your room."

Flashing a smile, she said, "Aww… Thank you. That's so sweet. I love them."

With Martin still standing outside the office to ensure nobody was watching, namely Sara, he added, "There's one more thing I wish to discuss."

Concerned, Abi asked, "Okay. What is it?"

"Have you made any plans for the holidays yet?"

"No. Why?"

His arms crossed over his chest. "Well, as you know, Nightfall Inc. is rapidly expanding worldwide. Recently, I received an invitation from a DJ in Japan who goes by the name Red Dragon. Apparently, he was approached by a young movie star, Riko Hattori, who asked if he was familiar with me. Hattori is tasked with hosting the high-profile NAKKA Museum fundraiser and is also responsible for attracting younger audiences to the exhibits. He figured my presence would draw in the Gen Z crowd, so he had Red Dragon reach out. Beyond the museum event, the guy has invited me to make guest appearances, and he's eager to discuss integrating the Vault app into some of his clubs."

"Wow, that's great! Congratulations," she said, despite being disappointed he would not be around over the holidays.

He nodded humbly. "I'm going there for three weeks over Christmas and New Year's. If you don't have plans, I thought you could join me. We'd be starting in Kyoto and Osaka before moving on to Tokyo and then spending Christmas and New Year's in Niseko. Maybe go skiing? We haven't done that together in a while." He could see her mind reeling.

"Me, go to Japan?"

"I figured you might want to avoid the holidays this year. What better way than to be halfway around the globe?"

She thought about his offer. "Is Sara going too?"

"Yes, she will be part of my security on this trip. If you come along, I will bring Andrew, Ted, and Matt with us."

Seeing her flash a worried expression, Burton wondered what she was thinking. "Not interested?" he asked, hoping to clarify.

"Despite Sara and me getting along better now, I remain very careful of what I say and do. That way, I don't upset things between you."

Rounding the desk to sit in his chair, he said, "About that." He leaned back and crossed his arms over his chest. "Thanks for being supportive of her and me. I know it hasn't been easy."

"It's fine. I get where she's coming from. The last thing I want is for her to feel threatened by me. So, I am really trying to keep the peace." She looked into his eyes. "It's nice to see you happy."

He humbly nodded his head. "I am. Surprisingly."

"Well, I'm glad to hear that."

"Getting back to Japan, would it help if Shane came with? That way, we are both paired up. Perhaps it would balance things out."

Abi shrugged her shoulders. "I don't know if he'd go. He has his university announcement before Christmas. I think he needs to be here for that."

Hearing her resistance to the idea, he leaned forward. "No pressure. Think about it. Just ask him and see what he says."

"Okay. I will."

"And don't worry, if you decide to go, I will take you shopping this week, and we can grab anything you need for the trip."

A million thoughts rolled through her mind.

"On that note." Turning around, he presented her with a vase filled with white and pink roses. "These are from the guys, Anton, Rosa, and Martin. I guess we all had the same idea."

Standing, she bent to smell their heavenly scent. "That was so thoughtful. They're lovely. I'll have to go and thank them."

Sara unexpectedly peeked inside the office before Martin waved her off, causing an awkward silence between them.

Abi noticed it.

"Don't worry about her," he said, knowing he'd now have to do damage control. "How about I help you take these upstairs?"

"Thanks. It will save me from making two trips."

Taking the one vase, he said, "Your friends will be here soon. It's going to be a fun evening."

"I think so too. I'm so looking forward to it. My first adult dinner party."

"The first of many."

Seeing they were ready to depart, Martin slid the doors open.

"The flowers are so pretty, Martin." She hugged the gentleman. "Thank you."

"You are very welcome, my dear." He paused. "Would you like some help taking those to your room?"

Interjecting, B said, "No, it's fine. I'll help her."

"Very well, Sir."

Burton took the white rose vase with her gift box in hand and followed Abi up the stairs as she carried his red flowers. Having stopped along the way to thank the guys, Rosa and Anton, on the way past, she spotted Sara in the family room off the kitchen and realized Burton hadn't included her in the list of gift givers.

Glaring, the woman watched like a hawk as they moved up the staircase.

At the end of the hall, Abi made a right into her room and set the vase on her side table.

"Where would you like these?" he asked while setting the precious box on her desk.

"There is fine." Doing as she asked, he noticed the letter of acceptance from Harvard and smiled. About to address it and congratulate her, they heard the doorbell ring.

"They're here!" Abi said excitedly.

He placed the gift box on top of the letter. "Let the party begin," he said. "Shall we?" Offering her his arm to escort her downstairs, she clung to it and happily walked with him.

Back on the main level, they found Martin welcoming the servers and the bartender before showing the guy where he wanted him stationed that evening. Catching sight of the two returning, he prompted, "Miss Abi? May I have one more moment of your time?"

She checked with Burton.

"You go ahead. I'm just going to check on Sara."

Abi watched as he walked towards his girlfriend. She was happy to have him back.

Meeting with her temporary guardian, she hugged him. "Thank you again for the flowers."

He joyfully said, "I am glad you like them. Just a short note on the other, umm, gift," he cleared his throat, "That was all, Master B. I am just helping to facilitate it. He didn't want you to worry about finances, especially when deciding which school to attend."

"It was quite generous of him."

"I hear you've applied to some very reputable institutions."

"Yes, I certainly did. Yale, Columbia, Harvard, Princeton, UCLA, Boston College, USC, Stanford, and Alabama."

Realizing one school stood out, he asked, "Alabama, Miss?"

"Shane signed with them on December 4th. Roll Tide," she said less enthusiastically, knowing her final decision was no longer up in the air.

"A word of advice, if I may?"

Abi flashed a serious expression. "Yes, please."

"At this age, do not sway away from your hopes and dreams and follow someone else's because, in the end, you will regret not forging your own path."

She nodded, noticeably taking what he said to heart.

"If it is meant to be, Miss, no matter where you are, love will always find a way."

With a smile, she hugged him. "Thank you for the great Fatherly advice."

When she stepped back, he divulged, "If I were lucky enough to have a daughter, I would imagine she would have been a lot like you."

Eyes glistening, she dabbed a tear before it fell across her cheeks. "That means a lot."

The doorbell rang again.

"You're guests have arrived, dear. Ready?"

Excited, the two walked to the door. Martin opened it as Abi greeted Jade and Reggie.

"Hey, girl! Happy Birthday!" She rushed over with open arms and hugged her tightly. "You look amazing!"

"Thank you! So do you!"

While the girls had their moment, Reggie shook hands with Martin. "Hello, Sir."

"Hello, Mr. Wilson. Welcome."

Once Jade stepped aside, Reg got his turn to greet the birthday girl. "Happy Birthday, Abs!"

Hugging the big guy, she said, "Thank you. Come in!"

"This is for you, my friend." Jade passed her the iconic Hermès orange gift bag. "You're gonna love it," she said excitedly.

"Wow, Jade... What did you do?"

"Only the best for my best friend."

The doorbell blended with the sound of conversation spreading through the home.

Martin answered it.

Abi found Mei clinging to Adrian, and Ming standing with Ben in the doorway. In minutes, Allan, Allie, Laney, and Shawn followed.

Greeted by happy smiles and delightful squeals, Abi hugged everyone, stepping forward. "Did all of you come together?"

"Yes," Shawn answered. "It's a hike to come all the way out here, so I rented a lux coach for us."

"Best idea ever," Laney interrupted, dressed to kill in a little black dress and red-soled heels with a fashionable cape to keep warm. "The drive didn't even seem that bad. We were so busy talking." Handing Abi a beautifully wrapped gift, she said, "Hey! Happy Birthday!"

Having captured everyone's attention, Abi beamed. "Thank you so much for coming, you guys. I know it's far, but I really wanted to spend some time here. It's close to the ocean, and on occasions like this, it makes me miss Boston a little less."

"Anything for you," Allie stated as her eye caught a glimpse of all the decor. "Wow, look at this place."

"Yes, it's pretty nice," she said humbly. "Come on in. Make your-selves at home. The punch is at the bar, and we should be seated for dinner shortly."

Laney walked in and found Burton standing with Sara. Wondering if the guy was still angry at her for sharing his secret, she hoped they'd moved past that. With a deep breath in, expelling it slowly, she grabbed hold of Shawn's arm for support and walked in the DJ's di-rection.

"Hey, Burton."

He inclined his head in a sharp nod, his piercing gaze locking on them with quiet authority. "Laney," he said calmly as the girl air-kissed him on both sides. "Good to see you." Offering a hand to Shawn, he shook it. "Welcome, man."

"Thanks for inviting us." The tall, blonde, well-dressed heir looked around. "Killer house, dude."

"Thanks." Without skipping a beat, Burton said, "You remember my girlfriend, Sara?" Placing his hand on her back, he added, "Sara, this is Laney and Shawn."

Remembering them from the Vegas incident, she smiled. "Oh, yes. Good to see you again. At least it's under better circumstances this time."

"You've got that right," Laney replied, recalling the girl in the SWAT uniform.

Hearing the doorbell, Burton walked over and opened it, seeing that Abi was busy talking. Finding Shane there with a gift bag and a bouquet in hand, he greeted, "Hey, Coppersmith."

"How's it going, B? Good to see you."

"Likewise. Come on in." Burton stepped aside. "Nice jacket," he noted, spying the guy's slate blue blazer over a black shirt and pants.

"Thanks. It's a bit out of my norm, but it suits the occasion, I think." Right then, Shane's eyes drifted past Burton. Finding Abi, a smile spread across his face as she approached. "Hey, you."

"Hello, handsome."

"Wow, you look beautiful," he said with a sexy smirk.

"You're looking pretty good yourself."

Handing her the flowers, he was at a loss for words. "These are for you."

"Aww... Thank you."

"Happy Birthday." One arm sneaking around her waist, he kissed her casually. "Love the dress."

"You like it?" she said, twirling once around.

"Very much." He stood back slightly. "I wore this in honor of your Birthday. I know you love this shade of blue."

"It suits you."

"I thought so, too."

"Come on in. Everyone is here."

Burton walked over with Sara clinging to his arm. "Congratulations on the Championship win," he said as Abi latched onto her man.

The team captain smiled proudly. "Appreciate that. Looking forward to a little R & R now."

Having kept up on Shane's NCAA journey, he asked, "Have you decided where you're heading in the fall?"

Humble, he replied, "I've secretly committed to Alabama. From what I'm told, I'll be officially announcing it in a week or so. Until then, we need to keep that under wraps."

"Congratulations. Best of luck there. They've definitely produced a number of NFL players."

"It's been a tough decision, but I feel good about it."

Moving along to say hello to Reg and Jade, Abi felt Rosa tap her on the shoulder. "Excuse me, Miss."

Abi stopped.

"Would you like me to put those in a vase for you?"

"That would be great. Thank you so much, Rosa."

Handing her the bouquet, the tiny woman left and disappeared into the kitchen.

The doorbell rang again. Martin answered it and found Marco and his new girlfriend had arrived. Before the man could say anything, Shane quickly made his way over.

"Wasn't sure if this was the place," Marco said with a grin, offering the Captain a handshake and a shoulder bump.

"Glad you guys could make it," the QB replied warmly.

Motioning to the striking blonde by his side, Marco introduced her proudly. "Shane Coppersmith, meet Sadie Costa."

Shaking her hand, Shane said, "Nice to meet you, Sadie." Studying her face for a moment, he added, "Track and field, right?"

The pretty girl smiled. "Yes, that's right. Eight hundred and fifteen hundred meters."

"Impressive," Shane said just as Abi walked over.

"There's the guest of honor," Marco announced with enthusiasm. He handed Abi a card. "Happy Birthday!"

"Thanks, Marco," Abi said, genuinely happy to see them. "Come in and join the party."

With an air of pride, Marco gestured to the girl accompanying him. "This is my girlfriend, Sadie."

Abi offered her a warm smile, recognizing her from school. "So nice to meet you," she said, a touch surprised by Marco's polished manners.

"Thank you for inviting us," Sadie replied graciously. "You have a beautiful home."

Not wanting to elaborate on the dynamics of her living situation, Abi hesitated for a moment, then nodded with a polite, "Thank you."

As she and Marco moved into the lively celebration, Shane caught Abi's eye and raised a brow, noting Marco's notable charm.

She just shrugged with a small, knowing smile, letting the moment pass as the night carried on.

"So, how does it feel to be eighteen, anyway?" Shane asked Reggie on their way over. "I still don't get how you guys are older than me."

"Since my birthday lands in December, my Mom didn't put me in JK until the following year. I technically should have started school the September before, but she held me back," Abi explained.

Overhearing them, Jade chimed in. "Well, around here, that's the norm. Every affluent kid I know, their parents did the same."

"Apparently, my Dad didn't agree with holding me back, but my Mom stood firm on it. Ultimately, she won," Abi clarified.

Satisfied with that, still not liking that Abi was slightly older than him, Shane asked, "Speaking of your Father. Have you heard from him today?"

"No, not a word since Burton overturned the court order, and the judge granted Martin guardianship."

"I still can't believe this all happened the way it did."

"How so?" she asked, standing by the bar.

"Well, Martin isn't exactly family. He had no connection to you but got temporary custody. Isn't that strange? Still don't understand how the judge came to that decision."

Burton overheard his comment. About to step in, he heard Abi immediately veer away from the subject.

"Oh, Jade. Your dress is so pretty."

"Aww, thanks, Abs. Yours is, too."

"It's actually my Mom's."

"Oh! I love that," she said with a sympathetic tilt of her head. The girl eyed up Shane's jacket. "Do you like this guy's ensemble this evening?"

"Yes, very much. It's my favorite color."

Shane confessed, "You can thank Jade."

"And me," Reg added.

"Yeah. They took me shopping."

"Well, all of you look great," Abi said before asking how her newly engaged friends were. "How are the wedding plans coming? Have you settled on a date yet?"

Both of them rolled their eyes.

Reggie addressed his fiancée. "Should you tackle that question, or should I?"

"It's your family..." she said with a hint of attitude.

"We've been trying to secure a venue, catering, flowers, and even her dress designer. But once we booked something, they call back a day or so later and cancel."

"How can they do that? I don't understand." Abi said to Jade.

"I'm convinced his Father finds out about it somehow and then calls the vendors to either pay them off or threaten them. Who knows?"

Reg lowered his head. "I don't know what to do here. At this rate, we will never get married unless we find a place on Venus or Mars, maybe another dimension, perhaps."

Amidst it all, Burton lent a keen ear and overheard their frustration before the dainty chiming sound of a crystal glass filled the room.

A flutter erupted in Abi's chest as Martin announced, "Ladies and gentlemen, please find your seats. Dinner is served."

| 2 |

The Celebration

Monday, December 11

Malibu House

The room quieted to a gentle hum while guests made their way to the long, gleaming dining table, their laughter and whispers floating above the strains of instrumental music. Admiring the silver and white décor, sparkling vases overflowing with white roses, lilies, and delicate sprigs of evergreen, the flickering candles in glass cylinders cast a warm, golden glow, their light catching the facets of the crystal and making them shimmer like jewels. Tiny snowflake ornaments nestled among the arrangements added a touch of whimsy, as if winter itself had lent its magic to the evening.

Abi watched her friends settle in. Taking her seat in the middle of the table, she caught Burton's gaze from the other end. His expression shifted from his relaxed demeanor to one of greater intensity. Unaware that he had overheard them moments earlier, and it had sparked a flurry of ideas to solve Reggie and Jade's problem, she noticed his mind was clearly racing, but couldn't decipher the reason why.

With everyone seated, their host remained standing. Their eyes glued to Burton, he announced, "Thank you for joining us this evening as we celebrate Abi's eighteenth birthday – a significant milestone in one's life." He paused and smiled. "Many of you know Abs and me are childhood friends. While living in Boston, despite being a few years older, I considered her an equal since she was far more mature than most her age. Not having siblings, we gravitated to each other. When I moved away, we, unfortunately, lost touch. After reuniting a few months back, I now believe fate has a way of bringing people into your life who need to be there. Abi, I am grateful to call you family." He raised a glass. "Please join me in wishing Abi a very Happy Birthday. May all your hopes and dreams come true this year and always."

Smiling through her tears, everyone clinked glasses so the festivities could begin.

Shane grabbed hold of her hand. Gently touching his glass to hers, he kissed Abi. "Happy Birthday," just as Anton and a host of servers brought the first course in from the kitchen.

Laughter and happiness filled the air as everyone began eating. The night was devoid of drama and grief.

Amidst the celebration, Abi caught Burton looking at her. Breaking from his trance, he took hold of Sara's hand while they ate.

Before the main course, Shane left the table to get the small gift bag he'd brought. Returning to his chair, he got everyone's attention by simply towering above them.

Confidently standing before his friends, he said, "Three months ago, my life changed when I saw a new student standing in the foyer at school." He turned to Abi. "For reasons I still can't fully explain, I felt compelled to meet her."

Reggie piped up. "I can attest to that," he chuckled. "He was pretty determined to speak to you."

With a bashful grin, Shane returned to Abi. "When we went to Allie's beach party, I waited for my chance to talk to you away from the crowd. Little did I know that was the start of - well, everything.

Now, I can't imagine my life without you in it. You inspire, motivate, and encourage me. But most of all, you love me."

The girls around the table melted and clutched their hearts while Shane pulled a small, beautifully packaged box from the gift bag. Presenting it to her, she took it and slowly opened the ribbon and the paper.

Burton's jaw tightened, and his broad shoulders stiffened. His sharp eyes lingered on the small box, causing a flicker of concern to flash beneath his calm exterior.

Afraid to peek inside and see what she'd find, Abi slowly lifted the lid and saw a diamond infinity band with a tied knot in the middle.

"Oh, Shane," she said as he took it from the box and slipped it on the third finger of her left hand.

"I promise to have your back through every game life throws at us—whether we're running up against the toughest defenses or fighting through the longest overtimes. Whatever comes our way, I'll be in your corner, supporting your goals like you've always supported mine. You're my MVP, my number one teammate, and the reason I give it my all every day. I love you more than I could ever put into words."

Teary-eyed, Abi stared at it, unable to speak as she stood up and lovingly reached her arms around his neck.

Before she knew it, he effortlessly dipped and kissed her like a scene out of a movie.

Proud to see his promise ring on her finger, Shane felt like he was on top of the world. It gave him a sense of accountability to someone other than himself. She'd won his heart, and he wanted everyone to know it.

The servers reappeared with steak and lobster tails, elegantly plated.

Shane pulled out Abi's chair and waited for her to sit before he did the same. "Do you like it?" he asked, leaning over to her, grazing her shoulder.

Admiring the beautiful ring, she replied, "Yes, very much. It's so pretty." Reaching to cup his cheek with her hand, Abi met him halfway as Shane leaned over to kiss her. "Thank you."

"Happy Birthday."

When they parted, Abi caught Burton staring at the two of them. Raising his glass to her, he offered a subtle nod and a half smile. She did the same.

Throughout the rest of the dinner, joy, happiness, and laughter filled the otherwise quiet home.

Once everyone had their fill, one by one, the guests mingled about the house.

Taking a moment, Abi stepped back. She was so grateful to have such a wonderful group of friends. While recalling everything they'd been through the past few months, knowing how close they'd all become, she felt so lucky.

"Abs?" Jade's voice cut through her thoughts.

"Yes?"

Excited, her best friend suggested, "Do you want to open your gifts now?"

"Sure," she said before taking a seat on one of the chairs as Jade and Laney handed the gift bags to Abi.

Given so many expensive presents, ranging from jewelry to silk scarves, clothing, and even a Hermès Mini Kelly bag, she was overwhelmed.

Handed Sadie and Marco's card, Abi smiled and opened it to find a gift certificate for Il Segreto. "Wow! Thank you so much!"

Sadie beamed. "We didn't know what to get you."

"This is perfect! Shane and I eat here all the time. It's our favorite spot."

The new girl was relieved to see her reaction.

"Thank you so much for coming. I'm sure it wasn't easy since you don't know most of us."

The blonde girl tilted her head. "I appreciate all of you welcoming me. Everyone is so nice."

Needing to say her piece, Laney spoke up. "Truth be told, Marco started off on the wrong foot at Gilderson but quickly made up for it in spades. He turned out to be not such a bad guy after all – no offense."

She laughed. "It seems we had the same initial experience. He didn't exactly come across well when he and I first met, either. Then I got to know him, and strangely, he started to grow on me."

The group giggled at what the track star said.

"Well, I think I speak for everyone here when I say we're happy for you two."

"Aww, that's so sweet of you to say." The girl blushed.

"We look forward to getting to know you better."

Having opened her gifts, Abi genuinely hugged her friends before getting everyone's attention to make a speech of her own.

"Thank you all for being here tonight. This isn't just a little pre-Christmas slash birthday celebration—it's a chance for me to express my gratitude to each of you for helping me through these past few months." Abi's voice wavered as she reached out for Shane's hand, which he tenderly took, his presence a steadying force beside her. "When I arrived in Los Angeles back in August, I was terrified. I never imagined I'd find friends here—friends who feel like family." She paused, her breath hitching as she fought back the tears. "But then I met all of you."

Shane gently wrapped an arm around her waist, pulling her closer as if to shield her from the weight of the moment.

"I don't want to bring the mood down, but... I've lost so much recently..." Her voice broke, and a heavy silence settled over the room. Everyone felt the weight of her pain while trying to hold back their own tears. Abi's sight veered to the left of the crowd. "Burton," she choked out, tears spilling over, "Thank you for giving me a home when I felt lost. Ever since we were kids, you've always been there, protecting me. Even after all these years, nothing has changed." Her voice was thick with emotion as she turned to the guy beside her. "And Shane...thank you for being the kind of boyfriend I always dreamed of. You're loving and supportive, sharing in all of life's ups and downs. God knows there have been plenty of those lately. I love you so much and can't imagine my life without you." She took a shaky breath, willing herself to continue. Sweeping the room, meeting the gaze of each person who had become so dear to her, she said, "Thank you for welcoming me into your lives. I couldn't have made it through without all of you. Your friendship means everything to me." Slowly, a smile appeared. "A special thank you to Burton and Sara for hosting tonight," she said, her voice steadier now as all eyes turned to the couple, hand in hand, listening with warmth and empathy. "Thank you for putting up with me during these tough times." That said, her attention shifted to someone who stood quietly near the edge of the group. "Dearest Martin," she said, her tone light. "Thank you for taking on the responsibility of being my legal guardian. You are the kindest man I know, and I am so grateful for everything you've done for me. You've been my grounding force when the world felt like it was falling apart." She looked at the small cluster of men nearby. "To Andrew, Matt, and Ted... I know I have not been the easiest to keep track of."

A chuckle rippled through the room, lightening the mood.

"But I am truly indebted to you for keeping me safe. You've watched over me with so much patience, even when I've pushed boundaries or stormed ahead without thinking. I see it now, and I thank you." Pausing and collecting her thoughts as the emotion swirled in the air, Abi added, "We've been through so much together in such a short time. I truly believe that has bonded us forever." She lifted her glass, her eyes shimmering with gratitude as memories rushed through her mind like a film reel. From surviving the explosion and fake kidnapping to facing the chaos of Eastwood's schemes and unraveling secrets that shattered their sense of safety, a wedding proposal brought a fleeting moment of joy, only to be followed by the crushing weight of death and grief that tested her resilience. Not forgetting the insanity of Vegas—where they teetered on the edge of disaster—through it all, Abi knew they withstood it together and weathered the storms. "To all my friends," she said, sounding composed despite the lump in her throat, the glass trembling slightly in her hand as she raised it higher. "Thank you for celebrating my birthday with me tonight. I love you all."

The gentle clinking of glasses and her heartfelt words washed the room in warmth as Dark Demon's music began to play, livening up the house as laughter and chatter threaded through. The tension dissolved as joyous conversations flowed. Small groups formed, sharing jokes and cherished memories.

The girls stayed in the living room while the guys headed toward the stairs to descend to the lower level for a game of pool and to watch the football game.

Witnessing Burton meeting up with Shane to shake his hand, she overheard him complimenting her boyfriend on his speech. Seemingly having a normal conversation, she was happy to see them getting along versus being at odds.

Eyes on the guys, Jade sat beside her. "They seem to be on good terms."

"Yes, finally." Turning to her friend, she asked, "So, tell me. Is the wedding planning really that bad?"

The rest of the girls listened in, including Sara.

Reiterating what she'd said earlier to bring the others up to speed, Jade explained, "I am not going to sugarcoat it. Honestly, it's been a nightmare," she dramatically revealed, fidgeting with her beautiful engagement ring on her finger. "Every time we try and book something or plan to, his father interferes, and suddenly, the vendors won't do business with us. At this rate, I worry our wedding won't happen. Like Reggie said, we would have to get married on Mars or Venus at this point. There's no hiding from his family."

"Don't say that." Allie tried to stay positive and encouraged, "There's gotta be a way."

"Exactly. The two of you are destined to be," Laney added. "Maybe his Dad will lighten up eventually."

Jade smirked. "I doubt that."

"At least you won the court battle against him, and Reggie doesn't have to pay damages for the company's losses," Abi expressed her thoughts, striving to maintain a level of optimism.

"But there was a price to pay for that. He's going to make our lives miserable for an eternity," Jade sighed. Not wanting to talk about it anymore, she said, "Okay, enough about me. Let's see that pretty ring of yours."

Abi reached out to show off the sparkly band.

"Honestly, that was the sweetest thing for Shane to do."

She smiled bashfully. "I think so, too."

"Have you decided where you are going to go next fall? Has he?" Jade asked.

"I believe Shane is leaning towards Alabama."

Laney was the first to comment. "Will you go with him?"

That piqued Sara's interest.

Abi looked down at the ring. "Umm, I'm not sure yet. Perhaps. The only problem is that the school doesn't have the pre-med program I want, so I'm waiting to see what acceptances come through first."

"Does he know that?" Jade could feel her friend's dilemma.

"No, umm, not yet," Abi said as her sight fell to the floor. "Please keep that between us for now…"

"Well, no matter where you applied, I bet you get in," Laney commented. "You're so smart. They'd be stupid not to take you."

"Thanks, Lane." Abi took a deep breath. "We will have to wait and see what happens. She scanned the faces around her, not wanting to stay on that subject. "So, on that note, what's everyone doing for Christmas?"

Laney answered, "Shawn and I are heading to Tahoe to ski with his family. Mine won't be around, given the drama with my Dad."

It wasn't hard for everyone to see that the girl was still hurting from her parents' split.

"My family is skiing in Switzerland over the holidays," Allie revealed. "They invited Alan and me to go with them. It's our first official family event together. I'm kind of nervous."

"I wouldn't worry. You guys will be fine," Jade said.

"How about you? Going away?" Laney asked Mei and Ming. "Or staying in town?"

Ming turned to her sister. "Well, the plan is to spend Christmas and New Year's in NYC with our family. The guys, too." She took a deep breath. "I know what Allie is feeling. This will be the first family event for Ben and me."

"Since Adrian has attended a few family functions thus far, I'm not worried. It'll be nice to spend some quality time together. Just him and me. We so need a break."

Happy to hear the good news, Abi heard her phone ring. Walking over to pick it up from the sideboard, she found the name 'Dad' flashing across the screen.

The girls saw the look on her face. It seemed the blood had drained from it. Silent, each assumed who was calling.

| 3 |

The Call

Monday, December 11

Malibu House

Heart beating a mile a minute, Abi's hands began to shake. Finally accepting the call, she managed to say the word, "Hello?"

"Happy Birthday, Sweetheart. I thought I'd reach out and see how you're doing."

Shocked by his nonchalant tone, an awkwardness loomed. "I'm, umm…fine."

Quick to respond, Abi could tell he was nervous. "Enjoying your day?"

She said confidently, "So far, it's been wonderful." Pausing, she wondered if she should elaborate further. Wanting him to feel a sense of guilt, she added, "Burton threw me a lovely dinner party to celebrate with all my friends."

"That was nice of him."

"Yes, it was."

The air went dead.

Suddenly, he blurted, "What are you doing for Christmas? Any plans?"

"No. I haven't thought about it."

He paused, then suggested, "Any chance you'd consider spending it with us?"

"What do you mean, us?"

"Jenna and I were hoping we could spend Christmas Eve together."

Abi was dumbfounded. "You're serious? It's my first Christmas without Mom…"

"I realize…"

"The last thing I want to do is spend it with you and your girl-friend."

The girls overheard that, and each glanced at the other, a look of stunned surprise on their faces.

Hearing this, the man huffed on the other end of the line. "Abi, you will have to get past this eventually," he said with quite an attitude.

"No. I will never get past this. Ever. If I recall correctly, as of today, I'm eighteen. That means I can make my own decisions. And that means I will never spend Christmas or any other holiday with you and her."

"Fine, but that doesn't change the fact I'm marrying her Christmas Eve."

The air escaped her lungs before she said loudly, "So, what? Did you call to tell me that so you could ruin my birthday? 'Cause congratulations. You've succeeded!"

The girls got up and surrounded their friend, whose hands shook as she held the phone.

"How could you! Seriously!" She yelled so loudly that Burton and Shane bounded up the stairs to see what was happening.

"Have a nice life, Dad! Don't ever talk to me again!"

When Abi ended the call, Shane was standing by her side. Seeing him, she fell into his arms and burst into tears.

The room went silent. Nobody said a word.

Not sure what to do, she let go of him and disappeared upstairs, needing a moment.

About to go after her, Burton felt Sara's hand hold him back. That is when he saw Shane follow and skip steps on the way to the second floor.

At the top, the football player proceeded down the hall. He could hear her sobbing when knocking on the door before walking in. There, he found her sitting on the bed before she suddenly popped up again and began pacing the floor. "How could he ruin my Birthday?" About to answer her, she interrupted Shane. "She's been gone less than three months, and he's getting remarried! Who does that?"

Unable to get a word in edgewise, Shane tried to speak. "Abs?"

"But the worst is, he actually thought I'd be happy for him!"

"Babe?"

"That will never happen! I will never accept that woman into my life!"

"Abi!"

She turned to him. "What!"

He rubbed his hands along her arms. "Take a breath." His eyes locked on her lovingly. "Shake it off. Don't let him get to you. Rise above that."

Thinking that was easier said than done, the pretty girl flopped her head back and huffed. "Fine." Hearing what he said, she inhaled deeply. "You're right. He's not worth it."

Shane stepped forward and wrapped his arms around her. Pulling Abi in close, he rested his chin upon her head. "You okay?" Comforting her, he spied the two floral bouquets and the white gift box on the desk.

When he veered that way, she held her breath. *Oh, no. The letter,* she thought. Thankfully, it was hidden under the box.

"So... Is that from him?" he asked. "What did he get you?"

Not sure what to say, she paused. "It's not important," and shot a look.

"No, seriously. What is it?" Walking over, he found the leather book atop the tissue paper and flipped it open to see the account summary on the first page. Shocked, he swiveled around.

"It's for school. He didn't want me to worry about expenses."

"I get that, but ten million? Come on..."

"Please don't be jealous." She lowered her head and stepped back, disappointed. "I don't want to do this today of all days."

"Sorry..." he said, placing the book back in the box. "You know he gets..."

"Under your skin? Yes, I'm aware." She sighed exhaustively. "Don't tell anyone, alright?"

Shane peered down at the ring on her finger. "He did that, and all I got you was a ring..."

Immediately shaking her pointer finger, she rebutted, "Don't do that. Don't diminish how special your gift is, especially the feelings that accompany it."

Hearing her, he rubbed the back of his neck with his hand and managed a smile.

Kissing his lips, she said, "I will treasure it, and you always."

The sincerity in her voice helped him forget about the bank statement.

"Come on. Let's go downstairs. I should get back to our guests."

He nodded before walking out of her room and over to the staircase.

When they reached the main floor, Abi could feel everyone looking at them.

With perfect timing, Martin, Rosa, and Anton appeared. Holding a cake with flaming candles, they prompted everyone to sing "Happy Birthday to you..."

The room erupted in song.

Shane stood stiffly beside Burton. His hands jammed into his pockets as if to anchor himself. The tension between them could have snapped like a live wire.

Able to feel anger off of the guy, Burton kept his composure and stayed unnervingly calm. "Is she okay?" he asked, straightening his jacket and crossing his arms, knowing something was up.

Jaw tightening, Shane muttered, "Umm, yeah. She's good." His thoughts churned furiously, debating whether to address the elephant in the room now or later. But he couldn't hold back. "So, she showed me your gift." His tone was low but edged with accusation as his stare fixed firmly on the cake instead of Burton's face.

The celebrity didn't flinch. His smirk was razor-sharp, slicing through the room's celebratory energy. "Don't start, Coppersmith," he said coolly, his voice just loud enough for Shane to hear. "Now's not the time or place. You'll only embarrass yourself."

What he said was like gasoline on a fire. Shane's desire to lash out—verbally or otherwise—was intense. Fingers curling into fists, about to explode, he saw Abi's joyfulness. It helped him refrain from starting something.

When the song ended, applause filled the room.

Shane forced himself to clap.

It seemed more mechanical and hollow as Burton's smirk widened. "Good decision," he murmured before stepping aside, leaving Shane standing there, his pulse pounding in his ears, with chest burning.

"Make a wish!" Jade announced.

Hands clutched together under her chin, Abi briefly looked at the two of them before closing her eyes and blowing out the candles. Smoke lingering, the room erupted in more cheers and applause.

Anton immediately cut the cake while Rosa started passing the slices around.

The girls gathered with Abi.

Jade could tell she was bothered. "Are you okay?"

It sparked a feeling of uncertainty. "Umm, yeah. I'd rather not talk about it."

She rubbed her friend's arm. "Alright. Come on. Sit down. Eat your cake."

Taking a seat, Shane joined her and tapped her knee with his hand.

At the same time, the newly engaged couple joined in and sat across from them.

"Now that we have a minute," Jade stated, "There's something we want to ask you both."

The two looked at their friends.

"Sure, shoot," Shane replied curiously. "What is it?"

"Well, if Reg and I are successful at planning this wedding, we want you to be our Maid of Honor..."

"...and Best Man," Reg added to finish her sentence.

Beaming uncontrollably, Abi reached across to take hold of Jade's hands. With eyes glistening, she said, "I'd be honored."

Shane got up and walked around the table. Giving Reg a manly hug and pat on the back, he said, "Yeah, me too."

"Thanks, my man." Reg was happy to hear that from his best friend.

Focusing on the large task ahead of them, Abi asked Jade, "So, I guess we need to figure out how to do this."

"It will be a tall order," her friend said, "It seems every Justice of the Peace in the state won't even marry us. His Father has connections everywhere."

Turning to Shane, she replied, "We will find a way."

Burton overheard their discussion from the corner of the room. His mind was still reeling a mile a minute as Martin walked up beside him.

"If I may, Sir. It seems your brain is smoldering."

He didn't react to his statement.

"What are you pondering?"

"Martin, when do we leave for Japan?" he said in a monotone voice, needing confirmation, not making eye contact.

"Thursday. Why do you ask?" Seeing Master B glued to Abi, Martin knew what he was about to do. "With all due respect, Sir, given the circumstances of the trip, I highly advise against it."

Always looking for solutions, Burton realized Jade and Reggie didn't fully know his secret but assumed he could help. "If I leave her here, I can't protect her. You know that. Besides, I'm sure you can help me keep business and pleasure separate."

Aware of the monumental endeavor he was about to agree to, Martin lowered his head. Strongly opposed to the idea, he was about to rebut it a second time. That is when his boss turned to him.

Eyebrows raised, he said, "Make it happen. Please…"

"I suppose we will manage, Sir."

Burton silently nodded. His eyes didn't leave Abi for a second.

Sara intently watched as her boyfriend disappeared into his office and closed the pocket doors.

Distracted by what had happened between the two men, Abi wondered what was going on before diverting back to their friend's conversation. "Maybe we should head to a remote island destination like Bora Bora. They do weddings all the time. We can have fireflies at an oceanside ceremony."

Suddenly, Burton emerged and continued to listen in.

"Or we can have pretty water trickling down the aisle like the wedding in Crazy Rich Asians." She released a whimsical sigh. "Wasn't that the most romantic wedding you've ever seen? I loved it." Distracted, catching sight of him also, she knew something was up.

"Yes, me too." Still contemplating Abi's suggestion, Jade repeated, "So, Bora Bora, huh? That's a thought." With a hint of hope, thankful they weren't alone in this, she said, "I don't know how we will pull it off. If anything, it will have to be in secret, I guess."

The big, burly DJ interjected. "Excuse me, Abs?"

"Yes?"

"Can I have a word?" Getting her attention, he asked, "Oh, and bring your friends."

When he disappeared inside the office again, each looked at the other, somehow feeling like they were getting called to the principal's office.

"Is he mad? What did we do?" Borderline fearful, Jade panicked based on the guy's bluntness.

"Just go," Abi said humorously. "Come on."

All four walked through the doorway.

Burton was already sitting behind his desk. "Close the doors behind you."

"What's this about?" Abi asked as Shane slid the glass panels shut.

"When were you hoping to tie the knot?" Burton posed point-blank.

Jade and Reggie turned to each other as the guy sat stoically in his chair.

"The sooner, the better," Reg replied, slipping his arm around Jade.

"Oh? Is that right?" she said, surprised.

Her fiancé smiled. "I've been waiting long enough. I just want to call you my wife."

She melted.

Throwing it out there, Burton suggested, "How about just before Christmas?"

The friends didn't know if the guy was joking or not.

Abi could tell by his expression that he was dead serious.

"If you want to get married, I can make it happen."

The engaged couple perked up.

"How?" Reggie asked.

"Sara and I have gotta be in Japan over the holidays. Why don't you join us? Get married there. I can arrange a quiet ceremony. Afterward, we can snowboard and sight-see." His eyes fell on Abi. "From what I gather, you're the Maid of Honor, correct?"

She nodded, "Yes."

"And you're the best man?" he pointed to Shane.

The football player nodded hesitantly, still angry about what was said earlier.

"So, then, both of you need to come too."

Nudging Abi, Shane wasn't sure how to react, as the guy further explained, "I'll take care of all the arrangements. That will keep your name off the books." He looked to Reggie. "That way, your Dad won't interfere."

The room went silent.

Burton could see Sara lurking nearby. He knew she wasn't happy with him.

The couple didn't know what to say.

To buffer the situation, Abi piped up. "Maybe you guys need a moment to think about it."

With a no-nonsense attitude, Burton said, "They need to decide tonight. We leave Thursday."

"Thursday?" Jade freaked out a little. "That soon."

Interested to know what Burton had in mind, Reggie attempted to calm Jade down. "I know this is fast, but it might be the only way."

She smiled and nervously replied, "I agree."

"So, it's settled?" Burton wanted confirmation. "Are we planning a wedding?"

The two nodded simultaneously and said, "Yes," before shifting their attention to their friends.

"So, Abi? Shane? Are you in?" Burton questioned.

Put on the spot, Shane grabbed hold of Abi's hand. "It's been a tough couple of months. I wouldn't mind getting away. I need to check with my agent and figure out how to make the university selection announcement remotely, but – yeah, I'll go if you do. What do you say, Abs?"

"I've never been there…" She looked up at Shane.

"Me either. All the more reason to go. It'll be an adventure."

Recalling Burton's invitation from earlier that evening, this new development helped her make her decision. "Okay, I'm in," she said.

Quickly turning to Reggie and Jade, Shane confirmed, "Guess you guys are getting married in Japan."

"Perfect." Burton slapped his hand flat on the desk. "Given the level of secrecy you need, don't tell anyone else." He pointed to their friends mingling in the other room. "Not even them," he added. "You can announce it when you return. The last thing you want is for your Father to get wind of it. Agreed?"

Reg immediately said, "Agreed," while putting out his hand to shake Burton's. "Thank you. We really appreciate this."

"No problem. Happy to help," he said as Jade hugged him.

"Yes, this is so kind of you."

Abi moved towards her childhood friend with open arms. "Thank you for helping them."

"Everything will go off without a hitch, I promise," Burton said confidently, his sharp gaze flicking over the group. "I'll have Martin send you our itinerary."

Leery of Burton's intentions, Shane caught the subtle way the guy lingered on Abi. Without warning, his protective instincts flared. Something felt off, a shift he couldn't quite place, but enough to make him uneasy, knowing he'd need to stay close to his girlfriend on this trip.

As they rejoined the group, their friends gathered around.

Sara studied their animated expressions. Though still unaware of what was happening, she could tell they'd apparently made some significant decisions.

Laney, always curious, leaned close to Abi as they returned to the gathering. "So, what was all that about? Why did you guys have a secret convo with our infamous friend?" she whispered.

Careful not to reveal anything, Abi played it cool. "He wanted to ask about Reggie's emancipation. That's all."

With that said, Laney seemed satisfied, and the festivities continued without further probing. Meanwhile, Reg and Shane made their way to the bar for a drink, then headed downstairs to join the guys.

About to follow, Burton stopped and addressed his girlfriend.

"So, what's going on?" Sara asked curiously.

Mindful of those standing nearby, he took her aside and said under his breath, "They are coming to Japan."

She rolled her eyes. "What? Why?"

"They needed my help."

Perplexed, she surmised, "Those two aren't aware of your profession. How is that going to work?"

"Not sure yet. I'll figure it out."

"But Burton…"

He held up his hand. "No buts, Sara. They're going. End of discussion."

While he walked away, Sara glared angrily.

Witnessing this, Abi noticed the threatening edge in the girl's contempt, but what truly surprised her was Burton's sharp reaction. She had never seen him speak to anyone like that before. From previous experience, she knew one thing about Burton—he hated anyone challenging him. It was something he would not tolerate. Not from anyone. Not even her.

| 4 |

Goodnight

Monday, December 11

Malibu House

While the evening slowly drifted to a close, one by one, the small group of friends bid the Birthday Girl goodnight just before the stroke of twelve.

Lingering, Jade, and Reggie snuck in a private exchange with Shane and Abi to discuss their secret plans for later that week.

"Guess we'll wait for more details," Jade whispered with a grin before bouncing excitedly. "I can't wait to pack—oh, and choose a wedding dress."

"Shhh..." Abi placed her pointer finger over her lips.

Lowering her voice, Jade covered her mouth and giggled. "I'm so excited," she whispered.

Passing out hugs all around, their guests departed, including Marco and his lovely girlfriend, Sadie, who'd fit in extremely well that night.

With their goodbyes said, the house emptied, leaving only the guys making the rounds with Abi, Burton, Shane, and Sara mingling in the foyer while the staff began tidying up, their movements quiet and efficient.

Taking Burton aside, Abi nervously asked, "Is it okay if he stays?"

Nodding, he paused briefly. "Yeah, of course." Despite his agreement, a part of him preferred that it be just the two of them, but Sara was already making herself at home upstairs.

Flashing a hopeful expression, Abi returned to Shane. "You're welcome to stay tonight if you want."

Not thrilled to sleep under the guy's roof, he apologized. "Sorry, babe. I can't. I'm meeting my agent in Huntington Beach early in the morning."

Surprised to hear that, feeling rejected, she replied, "Oh, okay... Will I see you tomorrow, then?"

"Maybe in the afternoon. Where will you be? Here or on my street?"

"I'm not sure yet, but I'll let you know in the morning."

"Sounds good." An awkwardness loomed. "On that note, I should head out," he stated.

With the cool night air brushing against her skin, Abi seemed noticeably down.

Shane paused when they reached the truck. "Sorry. If I'd known you wanted me to stay, I could've postponed the meeting." He wrapped his arms around her. "Now I feel like I'm missing out."

"It's okay. We'll have plenty of time together in Japan."

He smiled back. "I think this trip will be great. Honestly, I'm kind of excited—aside from *him* being there."

Abi tilted her head. "Hey..."

He cut her off with a playful kiss. "I'm just joking. Don't worry. I'll be on my best behavior. I won't fight. I promise."

"I should hope not," she replied.

A quiet moment passed between them, the only sound being the faint hum of the waiting SUV. "Happy Birthday, Abs," Shane said, his voice low and intimate.

He leaned in, his lips brushing hers with a tenderness that sent warmth coursing through her.

"Goodnight," he whispered. "I'll call you tomorrow."

She nodded. "Goodnight."

Watching as he stepped into the sleek SUV, the driver pulled away and blended into the darkness.

Abi stood there for a second in silence. Even though her heart felt full, at that moment, she felt a deep sense of loneliness.

Upon closing the front door and locking it, she removed her shoes from her sore feet. Waving to the staff on the way past, she bid them goodnight before slowly climbing the stairs one by one. Finding Burton's bedroom door closed, she made it to her room at the end of the hall and walked inside. Sitting on the bed before flopping backward, she folded her hands over her stomach and suddenly heard a knock.

Startled, she gasped. "Hello?"

Burton popped his head inside. "Hey, Abs. Can I come in?"

She sat up. "Sure."

Now dressed in a T-shirt and pajama pants, he said, "Just wanted to say goodnight." Having seen Shane drive away, Burton inched inside the room. "He didn't stay, then?"

She managed a small smile. "No. Apparently, he is meeting his agent early in the morning."

"Well, perhaps it's for the best. That way, you can get some sleep."

"Maybe you're right."

His eyes gravitated to his gift on the desk.

"He spoke to you, didn't he?"

Burton slipped his hands in his pockets. "Yeah... You could say that."

"I'm sorry. I didn't mean for him to see it."

"It's fine. I figured he would eventually find out."

"I guess..." she said before adding, "Thank you again for always being here. It means the world to me. You're the only family I have now, technically – well, aside from my friends and the guys, of course."

"I'm honored." A flicker of emotion broke through his usual stoic demeanor. "Only wish the best for you. Hope you know that."

"B?" Sara's voice echoed down the hall.

Abi looked at the door, knowing he had to go.

Hugging her firmly, Burton lingered. "Sweet dreams and Happy Birthday."

"Thank you."

On that note, he walked out of the room and closed the door. Alone yet again, Abi got ready for bed. Too tired to shower, she slipped under the covers. "Night, Mom," she whispered, feeling that she was close. "I survived the first Thanksgiving, and now my Birthday. Soon, it will be the first Christmas without you. Guess we will be in Japan for that. I hope you'll come along, too."

Her thoughts hung in the air as she closed her eyes, feeling a quiet peace settle over her. She didn't know what the future would hold, but for the first time in a long while, she felt like everything was going to work out the way it was supposed to.

| 5 |

Shopping

Tuesday, December. 12

Beverly Hills

The next morning, Burton and Abi left the Malibu house and headed East along the Pacific Coast Highway. Not having heard from Shane at all, she'd agreed to go shopping since Burton had time available.

As the ocean shimmered in the sunlight, waves crashed rhythmically against the shore as wetsuit-wearing surfers dotted the water. Driving in the back of his sleek black Bentley SUV, driven by Lorenzo with Andrew riding shotgun, Burton watched the scenery blur past. The salty breeze of the Pacific gave way to the bustling streets of Santa Monica as they transitioned from coastal cliffs to palm-lined boulevards. The plush leather seats and tinted windows insulated them from the noise outside, but the lively energy of Los Angeles seeped in as they neared The Grove. Soon, the quiet elegance of Malibu felt worlds away.

The hum of car engines blended with the rustle of palm trees swaying against a cloudless blue sky while Lorenzo eased to a stop in front of the sleek, modern Backcountry store.

Not needing assistance, Burton stepped out, adjusted his sunglasses, and offered his hand to Abi, who joined him. "Ready?" he said, scanning the storefront. "By the time we leave here, you'll have everything you need for the trip."

Nodding and brushing a strand of hair behind her ear, Abi could see their presence was already attracting unwanted attention as people walking by eyed them up from head to toe.

"Trust me," Burton replied confidently, ignoring the crowd. "I've got you covered."

Upon entering the Backcountry store, the air smelled faintly of new fabric and polished wood. The walls were lined with racks of weatherproof jackets, thermal layers, and hiking boots, while the center displays showcased chic, casual wear perfect for Après-ski. Abi's eyes widened as she took it all in.

"Where do we even start?" she asked, spinning slightly to take in the options.

"Outerwear," Burton said, heading toward a rack of insulated jackets. He plucked a misty-blue parka from the rack and held it up. "Try this. Lightweight but warm. Perfect for walking through Tokyo or skiing the slopes."

Abi slipped it on, looking at herself in the mirror. "This actually fits perfectly."

"Told you," Burton smirked. "Okay, next up—base layers. Can't let you freeze in the snow, can I?"

Seeing her gravitate to a white jacket with a fluffy fur collar, Burton checked for sizes and took one off the rack. "Here, try this."

With slight hesitation, she slipped her arms through. It was so cozy.

"You should get that too," he said as a salesperson approached.

"Can I help you today?" the well-built guy asked, knowing the two looked like they needed help.

"Absolutely," Burton replied, brimming with confidence. "We need to be outfitted for winter in Japan. Start with outerwear and work your way down to accessories."

The sales guy grinned. "Got it. Follow me."

That afternoon, Burton and Abi tackled their list piece by piece. After almost two hours, they emerged from the outdoorsy store with enough bags to rival a luxury boutique haul. From sleek city attire to fleece-lined leggings and outerwear for Niseko, Abi felt prepared for every scenario. He'd even picked up warm jackets for the men.

"Thank you for all this," Abi said as Burton stowed their bags in the back of the SUV.

"Don't thank me yet. We're not done," he said.

Abi raised an eyebrow but followed his lead, her curiosity piqued.

Moving on, with Lorenzo tight to their heels, they walked the streets of The Grove, ducking in and out of the stores. Admiring the over-the-top festive holiday décor at every angle, Abi realized Burton had more in mind than just practicality. If Backcountry was about function, The Grove was about style, ensuring she was equally prepared for upscale city adventures and laid-back mountain evenings, right down to a new LV tote and Rimowa luggage that would pack it all.

Exhausted, they made their way back to the SUV, where Andrew was waiting to help load the numerous bags as Lorenzo and Burton passed them along. Soon, the trunk was at capacity.

Abi climbed into the middle seat with a satisfied sigh, feeling the weight of the day's retail therapy as Burton settled in beside her.

He glanced over, noticing the excitement lingering from their successful trip. "You hungry?" he asked casually, leaning back. "We could head to Il Segreto for an early dinner. Drago's probably there prepping for the evening rush."

Abi perked up at the suggestion, grateful for the chance to escape the crowds. "That sounds perfect."

"Il Segreto it is, then," Burton said, nodding at Lorenzo to take them there.

As the SUV pulled away from the lively buzz of the mall, Abi gazed out the window, content to let the Christmas chaos fade into the background, replaced by the promise of a cozy meal and familiar faces.

The Bentley cruised onto the 405, the hum of the engine blending with the faint sounds of festive jazz playing through the car speakers.

Seeing the city's lights flicker on, Abi looked out the window as the early evening painted the skyline. The traffic was mercifully light, allowing Lorenzo to navigate up the freeway with ease, the hills of Bel Air visible in the distance.

While approaching the turn for Mulholland Drive, she broke the comfortable silence. "What does Sara think about us tagging along on the trip?" she asked, cautious but genuinely curious.

Burton's eyes stayed on the passing scenery as he leaned back against the headrest. "She's not happy about it," he admitted bluntly. "But it's not her decision. It's mine." He glanced at Abi, his expression stern. "She'll get over it. Besides, we have a lot riding on this trip. She needs to be on point from a security standpoint. I'm relying on her for that."

Absorbing his words, she shifted slightly in her seat, watching as the cityscape gave way to the winding curves and sweeping views. "I get it." But as she thought about the dynamic he described, a sense of curiosity lingered. "Your relationship with her... It's kind of strange. Isn't it? Mixing business and pleasure like that."

Burton's lips quirked into a faint smile. "Strange is one way to put it," he replied dryly. "Complicated might be another."

She nodded, letting the subject drop as the sun glimmered between the trees, the closer they got to their destination. While she appreciated his honesty, she couldn't help but wonder how Sara really felt—and whether her relationship with Burton would hold steady in his world.

Soon, they pulled into the Beverly Glen Plaza. Nestled within the hillside enclave, Il Segreto stood out with its timeless charm, its wrought-iron sign subtly illuminated against the stone façade. The scent of rosemary and garlic wafted faintly from the restaurant's kitchen, mingling with the cool evening air.

Lorenzo maneuvered the vehicle into a spot near the entrance.

Abi noticed that the terracotta planters were now filled with lush holiday greenery featuring tiny white flowers, which added to the rustic Italian theme.

"This place looks festive," Burton said with a small smile, stepping out of the SUV and holding the door open for Abi.

She slid out, the day's shopping bags temporarily forgotten as she stretched her legs and took in their surroundings.

Walking over to the entrance, Burton swung open the glass door for her. It didn't take long for the coziness of the restaurant to ignite their spirit. Golden lighting bathed the room, reflecting off the polished wood tables and exposed brick accents. The faint sound of Italian music played in the background, blending harmoniously with the low hum of conversation and clinking wine glasses.

"Ah, Mr. Baxter!" a deep voice called from behind the counter. Drago, the owner, emerged with a wide grin, his chef's coat slightly rumpled from a busy day. "And Signorina Abi, my favorite guest! You're becoming a regular."

Abi smiled warmly. "I have you to thank for that. No one can turn down your tiramisu."

"You are too kind," the Chef blushed, waving them toward a cozy corner booth. "Sit, sit. I'll make sure you're taken care of. What brings you here tonight?"

Burton glanced at Abi before answering. "We're getting ready for a trip. Heading to Japan for the holidays."

Clearly intrigued, Drago raised an eyebrow. "Ah, sounds exciting. And Mr. Coppersmith?"

Noting the subtle curiosity in his tone, she exchanged a glance with Burton. "Yes," she said lightly, suppressing a smile. "Shane's coming with us, too."

The chef chuckled, gesturing toward the kitchen. "I'll bring you something special. You'll need the energy for an adventure like that."

As they settled into their seats, Abi felt a sense of calm wash over her. The long day had been worth it, and with Drago's warm hospitality and the promise of good food, the evening already felt like a reprieve from the hustle of Beverly Hills.

The scent of simmering sauces and freshly baked bread enveloped them. Always eager to try whatever Drago had in mind, she knew his food was impeccable.

Leaning back in his chair, Burton inhaled, his eyes scanning the other patrons before turning to Abi. "What do you think about Shane coming with us to Japan?" he asked casually. "How do you feel about spending time with him, just the two of you, without all the usual distractions?"

Taken by his straightforwardness, she let out a small laugh, her voice light but thoughtful. "I'm kind of drifting into uncharted territory here," she said, glancing at him, her naivety shining through. "I've never been on vacation with a guy before..."

"Despite sneaking off to Cabo," he interjected.

"Umm, I suppose. But I didn't consider that a vacation. It was a day trip," she shrugged, a playful smile tugging at her lips. "Hopefully, after our time away, we will return to LA and won't hate each other."

Burton gave her a reassuring look. "It'll be fine, Abs. Trust me. You two will have a great time." His gaze revealed a hint of protectiveness. "But if you need anything, anything at all, don't hesitate. Just find me. I've got your back, always."

As their entrees arrived—Abi marveled at the plate of handmade pasta draped in a rich, velvety sauce—the delicate balance of truffle fettuccine was the comfort food she needed.

For Burton, the rigatoni Bolognese was a staple, and Drago knew it. The hearty sauce, robust and comforting, brought him back to his restaurant time and time again.

With each bite, she felt herself relax as her exhaustion faded.

The ambiance of the place and the attentive service allowed them to unwind, if only for a little while. There was a lot to do when they got home to the Beverly Glen house. Everything they'd bought needed to be folded and packed since they'd be heading to the airport early

Thursday morning. It wasn't long before they'd be flying over the Pacific en route to their first stop—Kyoto.

| 6 |

Departure

Thursday, December 14

Beverly Park House

Waking early that Thursday morning to gloomy skies, anxiety swirling in her chest about their departure, Abi rolled over and slowly eased herself out of bed. It had been two days since she'd seen Shane, and aside from the occasional text, she assumed he was shopping and packing on top of finalizing his football commitments.

Arms stretched above her, the weight of the past few days pressed heavily. Amidst it all, her alarm sounded. Rolling over, she reached for her phone on the side table, unlocked it, and saw a notification flashing on the screen. Her pulse quickened while she swiped to read it.

Atmospheric River Warning: Heavy rainfall expected to begin later this morning.

"Oh, no..." she mumbled, knowing the storm could potentially cause a mess at the airport. She quickly checked the time, then the radar.

"It will be close," she mumbled under her breath. "Please, just let us get off the ground." Hoping they wouldn't get stuck on the tarmac or worse, the last thing she wanted was a flight delay, which would make their already tight schedule even more stressful. Having seen Martin's itinerary for Day One, she knew that any delays could impact Jade and Reggie's ability to get to the Consulate and City Hall in time to process their wedding license. Without that, they would not be able to proceed with their plans legally.

Taking a deep breath, she put her phone down and started gathering the last of her things, trying to push the worry aside. She hadn't been on a real vacation in years and wasn't going to let anything spoil it.

With her suitcase packed and her backpack sitting nearby, she accounted for the things she would need to get her through the ten-hour flight that day before jumping in the shower.

As the water trickled over her, she recalled all the research she'd done that week to try and understand Japanese culture, including some simple phrases, rituals, and greetings. Determined to stay mindful, she knew, above all things, that respect was the highest priority.

Thinking about Shane and Burton and how well they'd been getting along recently, she prayed their truce would continue, and the drama would remain at a minimum.

Knowing Burton, she figured he had a number of experiences planned for everyone that a normal person would not be privy to. This sparked a little unease, but with Shane by her side, she knew she'd survive.

When she shut off the shower and wrapped herself in the towel, she quickly checked her phone. Upon finding a good morning message from Shane, her face brightened. Filled with warmth and affection, he always had the power to lift her spirits. Thankful for him every day, she could hardly wait to embark on this journey together.

She thought about exploring the many shrines and temples during their upcoming sightseeing tours. The idea of immersing herself in Japan's rich history and beauty was thrilling. But as much as she was looking forward to the adventures, the thought of being alone with him at times—just the two of them—made her heart race. The mere thought of it made her cheeks flush.

Taking deep breaths to stay calm, she got dressed. Double-checking that she had everything on her list, Abi closed her suitcase and zippered it shut. Packing a few essentials in her new tote, she made her bed and slung the bag onto her shoulder.

On the way down the hall, wheeling her luggage, she could hear voices coming from the main floor. About to swing around the corner at the top of the stairs, she caught the eye of Burton, who heard her suitcase rolling down the hall.

"Morning, Abs. Leave your suitcase there. I will bring it down for you."

Continuing to speak with Martin as the man updated him, Abi descended the stairs and set her bag down on the circular table in the middle of the foyer. Having a seat in one of the chairs, she took out her phone and texted Shane, wondering what his ETA was.

Almost here?

While waiting for his response, Burton turned to her.

"Ready?" he asked. "Excited?"

"Yes, on both accounts. Have to say, though, I'm nervous. I've never been on a trip like this before or on a flight this long."

He reached out his hand and rested it on her shoulder. "You'll be fine. Trust me. This will be the most amazing adventure you've ever had." He paused and offered his telltale confident smirk.

Anxious, she rubbed her palms together. "Oh, I can hardly wait."

"Let's just say I have some incredible things arranged, and I'm excited to share them with all of you."

"Any hints?"

About to answer her, Burton got a notification on his phone. Looking down at it, he said, "Looks like your boyfriend just arrived."

Abi turned and walked toward the front door. Opening it, she saw one SUV waiting with a Sprinter van bringing up the rear.

As Shane got his suitcase out of the back of the Jeep, she watched him sling his backpack on one shoulder and carry his luggage to the front step.

With a bright smile, he said, "Hey, you. Good morning. Sleep well?"

"Suppose so."

"I kept getting up, thinking I was going to sleep in. Finally, I set three alarms to give me peace of mind. Even increased the ringer to full volume, just in case," he laughed while approaching with open arms. "Sorry, I've been M.I.A the past couple of days. I've had a lot to take care of."

Seeing the sincerity in his eyes, she smiled. "It's okay. I understand. The important thing is, you're here now."

Lips touching hers, he backed off upon spotting Burton standing in the foyer, his arms crossed in front of his chest. Breaking from their embrace, he walked over and offered his hand. "Hey. Morning."

"Morning," Burton muttered somewhat coldly, surveying where the football player had parked his Jeep.

"Maybe you should put your truck in my garage while we're away. Keep it out of the elements." Attention gravitating to his device, he pushed a couple of buttons and looked out to the left of the property. "Bay four should be open. Go ahead and park there. I will close it when you return."

Shane nodded. "I'll do that. Thanks." Turning to Abi, he said, "I'll be right back."

An awkward silence erupted between Burton and Abi. "B, please be nice."

"What do you mean?" he smiled mischievously. "I offered space for him in my garage. That's nice of me, isn't it?" he glanced over and smirked.

She tilted her head. "Yes, I know. I'm just reminding you."

Seeing she was serious, he said, "I'll do my best."

"Thank you."

Disturbed by the gate notification again, Burton pressed the button a second time.

Spotting Reg and Jade arriving, she stood in the open doorway and waved to her friends as Shane returned from the garage.

"Hey, girlfriend!"

"Hello, bride-to-be!"

With arms open, Jade walked over and hugged her.

"I still can't believe this is happening," she whispered. "I'm getting married in a couple of days."

"I know! I'm so excited!"

Jade addressed Burton. "I don't know how we will ever be able to repay you for this."

"Don't worry about it. Just make sure it lasts."

Reggie overheard him as he placed their luggage on the steps. "That's a given. It's no secret that I'm determined to spend the rest of my life with this woman."

The comment suddenly hit Burton. Contemplating the gravity of what Reggie said, he looked at Abi and managed a half smile just as Shane walked up. In an effort to save face, he said, "The guys will load your bags momentarily." Leaving the foyer, he ducked into his study while Martin reappeared to give everyone instructions as Andrew, Matt, and Ted pulled up in their SUV.

One by one, the men placed their luggage in line with the others and greeted Martin.

"Morning, Sir," Andrew said.

"Morning, gentlemen." His eyes swayed to his iPad. "We are waiting for the rest of the entourage. When they arrive, I would like to have a quick meeting before we head out."

Acknowledging him, Andrew nodded. "Very good, Sir."

The other two did the same.

"Miss Abi?" he said.

"Yes, Martin."

"May I have a word with you and your guests?"

"Sure."

Overhearing that, Reggie, Jade, and Shane gathered around.

Making eye contact with everyone, he instructed, "We will be heading out to Van Nuys shortly. I trust you all have your passports?"

"Yes, right here." Tethered to a lanyard around her neck, Abi pulled hers from underneath her hoodie while each of her friends fumbled around to find theirs.

"Miss Abi has the right idea. Keeping it on your person is the best method."

"On your person? What does that mean? I'm sorry," Jade questioned.

Martin stood straight and prepared to educate the young lady. "It means in your pockets or attached to you, Miss." Looking at her, he waited for a positive expression to confirm she'd gotten it. "And, so that all of you are aware… You must have your passport with you at all times during your stay in Japan. Any failure to present your identification when asked by law enforcement will result in a six-hundred and ninety-five dollar fine per infraction."

"U.S.?" Shane asked. "That's heavy."

Jade eyed up Abi's lanyard. "Where did you get that thing? That seems like the way to go."

"Maybe somewhere along the way, we can find one for you." She assumed they could locate one along their travels.

"I will have a few of them sent to our first hotel. They will be waiting upon arrival. Until then, please check on the whereabouts of your documentation. Perhaps designate a pocket in your bag to keep the location consistent," Martin advised.

Jade secured hers in the interior pouch of her tote while Reg and Shane both zipped theirs into their joggers' front pockets.

When the sprinter driver approached, Martin's eyes veered away from the group. "Excuse me a moment," he said. "We must start loading the bags."

It wasn't long before Lorenzo, Bray, Ethan, and Rob emerged from the staff quarters, luggage in hand.

Giving them the same spiel that he'd given Andrew's and Abi's groups, Martin started checking things off his list and reading emails on the arrangements currently transpiring on the other end of their journey.

"Where on Earth is that Italian?" he whispered, spying the time on his watch. "The guy is late again."

All at once, he spotted a yellow taxi barreling through the gates. Inside, they could see Anton paying the driver before taking his baggage from the trunk.

"Don't worry! I'm here. So, so sorry! My car. It got a flat!" He looked frazzled. "Then I got it towed to my guy and called my friend to pick it up later..." Frustrated, he rambled on dramatically and took a breath while rubbing his hand across his forehead. "So, so stressful. Can't believe my luck. But I am here! Good to go." Fumbling with his soft-shell satchel of knives, Martin eyed him up.

"Those stay here," the older gentleman pointed out sternly.

"But..."

"No, buts! I am not going through another knife fiasco! Besides, aren't you supposed to be on vacation? You are not cooking."

"Yes, but I am doing research for Master B on Japanese cuisine. What if I need..."

Martin cut him off. "No."

Anton threw his hands in the air. "Martin, please!"

"This is not up for debate. The knives are staying, or you stay with them."

The chef sulked. "Very well."

Walking away, Abi giggled upon hearing him quietly speaking to the satchel as if bidding his knives goodbye. "Wow, he must be very attached to those."

"Typical chef," Martin commented under his breath. "They are lost without their tools."

When he said that, Abi saw Sara drive up in her Audi SUV. The girl made eye contact with her as she parked in front of the house.

Burton immediately walked over to help her unload her luggage. "Two suitcases?"

She smirked. "What do you mean? One is my stuff. The other is tactical gear."

"Tactical gear, huh?"

"Don't even think about it," she said, cracking a subtle smile.

Catching drips and drabs of their conversation, Abi watched Burton get behind the wheel and move her vehicle to the garage.

"Morning, Sara," Abi unnervingly said, watching the girl set her LV tote down beside the other bags on the step.

Casting a keen eye, she said with a monotone voice. "Morning."

Thankful her friends were standing close by, Abi continued talking with them since Sara wasn't interested in saying anything more.

Shane spotted Burton returning from the garage.

"Okay, Martin. Let's get this show on the road," the famous DJ ordered.

Anton grabbed his duffel bag and stood alongside one SUV to await further instructions.

Seeing the guy, Burton clarified, "You do realize we are gone for three weeks, right?"

The chef smiled. "Yes, Sir. I like to travel light."

While Martin belted out instructions, telling everyone they were riding together in the Sprinter, the men finished loading all the baggage in their flat-bedded SUV.

As their group climbed aboard and got settled in their seats, Abi saw Sara sit down beside Burton. The girl didn't look happy.

Still feeling like she'd forgotten something, Abi stared at the ceiling, racking her brain.

Noticing her worried look, Shane reached over. "Hey? You okay?"

Uncertain, she squeezed his hand and put on a brave face. "Yes. I'm good."

"It's gonna be fun. Just go with the flow. I'm sure Martin has everything under control."

"I don't doubt that," she laughed.

"I know it's your first Christmas without your Mom… Is that it?"

"Yes, and…" Pulling away from the house, a little panicked, Abi went over her checklist again. "I still feel like I'm forgetting something."

"Don't worry. If you did, we could always buy it when we get there."

Calming down as they exited the Beverly Park main gate, she said, "That's true. I'm sure it'll be fine." She turned to him. "And as for Mom, I'm not as sad these days, so this trip comes at a good time."

He slipped his arm across her shoulders and pulled her close. "I'm glad to hear that."

Wanting to lighten the mood, she quietly whispered so nobody would hear, "I was also thinking about the whole you and me…on this trip… Perhaps, spending time alone."

His sight snapped to her. "Is that right?" He could tell she was a tad uncomfortable, but more so curious. "Well, for me, I'm happy to have you all to myself for a change, apart from having to spend time with our friends and…"

"Come on," she giggled. "You can say his name."

"Rather not, if that's okay," he chuckled.

Heading north on the 405, Abi said, "Now, don't be mean. This is really nice of him to invite us. Would you rather be spending Christmas with your family?"

Quickly raising both hands to symbolize scales, the quarterback weighed in. "Hmm, let me see. My bossy father breathing down my neck steadily, while his wife criticizes my every move, or my self-absorbed Mother, who would go about her business not bidding me the time of day? That's a toss-up."

"Oh, my…"

"Without a second thought, I'd pick you over them any day." He leaned in and kissed her lips. "I just feel sorry for Jacob. Poor kid has to deal with that."

"Maybe when we get back, we should spend some time with him. Do something fun."

"Yeah. He'd like that, I'm sure."

When they pulled into Van Nuys' private boarding lounge, the Sprinter and the SUV passed through the main gates and circled the roundabout to wait for the airfield access to open. Making their way through slowly, they veered to the right. There, Abi noticed something odd.

"Wait? That's not Burton's plane," she said.

Jade piped up. "It's a long-range charter. He probably wanted more space and a bigger fuel and baggage capacity."

Abi nodded. That made sense.

Approaching the large Boeing 727 private jet surrounded by armed guards, their security team flooded the tarmac to secure the area before giving everyone the signal to exit the vehicle and ascend the stairs.

Given the green light, Shane and Abi bolted from the Sprinter, their laughter muffled by the rain pelting down. Andrew and Ted followed closely behind, holding umbrellas over their heads as they scanned the area with sharp vigilance. The cold rainwater streamed off the edges of the umbrellas as they hustled toward the steps of the plane.

One by one, their friends followed, moving quickly under the watchful eyes of the security detail.

The sleek private jet seemed dull under the overcast sky.

Inside, the cabin was a picture of understated luxury. Ivory quilted leather seats lined the interior, each complemented by plush burnt orange cushions that added a subtle pop of warmth. The light-colored walls and overhead lighting enhanced the airy feel, making the spacious interior seem even larger.

Seats were claimed quickly.

Burton and Sara sat two rows behind them, content with their quiet space. Meanwhile, Abi, Shane, Jade, and Reggie took a block of seats in the middle, facing each other. From there, Abi could see Burton adjacent to her as he looked over, smiled, and gave a thumbs-up. She did the same.

Comfortable, Jade immediately started scrolling through her phone. While she got immersed in social media, Shane leaned back in his seat and watched the rain streaking the windows as everyone prepared for their long journey ahead.

The gray skies darkened as the rain began to drum steadily.

Analyzing the data on her weather app, Abi frowned at the radar display. "Looks like we are on the edge of the storm, but might catch a slight break in thirty minutes if we're lucky," she said, turning the device toward Shane, hoping the pilot might get them off the ground then. On the map, a massive band of green and yellow stretched across the region, with vivid splashes of orange and red signaling heavy rainfall and powerful winds. "It's going to get nasty," she muttered.

Overhearing them, Jade asked, "Are we in the clear to leave?" Her voice was tinged with concern.

"Looks like a bit of a delay," Andrew replied, giving her a reassuring smile despite her own growing unease. "They're holding us on standby, but think we should be in the air shortly. Hold tight."

Near the baggage hatch, the ground crew worked hurriedly, shielding the luggage from the rain as they loaded it onto the plane. Water pooled on the tarmac, reflecting the swirling clouds above.

At the front of the cabin, Martin paced, his gaze flickering to his watch every few seconds. After a moment, he gestured for Reggie to follow him to a quiet corner near the galley.

The man leaned in, his voice low and urgent. "At this rate, I don't know if we will make the appointment at the U.S. Consulate."

Reggie's body went rigid. "And what happens if we miss it?"

"Then you and Jade won't legally be able to marry in the country," Martin said bluntly. "And I'd rather not explain that to her. So, keep this to yourself. If she finds out, it'll make for a very long flight."

The guy nodded, swallowing hard. "I won't say a word."

"Good man," Martin replied, tapping him on the shoulder. "I just wanted to keep you informed. Let's hope this storm doesn't set us back too much."

As the rain intensified, Abi, oblivious to the conversation up front, leaned her head against Shane's shoulder. Outside, lightning flickered in the distance, illuminating the heavy, slate-gray sky. She glanced again at the radar, biting her lip. Time was ticking, and tension hung in the air despite the luxurious surroundings. Saying a little prayer, she hoped God would part the skies sooner rather than later.

| 7 |

Come Fly with Me

Thursday, December 14

Van Nuys Airport

Within twenty minutes, a crackle came over the intercom, drawing everyone's attention to the pilot's announcement. "Ladies and gentlemen, we've been given a brief window in the weather. We're going to attempt to take off. Please buckle your seat belts and stow all baggage securely. Flight attendants, prepare for departure."

The cabin buzzed with muted activity as everyone quickly complied. The hum of the engines grew louder as the jet began taxiing toward the runway. Raindrops streaked diagonally across the windows, blurring the stormy landscape outside.

Abi double-checked her seatbelt and scanned the cabin. Martin had taken his seat at the front, his expression calm, but she could see his fingers drumming rhythmically on the armrest.

The jet slowed as it reached the end of the runway, briefly pausing as though gathering its strength. The engines roared to life, producing a powerful sound that reverberated through the cabin as the plane surged forward.

Thrust into her seat, Abi's grip tightened. "Here we go," she said with a mix of nerves and exhilaration while clutching Shane's hand.

He glanced at her and smiled, his thumb brushing over hers reassuringly, despite the tremors rippling through the aircraft.

Soon, the plane's nose tilted upward, and the wheels left the ground.

For a moment, her stomach dropped as they climbed into the gray, rain-laden sky. The world outside the windows dissolved into a haze of thick clouds, leaving them cocooned in the soft glow of the cabin lights. Exhaling slowly with knuckles white, she held on.

The jet bumped through a few pockets, drawing a gasp from Jade across from them.

Burton's voice drifted about, muttering something to Sara that got lost in the rumble of the engines.

Finally, the plane steadied, the turbulence fading as they climbed higher above the storm.

Abi sat up and released her grip on the armrest along with Shane's hand, giving him a sheepish smile. "Well, that was...terrifying."

Chuckling at her uncertainty, he held her hand, his fingers now loosely intertwined with hers. "Let's just hope that was the worst of it."

She nodded and peered out the window. The storm clouds stretched endlessly below them, a reminder of how narrowly they had escaped.

While the jet cruised northeast, smoothly gliding over the Pacific, Burton leaned back in his seat, casually pulling out his laptop. With a swipe of his finger across the touchscreen, he opened several news feeds from Japan.

Abi noticed his expression shift—subtle, yet unmistakably one of quiet satisfaction.

"What is it, B?" she asked, leaning forward curiously.

Sara glanced at Abi over the edge of her tablet, her gaze sharp and disapproving.

"It's nothing." A small smirk tugged at the corner of his mouth as he shook his head humbly. "Just skimming some Dark Demon media posts."

Not convinced, Abi pulled out her phone and did her own quick search for Dark Demon in Japan. Within moments, her screen filled with a string of articles and announcements. The headlines ranged from whispers about exclusive raves to cryptic references about cutting-edge technology that seemed too advanced to believe.

"Wow, the guy's buzz is crazy right now," Abi noted, watching how she spoke of him. "His upcoming raves are causing a stir."

Upon hearing this, Jade was intrigued.

At the same time, Reggie shifted his weight forward, somewhat interested as Abi continued flipping through the headlines, all of them centered around the mysterious DJ's upcoming events.

"*Japanese Fans Await Dark Demon's Appearance at NAKKA,*" she said, reading one. Another headline had a more skeptical tone: "*Is Dark Demon's Secretive Rave Tour a Scam? Many Still in the Dark About Event Details.*"

"Whoa!" Jade said excitedly, curious about the work Burton had done for the famous guy while also finding a few articles herself. "People are really hyped about this! But why are some of these headlines so negative?"

Burton shrugged. "Guess the concept is foreign to them, so there is bound to be bad press if there is a lack of understanding."

With a raised eyebrow, Reggie commented, "Makes sense. It is weird. Typically, for a concert, you purchase a ticket, receive it, and then know when and where the event is scheduled to take place. With Dark Demon, part of the allure is the mystery and the last-minute adrenaline rush you get on the way there."

"Exactly." Burton agreed. "The fans know it's legit. Look at the comments."

Jade scrolled down, reading through a flood of social media posts. Fans were fiercely defending Dark Demon, saying it was worth every penny. "If you get the invite, you'd better clear your schedule and go,"

Jade read what one fan wrote. "It's not just a rave. It's an unforgettable experience. You'll never see anything like it again."

Flashing a humble expression, Burton said, "The media don't like the secrecy. But the fans—people who've actually been to the events—know how it works and love the immersive atmosphere."

As her face lit up, Jade remembered the raves she'd attended while showing Reggie the screen. "Yeah, that is what makes the whole thing so wild! The buildup and the mystery—when we finally got in, it was like nothing else."

Removing his earbuds to join their conversation silently, Shane listened to his friend's comments.

"Maybe it's the fear of the unknown or the lack of control you have. Technically, you're at the mercy of the guy. If you want to see him perform, you gotta follow the DJ's rules, plain and simple. Many are afraid to go along with it, I think. In the end, it's not just a party—it's like stepping into an alternate universe. You create all that, right? All the technical stuff?"

"Yes, for the most part. But Dark Demon has a whole team that handles the set installs. I oversee the design." Clearly enjoying the topic of discussion, happy to get some feedback, Burton smiled as he scrolled through some more headlines. "I guess, from the look of it, Japan is just getting a taste of what's to come. Most are responding positively."

Smirking at what the guy said, knowing Burton was playing a role, Shane closed his eyes after placing his buds back in his ears.

"That's his marketing talking. Whoever is handling that should be given a medal. It's genius." Jade leaned in, her curiosity piqued. "So, when we land, will we get to go to one of the events? Maybe meet him? Can you get us in?"

Somewhat mischievously, Burton paused. "Actually, I've got something a little more interesting in mind for all of you."

"It better be a backstage pass," Reg suggested. "We all know you're well-connected, dude."

As planned, Martin interrupted their conversation. "A word, Sir."

Casually getting up, Burton stretched. "Sorry, excuse me a minute."

While he walked to the back of the plane, Abi knew what he was doing and noticed Sara didn't look impressed as the pocket door slid closed.

"Wonder what that's about?" Jade questioned, concerned by the gentleman's tone.

"I'm sure everything is fine. Martin does this often," Abi clarified.

Minutes later, Burton emerged—but not as they'd ever seen him. Wearing the signature Dark Demon hood, its intricate black design and striking lines cast a strange, magnetic presence in the cabin.

Jade shot up from her seat, almost fearful. "Oh, my god!" Her eyes widened, and her jaw dropped. "No freaking way!"

Abi laughed.

Reggie sat frozen, his mouth hanging open. "Wait... Holy shit." He thought they were pranking him. "Is this a joke?" He found Abi smiling from ear to ear. "Dude, are you telling me *you're him?*"

He slowly slid the hood back, revealing his face with a calm, steady grin.

Starstruck, Jade gasped and stood up. "I am..." She stopped and turned to Reg. "No! *We* are huge fans!" Her legs weakened, making her fall back into her seat. "I've been in the crowd while you've been up there on stage. How did I not know this?"

Reggie stared at Burton. "Man, this is...mind-blowing."

Confident, the DJ nodded. "With you coming along on this trip, I knew things would get complicated if you didn't know. Thought it was better to come clean now. I'll be too busy to deal with it later."

Throwing her hands up, Jade giggled joyfully in disbelief. "Wow, this is crazy! And here we thought you were just the brains behind the operation – not the celebrity, too. This is insane."

"Dark Demon, huh? Who would've thought?" Reggie slouched in his seat. "Suddenly, this trip has taken an unexpected turn." He hit Shane's arm. "Hey? Did you know about this?"

The football player removed one earbud. "Huh?"

Reg repeated. "I said, did you know about this?"

Shane looked over at Burton. "Oh, that? I've known since Vegas."

"And you never told me?"

Abi intervened and said to the guy, "Shane was sworn to secrecy."

The QB pointed at his girlfriend. "Yeah, what she said."

As the plane soared above the clouds, Burton slipped the hoodie off and returned it to the garment bag hanging in the back. In the aftermath of his reveal, excitement still hung thick in the air.

Wide-eyed, Jade and Reggie sat together as the excitement slowly faded, still grappling to wrap their heads around what they'd learned.

Just then, the flight attendant appeared, wheeling a cart of food and drinks. "Would you like something? I will be serving your meal soon," the woman asked the teenage girl, her voice calm and professional as the plane gently hummed through the sky.

"A sparkling water would be great. Thank you," Jade replied.

"Would you like it mixed with juice?"

Thinking about it, she added, "Sure. Something sweet would be awesome."

Mixing the San Pellegrino with strawberry and passionfruit, she handed her the orangey, pink drink. "Here you are, Miss. Enjoy."

"Oooh, thank you. This looks wonderful," Jade said excitedly.

One by one, the young woman satisfied their beverage requests before presenting the menu offering for the meal – a series of dishes, including sushi rolls, fresh salads, gourmet sliders, and delicate pastries.

Abi's eyes lit up. "Oh, this all looks so good."

While the attendant noted their preferences, Abi shot Burton a smile across the aisle.

He did the same.

Glad the reveal had gone perfectly, she took a sip of her sparkling water and said to Reggie and Jade, "So, are you guys ready to get married?"

The guy grinned happily at the love of his life. "I was ready the second I met her."

Reminded of their marriage license appointment, Jade checked the time on her phone. Confused by the time zone conversion, she raised her hand and waved to get Martin's attention.

"Yes, Miss Jade?"

"How are we on time? Will we make our appointment?"

Knowing the girl had an inkling there could be a problem, he said, "Be patient, Miss. We will ensure that you arrive in plenty of time. I promise."

The girl nodded happily.

The flight attendant returned with a mixed crystal jug of sparkling juice.

Burton raised his glass. "A toast to the happy couple, who will be married a week from now."

Everyone clinked their glasses with excitement.

Adding one final comment before they started eating, Reggie said, "And to this guy - for making it all happen."

Humbly acknowledging him, Burton silently bowed his head.

When the attendant served their food, the initial chatter subsided, allowing the atmosphere on the plane to settle into a smooth rhythm. The private jet cruised effortlessly above the clouds - the cabin bathed in soft, ambient lighting. A warm, tranquil energy settled over the group.

Martin leaned forward and flipped the cover on his iPad. An expression of focus crossed his face. "Alright, Miss Jade and Mr. Wilson. Since we've got time, let's go over the wedding plans. There are still a few details we need to lock down."

The two exchanged glances, ready to tackle the subject.

Eager to know what the man had planned for them, Jade listened intently. "Shoot," she said.

With his stylus pen in hand, Martin slid it over the screen in a series of strokes. "I've got a stunning venue lined up in Kyoto," he divulged, scrolling through his notes. "The chapel is nestled right beside a river and surrounded by a forest. It is a very secluded and quaint spot."

"That sounds perfect." Jade clutched her hands under her chin. "I like the idea of a natural setting."

Seeing the look on his fiancée, Reggie reached over and took her hand.

Martin smiled. "It is beautiful and picturesque. Now, let's talk flowers. Since it's winter, the wedding coordinator went with seasonal blooms. She's chosen this white flower with a black center. It is quite striking." He showed them the photo. "We will complement the bouquet with sprigs of festive greenery. It'll tie in beautifully with the winter theme and the natural setting of the chapel."

"That's gorgeous." Jade pointed at the picture and turned to Reggie. "Look, Babe. I love the idea of the black center; it's unique and elegant."

"Great," Martin said, jotting down a note. "Now, about your dress, Jade—it's Vera Wang."

She melted at hearing the designer's name roll off his tongue.

"The bridal salon found this. It's classic yet modern." He showed her the picture as Jade shielded Reggie's eyes so he wouldn't see. "And, as for the rings, you have a choice between Western traditional white gold or Japanese hammered platinum." Turning the iPad to them again, he showed them their options. "The hammered style has a unique texture that fits well with the natural, rustic feel of the venue. Also, it can be a reminder of your trip."

Loving the idea, Reggie said, "I like the sound of the Japanese ones."

"I like the hammered style, too," Jade agreed. "It adds a personal touch."

Martin made a note of their preference. "Perfect. I'll arrange for those. Everything will be ready for you."

With the details settled, they shifted back to lighter topics as they continued to enjoy their meal and drinks. The cabin soon filled with a warm, cozy ambiance as their attendant tidied up from the meal service. Jade and Abi volunteered to help the girl despite her declining their assistance.

Soon, a quiet blanketed the group as everyone watched movies and listened to music. Abi pulled the book she'd brought along – a young adult, apocalyptic, science fiction novel from a new indie author she'd gravitated to over the past couple of months. Starting chapter one, she got comfortable and reclined in the chair, raising the footrest.

A reader herself, the attendant noticed and brought over a polar fleece blanket. "Here you go, Miss."

Abi looked up from her book. "Thank you so much," she said.

"No problem. I'm a reader, too. There's nothing like being wrapped in a blanket while you immerse in the pages."

"I completely agree."

With chairs reclining, everyone settled in for a rest, knowing that with the time change, it would be another twelve hours before they would get to sleep.

| 8 |

Welcome to Japan

Friday, December 15

Tamayura Premium Gate, Kansai International Airport

With the sun shining brightly, Abi looked out the window of the plane as it circled the city. About to land on an island, seemingly man-made, the waters of Osaka Bay glistened in the light.

Stretching and checking the time on her phone, she noticed the time zone had changed. Registering Japan Standard Time, Abi realized it was now 12:15 pm on Friday. Up for more than seventeen hours thus far, she knew their day was technically just beginning.

As the plane slowly descended, Abi felt the wheels touch down on the runway. Taxiing towards the terminal, the pilot stopped outside Gate 98.

Burton opened his duffel bag, changed into a black shirt, and put on his Dark Demon sweatshirt, covering his head with the hood to hide his face.

Seeing Master B ready to go, Martin stood up. "Now, before we disembark, just a few things."

Everyone listened intently.

"Upon arrival, Master B will be meeting with DJ RED DRAGON. Our group will split up for this meeting and move through the same executive lounge. At no time will you look affiliated with Burton, his security, or me. This is a strict rule. No exceptions. Is that clear?"

They nodded.

"Miss Jade. You, Reggie, Miss Abi, and Shane will be with Andrew, Ted, and Matt upon arrival inside the terminal. I will be leaving with Burton after the meeting and joining you at the U.S. Consulate to submit the paperwork for the wedding. Afterward, we will file those documents at City Hall before continuing on to Kyoto." Turning to his Boss, he said, "While we are doing that, you, Sara, Anton, and your security will go on ahead to the Aman Hotel. It will be our home for the next few days and the secret location of the wedding."

Each man on the team acknowledged him. Burton included.

"A quick note. Always know where your passport is at all times and stick together. If you don't want to incur a huge cellular bill, consider turning off roaming or installing the eSIM Japan app on your phone. I emailed that information earlier. I strongly advise that you only communicate via WhatsApp from here on out."

Taking heed of his warning, everyone did as he said.

"I've created a group chat. If you haven't joined it, do it now. This is where I will be posting updates and status reports."

The pilot opened the door. A waft of cool air filled the cabin.

"Please gather your things. Do not leave anything behind," Martin added. "And for our couples, no PDA, please. It is frowned upon here."

They all looked around at one another.

"Guess I'll have to kiss you in the shadows," Shane mischievously whispered in his girlfriend's ear.

Looking into his eyes with a smitten smile, she replied, "I won't object," while grabbing her bag off the floor.

Surprised to hear this, his eyebrows shot up.

While the guys secured the area, Burton and Sara left with Martin and Anton first, as planned.

Staying on the plane, waiting for Andrew's signal to move out, Abi felt like they were still in the air. A little antsy, she stood in the aisle. Somehow, her feet still felt like they were flying.

Andrew motioned to them. "Okay. It's time to go," he said. "Remember, no communication with the other group."

Shane got Abi to lead the way. "It's showtime. Excited?" he asked.

She looked up at him. "More anxious, I think. This is a trip of a lifetime."

"I'm looking forward to our experiences here together."

Feeling his hand gently squeeze hers, she said, "Me too," before turning to Jade. "Ready to become Mrs. Reginald Wilson?"

The girl giggled lightheartedly and turned to her fiancé. "Yes, I can hardly wait."

Descending the steps of the plane, their groups moved inside Gate 98. Each was assigned a terminal guide upon arrival just inside the doors. Dressed in dark suit jackets and pants, both men communicated via radio to someone on the other end, spouting instructions in Japanese.

Spaced about fifty feet apart, Burton's guys surrounded him with two in the front and two in the back. Martin was to his left, and Sara to his right. Everyone wore something to cover their head, and sunglasses covered their eyes.

Following the gentleman through the labyrinth of hallways, Shane and Abi walked a few feet behind Reg and Jade, listening to the man inform them of the airport's arrival procedures.

When they reached the lounge entrance, walking side by side, the glass doors slid open as they entered a guarded area.

Abi took notice of Burton and Sara way ahead of them. The two weren't holding hands, nor were they speaking. She immediately felt something was off.

"We will stop at the main desk to do a passport check first before proceeding toward the main lounge," their guide said. "Once your transportation has arrived, your luggage will get loaded, and I will escort you out to your vehicles with additional security. The moment you are on your way, our contractual obligations have ended. Any questions?"

Taking point, Andrew acknowledged him. "Sounds good."

They watched Burton and his entourage breeze past the passport check without stopping.

"Wow, guess that guy is super famous, huh?" Reg joked, wondering if the guide would make mention of anything.

Under his breath, he said, "From what I know, he is here from America. Apparently, he is a famous DJ or something like that. Our boss instructed us not to speak to him directly."

Approaching the main desk, Burton disappeared around the corner while their group gathered and registered with Customs. Taking no longer than five minutes, they made their way to the circular lounge.

There, they found Burton standing with his head down.

Martin and Lorenzo were mere feet from him while the others gathered with their heads on a swivel.

A man dressed in a red hoodie with a dragon etched on it waited with a pretty Japanese girl with long, wavy dark hair. She was all smiles.

Avoiding the meeting at all costs, Shane and Reg stood together while Jade walked over to speak with Abi, who was curiously listening in as much as she could. It wasn't long before she noticed the woman with Red Dragon was wearing a wedding band. The Japanese DJ was also.

Huh? They're married, she thought. *Interesting.*

Bowing, the DJ in the red said to Dark Demon, "I'm sure our business venture will be successful."

"It will be," Burton replied in a deep voice from the shadows of his hoodie.

"I do not wish to keep you. When you arrive at Aman, I left some... What do you say?" he paused. "Swag...is it?"

"That's right," Burton confirmed in a friendly tone.

"Yes!" he pointed humorously. "I left some *swag* for you and your staff. Enjoy."

Offering a single nod, nothing else - Burton respectfully parted ways with the DJ and bowed, as did Martin. "Thank you, Sir. We appreciate your generosity."

They watched the two leave, waving casually with about ten security guards accompanying them.

"Wow, that guy has more security than we do," Reg speculated.

Spotting the refreshments bar, a Tamayura host greeted them with warm, essential oil-scented towels.

Jade grabbed Abi's arm. "I need to use the washroom."

"Me too. I'll come with you." Abi turned to Shane. "I'll be right back."

"Sure. No problem," the burly football player said.

Smiling at the QB, linking her arm with Abi's, Jade made sure they were far enough away before fishing a little. "I've been dying to ask."

"Ask what?"

"You and Shane will have a lot of time alone on this trip. Got anything specific planned?" Her eyebrows repeatedly raised, hoping her friend got the drift of what she was trying to say without asking directly.

Not letting on anything, Abi replied, "We haven't passed anything by Martin yet. Why?"

"Martin? Why would you..." Jade stopped, realizing she didn't understand her. "What I mean is... You and Shane will have *alone - alone* time. Understand?"

Hearing this, Abi lowered her head. "I'm trying not to think about that."

"Why? You guys have been dating for months."

"I know..." Abi ducked into a stall and closed the door.

Jade did the same. With the wall between them, she was concerned about her friend. "What's up? Are you scared?"

"No. Just nervous. It's a big step."

Flushing, they emerged at the same time to wash their hands and check their faces. Abi pulled her toothbrush and toothpaste from her bag. Jade watched as she brushed her teeth, thinking she was smart to have it in her carry-on.

"I should have done that."

Spitting, she said, "What?"

"Had my toothbrush in my bag."

Abi reached into the tote. "Here. I brought a spare just in case."

"Oh! Wow. Are you sure?"

"Absolutely."

"You're a lifesaver. My tongue was feeling a little pasty." Brushing her teeth, Jade looked at her. "So?"

"So, what?"

"Are you thinking of…you know…" She bumped her shoulder with hers. "…with Shane?"

Anxious, Abi stared at her reflection in the mirror. "Perhaps. If the time comes and it feels right. Maybe." She looked down at the ring on her finger.

"I gotta say, it was so sweet how he gave you that ring and announced his commitment to you that night."

Recalling his speech, she said, "Yes. It was."

With her eye on the time, Jade hurried. "We'd better get a move on. They may have left without us."

The girls opened the door and returned to the lounge. Burton's group had already departed.

Andrew immediately took notice of them. "Is everyone accounted for now? We need to move out. We are on a tight schedule. If we don't get to the U.S. Consulate before 2:00, there will be no wedding," he said point-blank.

Reggie rolled his eyes, knowing that would spark a fire under his fiancée.

"Wait? Why?" Jade panicked.

"Because of the storm, we were delayed over an hour. Now we're running behind."

"Please tell me you're kidding? Are you serious?"

"Calm down, Sweetness."

She looked at Reggie. "Why aren't you surprised by this?"

Figuring it out, she said, "Wait? You knew? Who told you?"

"Martin."

"When?"

"Before we left the ground in California."

"And you didn't think to share that with me?"

Reggie laughed. "Definitely not."

"Why?"

"Because we all knew you'd react like this."

Unhappy, Jade kicked it into high gear. "Enough talking! Let's move! We gotta hurry! Chop! Chop!"

On the way out, Abi grabbed a few complimentary bottles of water for her and Shane. Pointing it out to the men, they did the same.

As their group walked outside the terminal, they found two Blacklane chauffeur-driven SUVs waiting along the curb, with men loading their baggage in the back of a cargo van. Ahead of them, four more SUVs departed with Burton and his entourage.

"Looks like he got some additional hardware," Abi whispered to Shane in code, counting ten more heads dressed in black.

"Seems so."

With the last of their bags loaded, something unusual caught Abi's attention as she stood curbside. While moving with quiet efficiency, one of the men with modern, silvery-blue hair leaned over to grab the last suitcase from the trolley. On his neck, she noticed the edge of a red dragon tattoo just visible along the collar of his crisp dress shirt. The intricate design seemed almost alive, its fiery scales curling up from beneath the fabric. The ink, sharp and detailed, created a sense of curiosity as she studied it.

She recalled an article she read on Japanese culture. Knowing that tattoos were considered unacceptable in society, she was surprised the guy had one despite its obscure location. *Interesting*, she mused, her mind lingering on the mysterious symbol, wondering if it had a specific meaning. *Funny how Burton is here to work with Red Dragon. What a coincidence,* she surmised.

When the guy turned, Abi immediately moved from his neck to his flawless face. Staring at him, she was shocked to see that his eyes were different colors.

Pointing to her bag, he gestured for her to hand it to him.

She put up her hands, bowed, and kept her tote close. "Arigatō," she said, shaking her head, hoping she'd said it correctly.

The man understood what she wanted. "Dou itashimashite," he replied, bowing slightly.

She assumed he'd said, *You're welcome* while hearing her friend arguing with Andrew.

Initially told that she and Reg were in the second car with Ted and Matt, the bossy girl insisted, "But I don't want us to be in separate vehicles. I want to travel with our friends."

Going against Martin's instructions, Andrew looked at the time, then at the other guys. "This is not up for debate," he stated sternly.

"Look, I'm the bride, and what I say goes," she demanded as Reggie looked on, secretly wanting to travel with their friends, too.

Knowing they were wasting precious time, the big guy made an executive decision and humored her. "Fine. Hurry. Get in. We need to go."

Proud of herself, Jade got excited and climbed into the third-row seat behind their friends in the middle.

Andrew took point up front and instructed the driver where to go first.

As the SUV pulled away from the terminal, its tires rolling smoothly over the pavement, Abi's gaze drifted to the scene outside her window, where the crisp afternoon sunlight painted sharp contrasts across the winter landscape.

Her attention snagged on a figure across the street—a man standing near a glossy black Mercedes parked in the adjacent lot. He was dressed entirely in black, his tailored coat and polished boots lending him an air of quiet authority. Smoke curled lazily from the cigarette between his fingers, dissipating in the clear, cool air.

Abi's eyes caught on the object he held—a walking stick, intricately carved and faintly tinted with a reddish hue. It seemed an odd accessory, almost theatrical, but it suited him in a way she couldn't quite explain.

As their vehicle veered toward the exit, the man dropped the cigarette to the ground and crushed it underfoot. Without hurry, he opened the door of the Mercedes and slid inside. His movements were fluid, his head turning ever so slightly as if tracking their departure.

A flicker of unease rippled through Abi, her pulse quickening. She shifted in her seat, fingers tightening around the strap of her bag. *He's probably waiting for someone,* she reassured herself, though her mind didn't fully settle given the timing of it all.

Still paranoid to a degree after their run-ins with Eastwood, she mumbled quietly, "But...Nobody knows we're here."

"What was that?" Shane asked, glancing her way.

"Nothing," she replied. "Just talking to myself."

| 9 |

The Appointment

Friday, December 15

U.S. Consulate General and City Hall, Osaka, Japan

As they made the journey across the bridge, Abi marveled at the ocean below them. It was hard to fathom how they could create a man-made island that large and then connect the long bridge to the mainland.

Considering the scope of the project and its numerous challenges, she whispered to herself, "This is amazing," just as Jade bellowed from the back, "How are we on time, Andrew?"

"We are good, Miss."

The girl kept fidgeting, making everyone tense.

While merging with the highway on land once again, they made their way along Osaka Bay on the opposite side of the road. Mostly seeing countless industrial ports, they soon noticed the presence of high-rise buildings and residential areas. The traffic became increasingly dense as they approached the city center. Being stopped in the afternoon gridlock reminded them of the 405 back home.

Amidst the tall business buildings with trees growing in the spaces between, crossing yet another bridge overtop of a picturesque river running underneath them before exiting on Kitahama into the downtown core, they backtracked slightly, taking a narrow back alley of sorts. The driver put on his hazard lights and stopped at the corner of a large building guarded by police.

"This must be it," Shane said, peering out the window, spotting Martin standing alongside an SUV guarded by Bray and Rob.

"Wait here a moment," Andrew stated.

Leaving the truck, they watched the guys gather around and get further instructions while Martin walked over to greet a tall, middle-aged man with round, gold-rimmed glasses, dressed in a three-piece suit. When he reached out to her guardian, the two cordially shook hands, prompting Martin to signal Andrew.

"Alright. Everyone, take only your passports, wallet, and phones. Reg, please bring your forms with you. No bags allowed. Stay together," Andrew said as they got out.

Taking up the rear as Martin led the way with the gentleman ahead of them, Matt and Ted stayed vigilant on either side of the group.

Once they reached the main doors, the man turned to address them.

"Welcome to Osaka. My name is Hiro Matsumura. I will be your translator and English-speaking guide during your time here in Japan." With everyone greeting him kindly, he said, "We are about to enter the U.S. Consulate. First, we will pass through security, then make our way inside the Notarial Services Department. There, they will ask the happy couple for their documentation, and the witnesses will sign. Any questions?"

Not getting any inquiries, Hiro addressed the security officer at the door and said, "This lovely couple has an appointment at two o'clock in the Notary Department. Last names Webber and Wilson."

"Only the couple is allowed with two witnesses. Nobody else," the man said sternly while checking their names off his clipboard. Eyes on Abi and Shane, he pointed. "These are their witnesses?"

"Yes," Hiro said after seeing Martin silently confirm it.

"Are they over eighteen?"

Martin stated, "Mr. Coppersmith, you are not yet of age."

"So, what do we do? If Abi signs, we need one more." Jade and Reggie glanced at each other. "Can you, Martin? Maybe Andrew? We need to go. Our appointment is in two minutes." Each held out hope that they would agree.

Both nodded.

"Gentlemen," Martin instructed, "Take Mr. Coppersmith and Miss Abi back to the truck."

"Yes, Sir," Matt replied.

The Consulate security guard waved his badge over the reader and opened the door.

Anxious, Jade took hold of Reggie's hand before following everyone into the building.

"Good luck, you guys!" Abi shouted and waved as they were about to go in.

Jade crossed her fingers. "Thanks!"

Soon, their friends disappeared.

Walking alongside Abi, the QB said, "Guess we'll just have to wait. Hopefully, they won't be long."

"This way, you two," Matt gestured.

Following him back to their SUV parked around the corner, Ted on their heels, the guy opened the back door for them.

Settled in the backseat, Shane asked, "Do you think they are making the right decision?"

"What do you mean?" Abi nudged closer to him.

"They are still pretty young, considering," Shane paused. "Look, I know how much he loves her, and she loves him, but is it enough?"

"I think when you know, you just...know."

"Perhaps you're right." Ready to change the subject, he tightened his arms around her. "So, have you had time to think about what you would like to see while we're here?"

"Not really. It's been a bit of a whirlwind this week. Aside from shopping and packing, I haven't had much time to do anything else. Did you have something in mind?"

He smiled at her. "Truth be told, I've researched a few places I'd like to see with you."

She sat up. "Oh, yeah? Where?"

"I think I'm gonna leave that a surprise."

"You won't even give me a hint?"

"Nope," he grinned mischievously.

Abi knew then she would have to plan something also to return the favor.

"Hey, do you know where we are staying?"

"I think Martin said, Aman Kyoto. I have no idea where or what that is."

"Guess we can't use our phones to check either."

The driver turned around. "What would you like to search up?"

Abi leaned forward. "A hotel called Aman Kyoto."

In seconds, he handed them his device. "Here it is."

Taking hold of it, Abi showed Shane. "Wow..."

"Guess B didn't spare any expense."

Scrolling through the website, they perused the gallery of beautiful pictures.

"I'm really excited to get there now. It's not your normal run-of-the-mill high-rise hotel." Abi handed the man's phone back to him. When she did, she caught sight of a figure across the street leaning against the building. With sunglasses on, she thought he resembled the man in black from the airport, but she wasn't sure.

"Thank you for letting us use your phone," she said to the driver just as the dark figure took a drag from his cigarette. She sat up straight.

"Something wrong?" Shane asked, seeing her eyes locked forward.

Abi rolled down the side window. "Matt?"

"Yes, Miss."

"Don't look suspicious, but I see a man standing across the street, smoking. He's dressed all in black. I think I saw him at the airport when we left."

Matt made a routine sweep of the area inconspicuously, keeping an eye out for what Abi had described. "Sorry, Miss. I don't see anyone like that."

She peered through the front windshield again, but the man was gone. "He was right there a minute ago. I swear." A bit frantic, she leaned between the seats, searching the street up and down.

"I'm sure it was just a pedestrian, Miss," Matt said, his tone calm.

Sitting back, Abi exhaled as a strange unease settled in the pit of her stomach.

Shane tapped her knee. "We're far from all the drama back home. Try to relax, okay?"

"Yeah…umm… I'll try."

Thoughts of Eastwood engulfing her, Abi shifted uncomfortably in her seat. Surrounded by the sound of traffic in Osaka's bustling streets, she looked upward at the towering U.S. Consulate building beside them.

Watching the big guys walk around the truck, scanning systematically, Abi noticed movement out of the corner of her eye. She turned just as a group of teens emerged from the shadows between two nearby buildings. Their silvery hair and edgy, designer outfits made them stand out as if they'd just wandered off a runway. Two wore distinct hoodies with red dragons coiled around their torsos.

Spotting them, Matt and Ted took their positions.

The group fanned out, laughter spilling from them as they surrounded the SUVs. They didn't seem overtly dangerous, but mischievous energy lingered in the way they nudged each other and exchanged glances.

Shane sat up straight, counting the number of bodies. "What the hell?" he muttered, his eyes narrowing as one of the teens called out in a thick accent, "Hey!" Pointing to Matt, the kid smirked. "You American?"

Matt frowned, immediately stepping between them and the vehicle. His voice was firm but measured. "Back up. Now." His stance widened with hands raised in a controlled, warning gesture.

On the opposite side, Ted mirrored Matt's posture, forming a solid perimeter. "Step away," he ordered, scanning the group for weapons while continuously assessing the situation. Highly trained in handling threats, he and Matt weren't just security personnel. Their casualness was deceptive since both were capable of acting lethally at a moment's notice.

The teens, unfazed, exchanged amused glances. One of them sauntered forward with exaggerated confidence, smirking as he leaned close to the tailgate window.

Abi flinched, pressing herself against the seat as his palms flattened against the glass. He peered inside intrusively, his breath fogging up the window.

"What are they doing?" Abi whispered. Her pulse thudded in her ears as Shane kept an eye on everything going on.

"Get down, Abs. Just in case." He shielded her with his body, his head on a swivel.

Ted took a half step forward, blocking the teen's view. "Move back. Now!" he said, a degree harsher.

One of the other boys pointed past him, gesturing toward the SUV. "Who's in there?" His sinister grin sent a shiver down Abi's spine.

"Doesn't concern you," Matt shot back, his stance shifting as he prepared for things to escalate.

Alert, Shane's grip tightened on the door handle. About to get out and even the odds, he heard Abi gasp, and caught a flash of fear.

The click of the interior locks followed. They were locked in.

Flicking to the rearview mirror, Shane saw the driver staring, but not at the gang converging. Strangely, his eyes were on them.

Abi trembled as she clutched his arm. Her silent plea was clear.

Don't leave me.

That realization hit him like a punch to the gut. Immediately, he wondered if this was a setup. A distraction to lure him away from her. Quickly thinking things through, he knew if he stepped out, nothing was stopping the driver from pulling away with Abi left unattended.

That made him let go of the door handle, but his body remained rigid, prepared to spring into action.

They saw Matt slip his hand inside his jacket. It sent a strong message.

Able to tell the guy was armed, the gang exchanged telling looks. Some shuffled backward, suddenly aware they were out of their depth. But one boy didn't get the memo. Leaning sideways, he craned his neck to steal another peek inside the truck.

Seeing this, Abi shrank further into her seat, her pulse hammering as he zeroed in on her.

Too close, Matt saw red. In quick strides, he was on the kid, grabbing him by the scruff of his neck and pinning him against the vehicle. The sound of the impact against the SUV's side panel echoed through the narrow street, making Abi flinch.

His jaw remained tight, his knuckles white as he held the boy in place. "Do we have a problem?" he firmly stated, staring the kid down. "I told you to step away!" Matt's voice cut like a blade before he flashed his weapon.

"Whoa! Whoa!" the boy shouted. Wide-eyed and unsure, his earlier cockiness evaporated in the face of Matt's intimidating presence.

With five hoods around him, Ted communicated from the opposite side. "You good, man?"

Tightening his grip on the teen's hoodie, Matt shoved him backward. "Yeah, I'm good!"

Finally releasing his grip, pushing the kid toward his gang, the boy stumbled as his friends rushed to him and collectively stepped back.

Out of nowhere, another boldly shouted, "You gonna regret that, American! Big mistake!"

With it, another muttered something in their native language, and with a final sneer, they melted back into the alleyway.

The two men held their positions until the last of them disappeared. Only then did Matt glance inside the SUV. His eyes on Shane through the tinted glass, a silent understanding passed between them.

Danger wasn't always obvious. Sometimes, it came disguised as mischief.

Knocking twice on the window, their driver suddenly opened the locks as Matt got in the front seat.

"What was that?" the QB said, his shoulders tense.

"Not sure," Matt muttered, glancing around, expecting them to reappear with reinforcements. Turning, he looked at Abi. "You okay, Miss?"

Shaken, she nodded, unable to speak. That is when she spotted Martin. The others following him, she said, "There they are."

Not wasting time, the guys got out to brief their boss on the strange altercation.

Unaware that anything was wrong, Jade and Reg prompted Abi to let them into the third row. Hesitant, she got out before once again taking a seat and closing the door. Nervously watching Martin's reaction when the men took him aside, Abi was unable to hear what was said, but their body language spoke volumes. The four of them conversed for a brief moment before Martin stepped away to make a phone call.

"What's happening?" Jade asked from the back seat. Her voice filled with worry.

Shane answered. "We had a little problem."

"Little?" Abi tilted her head, unamused.

When Martin hung up, he approached. Opening the door, he glanced around, his focus gravitating to Abi mostly. "Everyone okay here?"

She nodded quickly, her hands still gripping the edge of her seat. "Yes, we're okay."

To diffuse any lingering tension, Martin nodded and offered a reassuring smile.

Abi didn't respond.

Glancing at his watch, he said matter-of-factly. "We've got less than forty minutes to file your papers at City Hall. Let's get a move on, shall we?"

He shut the door firmly, signaling to the other men.

The earlier commotion faded the second Andrew got in the front seat.

Engines roaring to life, the SUVs pulled away and left the Consulate.

It was hard for Abi to shake the uneasy feeling that clung to her as they drove off. Shellshocked, her eyes stayed locked to the rearview mirror until the building disappeared in the distance.

To sway everyone's attention, Shane nudged their friends and asked, "So? How did it go? Did you get what you needed?"

"Yeah, all good," Reg replied before Jade elaborated.

"Since we were both eighteen and seemed more mature, the guy didn't bat an eye at stamping the form. Thankfully, we didn't have to do much more. Just to be safe, not sure what roadblocks we'd run into, Reggie had his lawyer draw up papers when Martin said anyone under twenty years of age may have to provide parental consent to get married."

Reg added, "I sadly tricked my Mom into signing mine, but Jade spoke to her Mother and..."

"...she asked if I was happy." Jade looked at Reggie. "Without a doubt, I said yes. She could tell I was serious about this. From the moment she met Reg, she said she knew this day would come, so she signed it." Hugging her fiancé, the two watched as they moved south.

Crossing another bridge decorated with winter-themed planters along the center median, their driver signaled left and drove into the thruway in front of the large City Hall building.

Stopped, Jade and Reggie needed out again.

"Stay there, Abs. I'll get out." Shane opened his door and flipped the seat forward so they could exit.

"Wish us luck!" Jade said lightheartedly.

"Hurry!" Abi replied, hoping this process would be quick.

"Think happy thoughts!" Jade raised her praying hands.

The two joined Martin and Andrew, and the group headed up the steps for the final piece of the registration.

Matt and Ted surrounded the SUV.

"Hopefully, this won't take them too long," Shane commented.

Their driver peered in the rearview mirror. "This is the easy part," he said to them. "I'm sure they will be out in less than ten minutes unless there is a long line."

"That is good to hear." Clutching her hands together and tucking them under her chin to pass the time, she asked, "I'm sorry, Sir. We've been so rude. What is your name?"

The man turned slightly. His expression was neutral but polite. "Katsumi Kabe."

"Nice to meet you, Katsumi. I'm Abi, and this is Shane," she said with a small smile, motioning toward her boyfriend.

The man gave a curt nod. "Good to meet you."

Abi thought for a moment, then ventured, "So, for tourists, given what just happened to us... Any words of wisdom? Warnings, perhaps?"

The man considered her question. "In a city like this, tourists must be mindful of their surroundings. If you wish to avoid trouble, there are a few basic precautions you should follow."

Abi and Shane exchanged a look, both leaning in slightly as Katsumi continued.

"First, blend in. Avoid drawing attention to yourself. Dress modestly. Observe local customs whenever possible. Respect for our culture goes a long way."

Nodding, she committed that to memory.

"Second, never carry large amounts of cash or wear expensive jewelry—you will be a target."

Shane raised an eyebrow at Abi, subtly gesturing at her necklace, causing her to tuck it beneath her sweater instinctively.

"Be smart," Katsumi added. "Get to know the places you plan to visit. Some areas may have more petty crime and scammers." He chuckled. "I always say, *it's better to know before you go*."

Leaning back slightly, Abi was impressed by his straightforward advice. "That makes sense. Anything else?"

"Refrain from flashiness," Katsumi said firmly. "Keep high-end luxury items out of sight."

Crossing his arms, Shane pointed at her LV tote on the seat beside her as Abi shrugged.

"Lastly," their driver said, his voice dipping slightly, "Remain vigilant. Overly friendly strangers can be a distraction for pickpockets or worse. Stay alert and trust your instincts. If something feels off, it probably is."

Grateful for the practical advice, Abi said, "Thank you. That's really helpful."

He nodded. "You are welcome. Japan is a wonderful place, rich in history and culture. Despite the unruly behavior you just encountered, it remains one of the safest countries in the world. Stay mindful, but don't let that stop you from exploring its beauty and experiencing all it has to offer."

As they listened to the man's insight on local attractions, Abi leaned into Shane. It made him rest his arm around her shoulders. But that lighthearted chatter soon faltered the instant Matt's attention gravitated to something. Sitting up, Abi followed his line of sight. Not hearing a word of what Katsumi was saying, one by one, she watched four sports cars in formation slide up flawlessly along the curb across the street, as if choreographed.

The elaborately wrapped GTRs boldly made their presence known. They were hard to miss with decals of dragons and slashed kanji symbols. One by one, men dressed in black lounged suspiciously against the cars, bodies casual but eyes locked on them like predators sizing up prey.

Even with five lanes between them, the sight was enough to cause alarm.

"Uh...umm. Shane... Look." Abi gasped.

"What now..." Assuming the teens might have brought in reinforcements, Shane immediately rolled down the window to speak to the guys who were already talking on their comms.

"Don't worry." Holding up his hand, Matt reassured, "Martin's handling it."

Within minutes, the distant wail of sirens could be heard. Growing louder, accompanied by the unmistakable hum of helicopter blades overhead, engines roared as unmarked SUVs screeched to a stop, doors flying open. Officers poured into the street, weapons raised, shouting in Japanese. The GTR crew didn't fight back—they moved slow and mechanical, pressing palms to metal roofs like they'd rehearsed it.

Her skin prickled. She knew this wasn't random.

Dumbfounded by what was happening, Shane was about to say something, but Abi interrupted.

"Thank God. They're back," she said, happy to see her friends and Martin descending the steps. With his phone to his ear, her guardian scanned the scene with eyes of steel, unfazed by the situation unfolding.

Shane caught sight of him and leaned closer to her, his voice low. "Tell me the truth. Who is this guy?"

Unable to fully answer the question, she paused and said, "He's Burton's most trusted asset."

When she said that, they watched Matt and Ted scour the vehicles swiftly with handheld scanners while Andrew surveyed the commotion across the street. The devices, emitting a rapid series of beeps, zeroed in on the sources while Jade and Reg got in the third row.

Crouching near the wheel well of one vehicle, Ted carefully pried a small tracking device from its hidden position. "One down!" he said.

"What are they looking for?" Reg questioned as the men swept the truck.

Confused, Jade shrugged.

Hearing another second shrill beep, Matt ripped another from beneath the bumper of the second SUV. "We got two!"

Realizing the swarm of boys that converged on them earlier had a mission, Andrew waved to Martin and handed over the bugs in passing.

Briefly inspecting them, he offered a subtle, unreadable nod before giving them back to the guy.

Catching the entire exchange, Abi could feel her stomach tighten. She knew whoever was tracking them wasn't playing games.

In seconds, Andrew let the trackers fall to the ground, and he crushed them under his heel. Leaving the shards scattered across the pavement, he climbed into the passenger seat, breaking the tense silence. "Slight change of plans," he stated bluntly.

Glancing between him and Shane, she asked, "What do you mean?"

Andrew's smirk was thin and humorless. "You'll see soon enough," he said while buckling his seatbelt.

As they threaded through the barricades without question, the police assisted them while the GTR crew got handcuffed and loaded into squad cars. Watching them as they passed, each young man cast a sinister look their way.

That is when Abi saw it. Another crimson dragon tattoo on the nape of one guy's neck as the officer detained him. The sight of it was unnerving. *What is going on?* She thought to herself, wishing Burton were there.

Shane spoke up. "Is there something we should know here? None of this was accidental."

Head on a swivel, Andrew stared straight ahead. "No. Everything is fine." Knowing Shane was going to rebut him, he interjected. "There's nothing to worry about, Coppersmith."

His bluntness caught Shane off guard, so he left it at that. For now...

Abi noticed the compass embedded in the rearview mirror. The direction displayed was west. Frowning, she leaned forward. "Aren't we supposed to be heading north to Kyoto now?"

"Yes," Andrew replied casually. "Just hang tight."

While their SUVs maneuvered through the bustling downtown core, eventually they merged onto the main highway. The cityscape gave way to a scenic bridge, its view of shimmering water below briefly captivating Abi before they continued into a quiet, obscure corporate park. The wide road narrowed to two lanes, the surroundings growing more desolate until they spotted a fenced-in property with a sign that read: Ogawa Air.

Inside the confines of the place, rounding the corner of a sleek, modern building, Abi's curiosity spiked as a row of helicopters came into view, their polished frames glinting as the sun hit them.

When they came to a stop near two of the machines, Andrew announced, "Grab your things. We're heading out now."

Realizing they would be flying to Kyoto, Abi scrambled for her tote bag with heart pounding as Shane stepped out calmly to retrieve his backpack from the rear hatch.

Reg and Jade did the same.

"Wait a minute? We're flying there?" Jade questioned, a bit fearful. "Why?"

Martin approached with his usual composed demeanor. "It will help us save time, Miss. Nothing to worry about." His calm reassurance seemed to ease her nerves, if only slightly.

Pausing before walking away, Abi turned to Katsumi, who offered a small wave. "I guess this is where we leave you," she said.

"Yes." Katsumi gave her a warm smile. "Good luck."

"Thanks," Shane replied on their behalf, returning the gesture before guiding Abi toward the helicopter.

She followed, her mind swirling with questions, scared as to what really prompted the sudden change in plans.

Once they got settled into the spacious interior of the craft, the group fell silent, the tension thick as everyone mulled over the day's events.

As they donned their headsets, Shane broke the quiet. "So, did you get the paperwork filed?"

The hum of the engine filled the cabin as the pilot ran his preflight checks.

"Yeah, it was super easy," Reggie said, leaning back in his seat.

"Finally. We can get married now," Jade exclaimed, excitement laced with lingering apprehension. "One of the ladies there said, *Omedetō*." She pronounced it slowly, hoping she got it right. "It means congratulations."

Abi smiled warmly, reaching across to squeeze Jade's hand. "I'm so happy for you guys."

The helicopters lifted off one by one, their blades cutting through the Osaka skyline. Unbeknownst to them, the flight ahead, bound for Kyoto's peaceful, secluded hills, hadn't gone unnoticed.

| 10 |

Trip to Kyoto

Friday, December 15

Takagamine Heliport / Aman Kyoto

While the helicopter ascended over Osaka, the vibrant city below stretched into a sprawling maze of densely packed streets. Skyscrapers rose in every direction, their glowing windows catching the last rays of sunshine.

Feeling the rhythmic hum of the rotors, Abi marveled at the crowded cityscape before it soon transformed into snow-covered rolling hills. A patchwork of trees and scattered houses spread across the land, framed by gentle slopes that seemed to go on for miles. Partially frozen rivers snaked through the valleys, their winding waters shimmering like veins of silver threading through the earth.

Slowly gaining altitude, the farmland gave way to more rugged terrain and the distant outline of mountains emerging on the horizon. The rivers continued to carve through the landscape, guiding them toward the peaks. A sense of calm filled the air as the natural beauty unfolded before them while they flew deeper into a rural part of Japan.

Abi noticed a clearing coming into view. Nestled within the forest, it emerged from the sea of trees. While they circled, she saw two black SUVs waiting below and Burton standing by one of them—an unexpected but welcome sight.

Descending slowly, she felt a rush of relief the second the skids hit the ground with a moderate thud. The guys ushered them to disembark safely, ducking their heads to avoid the swirling blades, the reality of their unsettling event slowly sinking in. Even now, the memory made her chest tighten. Who were these people? Were the teen gang and the cars connected somehow, or was this just a coincidence? She glanced at Burton rushing toward her, wondering if he might have answers or if he was just as in the dark as she was.

When their machine lifted off the ground again, the low hum fading as the second helicopter descended, Burton rushed over and ducked. Meeting Abi partway, he pulled her into a brief, reassuring hug despite the tension between him and the football player.

"Are you okay?" he asked quietly, making eye contact with her.

She could see him reading her like a book while Shane, standing close by, glared in the guy's direction, keeping his distance, eyes narrowing in silent disapproval.

Offering reassurance, she said, "Yeah, we're good."

Jade and Reggie gathered around beside them.

Concerned about her, Burton walked Abi over to the vehicles.

Unable to keep the frustration at bay, Shane stepped forward. "So, are you gonna tell us why we got roped into whatever that was back there?"

With a level of indifference, the famous DJ didn't acknowledge the guy's question. Instead, his thoughts shifted to the next steps when the second helicopter landed.

"So, you don't have anything to say?" Shane reached out and firmly grabbed his arm. Staring him down, he did not let go.

Unimpressed, Burton stared at it. "Get your hand off me, Coppersmith," he replied angrily, not making eye contact. "Now!"

Not given a choice, the QB let go and watched as Martin and the others disembarked.

With a seasoned casualness, Burton approached his staff.

About to address his trusted advisor, Martin raised a hand to stop him from igniting any form of conversation. "Not here," he mumbled as Burton shot him a brief look before returning his attention to Abi.

Rejoining the group, nobody exchanged a word.

In an instant, they all gathered around the SUVs.

"Come on," Burton said. "Let's get you guys to the hotel. I'm sure you're hungry."

The last light of day spread over the forest as they settled into the vehicles. Reg and Jade willingly took their spot in the third row while Burton slid into the seat beside Abi, with Shane boxing her in between them.

The concern that had filled the air earlier suddenly faded.

When the doors slammed shut, the noise of it echoed in the clearing. As the engines roared to life, they began to roll forward and navigate the winding, desolate road ahead.

Threading through, barely wide enough for them to pass oncoming traffic, the dense tree line was so close that the gnarly branches scraped against the sides of the vehicles as they drove down the hill. The sound of tires crunching over the uneven gravel soon gave way to a smoother ride as they hit the pavement.

While descending the hillside, the road gradually widened to two lanes with sharp corners and towering retaining walls on either side. The stone seemed modern despite being covered in moss, which added to the feeling of isolation that hung over the journey. For miles, there were no signs of life.

Abi wondered how far removed they were from the city limits.

Eventually, as they reached the edge of a small town, the road narrowed to almost a single lane, forcing the driver to slow down. Cars coming from the opposite direction felt so close that Abi's heart raced as they squeezed past, barely inches apart. Fading light blurred the outlines of the buildings on either side as the SUV turned right and started to descend into a valley.

Inside the vehicle, the silence between them was strange.

Unable to tell if it was jet lag weighing on everyone or the worry of how things went in Osaka, Abi replayed those ominous events in her mind, making her eyes dart to Shane, then Burton, where she found each lost in their own thoughts.

Turning onto a narrow, one-way street, the world around them shifted into something almost surreal. To the left, a dense forest climbed the hillside, its towering trees casting long shadows over them. On the right, a wide river stretched out, its icy waters shimmering under the fading light. The further they went, the more it felt like they had left the real world behind and stepped into a place untouched, maybe even forgotten.

Not knowing exactly where they were heading, Abi asked Burton, curiosity surfacing, "Is it much farther?"

He glanced over at her, offering a reassuring smile. "We're two minutes out."

The vehicle followed the narrow road until the trees thinned. Light snow dusted an old stone fence, blending it seamlessly with the landscape. Overhead, bare Japanese maple branches wove a delicate canopy.

Soon, a number of residential buildings appeared, each signaling their reentry into some semblance of civilization.

The driver slowed, making a sharp right turn. Abi spotted a large boulder near the entrance, its surface engraved with the words: *Aman Kyoto*.

A quiet excitement filled the SUV as they moved forward.

Abi held her breath, knowing that hidden in the shadows was a beautiful five-star resort waiting for them.

"We're here," Burton said while driving up the laneway.

Arriving in a beautiful courtyard with an impressive stacked stone wall and tall hedges, their driver rounded the corner and parked in front of the main building, where four people were awaiting their arrival, with golf buggies standing by.

Dressed in a uniformed three-piece suit, a man promptly assisted them. "Welcome to Aman Kyoto," he said graciously upon opening the door as they slipped out and helped Reg and Jade escape the third row.

Martin was on the ball as usual. With his iPad in hand, about to walk into the building, he said, "Wait here. I will be back with your room assignments."

While standing around, the breeze was cool. Abi wished she had her jacket, but sadly, it was in her luggage, which she assumed had already made it there.

In minutes, the man returned. Handing them their card keys, he said as Burton looked on, "Please make sure you have everything from the trucks. Both of you are in a one-bedroom Takagamine suite. They are beside each other. Abi, this one is for you and Shane. And Jade and Reggie. This is yours. Your luggage is already in your rooms. Please verify that your bags were delivered properly. Inside your suite, you will also find welcome baskets compliments of Red Dragon."

Surprised to see the room number embossed on wooden cards inside a leather wallet, she acknowledged Martin. It was then, Abi realized she'd be sharing with Shane.

Noticing her staring blankly at the leather pouch, Martin asked, "Is there something wrong, Miss Abi?"

She quickly reacted, "No. Nothing."

Shane grabbed his backpack from the back of the SUV while Abi carried her tote.

"Very well. Off you go, then. Please make your way to the Living Pavilion for dinner within the hour. The concierge will drive you to your suites. They are on the hillside to the left."

"Alright," she said. "Thank you."

"You are very welcome."

Settling into the golf cart, Burton got into the back with Abi, forcing Shane to take a seat beside the driver. "I'll ride with you. Sara and I are staying just up from your room."

Moving past the hedges along a cobblestone path, the driver said, "This is the Living Pavilion, where you will be meeting for dinner."

Shane gave the man a thumbs-up while peering back at his girlfriend, who was sitting with Burton. Once again, a stroke of jealousy hit hard. Angry, he turned around and faced forward as they drove up the hill before arriving at a black-clad building nestled amongst the trees.

"Here we are. This is your room," the man said to them, pointing to the door on the right. They could see Jade and Reggie's driver a few feet ahead of them, pointing to the one next door.

"Should you need anything, please contact the front desk, and we will assist you."

"Appreciate that," Shane said, passing the guy a moderate tip.

"Thank you so much, Sir."

"Sure thing."

Turning to Abi, Burton said, "I'll let you two get settled. If you need me, I'm just in that building right there," he pointed a little further away.

"Don't worry. She'll be fine," Shane interjected, making Abi squint her eyes at him disapprovingly.

"I'm sure," the guy smirked before taking a seat in the golf cart beside the driver. "I'll see you shortly for dinner."

As he drove off, Shane tapped their key fob to the locking mechanism. It clicked, allowing them access.

"Hey, wanna meet back here in about forty minutes?" Reggie shouted to them, peeking out from their doorway.

"Yeah, man. Sounds good," Shane said upon swinging the door open for Abi to enter first.

When walking into the small vestibule, she peered around the corners while taking off her shoes at the door and placing them on the mat.

Scanning the sleek, modern space, she gravitated to the wall of glass offering a stunning view of the cliffside escarpment and the Living Pavilion below. The picturesque scenery added a sense of calm.

"Wow, this is really nice."

Shane walked up to her, mustering a bit of courage to address the elephant in the room. "Hey, umm, Abs…"

"Yeah," she replied while walking toward the windows.

"Are you okay sharing a room with me?"

Hearing that surprised her. "Of course. Why wouldn't I be?"

"You seemed panicked when Martin gave us the room assignment."

"I wasn't panicking. I'm just exhausted. Things aren't registering as fast as they should."

He wasn't entirely convinced of that. "Alright. If you're sure."

"Yes, I am." Abi let out a sigh as she stood by the window, taking in the quiet beauty of the landscape outside. The weight of the day, the tension, and the unknowns all seemed to melt away for a moment. Shane's presence felt comforting, and she didn't need to say anything more.

Walking in behind her, he wrapped his arms around her waist, pulled her in close, and nestled his head beside hers.

The warmth of his embrace brought about a smile.

"We made it. We're halfway around the world," he said with a hint of relief.

Abi's head turned slightly to meet his gaze. "Yes, I guess we are." For a moment, her troubles back in LA felt far away. "Let the vacation begin," she added with a quiet laugh, exhaustion mingling with a sense of excitement for what was to come.

Standing there a little longer, the two looked out the window, content to take in the beautiful view as snow gently began to fall.

| 11 |

The Room

Friday, December 15

Aman Kyoto – Takagamine Suite

Slipping her phone from her pocket, Abi said, "We should get moving. We don't want to be late for dinner."

Eyeing the bed over Shane's shoulder, to her surprise, she was thankful to see two twin mattresses adjacent to one another. Upon closer observation, she realized that if they slid together, it could become a king.

She left his arms to explore every nook and cranny of their new home for the next couple of days. Locating the welcome basket positioned neatly on a small table, she turned it around to see all the Red Dragon swag inside the cellophane and took a picture of it. Adorned with a thin, sturdy wooden card featuring elegant Japanese writing and a tasseled braided rope, she thought it would be perfect as a bookmark. Removing it, she slid the weathered card between the pages of her novel rather than dog-earing them.

Shane chuckled, noticing what she did. "I guess that's the perfect gift for you from the welcome basket."

She nodded, still intrigued by the card. "It's beautiful. I wonder what it says." Seeing what else was in the basket, she found a rolled quilted-down tote bag with the Red Dragon logo on it. "This was a thoughtful touch. It will come in handy here."

As they continued to settle in, their excitement for the days ahead bubbling beneath the surface, the room felt like a perfect blend of luxury and comfort, setting the stage for their adventure in Kyoto and beyond.

Collapsing on the one bed, Shane rested his head on the pillow.

"Don't get too comfortable," she giggled.

"I know. I think if I stay here too long, I'll fall asleep for sure."

Moving across the room, Abi found their luggage sitting on a bench outside the bathroom.

"Need any help?" Shane asked, hearing her unzipping the bag.

"No, I'm fine. Mind if I grab a shower? I'll make it quick."

"Sure. No problem. You go first, then I'll do the same," he said.

Venturing into the bathroom, she slid both pocket doors closed on either end but realized the area above the sinks was open to the bedroom. Starting the shower to warm it up, she said, "Umm, Shane?"

"Yeah." He got up to see her standing on the other side of the wall.

"What do we do about this?" she asked.

Joining her in the bathroom, he studied the space and found panels tucked in behind the mirrors. Each was on tracks that easily slid closed to partition the bathroom and give her privacy.

Closing the panels, he said, "There. Problem solved."

"Thank you."

The relief on her face was priceless. "Absolutely," he said. Closing the main pocket door behind him, he left Abi to have her shower. Returning to his suitcase, he pulled a fresh set of clothes to wear that evening before lying on the bed to rest for a few more minutes.

Feeling a bit uncomfortable, Abi got undressed and grabbed a towel from the hook embedded in the stone wall. Gathering her hair in a messy bun, she opened the glass shower and stepped inside, thankful to wash away their travel day.

After turning off the water and wrapping herself in the towel, she found a white robe to cozy up in and emerged from the room to see Shane with his eyes closed.

"All done. Your turn," she said, startling him.

"Yeah, okay. I'm up."

Watching him disappear into the bathroom and slide the door closed, she heard the water start. Sifting through her suitcase, she found a pair of black tights, a t-shirt, and her LuLu Scuba hoodie and feather-lite down jacket. As the water trickled on the tile inside the shower, Abi swiftly got changed before he finished. Slipping on a pair of socks before pulling on her Doc Martens, she heard Shane exit the bathroom. Suddenly, he appeared with just a towel wrapped around his waist, completely bare-chested.

"Oh…" she said, turning her back to him and clearing her throat.

"What's wrong, Abs?" Shane laughed at her reaction but soon clued in. "Sorry. It's a force of habit. Guess I'm used to the locker room environment." Taking his clothes, he pointed and said, "I'll just change in there."

"That's okay. You stay. I need to fix my makeup anyway."

"Alright."

Taking her cosmetics bag into the bathroom, she stood in front of the mirror and whispered, "Abs, you've gotta chill. What is wrong with you?"

"What was that?" he asked, having overheard her say something.

In an effort to save face, she replied, "Umm, nothing. Didn't say anything."

Minutes later, about to return to the room, she hesitated. "Hey, are you decent?"

"All good."

Rounding the corner, she was thankful to find him tying the string on his black joggers and wearing a white hoodie. His winter jacket was lying on the bed.

"Ready to head out, then?"

She nodded. "Yes. You?"

"Yep." He took the card key wallet from the table and zipped it in his jacket pocket before holding out his hand to her as they walked toward the door. "After you," he said, opening it.

It was almost dark as they stepped outside. Because they'd showered, the cool air hit them hard.

"Oh, man. It got colder." Shane flipped his hood over his head.

Having lived in Boston, where the winters at times were beyond frigid, Abi laughed. "This is nothing - wait until we head north to Niseko. If you think this is bad, you haven't seen anything yet."

"Glad I bought all that winter gear this week."

"I'm sure we're gonna need it," she giggled.

Jade and Reggie appeared from their room.

"Hey, man," Shane greeted Reg. "Thought you guys would be asleep by now."

Dressed in her ankle-length winter parka, Jade answered, "If my stomach weren't growling so much, we would have."

"I know. I'm starving, too." Barely able to fashion a sentence, Abi added, "I think we should eat and then head to bed. I'm exhausted."

"Is that right?" her friend said mischievously.

Understanding what she was implying, she clarified, "You know, jet-lagged?"

Jade tilted her head. "Hmm, I'm sure you are."

Hearing this, Shane knew Abi was not exactly comfortable with their sleeping arrangements. Not wanting to ruin dinner, he figured he'd address it when they returned later that night.

At the bottom of the hill, they rounded the building to find everyone gathered on the raised wooden deck with a sunken stone fire pit. Immediately, she found Burton.

He, too, gravitated to her. Walking over, he said, "Hey, you made it."

"It's been a long day. Both of us are beginning to fade. Right, Abs?" Shane answered first, taking hold of his girlfriend's hand.

"Yes, that's right." Abi saw Sara glance over sinisterly.

With a snicker, Shane added, "After dinner, I'm looking forward to getting some sleep."

Not rewarding the comment, Burton focused on the engaged couple and asked Abi, "So, did they get their marriage license, okay?"

Uneasy with his girlfriend staring at her, Abi answered, "Umm, yes. They did."

"That's good."

Picking up on his strange, still confident façade, she felt like he seemed off. "Hey, are you okay? Is there something wrong?"

Immediately waving her off, he said, "Yeah, everything is fine." Leaning towards her ear, he whispered, "We'll talk later, alright?"

She looked up at him and nodded, just as Martin surfaced from inside.

"Please come in. Dinner is served."

Approaching the floor-to-ceiling glass windows showcasing the beautiful dining room, they walked through the doorway at the far end. Surrounded by black panelled walls, the natural wood furniture stood out in contrast. With an open fireplace in the middle of the room, their group of sixteen gathered at the long table set for them. Their security stayed together to talk among themselves while the rest of the group got comfortable on the opposite end.

One by one, the staff carried out trays of food.

Anton assisted them, having eagerly watched Chef Ozawa's culinary expertise that afternoon.

With the dishes placed in front of them, each tiny white plate held a bite-sized treat nestled in a wooden bento box. Everyone's faces lit up. There was miso soup, crispy fried shrimp, and tender sautéed fish. The smoky cedar-roasted Kyoto Wagyu beef was rich and flavorful, and a bowl of hearty rice risotto with edamame tied everything together, leaving them feeling warm and satisfied.

Up for almost twenty-one hours, the atmosphere around the table was less lively than they were used to. With most of them hitting a wall, it was hard to string a sentence together.

Abi kept an eye on Burton and his interactions with Sara. For whatever reason, throughout dinner, they didn't speak to each other. Intent on being upfront with Shane, Abi leaned over and whispered, "Umm, don't be mad, but Burton needs to talk to me. Something is up with him and Sara. Do you mind if he and I go for a short walk?"

He peered into her eyes and could tell she was worried about what he might say. Determined to be confident in their relationship, he answered quietly, "Sure. No problem. Thanks for the heads up."

She tapped her hand on his forearm. "Thank you for understanding."

The QB nodded.

Making eye contact with Burton, she nudged her head toward the door.

He took the napkin from his lap and placed it on the table before getting up.

Abi did the same. As the two of them moved toward the entrance, she realized there was no discreet way to leave.

Swinging open the door, Burton had her lead the way. They each could feel everyone's eyes on them, primarily Sara's daggers plunging into their backs.

Snowflakes drifted lazily from the night sky, settling on the mossy stone paths and bare branches of the Japanese maples as they began their stroll through the serene grounds of Aman Kyoto. The tranquil beauty of the resort stood in stark contrast to the events that unfolded that afternoon in Osaka. She wrapped her arms around herself, not entirely because of the cold.

"Sorry, we haven't had a chance to talk much until now," Burton said, his voice gentle against the quiet of the forest. "How are you holding up? It's been a chaotic day."

"To say the least," Abi replied. "Thankfully, we made it in time for them to register their documents and get their marriage license. That's what matters."

"One less thing to worry about."

A million questions in her mind, Abi glanced at him, her eyes betraying the fear she couldn't shake. "What happened today? That was not random..." She paused, her words trailing off as she replayed the day's events.

Burton slowed his steps and turned to her.

She exhaled, her breath visible in the crisp air. "Those teens attacked us. And the cars? Those men? Are the two events connected?"

He did not respond, but she could tell he was mulling over a list of explanations.

"And there's something else I need to tell you."

Stopping dead, he slipped his hands into his pockets. "What is it?" he focused in on her.

"I saw two strange men today, aside from everything else."

"Where?"

"The one with the red cane was standing in the parking lot as we left the airport, and the other was across the street, dressed in black with dark sunglasses and a hat while we waited for Reg and Jade at the Consulate."

"So, two men in two different locations?"

She nodded.

A scowl crossed his face. "Have you shared this with Martin?"

Her voice quieted. "No, not yet. I wasn't sure if it was just my imagination. But I'm pretty sure it wasn't. They had eyes on us."

His jaw tightened, his gaze searching hers. "If I had known, I would've had the team sweep the area sooner."

Biting her lip, Abi peered down at the snowy path. A hint of terror hit her at the same time. "Burton, why did you have us flown out of Osaka in helicopters instead of driving?"

He hesitated, his usually composed demeanor slipping slightly. "I didn't want to stake any chances. The city's too crowded - too many variables we couldn't control. This way, I knew we could avoid..."

"Avoid what?" Eyes narrowing, she attempted to read between the lines.

"Complications." His response was blunt and devoid of emotion. "I don't want to scare you, but the tables are about to turn. We need to stay vigilant, Abi. That's all I can say right now."

A shiver ran down her spine, though she wasn't sure if it was from the chilly gusts or his words. "So we're not safe here?"

Expression softening, he said, "You're safer now than you were this afternoon. You're with me. That's what matters. I swear I won't ever let anything happen to you. I promise."

"Why did you bring me if it's not safe?"

"It was the only way I could protect you and still do my job."

"How bad..." she asked.

Resting his hands on her arms, he confessed, "We're on top of it. I promise you've got nothing to worry about."

Not exactly receiving the answer she wanted, Abi paused a moment before her steps resumed beside his as they walked the grounds.

The wind whistled between the trees toward the far end of the resort.

"On the way through the city today, I saw a few Shrines." When he said that, he could feel his attempt to sway their conversation was about to fail terribly.

"Despite flying above it all, I didn't see much." She was still perplexed by what he'd said. "I was excited to experience the history here..."

"And now?"

Unable to share her true feelings, she danced around the subject. "We will take one day at a time. Tomorrow, I wouldn't mind relaxing a bit if we can. I'm exhausted."

"From what I understand, Martin has plans for us, but maybe I can tell him to keep things light."

"That would be good." She saw how far they were from everyone. Hidden amongst the trees, passing two other pavilions, she turned and said, "Can I ask you something?"

"Sure."

"Don't be mad."

Worried, he stopped again. "Why would I be mad?"

"I noticed Sara is acting a bit strange. Did something happen?"

"It's nothing..." he said dismissively.

Running a hand through his hair, about to keep walking, she reached for his arm and brought him back. "Hey," she said. "You can trust me."

Jaws clenched, he started walking again, his stride strong and determined as they looped back toward the Living Pavilion. The faint glimmer of uplit trees and scattered pathway lights created flickering shadows around them.

Finally, amidst the darkness, he muttered, "She's just jealous."

"Of who?"

"You," he said unapologetically.

She didn't know what to say. "Have I done something wrong for her to feel that way? I've tried to be so careful."

"I know you have. That said, she may have a different opinion on it. To me, it's just your presence and her insecurities."

Abi looked back toward the pavilion. "I guess taking this walk is probably fueling the fire, then?"

"Most likely," he said point-blank. "But I don't care. She doesn't dictate what I do."

Frustrated, she pressed her hand to her forehead. "Oh, Burton. I'm sorry."

"Why should you be sorry? You've done nothing wrong."

"So what are you gonna do?"

"Not sure." He glanced up at the night sky. "But I'm glad I've got a two-bedroom suite."

"That bad?"

"Unfortunately."

Stopping, Abi approached and wrapped her arms around his waist as he instinctively encircled her with his.

"How did life get so damn complicated?" he asked quietly. "A solid relationship shouldn't be this hard."

"No, it shouldn't."

Clearing his throat, he let go of her and stepped back. "Thanks for listening."

"I'm always here, you know."

"I know."

Continuing around the property, with a stone wall to their right and a line of towering slender trees to the left, Burton said, "So, how are you and Shane? Everything good thus far?"

"It's only the first day. A lot can happen. We'll see."

Almost reaching the end of the path, they found an uplit extension leading deep into the forest.

"Feeling adventurous?" he asked. "Want to see where that leads?"

A little creepy in the dark, she hesitated but felt safe with him. "Sure. I'm game."

Climbing the hill, Burton said, "I know Martin booked you guys a room together. Guess he just assumed..."

She was surprised he brought it up. "Umm, yeah. Don't worry. It's okay. They split the king-sized bed into two twins, so it worked out."

Feeling he'd overstepped his bounds, he nodded. "So, that's good, right?"

"Umm, yeah." About to say something more, Abi quickly opted to change the subject. "So, what's on tap for Dark Demon on this trip?"

He smiled and spoke of him in the third person. "Well, he's making a two-hour appearance at a private venue hosted by Red Dragon. Then it's on to Osaka, where he's headlining the NAKKA Museum Gala. It's an incredible, newly built facility – this black cube in the middle of the city. The guest list is tight. Only the who's who of Osaka will be attending."

"Sounds exciting," she said, knowing how busy he'd be.

"On Saturday, we head to Tokyo, where I have four appearances. Three of which are public, and the others are private events at undisclosed locations."

"So, your vault system will be available?"

"It's a trial run to see how it's received."

"Are the events fancy?"

He chuckled. "What do you mean by fancy?"

Seemingly daydreaming, she whimsically said, "You know, glamorous. Women in luxurious dresses. The men in suits or tuxes. Champagne. Hors d'oeuvres."

"Maybe not that fancy, but I'm assuming most will be showing off a bit a the NAKKA Gala for sure, yes. The others will be the typical elite rave crowd."

"How does it work? I've never asked you."

"What do you mean? The vault system?"

"Yes. How do people access it?"

"I've got a team of tech geniuses working with Martin to keep everything running smoothly. Each one I carefully vetted, and they know crypto inside and out—especially how my app works. When attendees register, they get a one-time access code linked to a QR key. That's their ticket into the vault, which possesses the best security—encryption, multi-factor authentication, and even optional facial recognition as an extra precaution for those willing to risk it."

"Risk what?"

"Leaving their biometrics and attaching them to their transactions."

Thinking about what he said, he asked, "And that would be a problem because?"

He smiled. "Because some transactions aren't, let's just say, above board."

Abi nodded. "Hmm..."

"Once inside, they can transfer their crypto straight from their hot wallets into the vault. That's when the real security kicks in—time-locked transactions, smart contracts, and multi-signature approvals for anything they want to move. It's like a digital fortress. Nothing slips through the cracks. And the best part? It's all woven into the event. As they dance and get lost in the music, their devices light up with real-time updates, connecting them to the tech in a way that feels alive and electric. It's everything they came for—cutting-edge, secure, and unforgettable."

"Sounds complicated."

"To tell you the truth, the only thing complicated is the Nightfall set installations at each location. That reminds me, before I forget, I'll be checking up on the Osaka event setup on Friday afternoon, so I won't be here. At least when we go to Tokyo, the appearances are Red Dragon bases, so we won't need to set anything up until my guys move onto Niseko for the Andaru event."

Reaching a spooky flagstone staircase, like something out of a movie, Burton said, "Want to keep going?"

Curious as to what was at the top, she replied, "Yeah, let's check it out."

While they started climbing the steps, she felt the need to ask again, "So, back to Sara…"

He stopped her right there. "Please don't worry about her. She hates that you see me in ways she doesn't. I've tried explaining our friendship, but she doesn't see it that way. Ever since your birthday party and the speech I gave that night, things haven't been the same between us."

Abi recalled her conversation with Martin on their way to the new Beverly Park house. "One more thing…"

He stared her way and squinted his eyes. "Wow, you're full of questions tonight." Chuckling lightly, he was afraid to hear what else she would say.

"When we returned from Newport and arrived at the Beverly Park house, Martin told me your relationship with Sara was *of convenience.* What did he mean by that?"

Burton exhaled. "It's complicated."

"Sorry, I don't mean to overstep."

Hesitating, he considered his answer. "Don't take offense, but that's something I can't share."

Not pushing him, she conceded.

Finally making it to the top of the stairs, they found a dead end with an open clearing, a falling water wall, and a cobblestone square in the middle.

"This must be a meditation space," she said.

"Looks that way."

Surrounded by darkness, only the uplighting along the path was visible. Abi heard something rustling in the bushes. Launching into Burton's arms, she clung to him tightly. "Oh my gosh! What was that?"

He didn't answer her.

Finding his eyes locked on hers, as he held her protectively, for a moment, a charged silence developed.

He cleared his throat. "I'm sure it's nothing," he whispered, releasing her. "I think we should get back. Shane will be worried."

"Yes, you're probably right."

On their way down the uneven steps, they didn't say much.

Burton filled the dead air between them. "Are you glad you are away for the holidays?"

"Kinda have mixed feelings on that. I miss Mom. There are still a number of firsts to endure this year without her. And then, there's Dad and that woman."

"I know it's tough. But, hey, I've got something special planned for Christmas once we get to Niseko. You're gonna love it. A little skiing. Maybe some tubing. Snowmobiling. Even some great Michelin-star meals. You won't even think of anything else."

"Well, that sounds really nice. I can hardly wait."

"There is one more thing I want to run by you."

She turned to him and said, "Oh? What's that?"

"The bachelor and bachelorette parties. Martin and I had a few ideas that we were kicking around. Wanted to know your thoughts."

She stopped on the path as the snow fell lazily above them. "Okay. Shoot."

Seeing that she was all ears, he said, "Well, Martin suggested a Sumo Wrestling experience at the National Sumo Arena in Tokyo." Pausing, he looked to her for any type of reaction.

"Sumo?"

"Yes, it's a huge sport here. Thought I'd fly the guys out to see a private matchup. You know, a sparring session."

"I'm sure they'd love that, but us girls...not so much."

"No, you ladies will be doing something different."

Curious, she asked, "Like what?"

"How about shopping in the Ginza Six at stores like LV, Cartier, and Chanel, just to name a few?"

"Those are pretty expensive stores, Burton."

"Don't worry. It's on me."

Thinking about what he said, Abi figured spending so much money on themselves didn't seem right. "Why don't we skip the shopping and the Sumo and do something that makes a difference? Before coming here, I read a lot about the challenges facing children's charities and nursing homes for the elderly..." she paused. "Maybe we should volunteer and do something along those lines instead. Places that need help or a light shed upon them."

"A charity, huh?"

"Yes. I'm sure Martin can vet a few places and see what works best."

His mind reeled.

"For the kids, we can go shopping in a toy store or grab children's clothing and shoes. Bedding, pillows, blankets. Teddy bears? After all, it's Christmas, remember?"

Staring at her as she rhymed off the list made his heart swell. "That, umm, sounds like a great idea."

Excited, she clapped her hands together. "Really?" she said, clutching them tightly.

Her sheer excitement caught him off guard. "I'll ask him to look into it."

"It's something we can all do. There is no need to separate. Besides, the main reason for getting married is to experience life together. I've never understood the bachelor and bachelorette thing. I mean, why? Why celebrate your last night of being single? Doing what you want because, from the next day on, you'll never get to? It makes no sense. Defeats the purpose of the commitment you're making."

Somehow, her idea grew on him by the minute. "I agree," he replied.

"Shouldn't this be the first thing they do before becoming man and wife? Conquer something big and work together – not apart?"

"I hear what you are saying. That's a refreshing take on it."

"That's good. So, you're in?" Abi smiled.

"Yes, I'm in."

Bubbling, she giggled, "Let's keep it a surprise. What day were you thinking?"

"Martin mentioned Tuesday. The day before the wedding."

"That's perfect. It gives me time to do some research of my own." Grateful for his help, she said, "You won't regret this. I promise."

Unable to avoid her, he wondered what it would be like to share all of life's experiences as she described. In that instant, the energy she exuded seemed to fuel him.

Catching her shivering, he said, "Come on. We should let you warm up."

Continuing, they reached a fork in the path.

She pointed, "Straight ahead, correct? Is that the pavilion there?"

"It is." Needing to say his piece, he added, "Before we go inside, as always, if you need me for anything, please text or call me. Don't hesitate, no matter what time, day, or night."

"I will. Thank you."

Climbing the steps onto the wooden deck, Abi could see Shane scanning the premises, looking for her. Sadly, Sara was nowhere to be seen.

Burton noticed. "Guess I'll head back to my place and face the music." He tried to chuckle lightheartedly. "No pun intended."

She smiled and pointed at him.

"I'll see you at breakfast in the morning."

"Sounds good. I hope you don't have a bad night."

He smirked, "Well, I hope yours isn't bad either."

Not sure what he meant, Abi let it go as he opened the Pavilion door for her before walking away.

"Goodnight, Abs," he said, making eye contact with Shane. The guy wasn't happy.

"Night, Burton," Abi said before walking inside.

Gravitating to her, Shane pulled out the chair beside him. "You were gone a while."

"Sorry. He and I had some things to discuss." Warming herself by the fire, she could see him go stoic.

Not about to share what Sara had told him only moments ago, Shane realized that the couple's relationship was on the rocks. That meant he'd have to stick close to Abi from now on.

More than ready to leave, he suggested, "Want to head out?"

"Sure."

The two stood up.

"You love birds going back to your suite?" Abi asked Jade. "We are heading that way if you want to walk with us."

"Sure. We're coming," the girl said.

"Oh, Miss Jade?"

"Yes, Martin."

"Be a dear and meet for breakfast at ten. We need to visit the chapel tomorrow," Martin instructed.

"Will do."

Bidding him, Anton, and the guys - goodnight, the four of them left the building. Walking around to the left of it, they climbed the path, barely able to muster the energy.

As the girls fell behind, the guys gained distance from them.

Jade turned to Abi and said, "So, is tonight the night?"

"What do you mean?"

"You know, your first night together?"

"Not sure." Feeling a bit of pressure fall upon her, she didn't know what to do.

"Don't worry. You're safe with him. He really loves you, you know?"

Abi nodded. "I know."

"Don't be afraid. Afterward, you'll see. The love you share deepens. It's beautiful. Not scary."

What she said struck a chord, sparking Abi's curiosity slightly.

Almost at their building, she watched the guys give each other a bit of dap while waiting for the girls.

"Goodnight, my friend," Jade said, hugging her and giving her the eye.

"Night. We will see you in the morning."

"Yes, you will," she winked before whispering, "Good luck."

| 12 |

First Night

Friday, December 15

Aman Kyoto

Waving to their friends, Shane touched the card to the reader as it opened with a click. Abi walked inside first. Hearing it close behind them, she saw Shane lock up. Not very talkative, she quietly grabbed her pajamas from her suitcase. About to go and change, Shane stopped her in the middle of the room.

"She spoke to me, you know."

Confused, Abi asked, "Who?"

"Sara."

She was afraid to hear what the girl had said.

Slowly sitting on the bed, he couldn't look at her. "She asked him if something was going on between you and him."

Immediately, she pounced on that. "There isn't."

"What would make her think that?" he paused. "Perhaps the two of you taking a twenty-minute walk in the dark – alone tonight?"

"So, I can't take a walk with my friend when he needs to talk?"

"At one point, she asked him if he loved you."

Abi stopped in her tracks. "And?"

"Burton told her that he couldn't say he didn't."

Huffing it off, she answered, "Of course, he loves me. We're family."

"She doesn't see it that way."

"Well, how do you see it?"

Unsure how to respond, he replied, "I'd like to think I'm the only guy you love."

Seeing the desperation on his face, she tilted her head empathetically. "You are." Abi leaned against the wall. "You do realize that Burton is the only person I know who actually knew my Mother, like physically spoke to her. Nobody else, aside from my father."

"I know. I get it."

Tired of the drama, she firmly put things in perspective. "We've been over this before. If you want to be with me, you need to accept him, too. If you can't, there's nothing more to say. I refuse to cut someone out of my life just because you're jealous or insecure. Sorry." Abi abruptly left the room and ducked into the water closet to change.

Emerging minutes later, folding her clothes, she found Shane in pajama bottoms and a white T-shirt, brushing his teeth.

The casualness of it felt calming for some reason. "Mind if I..." She raised her toothbrush in front of the second sink.

He nodded with his mouth full of toothpaste, making a sound that resembled a muffled - *Yes.*

Her heart pounded in her chest. She could feel the tension rising between them.

Abi finished washing her face as Shane left the room. She could hear the sound of him climbing into bed. With a steadying breath, she turned out the lights and adjusted her eyes to the dim glow from the large windows, guiding her back into the bedroom. The quiet of the night wrapped around them. The only sounds now were the rustling of sheets as Shane adjusted his pillow.

About to get into bed, she paused when he said, "I'm sorry. I didn't mean to..."

Caught off guard, Abi froze. "Me too," she whispered, too quick, too unsure.

Shane pressed gently. "I would never ask you to cut someone out of your life."

Finally slipping into her bed, she pulled the duvet around her and lay still for a moment, staring up at the ceiling. "I'm glad to hear you say that."

Their eyes met across the small space between the beds, and for a moment, it was just the two of them.

Reaching out, Shane tapped her arm gently. "I love you." Leaning forward, drawn by an invisible connection, he waited.

Abi felt a flutter in her chest as a warmth spread through her. Meeting him partway, putting their differences aside for the time being, she closed the gap between them, unable to resist him.

Their kiss wasn't rushed or passionate. It seemed familiar, gentle, and full of promise as time seemed to blur amidst the quiet.

When they pulled back, the tenderness remained.

He smiled slightly. "Sweet dreams, Abs." Rubbing her arm as it grounded him, he asked, "Are we good?"

"Of course," Abi replied, despite the secrets she was keeping from him.

Rolling onto his back, Shane stared at the ceiling. "Can you believe we've been together almost four months?"

Abi's mood brightened a little. "It's gone by fast. A lot has happened."

"Sure has." The room went quiet. "Oh, forgot to tell you. Got an email from my agent. I need to go on Instagram Live, Thursday at some point, to officially announce which school I'm attending."

Abi's stomach knotted.

"I'm excited about playing for Alabama. I think we'll like it there," he said with enthusiasm. "The stadium is legendary. My agent said he got me in on a two-bedroom suite in Bryant Hall. The whole football team stays there. Apparently, it's dressed in Alabama colors and fully furnished. Even has a queen-sized bed."

Hearing that made her heart sink. "It sounds exciting."

"Yeah...I guess. A lot of pressure, though," he admitted.

Turning his way slightly, she tried to offer some comfort. "It will be, but you have never backed down from a challenge. I think you'll be just fine."

"They even have an athletic tutoring center with quiet areas where you and I can study. It will be like we never left Gilderson," Shane continued, his assumptions clear.

Abi's breath caught, the brick on her chest growing heavier. He hadn't even asked her. Not one word about what she would like to do, or where she saw herself next year. He just assumed they'd be together. Conflicted, she knew she had to tell him she'd gotten accepted to Harvard eventually. Forcing herself to smile in the darkness, she tried to remain positive. "Your dreams are coming true."

Shane's hand found her arm again, a gesture of gratitude. "I owe this all to you," he said softly.

"No, you did this all on your own, Shane. I didn't help you on the field."

"See, that's where you're wrong. You do. Every time I step out there, I hear you inside my head, encouraging me and keeping me focused. So, thank you."

Her heart skipped a beat. "That's so nice of you to say," she replied, torn between his sweetness and the secret she still hadn't shared.

He quieted. "Well, it's the truth."

After hearing that, she couldn't bring herself to say anything more. Quietly lying there, with her heart racing, she knew she couldn't keep this from him much longer. About to share her news, she suddenly heard him say - "Night, Abs," assuming he was surrendering as fatigue took over.

"Night."

"Love you," he whispered.

Abi swallowed against the knot in her throat. "I love you, too," she said, her voice trembling ever so slightly. With a quiet sigh, she closed her eyes and let the silence fill the room. *Tomorrow,* she told herself. *I will tell him about Harvard - about my dreams, about the path I want—no need—to take.* But for now, she let herself drift into the comfort of the night, knowing this moment of calm between them might not last much longer.

| 13 |

The Next Morning

Saturday, December 16

Aman Kyoto, Takagamine Suite

Abi heard a door close lightly. Looking around the room, she realized Shane wasn't there. Slowly stretching in bed, still tired, she wondered where he'd gone. Getting up and rounding the corner into the bathroom, she found a note sitting on the black slate counter.

Morning, Abs, Reg, and I went for a run. Be back soon.

Believing they'd be out for at least thirty minutes, in need of a soak to work through her problems, Abi turned on the water of the traditional Japanese tub similar to the one at her home on Stradella and added some of the aromatic bubble bath. As it filled from the waterfall ledge, she recalled Shane's conversation with Sara. Immediately, she wondered how Burton was doing that morning. Afraid to text him just in case the girl saw her message, Abi figured she'd wait until breakfast to speak to him.

With the water halfway up the side, bubbles quietly popping, she closed the pocket doors on both ends of the room. Grateful for the peacefulness, so many thoughts raced through her mind. Their first day ended in an argument, and Sara's drama continued to cast a dark cloud over them.

"The girl has to get a grip," she said aloud. Despite his tough-as-nails exterior, she could always see Burton's heart on his sleeve. Wishing she had never suggested that he give the girl a chance while they were in Tahoe, she felt responsible and regretted the decision. "You should have stayed out of it," she whispered, believing they could have avoided all the drama if she hadn't interfered.

Through the frosted glass wall towering adjacent to the tub, she heard the guys returning. Their friendly banter was unmistakable. Soon, their room door opened.

"Abs?" Shane said before knocking.

"I'm in here," she replied. Sliding the door open a notch, he asked, "Did you get my note?"

Thankful for his thoughtfulness, she replied, "Yes, I did."

"I'm sorry I wasn't here when you woke up. Figured I'd be back before that."

"It's fine. No worries."

He was curious as to where things stood between them. "So, are you doing okay?"

"I suppose," she paused. "How about you?"

"I'm feeling better after the run."

"I'll be just a few more minutes," she said, "then the bathroom is all yours."

"Take your time. It's fine."

Abi heard him move some furniture. Unable to enjoy the bath with the peacefulness gone, she sadly pulled the plug and got out. Wrapped in a towel, she continued her morning routine before walking out in a white robe.

"All yours," she said with less enthusiasm.

He knew right away she was upset. Determined to do better, he said, "Hey, umm..." while she rummaged through her suitcase.

Not looking his way, she answered nervously, "Hmm?" Returning to the room, she placed her clothes on the chair and noticed he'd moved the beds together.

Cautiously coming up behind her, he ran his hands along her arms. "I'm sorry about last night."

She turned to him as their eyes met. "Me too."

Pulling her in close, he asked, "Do you want to do something fun today? Just you and me?"

Liking the idea, she remembered Martin's itinerary. "Maybe after we see the chapel." Unsure of what they'd do, she asked, "What did you have in mind?"

"I searched up a few attractions this morning. You know, stuff close by. There are a few shrines and temples. Also, I put in a request to Martin to do something special on Sunday night."

"Oh? What's that?" she asked, peering up at him as they swayed gently back and forth.

"That is a surprise," he revealed rather mischievously.

"A surprise, huh?" Abi suddenly got a glimpse of the California boy she had fallen for months ago.

"I promise. You're gonna love it."

Elated, she smiled brightly, hoping they'd get past all the heaviness. "Well, then. I can hardly wait."

Kissing her forehead, then her cheek, he inched her backward ever so slowly until Abi felt her calves hit the mattress behind her. Swiveling her head around, she fell into the covers.

"Thought we needed some time to cuddle. Up for it?"

About to kiss her lips, she panicked. "Umm… Shouldn't you have a shower first?"

He stopped and lowered his head. "Hold that thought."

Disappearing into the bathroom, he closed the door.

Lying there, propping her head on two pillows, Abi whispered, "You've gotta be honest with him." She knew that if she weren't, moments like these would become increasingly complicated.

The sound of water trickled against the tile floor. Somehow, it reminded her of a ticking clock, keeping time. Wondering how to phrase what she needed to say, Abi exhaled.

Seconds later, the water turned off. Her chest was in knots. Knowing how patient he'd been, she suddenly felt pressured. Assuming he expected things between them to move to the next level at some point on this trip, her body started to vibrate inside with nerves.

Why am I feeling like this? It's not the way it should be, she thought to herself.

Hearing him brushing his teeth, she tried to formulate a plan, not fully knowing what to say. Wanting to offer some reassurance, careful not to hurt his feelings or make him question their relationship, the pocket door suddenly slid open, and she saw Shane emerge wearing a bathrobe as well.

Sliding the beds even closer together, he sat down and inched closer to rest his head on the pillow beside her. An awkwardness loomed. Easily reading the slight panic on her face, her body rigid, he backed off.

Forced to roll onto his back and give her space, he took his phone from the side table and said, "So, I'm not sure what the plan is today, but this is what I thought we could see." Scrolling through the bookmarked pages, he skooched over a little and showed her the screen. "This famous bamboo forest is interesting, but not far from it is another one. Something similar. Apparently, that place is less crowded and more peaceful."

Abi looked at the pictures. "I see," she said as a spark ignited between them, and her body started to relax. "It's very pretty, but I'm sure Martin has an itinerary prepared, aside from the chapel visit."

Flipping to the next bookmark, he said, "And this is the Golden Temple. It's along the same route." He turned to her. "Thoughts?"

"Honestly?"

Worried, he leaned on his side and propped his head in his hand. "You don't want to go with me?"

"It's not that. This is only our second day here, and we are on a group trip. As much as I would like to do things alone, I feel like it's rude to take off on our own. Can't we steal some time together while still doing things with everyone else? I believe Jade and Reg expect to tag along wherever we go. Then there's...Burton."

Shane exhaled upon hearing his name.

"Despite what you think of him, he is paying for this trip. At the very least, we can be civil. If he and Sara go off and do something together, then that gives us the green light to do the same."

Once again, always thinking of others, he heard what she said. "You're right." Loving that side of her, unable to contain himself any longer, Shane's muscles tensed beneath his robe as he reached out to brush a loose strand of hair from Abi's face.

The warmth of his touch caused a shiver, while the scent of his body wash - undeniably masculine - kindled her senses.

When he leaned in, the space between them disappeared as his lips met hers. Filled with heightened intensity, Shane poured all of his feelings into that single moment, then rested his forehead against hers.

Bodies pressed firmly together, their legs tangled - the heat between them increased. Yet, amidst it all, Shane stayed mindful of her, his movements careful, never pushing too far.

"I just want to be close to you," he whispered, tightening his hold slightly.

Wrapped in his arms, she could feel her heart swell. With only the quiet hum of emotions between them, she allowed herself to let go. Then, without warning, she flinched, making him back off.

Realizing what she did, Abi mumbled, "I'm, umm..."

At a loss, Shane rolled onto his back, staring at the ceiling. His voice filled with concern. "Abs...you've gotta tell me what I'm doing wrong. There are times I feel like you're right here with me - like we're really connecting. And then, you abruptly pull away, and I don't understand why. After all this time, I feel like I'm messing up. That said, I don't know what to do about it." His eyes flickered to hers, vulnerability showing through. "I just... I don't know what you need me to be."

Struggling, Abi felt her throat tense. "It's not you, Shane." She hesitated before admitting, "Ever since my mom died, I feel like she's still watching me—like she's guiding every choice I make. And I don't want to disappoint her."

Shane's brows furrowed. "Disappoint her how?"

"Before she went into the hospital," Abi exhaled slowly, "she told me that love isn't about rushing or second-guessing—it's about knowing, deep down, that it's right." Rolling on her back, she said, "Mom wanted me to wait. She was afraid I'd make the same mistake she did."

"What mistake?"

"I've never shared this with anyone, but..." she paused, somewhat ashamed to say it. "She got pregnant with me before marrying my Dad. The last thing she wanted was for me to have the same experience."

Sitting up slightly, Shane replied, "But, Abs, that was years ago. Things are different now."

"I know," she whispered. "But in my head, she's always there, reminding me. Watching me. If I let things go too far, I feel like I'm letting her down. The thought of it just, umm, stops everything for me." She rolled to face him.

He studied her for a moment, then reached for her hand between them. "I get it."

Grateful for his understanding, her emotions remained tangled inside her.

Running a hand down her arm, his touch was warm and steady. "I just wish I knew how to make you feel safe with me." Then, with a small smirk, he added, "Because if I'm being honest... It's really hard being this close to you and not loving you up."

Abi's heart pounded as she searched his eyes, torn between the comfort he gave her and her Mother's expectations.

He flashed her a playful, sexy smirk. "Because I really do want to..."

Unsure how to respond, she fell silent.

For a second, he turned away.

Inches apart, she whispered. "I'm trying to make sense of these feelings... Somehow, it is all so complicated."

Analyzing that, he remained quiet.

She added, shaking her head, "And I know it shouldn't be."

"Abs, it's okay." Shane reached over and wrapped his arms around her and pulled her close. For a moment, the world outside seemed to fade away as he rested his chin gently on the top of her head, holding her like he never wanted to let go.

Nestling in with her head resting on his chest, Abi heard the steady rhythm of his heart. Something was reassuring in the way he held her—like no matter what, they'd figure out their problems together.

His hand stroked her hair. "Maybe you shouldn't think about it so much," he murmured. "Just be here with me."

Closing her eyes, she tried to let her worries melt away. She listened to him breathing and felt the gentle rise and fall of his chest beneath her hand. For the first time in a long while, Abi allowed herself to stop analyzing and questioning. Simply lying there in his arms, she trusted him wholeheartedly.

"Maybe I'm just looking for that flawless, happy ending?"

"How so?"

"That special moment where it's just the two of us, overwhelmed by love."

Hearing what she said, knowing they hadn't had a lot of time alone the past two months with so much going on in their lives, he understood where she was coming from. "See, that's why I love you. Other girls don't think like that."

She felt a sense of relief.

"Since we met, I feel like we've built a strong foundation, and despite the Burton drama, we trust each other. Am I wrong?"

"No," she shook her head. "You're not wrong."

"That's good. I'm glad to hear that." Shane slipped his arm behind her head and cuddled up. "Hey, it's only eight o'clock. Maybe we should sleep a little bit longer. I'm kinda liking this, right here." He tightened their embrace.

Loving the closeness, she nodded, "Me too."

| 14 |

Breakfast

Saturday, December 16

Aman Kyoto - The Living Pavilion

The phone on the bedside table rang loudly, startling them to bits. Dazed and disoriented, still half asleep, Shane let go of Abi, rolled over, and grabbed the receiver. Bringing it to his ear, he said groggily, "Hello?"

"Where are you guys? We expected you for breakfast fifteen minutes ago," Jade questioned. "We are heading out to the chapel soon."

"Don't worry. We're coming," he said before hanging up the phone.

"Who was that?" Abi asked sleepily.

"It was Jade. We're late. Everyone is waiting for us."

Frantically getting out of bed, Abi located the outfit she'd taken from her suitcase while Shane did the same. About to strip down, they both stopped.

She grabbed her things. "I'll change in the bathroom. You change out here," she said on her way past him.

He gave her a thumbs-up. Assuming she'd gone, he dropped his robe, not knowing she'd gotten a glimpse of him before ducking into the bathroom.

Frazzled, instinctively closing her eyes, she almost ran into the doorframe. Steadying herself while getting her bearings, she stumbled about and got dressed as fast as she could. Before long, she heard a knock.

"Hey, can I come in?"

Slipping her hoodie over her head and threading her arms through the sleeves, she said, "Yep. All good."

Both brushed their teeth quickly and fixed their hair.

Abi pulled hers into a tight ponytail. After securing it in place, she had just enough time to splash a bit of gloss on her lips, accentuate her eyelashes with some mascara, and brush her cheeks with a hint of blush.

Feeling cozy in black tights, a white tee, and her Lulu scuba hoodie, she zipped it up and returned to the bedroom to put on her Doc Martens and her down vest.

"Ready?" he asked, flipping the hood over his head, grabbing his feather-lite down jacket in the process.

"Ready."

Grabbing her LV tote, Abi put her romance novel inside, just in case she found a quiet place to read.

Shane took the card key off the table and stuffed it in his pocket before reaching out to take her hand and walk out the door.

The minute she took hold, she felt things shift again.

Is this the feeling Mom described? Suddenly wanting to be near him, nothing else mattered.

Lightly jogging down the path toward the Living Pavilion, they soon climbed the steps to the deck.

All eyes were on them as Shane pulled the door open and rested his hand on the small of Abi's back to escort her inside. This gesture did not go unnoticed. Aware of their friends staring, the first person she made eye contact with was Burton. Unfortunately, to his left was Sara.

Well, at least they're together, she thought as they met up with Jade and Reg. "Sorry, we're late. We slept in," Abi said, taking off her vest and hanging it on the back of her chair.

"Oooh, you did, did you? Busy night?" Jade asked in front of everyone.

Taken off guard, she witnessed Burton's head snap in their direction.

In an instant, she missed the opportunity to rebut the comment innocently. Not doing so made them look guilty.

Moving along to the breakfast buffet, Shane took a plate from the stack and handed it to Abi before taking one for himself.

Burton took notice of the apparent closeness between the two. Watching as they dished out their plates and found a seat together, he saw Shane pull out her chair and ask if she wanted a coffee.

"Yes, please."

He left and got that for her, along with some juice for himself. Returning minutes later, the two started eating and didn't say much.

Without warning, Abi found Burton's eyes locked to hers. Before long, her thoughts got away from her. *Your best friend invites you on this luxurious vacation, and you can't even speak to him. How messed up is that?*

Practically downing the first cup, Abi got up from her chair and returned to the beverage area. Unbeknownst to her, Burton followed.

"Morning," he said, taking a packet of sugar from the basket.

"Morning." Assuming people were looking at them, she asked, "How did you sleep?"

He smirked. "Not as good as you, apparently."

Hating the snarky comment, she cleared the air. "For the record, nothing happened."

"I don't want to know your business." Pouring his coffee, he stirred in some cream. "But I am happy to hear that." He peered over his shoulder. There, he found Shane's eyes on them, Sara's too.

Abi finished up and carefully walked away, making sure she didn't spill it. Returning to the table, she hoped she could talk to Burton again at some point today without any drama.

Martin stood up. "Can I have your attention, if I may?" Seeing all eyes gravitating to him, he continued. "In about thirty minutes, we will be leaving for the chapel, where our happy couple plans to tie the knot. It is just down the road. Not far. While there, the chaplain requested a meeting with them. Afterward, we will return, and you have the option of a leisurely afternoon or a short sightseeing excursion to a few attractions nearby. At some point within the next hour, please let me know your intentions so I can arrange transportation. Dress accordingly. The weather is expected to get colder this afternoon. Additionally, for those who wish to stay behind, the staff would like to inform you that they have availability in the Spa, should anyone like to make an appointment. Simply call and book directly with the Concierge. Moving on to dinner this evening, we are dining at Taka-An. It is located just outside the main gates. Please meet outside the Welcome Center by six o'clock. Thank you. As you were."

Abi saw Burton steal a glance at her. She wished she knew what he was thinking, but he was his usual, mysterious self. Spotting Sara, cracking a hint of a smile, she hoped they were working things out.

Maybe I should talk to her today and reassure her that I am not a threat. Thinking more about it, she figured if the opportunity presented itself, she would give it a try, hoping by doing so, she wouldn't cause more harm than good.

| 15 |

The Chapel

Saturday, December 16

Roku Hotel / Shozan Chapel, Kyoto

Their group parted ways after breakfast. Moving to the Welcome Pavilion, Shane and Abi joined Jade and Reg, ready to head over to the wedding chapel. To their surprise, Burton tagged along with three of his guys. Upon seeing this, a small smile appeared on his face.

To spark some conversation, he approached the bride-to-be. "So, are you ready for this? Excited?"

"Yes, very much. A little nervous, too."

"Don't worry, Babe. We got this," Reggie encouraged.

A luxury coach pulled into the courtyard, its sleek design catching the winter sun. One by one, they boarded and found their seats.

"We are going to the Roku Resort," Martin instructed the driver.

"Very well," the man said, dressed in black and white attire.

The coach pulled away from the Aman compound and onto the main road. The short journey was peaceful, the group quietly chatting as they watched the snowy world outside. In minutes, the vehicle turned into the parking lot of the modern hotel.

To their left, nestled among the towering trees, was the small stucco chapel. Its creamy exterior blended harmoniously with the surrounding landscape, giving off a rustic charm. Snow blanketed its roof and framed its arched windows, while lazy flakes fell gently from the sky, making the entire scene feel magical.

Beyond the chapel, the river wound lazily through the trees, its surface shimmering under the pale winter light. Frost clung to the branches overhead, their tips heavy with snow that occasionally drifted down in clumps. The woods beyond stretched in serene beauty, their silence broken only by the ice crunching underfoot as the group stepped off the coach.

Taking it all in, Abi stood for a moment, the wonder of it reflected in her expression. Burton could see she was analyzing the place.

With eyes on her, a knowing glance passed between them.

Standing on the steps, Jade folded her arms, disappointed. To her, from the outside, it was nothing remarkable—just a small building nestled beside a river, with thick trees looming over it like sentinels.

She found Reggie chatting with Martin. Both were oblivious to her friend's mood.

"I'm not sure about this," Jade muttered under her breath. "I thought it'd be more... I don't know... Grand?"

Reggie glanced at her, sensing her unease. "Give it a chance, Babe. Martin says it's incredible inside."

Sighing, Jade gave a half-hearted nod and followed the group as they moved through the glass doors to escape the cool air. The main lobby wasn't much to look at, but when they entered through the wooden doors, the large floor-to-ceiling cathedral window bathed the room with natural light.

Her breath caught in her throat. It was far more than what she expected. An intimately elegant place with timeless simplicity. The vaulted ceiling drew her eyes upward. Surprisingly, the space was decorated in a modern monochromatic black-and-white color scheme, with the ceiling, walls, and floor all white and the arched beams jet black to match the pews.

Jade's eyes teared up.

Reggie approached. "So, what are you thinking now?"

The scent of fresh, winter-white flowers in the tall glass cylinders lining the aisle added to the scene before her.

"This...this is perfect," she whispered, her mood shifting entirely.

Squeezing her hand, Reg walked with her toward the altar, where the clergyman awaited them for introductions.

Martin joined, making sure everything was in order for the ceremony, discussing last-minute details while Jade wiped away her tears.

Leaving them to have their meeting, Shane, Abi, and Burton left and decided to explore the Roku Resort.

As they walked along the path together, Abi asked cautiously, "Where's Sara?"

"She decided to take advantage of the spa for a bit."

"I'm sure she'll enjoy that."

"From what she says, it's pretty nice."

Abi could feel the tension, knowing they were acting this way for Shane's benefit.

Approaching the sleek yet cozy entrance, the stone and wood details, along with holiday-themed planters, mixed old-school Japanese style with modern vibes.

As they drew closer to the main doors, the natural slate and wood textures gave the entrance a calm and relaxing energy.

Upon entering the large breezeway with a shallow reflecting pool, they noticed a few lazy flakes fall through the open roof and melt into the water below. A Christmas evergreen with crisp white lights stood front and center.

With Shane by her side, Abi followed Burton into the TeaHouse, a space with wooden slat walls, contemporary furniture, and huge windows. Captivated by the perfectly arranged gardens and the expansive shallow pools beyond the windows, she sat down, feeling like the indoors and outdoors flowed beautifully together.

Taking out his phone, Burton perused his messages before double-checking the whereabouts of Lorenzo and Bray on the premises. Having received something from Sara, he sighed.

At the same time, Shane mentioned, "I want to see if they have a gym. I'll be right back."

Left alone with Burton, amongst the hum of conversation in the background, Abi pulled her book from her bag. The quiet between them wasn't uncomfortable but rather a rare moment of peace despite everything going on.

"I should probably head back to the hotel and meet up with Sara," he said, standing up, slipping his hands into his pockets.

Removing the bookmark and setting it on the seat beside her, Abi opened the novel and smiled. "That's okay. I'm just going to stay here and read. It's peaceful."

The tasseled card suddenly fluttered to the floor with the breeze from the doors opening.

Burton bent down and picked it up. Staring at the Japanese letters, he noticed the red dragon embossed on the bottom. "Where did you get this?" he asked firmly.

"It was in the welcome basket from Red Dragon," she replied. "Why?"

Not responding, his face hardened. A sense of concern followed. Studying the elegant Japanese script etched on it, he muttered, "No reason."

"Didn't you get one, too?"

Not wanting to cast caution her way, he said, "Maybe. I'm not sure. I'll ask Sara. She was more interested in the swag than me."

Handing it to her, Abi said, "Thanks."

"Guess I'll see you after?"

"For sure." She crossed her legs and opened her book to the chapter where she'd left off.

He waved before leaving. On his way out, he stopped by the concierge desk.

Abi watched as he floated his hand through the air, signifying that he needed a pen. Given one, she saw him write something on the paper. When he'd finished, he pointed at it. The man looked at him, perplexed. Burton's eyes were glued to his intensely.

What is he doing? she thought.

Spotting Shane walking into the room in search of her, she raised a hand and said, "Over here!"

"I found the gym. It's pretty impressive. Even has a view of the outdoor pool and the chapel."

"Good to hear," she replied, her attention gravitating elsewhere.

The closer he got, Shane's expression shifted from casual curiosity to mild concern as his eyes flickered between Burton's tense face and Abi's troubled demeanor. "What's up with him?" he asked.

"I'm not exactly sure." Her instincts told her something was wrong.

"If something is going on, you need to tell me."

"I don't know yet." She pulled the thin wooden plaque out from the pages of her book. "His mood changed when he saw my bookmark. After that, he walked to the main desk and asked the guy for a pen and paper."

"Do you want me to go and..."

She stopped him right there. "No, absolutely not."

"Why?"

With a tilt of her head, she said, "You know why."

For a moment, he contemplated going against her wishes, but stopped. "Fine. I won't interfere."

"Thank you," she said, seeing Martin emerge from around the corner.

Closing his iPad cover and removing his reading glasses from the end of his nose, he tucked them in his inside pocket.

Burton didn't waste any time pulling him aside to speak to him in a hushed tone. Moving to where he thought nobody would see, Abi caught their reflection off the glass. Deep in conversation, things seemed to escalate.

She wasn't the only one who noticed.

"What do you suppose that's about?" Shane pointed out. "Must be big."

Looking down at the bookmark again, she recalled something Martin had sent them. Not wasting any time, she pulled up their WhatsApp group chat and clicked the Google Translate link. Joining the hotel's WiFi, she downloaded it.

Waiting for it to install, her fingers tapped anxiously against the edge of her phone. The second it popped up, she opened the app and pressed the camera button. Heart pounding, she ran the lens over her bookmark.

Suddenly, the kanji Japanese letters morphed into English.

"Death to her…" Her voice was barely loud enough for Shane to hear.

"What did you say?" His tone was razor sharp.

"Look." She turned her phone, showing him the words on the screen.

The QB's face drained of color as his eyes darted to Abi alarmingly. "Are you serious?" His casual stance stiffened.

Finished with their meeting, Jade and Reggie bid the clergyman goodbye and joined Abi and Shane.

Seeing Burton and Martin talking, Reggie cut through the quiet. "Hey… Are they fighting?"

Not fully explaining, Shane answered before Abi could. "We aren't sure."

"Stay here," she said, "I'm going to find out."

Martin's expression mirrored Burton's—grave and noticeably worried.

"I'm telling you, it's Yakuza."

"Perhaps, but we need proof," the wise gentleman stated.

Having overheard everything from a few feet away, Abi felt a cold shiver run down her spine. With her heart racing, a level of paranoia set in as she rounded the corner to confront them.

Shane was close behind while their friends watched from afar.

Pulling on Burton's arm, she asked, "What are you two talking about?"

Immediately, Shane came up behind her. "And what is Yakuza?"

Neither of the men answered.

The concern in Burton's eyes was undeniable. Taking a deep breath, he knew he needed to stay tight-lipped for now. Part of him thought there was no reason to suspect anything—not yet, at least. But that said, the message on the card was clear.

He attempted to ease her worry. "It's nothing."

The girl frowned, unconvinced. "Well, I'm not leaving here until you tell me the truth." She stared Burton down and crossed her arms accusingly. Pulling the wooden plaque from her book, she held it up. "I saw you talking to the concierge. The guy seemed as though he'd seen a ghost. I know what it says."

"Abi..." he said, about to invoke reason.

The girl interrupted him. "It says *Death to her*. Is this true?"

Inspecting the unassuming design, Shane turned to Burton, waiting for him to respond. "Answer her. Is that translation correct?"

Martin gravely nodded at his boss.

"Yes," Burton revealed. "That is what it says."

The words engulfed them suffocatingly.

"Why would Red Dragon put that in our welcome basket? Is this some kind of sick joke?" she asked.

"Don't worry, Miss. I am looking into it." With a sense of urgency, Martin added, "We will find out more soon. In the meantime, Master B, why don't you and Mr. Coppersmith take Miss Abi back to the hotel? Send the driver for us afterward. We are almost done here."

She could see Martin was doing his best to distract her.

Straightening his posture, with hands buried in his pockets, Burton leaned in close and said, "I think that's wise," in a low, concerned tone. "We might be blowing this out of proportion. But will take precautions, just in case."

Gaze narrowing, Shane focused on Abi. His chest puffed to counter Burton's stature. He knew the guy would refuse to divulge anything more.

Feeling Abi's hand on his arm, Shane knew she was silently telling him to let it go and walk away despite his blood boiling.

Still clutching her book against her chest, she hesitated. Her fingers, gripping the spine tighter. "Fine. Let's go, then," she said, not questioning their reasoning.

Motioning to his security detail, Burton said, "Let's move."

From across the room, they waved to Jade and Reggie as Martin went to join the couple and finish the business that needed tending to.

Hurrying along with the guys, Abi saw the shuttle waiting for them. Her pulse raced. The once beautiful chapel and the serene atmosphere around it now seemed menacing.

"Stay close," Shane whispered as he kept his hand on her back, his touch both comforting and tense.

When they climbed aboard the vehicle, two of Burton's security in tow, Abi had so many unanswered questions.

Shane sat beside her. His legs spilled into the aisle and bounced with pent-up energy while Burton remained stoic and took the seat across from them.

As the shuttle pulled away, leaving Martin, Jade, and Reggie behind, Abi couldn't help but glance down at the tassel dangling from the book.

Nobody spoke on the way back. Both guys kept their eyes on the road ahead.

Out of the blue, Shane said, "Let me see that thing again."

Abi fanned through the pages and handed it to him.

Examining the front and the back, he didn't know what to make of it. When he looked at Burton, the guy shook his head subtly to signal him to stay quiet. Taking heed, Shane handed it back to her. "I'm sure these are a dime a dozen. Maybe it's just a trinket for tourists. Nothing more."

When he said that, Burton nodded in agreement.

Upon entering the gates of Aman, they soon pulled up to the Welcome Pavilion.

The driver opened the door. Before leaving, Burton instructed him to return for the others and added, "I'm gonna check on Sara. Maybe I'll see you two at lunch."

About to go their separate ways, Abi replied, "Sounds good."

Stopping at the Living Pavilion, they grabbed some tea and a few snacks to go before they returned to their suite along the hillside.

With the breeze hitting their faces, Abi tucked her chin inside her coat. Her cheeks tingled in the cold. On the way up the incline, an ominous feeling struck her as she walked along in silence. Instincts sounding the alarm, she knew there was something dark on the horizon and didn't notice that Shane wasn't by her side.

| 16 |

The Bookmark

Saturday, December 16

Aman Kyoto

Almost reaching the top of the hill high above the resort, Abi turned and found Burton walking with Shane, mumbling a good ten steps behind her.

"What are you two doing?" she asked suspiciously.

"Nothing," Shane replied, trying to sound innocent as Burton gave her a thumbs-up at the same time, adding, "Don't worry, Abs. Everything's fine."

Just as she reached their room door, Shane approached and pulled the key card from his pocket to tap it to the reader.

Not happy about leaving her, Burton knew he didn't have a choice. "I'm just gonna work for a bit. If you need me, I'll be over there," he said, pointing to his building.

"Okay," Abi said as the QB looked on.

Before going inside, she caught them exchanging worried looks. "What about our sightseeing excursion this afternoon?" she asked, wanting to make the most of their time in the historic city. "I refuse to be huddled up here out of fear."

The guy flashed a stern expression. "We are contemplating keeping a low profile for the time being."

Unhappy with that, she said, "No, I don't want paranoia ruining this trip."

Before he could respond, they saw Martin walking towards them with Jade and Reggie.

Raising a steady hand, Abi zeroed in on Martin. "So, what's the plan for the rest of the day?" she asked, throwing the onus on him.

Their trusted friend referred to his iPad. "After some deliberation with the guys, we decided to remain vigilant but not impose restrictions. We'll keep security tight until we have something concrete to worry about. Meet at the Living Pavilion in half an hour. Dress warm because we are going to see the Arashiyama Bamboo Forest and the Golden Pavilion."

"Perfect!" Thankful to be moving on with their day, Abi was excited by the itinerary.

"Yeah, that sounds fun," Jade replied, clutching Reggie's arm, not knowing what was happening. "Want to meet back here in fifteen minutes to walk there together?" she asked her friend.

Noticeably preoccupied, Abi agreed. "Sure. We will see you shortly."

With that said, the happy couple disappeared into their room.

Doubting his advisor's assessment, Burton asked quietly, "Martin. A word."

With her interest piqued, Abi tried to listen in.

Moving away with their backs to them, he muttered, "You and I both know this was a possible warning shot."

"Yes, and I've got a number of people working on it," he replied calmly, his hands cupping the iPad in front of him. "No need to cause a frenzy until we know more."

Adding to his case, he said, "They are dangerous."

"I am well aware."

Burton stared into the man's eyes, understanding all too well that he had extensive experience in dealing with these organizations.

With a keen eye on both Burton and Martin, she could tell there was more to this than what they were letting on. It was clear they wanted to protect her from something. But what?

"Come on, Abs," Shane prompted, hoping to break her from the drama. "Let's go and get changed."

She watched the men as they walked toward Burton's pavilion.

Finally able to corral her inside, Shane closed the door behind them.

"What was that about?"

Unable to look her in the eye, he said, "Nothing...umm...we were just discussing the bookmark thing."

Taking off her boots and jacket, Abi sighed. "Oh..." Letting it go for now, she walked into the room and noticed the maid service had already visited. Running her fingers along the duvet cover on the way to the window, she realized they'd converted the bed into a king. Sadly, it felt like this was the least of her worries right now.

While watching her in silence, Shane could see she was afraid despite her tough exterior. Slowly stepping forward, he gently took her by the hand and pulled her in close.

Her eyes met his. "I know what you are gonna say," she whispered, "but it's more than that. Once again, I feel this darkness hanging over me, and it seems I can't escape it, no matter where we go."

"There's only one person to blame for that." Those words slid off his tongue too easily.

Abi tilted her head. "This isn't his fault." Recalling Burton's reaction to it all, she knew he was just as surprised.

"You and I both know whoever *he* works for puts him in danger and ropes you in by association."

"If I recall, the last thing I got roped into started as a riff between you and Eastwood. Burton got involved because he needed to save me."

What she said hit him hard. It was a reminder that he'd failed her. "And I've regretted it ever since. Do you know how much I hated myself that I wasn't there to protect you - how the guilt has eaten at me all this time? If I could go back and change that night, I would. In a heartbeat."

Turning around, she knew what had happened at the Black Lyon rave was not entirely his fault. She should never have wandered off alone. It was a mistake that could have cost her everything. "I'm sorry... I shouldn't have said that."

"But, you're right. I should've been there," he replied. "I can't change the past, but I promise I won't let anything happen to you," he whispered as his arms encircled her waist.

Swiveling around, hands resting on his chest, she felt his heart beating. "I'm scared, Shane," she said, "And I hate it."

He was determined to get her out of harm's way. "Just say the word, and I'll take you home. We can go back to LA."

As much as she wanted to do that, Abi knew they couldn't leave now. Whatever was happening, they needed to stay with Burton and Martin to be safe. "No, we can't. We don't have a choice."

"You always have a choice, Abs." His thumb brushed across her cheek gently.

Sighing, she knew otherwise. "We need to stay."

"Fine. But from here on out, you will not leave my sight, ever. Is that clear?" he smirked to lighten the air around them.

Nervous, she nodded.

"Let's take it one hour at a time. Everything will be okay. I promise." His lips met hers in a tender, lingering kiss. Not rushed. Just slow, filled with a quiet assurance. As the moment stretched, the world outside their room faded into the background while the snow continued to fall lazily outside the window.

When they parted, Abi rested her head on Shane's chest, feeling the warmth of his body against hers. His arms wrapped around her, cocooning her in his presence.

The looming uncertainty melted away briefly as Shane kissed the top of her head, his voice low. "This whole thing is probably nothing. So, don't worry."

Abi managed a smile. The tension in her body slowly began to ease. "I believe you," she whispered, despite her gut feeling telling her otherwise.

"Come on. Bundle up, and we will get moving."

She disappeared into the bathroom and heard Shane fumbling in his suitcase. Staring in the mirror, she got a sinking feeling. It was similar to when she found the rose in her Mother's hands.

"Don't psych yourself out. Everything will be okay," she mumbled while brushing her teeth.

Dressed in winter gear, his hat and mitts in hand, Shane peeked around the corner. "Are you good to go?"

A knock came on the door. Shane opened it. "Come on in, guys. Give us one more minute. We are almost ready."

Their friends scooched inside. Jade looked around. "Hey, our room is exactly the same. It's a mirror image." Spotting the Red Dragon welcome basket, she asked, "So, what did you get in yours?" Nosily perusing through it, she said, "Wow! You got a quilted down tote bag? That's pretty cool. We got a hoodie." Jade unzipped her jacket, revealing the Red Dragon swag she was wearing. "What do you think? Does it look good? Is the red too much? I figured it would keep me warm."

"If anything, it's festive given the holidays." With her coat and hat on, Abi grabbed her mittens. "I think it's great."

"Thanks," Jade said, knowing they had to get going.

With their room key zipped in Shane's pocket, they all walked outside, ready to make their way to the Living Pavilion.

Abi couldn't help but notice Reggie's strange look.

Shane saw it, too. "What's up, my man?" he asked. "You seem like you have something on your mind."

Reg couldn't help himself. "So, we get the feeling something went down earlier. And we're just wondering what happened. You guys seemed stressed when we returned from the chapel. Martin didn't say anything."

Glancing up at Shane, Abi revealed, "Did your welcome basket come with a wooden plaque with a braided tassel?"

Jade thought a moment. "No, I don't think it did."

"I thought it would work well as a bookmark." Recalling the makings of that moment, she described, "While we were waiting for you, Burton saw that it had fallen onto the floor. When he picked it up, he was curious as to the writing on it and had it translated by the concierge desk."

"What did it say?" Jade asked as they walked along the path.

Abi took a deep breath. "It read - Death to her."

"Wait?" Jade's face went blank. "What did you just say?"

Shane interjected. "She double-checked with the Google Translate app. That confirmed it."

"Death to her?" Reg questioned. "Meaning you?"

Immediately shooting his friend a disapproving look, Shane figured the guy would rebound in his usual way.

"Did I say something wrong? It's a valid question. Isn't it?"

Jade hit his stomach with the back of her hand.

Partially knocking the wind from him, he blurted, "Wow, you have seriously bad karma, girl."

His fiancée smacked him again. "Are you insinuating that this is her fault?"

"After everything that's happened to her, how can you not think that?"

Turning to Abi, Jade said, "Ignore him." Needing to say something positive, she rested her hand on Abi's arm. "I'm sure it's nothing."

"But why would they get a card and not us?" Reg questioned point-blank. "I mean, did Burton, Martin, or Anton get one? Or just them?"

Angry at the guy for his unfiltered comments, Jade pulled him back. "You guys go ahead," she instructed. "We'll catch up in a minute."

Abi nodded, knowing Jade was about to scold him.

Overhearing the girl, Shane chuckled, "The guy brought that upon himself. Sucks to be him."

"In Reg's defense, he does have a point."

He was surprised to hear her say that. "Honestly, I was thinking the same thing. You should take inventory of everyone's basket and see if we were the only ones to get that plaque."

"I'll talk to Martin and Burton about it at lunch."

"I think you should," he replied, taking hold of her hand as they descended the hill.

Approaching the Living Pavilion, Shane reached out and opened the door, allowing Abi to enter first.

Inside, they found the guys gathered, seemingly having a serious conversation with Martin, Burton, and Sara.

Not wanting to interrupt, Abi opted to avoid them and found a table for four. Draping her jacket along the back of the chair, she had a seat and perused the menu card resting on the plate.

Soon, their friends joined them. Reggie seemed a little worse for wear.

"What are you going to have?" Abi asked, contemplating it herself.

Reading the descriptions, Shane looked over at her. "At this rate, I'll probably end up losing twenty pounds if I don't get some pasta and steak soon."

"That's a bit of an exaggeration," she pointed out humorously.

His friend confirmed, "No, he's right. We need to consume at least thirty-eight hundred calories per day during training. Sometimes more. In the off-season, it's less, but not by much."

Martin overheard them. "Would you like me to submit a request, Mr. Coppersmith? Anything specific you'd prefer?"

The football player turned to him. "The food last night was amazing, but my stomach was growling half the night. Guess it's just that we aren't used to eating like this."

"Something a bit more substantial, then?"

The DJ pointed at him to indicate he felt the same.

Every security guard nodded their head.

"I see you are not the only one?" Martin took note. "Very well. I will pass this along to the chef."

When their waitress stopped by their table, the girls didn't hesitate to order the much-anticipated afternoon tea boxes. Sara included. Following suit, the guys did the same, hoping they'd eat again within an hour or two.

The meal was a feast for the senses, showcasing the season in two elegant wooden layers. The first box featured savory bites made with local ingredients like Shogoin turnips and tangy Sugukizuke pickles. The second held sweet delights—peony-flavored treats, creamy cheese bites, and strawberry daifuku, capturing the essence of early spring. Freshly made dumplings, cooked tableside by our pastry chefs, made the experience even more special.

With the list of teas given to them, each of them placed their order and enjoyed the aromas and warmth each cup granted before Martin announced, "We will be departing shortly for our excursion this afternoon. If you haven't done so already, grab your warm layers and accessories. We will be meeting outside the main gates in ten minutes."

About to leave the table, a pretty young lady asked, "Would you like tea to go, Miss?"

Abi's face brightened, having enjoyed the Jasmine Pearl flavor she'd tried. "Yes. That would be great if you don't mind."

"Not at all." Making eye contact with Jade and Sara, she asked, "Anyone else?"

The two girls nodded and showed her what tea they'd prefer before she disappeared to prepare their orders.

When she returned, she had with her three Aman-logoed, earthy green, insulated bottles with a flip-top. Around each, she'd fastened the tea pouch to identify who they belonged to. On the tray, she also had bottles of water, which she passed around to everyone who wanted one before their departure.

"Are you going to ask everyone about the baskets?" Shane stood tall beside her, his broad frame clad in a warm black Boda puffer, his protective nature evident as he glanced her way. "I can throw it out there if you want?"

"Sure. Do you mind?" she said.

"No, not at all." Not wasting time, he said, "Can I have your attention for a second?"

Multiple sets of eyes converged as he spoke. "Abi and I just wanted to check with all of you and see if anyone noticed a wooden plaque in their welcome baskets. It had hand-painted Japanese letters on it with an embossed red dragon and a corded tassel."

The room fell silent as the others glanced at one another. One by one, each person shook their head.

"No, not in mine," Anton said, looking puzzled.

"Same here," Bray and Ethan added, shrugging.

Andrew and Matt looked at each other. "Nothing like that in ours either. Just the usual stuff—snacks, maps, and the itinerary."

Martin surveyed everyone's answers while Burton's gaze shifted back to Abi. Her expression mirrored his concern as the realization settled in. Not one person in the room had received the card they had.

Returning to Abi, Shane ran a hand through his hair, clearly at a loss. "I don't know what more to say," he muttered.

She shifted uncomfortably, her fingers brushing the edge of the chair. "Maybe it was just a mistake," she offered, sounding highly doubtful.

"Maybe," he replied, but he sadly didn't believe it was.

Unable to do anything more for the time being, Shane and Abi watched as everyone gathered their things and slipped on their jackets as a light dusting of snow began to fall.

Peering out of the floor-to-ceiling glass walls, she watched the mesmerizing snowflakes - their lazy descent a temporary escape from the morning's events. "The calm before the storm," she mumbled quietly. Right then, her thoughts were anything but serene.

Burton and Martin exchanged a brief look.

While stepping toward her, Burton's voice cut through the mayhem. "Don't worry about this too much. We'll figure it out."

She forced a smile. "I'm fine," she said, uncertainty churning inside. "Really, I am." She took a deep breath, looking out at the snow-covered grounds again. "Let's just go."

Despite the lingering doubt, they left the Living Pavilion and walked along the path to the main gates. Outside that, in the driveway, was the luxury Mercedes Sprinter and their translator, Hiro Matsumura, awaiting them.

"Good afternoon, Miss," he said pleasantly before looking at Shane. "How are you doing, Sir?"

"Hey, Hiro," Shane addressed, while Abi smiled.

"We are good," she replied, hiding things well.

Guiding them to the door, he said, "Feel free to find a seat. We have an exciting afternoon planned for all of you."

The two stepped aboard and found a spot near the back. Getting comfortable, they waited for everyone else to join them.

Each time the driver opened the door, the crisp winter air drifted into the vehicle.

Attached to the hip, Jade and Reggie boarded and walked down the aisle to sit in front of them.

"Do you know where we are heading first?" the girl asked, peering between the seats.

"Not sure," Abi replied. "All I know is we are seeing the bamboo forest and the golden temple." Thankful for the warmth of the insulated bottle keeping her hands warm and the plush cashmere scarf around her neck, Abi felt her cheeks already tingling from the cold.

Guarded by his men, Burton and Sara got in and grabbed their seats near the front.

Happy to see them getting along, she noticed his usual calm demeanor while he offered Sara the window seat.

Dressed in a tailored navy parka, he kept an eye on their surroundings before making eye contact with Abi.

When he was about to sit, she saw Sara's head suddenly pop up over the seats. Unfortunately, she caught her smiling at Burton. With blonde hair cascading over a royal blue scarf that accentuated the color of her eyes, Sara glared, making Abi quickly divert her attention elsewhere. A slight edge to her gaze, she knew the underlying jealousy Burton spoke of hadn't faded.

Their forever-polished planner, Martin, stepped aboard regally in a sophisticated black wool coat. With a plaid scarf wrapped around his neck, he stood in the aisle, ready to give a few last-minute instructions to the security team and their driver. The glue that was holding everyone together on this trip, Abi felt that he stayed fairly level-headed despite the tension looming that morning.

Grabbing one of the single seats with the guys, Anton quickly sat down and swiveled his side satchel onto his lap, more than ready to get the show on the road.

With everyone now accounted for and ready to depart, Martin gave the signal for the driver to proceed to their first stop—the famous Arashiyama Bamboo Grove.

| 17 |

Arashiyama

Saturday, December 16

Arashiyama Bamboo Forest

Winding through Kyoto's quiet rural outskirts, the Sprinter slipped past a blend of sleek modern homes and timeless architecture.

Martin conversed with Hiro the entire time, intrigued by the city's history and its many traditions.

Buildings to their left and hills of snow-dusted green to their right, they noticed most residential homes took great pride in their sculptures, Bonsai-shaped shrubbery, and ornate maples.

Escaping to the country and rounding a small, picturesque, partially frozen lake, their driver needed to stop countless times for oncoming traffic. As each passed by, mere inches from Abi's window, she hoped the Sprinter wouldn't get damaged. Crossing over a set of train tracks, they saw two athletic men pulling rickshaws dressed warmly in athletic gear. Able to see their breath expelling from them in the cold, it was surprising to see them still operating in the winter.

"Wow. That would be a good job to stay in shape," Shane commented, noticing the guy was in peak condition.

"Yes, but I'm sure it is killer in the summer."

A few crowds meandered through the many businesses lining the street as they drove along slowly. Soon, their driver stopped in front of a chocolate shop.

"Here we are," he said. "Follow the path straight through here, and you will find the entrance to the Arashiyama bamboo forest." Giving Martin his cell number, he said, "When you are ready to leave, I will park at the Tenryn-Ji here." Pointing to the map and showing Martin the location, Andrew and Lorenzo listened in and prepared their route accordingly.

As he opened the door, the guys stepped out to secure the area while a few tourists watched. The alley led to a row of shuttered shops, likely closed for the winter. Snowflakes drifted down as they reached the tree line, where towering bamboo swayed in the breeze. A low stone wall lined the path, with thick shrubs held back by bamboo beams. The canopy overhead shielded them from the falling snow as they walked.

Hand in hand, Jade and Reggie followed Lorenzo and Matt, who were leading the group. Abi and Shane strolled along with them as Martin, Anton, Burton, and Sara took up the rear.

Coming upon a shrine with red fences and traditional buildings, Abi read the sign. "Nonomiya," she said, struggling to pronounce it.

Hiro stopped them before the group entered the main gate. "I assume most of you are new to learning Japan's traditional Shinto customs when it comes to visiting the shrines. Here, it's best to honor the deities by practicing prayer correctly." Raising his hand, pointing to the weathered gate, he said, "Before entering, through any torii gate, consider it a boundary between the human world and the sacred holy grounds. Briefly, bowing is a form of respect."

One by one, they did as he said upon walking under the arch.

"Now, it is custom to wash your hands at the chozuya." Showing them what to do, he scooped up the water with the ladle and poured some into each of their hands. "By doing this, you purify yourself." Hiro stepped aside to allow everyone to perform this sacred act.

Once the group had done this, he said, "Upon entering the main area through the red torii gate, bow your head twice, clap your hands twice, offer a prayer, and bow once more. If you would like to give an offering, you may do so by placing it in the offering boxes. Upon giving your offering, ring the bell and repeat the bowing and clapping sequence."

Standing before the bright red torii gate, leading to what looked to be a sacred garden amidst a few old Japanese umbrella pines, each of them did as Hiro instructed. Inside, smooth stones with Japanese writing etched into them sat atop the snow-dusted carpet moss.

"Feel free to pray at smaller shrines in the temple precinct. Once you have visited the main shrine, you're free to stop by any of the other smaller shrines on the grounds. If you do, make sure to repeat the bowing and clapping sequence at each one."

Mingling among a sparse number of visitors, Abi noticed that opposite the garden were red wooden racks arranged in rows with hundreds of layered wooden plaques hanging inside them.

"These are Emas, wooden wishing plaques," Hiro pointed out.

Burton listened to their conversation, interested in what he had to say.

"Visitors write their wishes, prayers, or messages of gratitude on the *ema* and hang them on these holders as offerings to the deities. As you can see, the plaques themselves have traditional images, such as torii gates, cherry blossoms, or representations of local culture. Would anyone like to write down their wishes and hang them here? If so, please visit the little shop and purchase your plaque. They range from four to seven dollars, depending on the design."

Abi looked at Shane. "Want to do that?"

He smiled. "Sure."

Walking over to the little building, Abi said, "Konnichiwa," and bowed politely in front of the older woman working there.

A shy grin appeared on the woman's face.

Abi pointed to the plaques.

The woman nodded and set a few on the counter in front of them. "Dore?"

Standing nearby, Hiro translated, "She asked you - which one?"

"Oh, umm..." Abi said, looking at what she'd presented to them. "What do you think?" she asked Shane.

He pointed to the one with the colorful stamped scene on it. "How about that one?"

She agreed and pointed to what they'd selected. Handing her some money, the woman nodded and smiled before slipping the card across the counter.

"Doumo arigatou gozaimasu."

Hiro translated. "She said Thank you very much."

Turning and bowing their heads politely, Abi and Shane waved to her before allowing Jade and Reg to do the same.

Walking to a makeshift table, Abi asked, "What shall we write?"

Thinking a moment, Shane said, "Together, always and forever."

Her heart fluttered upon hearing this. "Ohhh... That's so nice." Wanting to kiss him, knowing she couldn't, given the PDA rule Martin instilled, she simply rubbed her hand on his arm as he gave her a side hug.

Writing that on the plaque, he held up his phone and took a selfie of them holding it before taking another as they hung it on a peg on the rack.

To her surprise, when she turned, she found Burton's eye on her. Smiling slightly, he quickly broke away and looked for Sara.

Taught by Hiro what to do when leaving the shrine, each of them visited the Kameishi stone before bowing and passing through the torii gates.

As their group moved on, amongst the peaceful beauty of the bamboo forest, a little warm, Jade unzipped her jacket. Exposing the Red Dragon hoodie, the symbol on the front visible, they walked along the path, passing a Buddhist Temple, admiring the craftsmanship of its traditional roof.

Meandering through a narrow section, Abi couldn't help but notice the lingering glances cast their way. Most directed towards Jade, she assumed they were simply admiring the girl's beauty. Not thinking much of it, they carried on unfazed by the attention.

While passing a cemetery, they read the inscriptions on many of the monuments.

Soon, the path darkened with the thick bamboo, creating a living tunnel through the forest. Like being in another world, they kept walking. Abi sipped her tea, admiring the grass-like, frosty-tipped reeds.

Following the path, they came upon a clearing before descending the hillside.

"Some of the trees are so uniquely shaped," Shane said.

"I wonder what type of leaves they have in the summertime?"

Finding the water's edge at the bottom of the cobblestone staircase, Hiro said, "Boats frequent this river to immerse guests in nature. In my opinion, the best time to visit is in the fall, when the trees change color. It is quite splendid."

Almost at the end of their visit, they made their way to Tenryu-ji to meet their driver. On the path leading to the temple, they passed a restaurant with a Japanese garden filled with a number of carved statues.

"There must be hundreds of them," Jade marveled.

Walking up the street and around the bend, they arrived at the temple and spotted their Sprinter parked nearby.

"Before we continue to our next destination, those of you who would like to see the temple quickly, follow me," Hiro said, leading the charge.

Not wanting to miss anything, Abi followed their guide down the ornate path despite the cold and her toes becoming numb. Holding Shane's hand as they walked, Burton and Sara weren't far behind, while Jade and Reggie, intent on warming up, retired to the vehicle with sore feet.

Their group stopped in the courtyard beside a pretty garden.

"Welcome to Tenryu-ji Temple, a UNESCO World Heritage Site and one of Kyoto's most important Zen temples. Founded in 1339, it's famous for its stunning Zen garden, designed by Muso Soseki, which has remained unchanged since its creation. The garden features a tranquil pond in the back and beautifully arranged rocks and plants, with the Arashiyama mountains as its backdrop. It is an ideal spot to experience both history and nature. This way, everyone," he said.

Snowflakes tumbled from the sky, their descent casting an ethereal hush over the sacred place. Upon rounding the corner to the pond, they found snow clinging to the sloped rooftops, with some settled on the manicured Zen garden. The fine dusting softened the edges of the stone.

With the crisp winter air filling her lungs, Abi breathed in and let her gaze drift over the still waters as the trees rustled quietly around them. A rare calm settled over her, loosening the ever-present coil of tension in her shoulders. *Maybe,* she thought, *for once, the day would be uneventful.* Enjoying the experience, Abi realized the ominous wooden card was now the furthest from her mind.

Taking pictures, she exhaled. "This is so pretty."

Shane peered over the bamboo railing lining the water. "There are carp in here. Look a the size of them. They must be a foot and a half long."

As Sara and Burton moved past, Martin followed as half of their security detail fanned out strategically.

Finding Anton at the edge of the roped-off area, in front of the pebble raked in a linear pattern lining the pond, it seemed the Chef was drinking it all in.

It was a sight to see.

Standing under the traditional Japanese sloped roof, they heard the wind whistle through the trees and noticed the ripples dancing across the water from time to time.

Abi took a seat. Taken by the scenery, she'd almost forgotten about all the negatives.

Intrigued by the look on her face, Burton approached, despite Shane sitting beside her. "What do you think of this place?"

She broke from her daze and smiled.

"Pretty incredible, huh?"

Taking a cleansing breath, she replied, "Yes. Stunning."

Happy she was enjoying the experience, he flashed a pleasant expression.

"Thank you for bringing us here, Burton. I could never imagine anything like this. You need to immerse yourself in it to appreciate its beauty fully."

The big guy nodded. "I agree."

Beyond the temple grounds, the hillside, usually so vibrant against the sky, was gradually vanishing under the quiet weight of the snow falling, as if nature herself sought to conceal it. The Arashiyama mountains soon became cloaked in a gauzy veil of misty snow. Slowly fading into the distance, the once sharp lines began to blur into the winter haze.

"Not to rush you, but I believe we should continue to our next destination, given the impending storm. Otherwise, you may not get to see the Golden Temple today."

Listening to Hiro, everyone made their way back to the Sprinter.

"Jade and Reg don't know what they just missed," Abi said while walking with Shane alongside Burton and Sara.

"Maybe I should put a garden like that in my backyard. What do you think, Abs?"

She looked over at him. "I would not object. How beautiful would that be to look out and see that view every day?"

"Inspiring," he replied.

"Absolutely."

When she said that, Sara shot her a look again, making her feel uncomfortable. Quickly looking away, they returned to the Sprinter and climbed aboard, more than ready to warm up.

Taking their seats in the back of the luxury coach, to her surprise, Burton sat in the single seat across from them.

"Next stop, the Golden Temple," he said excitedly, peering forward at Sara, who was not happy that he had deserted her.

| 18 |

The Golden Temple

Saturday, December 16

Kinkaku-Ji Temple

Leaving the Tenrju-Ji Temple, Abi showed Jade her pictures of the pond and gardens.

Looking at what she'd captured, Jade was stunned. "Oh, wow! That was behind the building? Are you kidding me?" she whined. "I should have gone."

"Yes, you should've seen it. It was so beautiful and peaceful."

The girl turned to Reg. "From now on, any time I want to rest and not keep going, please force me. Deal?"

"I will do that, but you can't fight me on it. That means no kicking and screaming," he said humorously.

"You might have to carry me."

He laughed. "Not a problem, but that may be considered PDA, there, Jade."

The drive back toward the outskirts of town, close to Aman Kyoto, did not take long. Slowly, Abi's feet finally started to unthaw just as they were pulling into the parking lot.

Driven to the far left side, the driver stopped adjacent to the main gate.

Hiro stood up at the front. "Welcome to Kinkaku-ji, home of the famous Golden Pavilion, here in Kyoto. This stunning Zen temple is one of Japan's most iconic landmarks. Originally built in 1397, the temple's top two floors are covered entirely in gold leaf. The gardens create a perfect harmony with the temple's golden beauty, showcasing the principles of Japanese landscape design. Since it is winter and the Golden Pavilion is dusted with snow, it adds a magical touch to this already breathtaking sight. Take your time to stroll around the grounds and enjoy one of Kyoto's most unforgettable spots."

Leaving the Sprinter, the snow still falling lightly, Abi flipped her fur hood to cover her head. With two guys leading the way, both on high alert, the others encircled their group from all angles. Hiro, Martin, and Anton were all deeply engrossed in the history of the place.

The path to the temple curved gently through the snowy grounds. The gardens, once full of life, were now bare as the twisted branches of the ancient trees spread out above them, their bark rough and frosty.

They crossed a dark wooden bridge and stepped through the traditional Japanese gates.

Martin headed straight for the ticket counter and purchased passes for their group. With no lines, they were able to get inside quickly. As they walked around the corner, the Golden Temple came into view through the evergreen trees. Martin, Hiro, and Anton stopped by the bamboo fence, chatting excitedly about the temple's history.

Abi took a few pictures, then caught Burton taking one with her in the foreground.

"Can you take one for us?" Jade said whimsically. "It's so pretty."

Handed her phone, Abi snapped a few angles for them. "How are those?"

Jade scrolled through what Abi had taken. "Perfect. Thank you."

"Can you do the same for us?" Shane asked.

"Sure." The girl took his device and stepped back while Shane wrapped Abi in his arms. Both smiled for the picture.

"There you go," she said, handing it back. Hot in her down jacket, she unzipped it. The bold, striking logo emblazoned in red across her chest suddenly seemed to draw more eyes than the natural splendor around them.

At first, Abi didn't think much of it. After all, Jade often attracted attention with her chic, fashion-forward style. But unlike earlier today, this seemed different. There was an edge to them, something darker than mere curiosity. A group of tourists passed by, their eyes lingering on Jade a little too long, whispers exchanged in a language Abi didn't understand. One of the women even pulled out her phone and snapped a photo of Jade from a distance before quickly turning away.

Her stomach twisting with unease, Abi stepped closer to Shane. "Does it feel like people are staring at her?" she questioned quietly.

He looked up from the map he was holding and frowned. "Yeah... now that you mention it." His gaze flicked toward the girl, then back to his girlfriend. "It's probably the hoodie. Perhaps they recognize the Red Dragon logo."

Suddenly, Hiro spotted her sweatshirt. "Excuse me, Miss?" He was quite concerned.

"Yes," Jade replied, with Reggie holding her hand.

"Where did you get that?" He pointed to her sweater.

"It was a gift from..." She stopped, unsure what to say, not wanting to reveal too much, given Burton's secret.

"A friend," Abi added.

Jade followed suit. "Right... A friend. Why?"

Their guide pulled Martin aside. The two whispered secretly before the man waved her over.

Burton followed. "What is it?"

"The dragon on her sweater is a known symbol of a very powerful family. It is unmistakable."

Not sure what the problem was, Martin asked, "What does this mean?"

"Anywhere she goes, she will invoke fear in those who know of it. Truthfully, it is considered extremely threatening."

Overhearing what he said, Jade quickly zipped up her jacket. "I'm sorry. I didn't know."

"Crisis averted," Hiro nodded, not wanting to embarrass the girl. Casually, he continued the tour.

Now on edge, Jade kept her jacket tightly closed, trying to avoid unwanted attention as the four of them approached the radiant building.

Amidst the pretty scenery, on the path opposite the Golden Temple by the edge of the forest, Abi's attention shifted. She had been thinking about Sara. The subtle tension between them had gone on too long. She wanted to clear the air, hoping it would help ease some of the pressure on Burton, who was already juggling so much.

"Shane?" Abi whispered, "I'm going to talk to Sara for a second."

"Are you sure you want to do that?" he asked, believing it wasn't a good idea.

She nodded. "I have to." Squeezing his hand, she soon made her way toward Burton's girlfriend, who was standing alone while he spoke with Martin, Andrew, and Lorenzo.

Easily locating the girl, quietly taking in the view with arms crossed, her blonde hair caught the light.

"Sara?" Abi began, her tone light but sincere. "Can we talk for a minute?"

She turned, her blue eyes quite striking. "Sure," she said, not sounding particularly enthusiastic.

Seeing Shane watching her every move, Abi took a deep breath and said, "I feel things have been tense between us, and I don't want there to be any misunderstandings."

An attitude-filled "Hmm..." is all she expelled.

"Look, I care about Burton, but not in the way you might think. He's important to me, but I consider him family—nothing more. And I don't want you to feel threatened by that."

Smirking, Sara tilted her head slightly, her expression flaming. "Threatened? By you? Hardly..." she said dismissively. "So that you know, I'm not worried."

Abi blinked. Caught off guard by how arrogant Sara came across, she once again regretted encouraging Burton to give the girl a chance. In this instance, she was terribly wrong about her. It made her wish she had taken the time to know her first before giving her the benefit of the doubt. Swift to break the silence between them, she added, "Well, I'm glad we're on the same page." Unable to shake the seed of doubt taking root in her mind, she found Burton looking at them, concerned.

Sara saw him, too.

There was something in her eyes that Abi couldn't quite place. It was fleeting, almost as if the slight warmth she was projecting was just a mask.

As she rejoined their group, Abi couldn't help but feel a creepy unease settling in. Had she really gotten through to Sara? Or had she just made things worse?

Having seen what happened, Shane leaned in and whispered, "Well, that conversation went over like a lead balloon."

With a roll of her eyes, Abi huffed. "Yeah, it didn't turn out the way I imagined it would."

"Well, at least you tried."

Arm and arm, they walked toward the Golden Pavilion on the other side of the pond.

Noticing Sara chatting with Burton up ahead of them, the girl's demeanor seemed sweet as sugar as she glanced at her from time to time, almost out of spite. As she linked arms with him, Abi noticed the girl spreading the charm pretty thick. But by the look on Burton's face, he didn't seem convinced.

Snowflakes covering her hood, Abi pulled it back and shook off the iciness that clung to it. The Golden Temple shimmered in front of her, glowing against the stillness of the pond. It should've felt magical, but her conversation with Sara put a damper on it all. Flipping the hood upon her head, she heard a growl slice through the crisp air.

"Death to her..." The muffled words trailed off, venomous and haunting.

Abi's head snapped around. Frozen, her wide eyes scanned the crowd.

Only finding tourists bustling by, most were oblivious to what had happened. Laughter, chatter, and the click of cameras seemed distant, muted against the thunderous pounding of her heart.

Her hand tightened around Shane's. "Did you hear that?"

Brows pulling together, he looked down at her as concern flickered in his eyes. "Hear what?"

Had she imagined it? She tried to shake it off, but couldn't as her body trembled. "Nothing," she mumbled, forcing herself to move.

They followed the path around the temple. The scene was beautiful, but Abi couldn't help but feel a sense of paranoia creeping in.

Suddenly, a few teenagers dressed in school uniforms caught her attention as they lined the edge of the pond. Their laughter carried on the open spaces, carefree and loud. A frown tugged at her lips. *It's Saturday. Why would they be in uniform?* she thought. *How strange...*

While assessing it all, she saw him.

The man.

Tall and thin, he stood near the trees, dressed in black. A wide-brimmed hat cast a shadow over his face, but the bright red cane in his hand burned like a warning. He took a slow drag from his cigarette, the ember briefly flaring in the shadows before he exhaled a stream of smoke and flicked the butt to the ground.

As he stared her way, the blood drained from Abi's body, causing a numbness to set in. "Oh, my God." Her legs locked.

"Abs?" Shane's voice barely registered. "What's wrong?"

"There," she whispered, pointing shakily. "By the trees."

Shane's gaze followed hers just as the man disappeared behind the branches. "I see him. Is it the same guy?"

"Yes," she nodded fearfully.

"Andrew! Matt!" Shane called out sharply as their security detail materialized.

"What's going on?" Andrew's hand hovered near the comm earpiece.

"Black coat, red cane! Tall guy!" Shane shouted. "Matt, stay with her!" In an instant, the football player bolted in that direction.

"No, Shane! Don't—" Before Abi could finish, he was gone with Andrew flanking him. Unable to tear her eyes from the spot where the man had vanished, her pulse thudded in her ears, drowning out the chatter around them.

Burton rushed to her side. "What's going on?" Finding her shell-shocked, he said, "What did you see?"

"It was him," Abi said fearfully. "The man..."

Confused, Burton's eyes narrowed. "Whoa, whoa. Where?" He immediately scanned the area. So did his security.

She opened her mouth, but nothing came out.

Matt stood close and inspected the crowd, his posture tense as he updated his boss.

"Apparently, it was the man with the red cane. Shane and Andrew went that way." He pointed in their direction.

Overhearing what had happened, Martin shot Burton an eye as the guy's expression hardened. Taking Matt's place, he reached for Abi protectively. Wrapping his arms around her, he went on high alert as Sara looked on with disdain.

The guys gathered their group, each listening to Andrew's play-by-play coming through the comms.

"What is he saying?" Burton ordered.

"The man just...disappeared," Matt said. "He's gone. No sign of him."

Every nerve was on edge. Abi's body remained frozen. The moment stretched while she waited for Shane to return.

Finally, just as he and Andrew rounded the corner, deep in conversation, a deafening CRACKLE ripped through the air, followed by a rapid series of POPS—sharp, relentless, like gunfire. The once-tranquil scene detonated into chaos. Tourists screaming, instinctively diving for cover, the acrid scent of smoke curled into the air.

Abi's heart slammed against her ribs as her body seized in fear.

"Get down!" Shielding her and ducking low, Burton covered her head with his hand.

Amidst the loud bursts, Abi's mind flashed back to the night of Reggie's party.

The heavy bass rattling everything around them.

The music so loud it vibrated through her chest.

Laughter.

Dancing.

Then—BOOM.

A blinding flash.

The shockwave knocking the air from her lungs.

Her body crashing to the ground.

Shattered glass slicing through the air.

The heat of the explosion roaring past.

It's orangey flames clawing at the darkness.

Screams.

Terrifyingly raw.

The scent of sulfur burning, choking her.

Panic surging through her veins.

Was she even breathing?

Was anyone?

Then—just as quickly—she snapped back to the present as the world came into focus. Faintly, she heard Burton's voice.

"What's happening!" she screamed, feeling a firm hand tightening its hold on her.

"I got you!" Trying to keep her calm, he shouted, "It's just fireworks! You're okay! Stay close! Don't move!"

Hands covering her ears, Abi's heart slammed in her chest. *Fireworks! Just fireworks.* That repeated in her mind while her body shook and expelled ragged gasps.

Still covering Abi with his body, Burton saw Reg do the same with Jade.

Making eye contact with Shane fifty feet away, she saw his desperation and watched him quickly scan the area before courageously staying low and running to her.

Pulling Burton off, releasing her from him, he took his place. "I got her!" he shouted through the mayhem.

Roughly grabbing Shane's jacket in retaliation and holding him there as he stared him down, Abi looked up at Burton with fearful eyes. Anger aside, he knew they had to get them out of there.

Seeing the commotion stemming from a garbage barrel erupting with smoke curling upward, it soon caught fire.

The uniformed teens scattered, their laughter echoing as they ran away.

Martin's command rang out. "We are leaving! Now!" he said. "Everyone, stick together. This way!"

With his arms protectively wrapped around her waist, Shane guided Abi out. "Stay close to me," he said confidently. "I got you."

The group fell into step, their security detail forming a protective perimeter around them.

Reg kept Jade close, his jaw tight as he navigated through the frantic scene unfolding.

Eyes darting from person to person, Abi searched for any sign of the sinister figure as they got closer to the parking lot. But there was nothing. The words *Death to her* kept echoing in her head, the chill of it causing more and more fear to surface.

Back a the Sprinter, everyone piled aboard and found their seats.

Safe inside, Martin approached Abi and instructed, "You need to give me a full description of that man. There is a live feed that is updated every three minutes on the cameras here. We will try and identify him from the footage." He paused a moment. "There is no indication that the fireworks set off by those teenagers are in any way connected to the man with the cane." His expression went blank. "So, for now, we assume the two incidents are simply coincidental unless proven otherwise."

Flashes of the sinister figure gnawed at her. The craziness wasn't far behind as she noticed Martin's expression. He looked concerned despite putting on a brave face.

Even though the man had vanished, she wondered what he wanted and why he was following them. Even being halfway around the world amidst the perfect winter scenery, the falling snow and the glistening temple didn't stop the darkness from hovering, waiting, and watching.

Giving Martin what he needed, Shane offered up the description of the man while Abi listened in on their strained conversation.

When he returned to her and had a seat, Shane said, "It's gonna be fine. Don't worry. They're on it." Still curious as to the true nature of the men's jobs, he knew their actions went beyond usual security protocols.

Diverting their route away from the hotel, they circled the city a few times before returning to Aman. The precautionary process took forever as the snow began to fall more heavily.

As they drove down the laneway of the exclusive resort, the first thing they noticed was an increased presence around the main gates and welcome pavilion.

Arriving safely inside the compound, Martin stood up when the Sprinter stopped. "As you can see, we now have more security on site. Despite the added presence, please stay mindful of your surroundings." Determined to keep those in their care calm, Martin added, "That said, onto other business. We have a reservation at Taka-An tonight and plan to visit the Kifune Shrine's illumination display later this evening." He looked at Hiro. "From what I understand, this heavy snow will be short-lived, so I will update you on the status of that over dinner. Everyone, please bring your outdoor gear with you, so if we do decide to head out, we are ready promptly. Until then, you have free time. I will see you in an hour."

Leery about going out again, Shane asked, "Martin?"

"Yes, Mr. Coppersmith."

"Are you sure it is safe to..."

The gentleman raised a hand to stop him, assuming what he would ask. "...stick to our sightseeing plan?" With a smile, he said, "I would not take a chance if it weren't."

Trusting her guardian, Abi overheard him and nodded in agreement.

Unsure of his recommendation, Shane wondered if the guy knew something he didn't. "Weren't we targeted?" Thinking back, he still couldn't help but wonder if there was a connection between the creepy man and the meddlesome teens. "How can that be considered random?"

"Leave this with me, my boy. Everything will be fine," the wise man said with certainty in his eyes. Reassuring Abi, he placed a hand on her shoulder. "You are safe with us, my dear. I promise."

Believing him, Abi turned to Shane and nodded before the two headed back to their room to get ready for dinner.

While climbing the inclined path, the big QB kept glancing her way. "How are you holding up?"

She didn't know how to answer him.

Offering her his hand, he said as she took hold, "Don't worry. Nothing is gonna happen."

With all her heart, she wished she could confidently believe him. The gut feeling in her chest said otherwise.

Making it back to their pavilion, Shane opened the door for her.

Abi slipped off her boots and shrugged off her heavy coat, the warmth of their suite instantly soothing her chilled skin.

Standing behind her, Shane rubbed his hands together to bring some life back into his fingers. He watched as Abi wandered over to the window.

Mesmerized by the snow falling outside, despite the beauty of it, her mind kept circling back to the ominous card and the unsettling shadow of the thin man she'd seen. The memory of the black rose resurfaced, sending a wave of nausea through her stomach. She sighed, hugging her arms around herself to shake the creepy, dreadful feeling.

Shane set the wallet key on the side table. "Let's just try and stay positive and not get too caught up in all the negative." Approaching her from behind, he wrapped his arms around her waist. "Hey," he mumbled into her hair. "Come here," he said, pulling her in closer. He could sense the worry gnawing at her thoughts.

"I just have a bad feeling…"

Shane turned her around gently, noticeably concerned for her well-being. "Abi, listen to me," he said, trying to remain calm. "If Martin says we are good, then I believe him. Even the guys don't seem to be phased by it." Hugging her tightly, the warmth and strength of his arms were a silent promise that eased some of the fear weighing heavily.

She clung to him, drawing comfort from his presence.

After a moment, she stepped back with a quiet sigh. "We should get ready for dinner," she said wearily.

Letting her go, he watched her move about the room in silence. Respectfully sticking to his own corner, Shane got changed and kept a discreet eye on her. Careful not to hover, he let her do her thing and get ready in peace.

Once they were both nearly set, they met by the door.

Shane asked while pulling on his jacket, "I wonder what's on the menu tonight?"

"I'm not sure. But I bet it will be impressive," she replied while slipping on her boots.

Before walking out, prepared for the evening's frigid air, both of them flipped their hoods to shield themselves from the weather. The snow-covered resort felt magical as the flakes continued to fall, dusting the pathways and turning the entire landscape into a winter wonderland. Lights twinkled along the stone paths, reflecting off the snow, guiding them toward Taka-An, the restaurant nestled within the resort.

The wind gusts nipped at their faces as everyone converged upon the restaurant at the same time.

When Abi saw the guys and the extra security nearby, a sense of calm washed over her. She recognized the feeling well, having experienced it many times before. Stepping into the restaurant, she pretended like nothing was wrong and was determined to enjoy the evening despite the unease lingering in the back of her mind.

| 19 |

The Curse

Saturday, December 16

Taka-An Restaurant / Aman, Kyoto

Kifune Shrine

One by one, the rest of their group arrived behind them, each ridding themselves of the shivers as they dusted the snow off their hair and removed their jackets at the door.

Struck by the serenity and minimalist beauty of the place, Abi rounded the corner and walked in.

The large lanterns hanging from the cathedral ceiling and the up-lighting along the walls cast warmth on the natural wood paneling and black-clad accents, creating a striking balance between light and dark. As they stepped further inside, the hushed sounds of the staff's voices blended with the gentle clinking of dishes - the tranquilness quickly wrapping them like a comforting embrace.

Hiro stood beside a man in a white chef coat. "Good evening, everyone. I will be assisting Chef Takagi."

The man bowed to the group as each of them did the same out of respect.

Relaying something in Japanese, Hiro explained, "Chef says, welcome to Taka-An. Please have a seat. I will be preparing your meal tonight. As you can see, there is no menu card. Here, we create tailored dishes." Hiro paused as the Chef continued. "From what I understand, he says, he knows you require more meat and something hearty, especially after a long day in the cold weather."

Excited to hear that, Shane anxiously rubbed his hands together.

Asked to take their seats at the long table in front of the granite counter, Abi sat down beside Burton and noticed a number of sous Chefs ready to get started. Able to see the snow falling lightly outside, she wondered if they would still be going on their evening illumination excursion as Shane, Jade, and Reggie sat adjacent to her.

Finally able to sit together, Burton leaned in and said, "This place is supposed to be amazing. The guy is a Michelin star. Been looking forward to this all day."

"I'm excited, too," Abi said, spotting Sara sitting quietly to his right.

"I'm sure you are," the girl said under her breath.

Burton quickly flashed a disapproving eye.

Nudging Abi with his arm, Shane whispered to her, "Don't play into it. That's what she wants."

With beverages served to them one by one, accompanied by an aromatic cup of green tea to soothe their souls, the Chef soon set their first course before them. An array of beautifully presented dishes followed, each more delicate and artful than the last.

Keeping up her conversation with Burton, brushing off Sara's glares, she was thankful Shane stayed neutral. Catching Sara's snide comments muttered here and there, Abi knew that despite trying to make peace with her, it was clear she wasn't interested in making amends. Given no choice but to ignore her, she tried to rise above all the pettiness.

From fresh sushi to baked fish and flavorful brothy soup to the Hirai beef, they finished their tailored meal beyond satisfied.

Sipping her tea, Abi smiled, the tension from earlier easing as she basked in the warmth of the evening. Over the past hour, it was easy to focus on the laughter of her friends and the exquisite food, letting the worries of that strange afternoon fade into the background.

When dinner ended, they graciously thanked the Chef and Hiro for the incredible dining experience before leaving the table and gathering their things.

Bundling up, the group watched as Martin stood nearby and announced, "They tell me it is possible to visit the Kifune Shrine this evening despite the weather. We have arranged for a private showing. With the freshly fallen snow, it will not disappoint those wishing to join us."

Turning to Shane, she said, "Want to go?"

He nodded. "Sure, if you're up to it."

"Yeah, I am."

Burton overheard. Intent on convincing Sara, the girl hesitated.

Aware that Abi was going, she perked up. "Fine. I'll go."

Whining a little to Reggie, stating that she was tired, Jade was about to decline.

Abi quickly stopped the girl in her tracks. "Remember what you missed out on earlier today. From what I understand, this place is mega Instagram-worthy."

That piqued Jade's interest. "Really?"

Hoping she'd join in, Reggie waited to hear what she'd say.

"Alright. Sounds like an adventure," the pretty girl said, zipping up her jacket and draping a scarf lightly around her neck.

Standing by the main entrance, Abi tugged her coat tighter as snowflakes swirled around her, blanketing the resort in a pristine layer of white. Finding their luxury coach waiting, the headlights made the snow sparkle, adding to the fairytale-like atmosphere that night. Upon stepping aboard, the warmth inside was a welcome contrast to the nip in the air. Quickly taking a seat, Shane joined her, his long legs stretching into the aisle.

Overhearing him talking with Reg as they got underway, she peered through the frosted window as the once-bustling streets now felt serene. Buildings on either side glimmered gently, their light reflecting off the snowy rooftops. It felt like stepping into another world, one that belonged to a storybook rather than reality.

Soon, the road narrowed. Mountains looming above them, they climbed higher, their dark silhouettes sharp against the moonlit sky. Abi's fingers gripped the edge of her seat as the coach carefully maneuvered the winding paths, skirting the river to their right and the shadowy homes to their left. Her heart raced when they passed a particularly long stretch, the wheels seemingly brushing the very edge of the traditional bridge before maneuvering a tight bend.

Then, glowing in the dark was a red torii gate. Tall and proud, bathed in an ethereal glow from hidden uplights nestled among the towering trees, the snow clung to its edges, accentuating its shape against the inky forest behind it.

Abi pressed her hand to the window, drawn in by its quiet majesty. She couldn't look away.

Everyone exited the vehicle as their security fanned out to keep watch.

Abi flipped her hood over her head and took hold of Shane's hand as they walked up the deserted street. The air was crisp and cold, but something was soothing about the way the world felt covered in white. As the icy patches crunched beneath their boots, the magical red lanterns brightened the stone staircase. The branches hanging above them created archways to thread through.

Abi looked up at the line of lanterns and pulled out her phone. Taking a few pictures, Shane took out his device too and took the best selfie. With their faces at the bottom of the shot, he was able to capture the magical staircase behind them perfectly.

Impressed by the pic he took, he showed it to her. "Hey, look at this."

"Oh, wow. That's a great one." Seeing Burton and Sara just ahead of them, Abi said, "Hey, you two. Say cheese."

Hearing her, they stopped on the stairs. Finding Abi with her phone pointed their way, they struck a pose. Burton put his arm around Sara. But she hesitated to do the same. Both of them smiled brightly for Abi to snap the picture with the line of red lanterns faintly shining behind.

Showing them, she said, "It turned out really nice."

"Yes. Perfect," Burton said as Sara looked on.

"Thank you for bringing us here. It's so pretty in the snow," Abi smiled.

Content to see her so happy, her childhood friend said, "I can't take the credit. This was all Martin."

As they climbed to the top, they spotted two medieval-looking iron torch baskets all ablaze. Beyond that, the enchanting shrine, embellished with gold accents, uplit the canopy of trees above it.

Stopping, Abi stood before the sacred building and soaked it all in. Not overly big, she loved the carved wood beams and posts. Something about it felt powerful. Completing the purification rituals, she prayed before moving down the staircase again. That is where she spied the Shimenawa rope wrapped around an ancient tree, marking it as holy. The way the light hit the mangled branches revealed something hidden amongst them. Inching closer, she spotted a small, eerie figure lodged within.

With Abi's attention swayed, Shane remained beside her as the girl squinted to focus.

"Is that a doll?" she stated, moving her head left, then right to get a better look.

Impaled with a large nail through its chest, positioned about five feet off the ground, it had long brown yarn for hair, wore a white gown, and had a tasseled wooden plaque around its neck.

The air expelled from her lungs as her throat went bone dry. The symbols carved into the plaque resembled the Japanese letters she'd seen on her bookmark.

Reading her troubled expression, Shane locked onto her.

Before either could say more, Hiro, their guide, approached them from behind. His usually calm demeanor shifted as his eyes fell on the doll.

"Oh, my... This..." Hiro pointed, "...may be the work of a Ushi no Toki Mairi."

Abi and Shane traded glances between them and the tree.

"A what?" the football player asked, hoping he'd elaborate.

"It's an ancient ritual," Hiro explained. "A curse, really...performed during the hour of the ox, between one and three in the morning."

"Like the witching hour?" Abi asked.

"Yes. Local witches perform the curse for someone seeking revenge. They make a straw doll—like this one—and impale it with nails before attaching it to a sacred tree or shrine. The doll represents the person they wish to harm, and the nails drive the curse into them. Legend says, once the powerful spell is cast, it is irreversible."

Upon hearing this, Abi felt uneasy. "So it's like voodoo or a witch's spell?" she asked, skeptical.

He nodded gravely. "Yes. Whoever placed this intends to bring suffering or death to the person the doll represents."

"I swear that is the same writing as my bookmark," Abi said alarmingly, while examining the small plaque.

Overhearing them from a few feet away, Burton noticed the commotion. "I'll be right back," he told Sara. Approaching them, he asked, "What's going on?"

Abi pointed at what they found. "It's a cursed doll."

He looked at it. "Well, that's interesting."

"What's weird is that it has the same wooden plaque as the one I got on Red Dragon's welcome basket. Look..." Pulling up the picture of it on her phone, still laced to the top of the basket, she added, "See..." Magnifying it, she held it up. Comparing the close-up of the symbols, Abi felt a cold chill run down her spine. It wasn't just similar—it was the same, right down to the Red Dragon painted along the bottom edge.

Burton zeroed in on it. "It's identical," he said as Sara came up behind them.

The girl snickered. "It resembles you, too," she said, "Doesn't it?"

Shooting his girlfriend a look, she knew he wasn't impressed. In an instant, Sara's attention gravitated elsewhere, and she walked away.

"The hair... the face... the blue eyes." Abi scanned its features. "Is that me?"

Burton's expression darkened as he stared at what hung around the doll's neck. "Hiro," he said, turning to the guide. "Does this say the same thing as her bookmark?"

Hiro stepped forward, peering at both the photo and the plaque on the doll. He went white as a sheet. He took a small step back, clearly disturbed.

Pressing the guy for answers, Burton demanded, "Can you confirm what this means?" despite already knowing the roundabout definition.

The young man hesitated and swallowed before answering. "It, umm... It's a traditional Yakuza mark that reads ***Death to her.*** It is how one man takes revenge on another. They go after that man's prize possession – usually, the woman he loves."

Abi's heart almost stopped. And just like that, she felt the ground beneath them seemingly vanish. All she could hear was her own heartbeat thudding loudly in her ears. This was the second time she'd heard those revengeful words spoken in that way.

Staring Burton down, Shane immediately wrapped Abi in his arms to diffuse her fears. "This has nothing to do with you," he whispered, strained with doubt.

Recalling how Eastwood conducted business, Burton said, "There's no way it's them... Korolev is gone. They both are."

"But whoever is at the helm now, could they still want this?" Abi questioned.

With eyes affixed to the doll, she wasn't fully listening anymore.

They could blatantly see her mind racing and her breath shallow - the urge to leave overwhelming her. The eerie curse and Hiro's haunting explanation—it was all too much.

Her voice trembled. "Can we go now?"

Grabbing hold of her hand, the QB said, "Sure."

She pulled on him. "I need to leave."

Without waiting for a response, Abi hurried down the narrow staircase lined with red lanterns. Once mesmerizing and magical, they now seemed cold and threatening.

Passing by Jade and Reg as they took videos and pictures, her friend stopped what she was doing. "Abi? Abi, what's wrong?"

She did not answer her.

The two saw Shane bounding down the steps. "Abs, wait!" he said, his footsteps hitting heavily on the stone as he tried to catch up.

Still at the top of the hill, lingering a minute longer, Burton's eyes were affixed to the doll. Thoughts reeling, he spied a short, frail woman approaching Sara. Dressed all in black, her hair, long and wiry, blew in the breeze. As he got closer, the woman turned. Her eyes, ice blue, met his before she walked away.

"What was that about? What did she want?" he asked, making sure Sara was alright.

"Just a resident trying to sell me some incense." Then, with forced casualness, she added, "What happened with Abi? I saw her take off."

He didn't answer right away. Instead, he led her back to the tree and pointed to the ominous doll. Pulling out his phone, he snapped a picture of it. "It's a curse, apparently." His reply was grim.

"You don't really believe that, do you?" Sara asked, barely feigning interest. The cold edge in her tone was unmistakable. Without missing a beat, she added, "I think it's just another way for her to garner sympathy from you and the football player. Sad, really, how easily you fall for it every time."

Scoffing angrily, his patience wearing thin, Burton slipped his phone into his pocket and said, "Come on. It's late. We need to go so I can check on her. She's pretty shaken up."

Huffing dramatically, Sara crossed her arms. "I'm sure she is," she said, dripping with sarcasm.

Not bothering to respond, he headed off down the stairs, leaving Sara behind to stew in her own bitterness.

Carefully descending the icy steps, the girl followed him as the group began to gather at the base of the large torii gate. Their coach bus was waiting at the entrance.

Having already taken refuge inside after the unsettling experience, Abi peered up at the red-lanterned staircase. The beauty of Kifune Shrine, which initially captivated her, had now been cloaked by a creepy sense of dread. A growing trend, it was hard to shake the unease that clung like shadows in the night. Arms wrapped around herself, the phrase, *Death to Her,* echoed in her mind. Recalling the black rose in her Mother's hands, the same sinking feeling of doom surfaced. She didn't want to admit it, but the whole thing terrified her.

While their group boarded the bus, Martin took inventory of everyone before he gave the driver the signal to depart.

Shane watched as Burton and Martin had a quiet conversation across the aisle. He was sure they were discussing what had transpired since the guy glanced back at him a few times before catching sight of Abi staring out the window.

Slowly making the winding journey down the tight, curving roads away from the Kifune Shrine, the darkness closed in around them. The air inside the bus was light for those who had yet to know about their finding. For Abi, it was thick with tension as she replayed the eerie discovery over and over. Resting her head against the window, she watched the world outside blur.

Not saying anything, Shane reached over and gently took her hand in his.

"A curse..." This shocked her. "Who would want to hurt me?"

Willing to make a strong case to the contrary, he said, looking deep into her eyes, "We are thousands of miles from home. Nobody from Japan wants to harm you. It doesn't make any sense."

"But the plaque is identical. Doesn't that strike you as odd?"

He couldn't argue that fact.

She tilted her head.

"Look, maybe, like I said, it's just a tourist trinket sold for a dime a dozen? Who knows?" He was desperate to calm her down. "Besides, we only got here yesterday. That doll seemed like it had been there a while."

Not convinced, Abi leaned uncomfortably against the window again.

Immediately, Shane took his jacket off and reached in front of her, offering it as a pillow. "Better?" he asked, his eyes locked on hers.

"Much. Thank you," she whispered, barely audible.

Eyes locked on Burton while the men and Martin talked with him, Shane wondered if they knew something he didn't.

Soon, they approached the familiar gates of Aman Kyoto. Passing through the line of security, the comfort of the luxurious resort couldn't wash away the fear that had settled deep within Abi.

When the bus stopped at the entrance, Martin stood and said, "Before you all go your separate ways, please be at breakfast no later than ten tomorrow morning. We have a full day of sightseeing planned. The first stop is the Fushimi Inari Shrine, famous for its red torii gates. Depending on the time, we may also visit the Kiyomizu-dera Shrine and the traditional town located below it. On that note, I will see all of you bright and early." Stepping off the bus, he waited for Anton and a few of the guys.

Gathered together, the group disembarked and began making their way to their respective pavilions. Burton and Sara walked ahead, a notable gap between them despite their attempts at casual conversation. Jade and Reggie strolled hand in hand, their carefree laughter weaving through the crisp night air, and close behind them were Shane and Abi, the crunch of snow underfoot filling the silence between them.

"See you in the morning," Jade chimed, pulling Reg along as they disappeared into their building.

Ahead of them, near the top of the incline, Burton turned while Sara did not look back. "Have a good night, guys," the infamous DJ said, eyes flicking briefly to Abi. Worried about her, he hesitated before giving a brief wave.

She met his eyes for a moment, her stomach twisting. Silently, she raised a hand in response. "Night," she said, the sentiment carrying more weight than intended.

He nodded but lingered just a beat too long before turning to go.

Watching him walk away, she caught him glancing over his shoulder. In that split second, his concern clung to her as if he were trying to decipher something.

"You coming?" Shane asked, cutting through her thoughts while holding the door open for her.

"Umm, yeah," Abi mumbled, snapping out of it and stepping inside. The door clicked shut as Shane locked it behind them.

Removing her boots and hanging up her coat, her hat, and mittens found their place in the closet to dry. Quietly crossing the room, her focus landed on her book sitting on the side table. Picking it up, she looked at the cover briefly and pulled out the bookmark.

Holding it in her hand, Abi released a small sigh while staring at it. Then, in an instant, she slowly tossed it in the trash.

Needing to snap her out of the seemingly terrified mindset she was exhibiting, he came up to her as she ran her hand along the bed, now made into a king.

"Guess they saw we'd shifted them closer together," she analyzed.

"Yes, they must have assumed we wanted it like that." Shane rested his hands lovingly on her shoulders. He could feel the fear and worry still pressing on her and knew he needed to make the girl see reason. "Abi, listen to me," he said, calm and steady. When she caught his gaze, he tried to anchor her back to reality. "Let's think about this logically. A random doll, cursed and left in some forest? It's nothing but a person's twisted idea to scare tourists with some crazy folklore, that's all."

Hearing this, Abi exhaled slowly despite having that distant, haunted look.

Determined to ground her, Shane kept going. "Whatever it is, it's not real. There is no curse. Period." Coming right out with it, he said, "This is very unlike you to get caught up in something so crazy."

When she nodded, her face softened slightly, though the worry hadn't entirely left her.

"Trust me." He squeezed her hand. "Everything will be fine."

After a moment, she sighed and whispered, "Okay."

Opening his arms, he hugged her as she clung to his waist. "Come on, let's get ready for bed. I'll run you a bubble bath to help you relax."

Steps, slow and robotic, Abi followed him without protest. She was still processing everything, but she hoped he was right.

Turning on the tap on the large wooden tub, he watched the warm water cascade out of the spout. Upon adding lavender-scented spa beads, suds soon began to form and grow bigger by the second. Hoping the bath would drown her worries away, he said, "I'll leave you to it. Call me if you need me."

As the bubbles frothed, filling the air with the soothing scent, she said, "Thank you. I won't be long."

"Take your time. No rush." Leaving her, he slid the bathroom pocket doors closed to give her privacy.

Abi undressed and slipped into the soothing water. She let out a soft sigh as the heat enveloped her, easing the knots in her body and taking the chill away. Leaning back with her head resting on the edge of the tub, she closed her eyes, wishing her mind would stop racing. But she couldn't stop thinking about the doll. The card. The curse. What if it was a warning? What if it wasn't a coincidence after all?

It didn't take long for the bath to make her limbs feel heavy, but her thoughts wouldn't quiet. As she ran her fingers absentmindedly through the bubbles, staring at the rising steam, Shane knocked, wanting to check on her.

He opened the pocket door an inch. Leaning against the doorframe, he asked softly, "How are you feeling? Doing okay in there?"

She opened her eyes and glanced over at him, her expression tired but calmer. "I think I'm ready to get out."

"Alright," he said, closing the door again.

Pulling the plugs on either end of the tub, she sat on the edge and wrapped herself in a towel before slipping on a white robe.

Quickly brushing her teeth and washing her face, she walked out of the bathroom and found him sprawled out on the covers, surfing the net. "All yours. You can have your shower now."

He nodded, "Sounds good." Swinging his legs off the bed, he walked around to her side and helped pull back the covers as she slipped between the sheets. Kissing her forehead, he said, "Sweet dreams, Abs."

"Thank you."

Leaving her, having turned off the lights, Shane disappeared into the bathroom and started the shower. With time to think as the water trickled down his skin, he, too, thought about the eeriness of the evening's events.

Turning off the faucet, steam trailing behind him as he opened the door, Shane emerged a few minutes later to find Abi already fast asleep. Her breathing was slow and steady. She looked angelic despite the chaos that had consumed her earlier. Happy with that, he smiled and turned off the rest of the lights before crawling into bed beside her.

His arm slipping around her waist, he pulled her in close. Cuddled up, the sweet guy kissed the back of her head before closing his eyes.

"Sleep tight," he whispered before drifting off, thankful that the worries from that day had faded into the quietness of the night.

| 20 |

At Odds

Sunday, December 17

Aman Kyoto - Living Pavilion

Met by lazy flakes falling outside the floor-to-ceiling wall of windows, Abi opened her eyes before rolling over. Shane's back was to her. Still tired, she quietly looked at the time on her phone. With a half hour left before their alarm would go off, she buried her head in the pillow again, thankful to have a few more minutes to rest.

Death to her, she thought, still haunted by it.

When she stirred slightly, it caused Shane to wake.

Rolling over, he reached for her hand. "Morning," he said, somewhat groggy.

"Morning," Abi replied softly, her thoughts elsewhere.

"Did you sleep okay?"

"Yes. You?"

"Not bad."

Both lay in silence, waiting to get up and greet the day.

Shane could still feel her anxiety. "About last night," he said, wanting to elaborate.

Abi flung back the covers. "I'm fine. Let's not talk about it, okay?" Having said her piece, she disappeared into the bathroom.

Despite being happy to hear her say that, deep down, he wasn't fully convinced. Brushed off, he sighed, grabbed his phone, and searched for the curse Hiro had described. His brow furrowed as he skimmed through the pages, reading about the legend.

"It can't be real," he whispered to himself, the hum of the shower echoing throughout the room.

After perusing several websites, he saw Abi emerge again, her long hair wrapped neatly in a towel. Wearing a white robe, she silently moved about. She did not say much but offered him a small smile before heading toward the water closet to blow-dry her hair.

Getting out of bed, he grabbed his clothes for the day and slipped into the bathroom before sliding the pocket doors shut behind him.

Alone again, Abi focused on drying her hair in front of the sink, the warm air blowing against her face.

"Forget about it. Move on, and don't let it bug you," she faintly whispered while running the brush through her long locks, the heat drying every strand. With it now sleek and shiny, she applied light makeup and selected an outfit from her suitcase. Behind the door, she could hear Shane drying off after his shower.

Soon, the barrier between them slid open. Wearing a thick sweatshirt and jeans, he tossed his pajamas in his suitcase. Still not having said anything, he could feel an awkwardness between them.

Both moved with quiet efficiency, as though the snowy morning outside had cast a calming, almost solemn mood.

Dressed and ready to head out on time, Abi sat on the bench to slip on her boots before grabbing her coat from the rack. Sliding each arm into the sleeves, she bundled the furry collar around her neck.

"Hey..." Afraid to ask, he reached out and held her arm. "Are you sure you're okay? What can I do to help?"

She peered up at him. "Nothing." With a sincere look, almost forced, Abi replied, "Don't worry. I'm good. Just tired."

Giving her space, he knew he'd have to let it go for now.

She smiled briefly before opening the door and walking outside to a world awaiting them under a blanket of fresh snow.

Light flakes falling gently from the sky dusted the evergreens, making the path ahead shimmer in the pale light. The air was crisp but not bitterly cold. Abi took in the quiet beauty.

About to leave, Shane's phone rang. He glanced at the screen, frowning slightly. "Sorry, umm... Give me a minute. I've gotta take this," he said before stepping away.

Abi watched him slowly walk up the snow-covered path. His head lowered as he listened intently. Occasionally, he raised his sight to the sky and shook his head. The tension in his shoulders was unmistakable.

"What is going on?" Abi whispered.

Far enough away from her, Shane's breath fogged the air as he listened to his agent explain the situation. "Wait... What do you mean, transferring?" His voice stayed low so Abi wouldn't hear him.

The man kept talking as Shane ran a hand through his hair. "I—I get it, but... can't this wait until summer?"

The agent's response left him little room for negotiation. He was pressuring him whether he liked it or not.

Just then, Burton stepped out of his pavilion and stood on the porch by the doorway to wait for Sara. He immediately overheard Shane's conversation, his keen ears picking up more than he probably should have.

With a frustrated sigh, Shane ended the call, staring at the screen for a moment before turning. When he saw Burton standing there, his eyes widened slightly.

"How much of that did you hear?" Shane asked sheepishly.

"Enough." Burton stood tall, crossing his arms.

Shane panicked for a second. "Please, don't say anything to her. I don't want to ruin her Christmas. Besides, nothing's set in stone yet."

"Fine." Burton raised an eyebrow. "But eventually, you've got to tell her."

"I will," Shane said, quieter now as he headed back toward Abi. He tried to compose himself, but his mind was racing.

Concern etched on her face. "Everything okay?" she asked when he approached.

"Yeah, umm…" Shane forced a smile just as Burton and Sara passed by.

"Morning, Abs," the famous DJ said, his gaze moving from her to Shane disapprovingly.

"Morning," she greeted, catching their strange interaction. When they were far enough ahead, Abi asked, "What was that about?"

Not letting on that anything had happened between them, Shane divulged, "Just my agent going over details for the signing announcement."

Realizing the two guys were once again at odds, Abi nodded uneasily. "I see," she replied.

Taking hold of her hand, they walked down the path, hearing only their friend's muted conversation ahead. Still walking a few feet apart, Abi heard the combativeness in Sara's voice. It made her skin crawl. She hated that Burton not only sounded unhappy but now looked it, too.

Surrounded by snow-laden branches hanging all around them, they soon crossed the deck at the Living Pavilion.

Burton held the door open for Sara, then gestured for Abi to go in as well. With Shane close behind her, Burton stepped aside. "After you, man," he said, allowing the QB to enter before following them.

Martin, Anton, and their security were already present and accounted for.

"Good morning, everyone," Martin greeted.

"Morning," Abi replied with a smile on her way to pour a coffee.

"They have prepared a variety of dishes for us. Help yourself when you're ready."

The large windows framed the winter gardens outside, a peaceful contrast to the warmth and quiet buzz indoors. The calming sounds of traditional Japanese zen instrumental music floated through the room, creating a harmonious atmosphere.

With the murmur of conversation mixed with the clinking of plates and cutlery, the waitstaff, dressed in immaculate, dark uniforms, moved gracefully between tables, attending to guests with soft-spoken words and polite bows. There was an air of refinement, yet the comforting smell of breakfast—a blend of savory and fresh—grounded the room in warmth and hospitality.

The buffet was a mix of Western and traditional Japanese favorites. Silver warming dishes held fluffy scrambled eggs and the rolled Japanese version, known as Tamagoyaki, along with sausages, fresh pastries, grilled fish, miso soup, rice, and more.

Shane's eyes lit up when he spotted the eggs and sausages. "This'll do," he said with a small smile, picking up two plates—one for Abi and one for himself.

"Scrambled or Japanese style?" he asked, offering the plate to her.

"I'll try the rolled." Abi smiled. "Thank you."

Placing one on her plate, he handed it over, unsure what more she wanted. Adding two slices of grilled fish out of curiosity, the aroma alone enticing, he said, "Can't hurt to try something new," before taking a slice of baked matcha bread.

With Sara hovering nearby, Abi kept her distance and watched Burton gravitate to the more traditional options.

On the way back to their tables, he smiled at her upon seeing what Abi had taken. "Looks good. Doesn't it?" Burton asked.

"Certainly does."

Veering away from her to sit with Sara, he watched her join Shane, who had already taken the fork from the cutlery rest.

Quietly enjoying their meal, the QB let out a content sigh. "These eggs are incredible."

Abi agreed while savoring the first bite of hers.

He leaned back slightly and looked outside. "It's a nice change of pace, isn't it?" he said, trying to forget his early morning phone call.

"You can thank *him* for that." Abi raised her fork and pointed to Burton.

"Suppose you're right."

They ate in comfortable silence, appreciating every dish as a peacefulness unfolded before the day's adventures began.

Reg and Jade waltzed in late.

Martin quickly eyed them up and tapped his watch.

"So sorry, Martin," Jade greeted. "We will hurry and eat."

Finishing his last bite, he raised his hand. "No need. Take your time. We will wait."

Reggie nodded and escorted Jade to the table before grabbing some food.

Refilling her coffee, Abi noticed Martin standing with his iPad in hand. "While we are wrapping up here, I will share the details of our plans for today."

Everyone sitting around him was all ears.

"As I mentioned last evening, we will be visiting the Fushimi Inari Shrine. It is famous for its iconic red torii arches. Afterward, we will have an early dinner at the Ritz-Carlton's La Locanda restaurant, where we will enjoy an eight-course preset menu. Because Mr. Coppersmith has submitted a request, we will not be visiting Kiyomizu-dera today. Instead, our evening will consist of a special event to honor Miss Abi."

When he said that, Sara rolled her eyes.

"Does anyone have any questions?"

Turning to Shane, Abi smiled. "A special surprise, huh?"

"Yeah," he said bashfully. "And don't ask for any hints," he chuckled.

She looked at him sitting across from her. "Hmm..." she said, while closing one eye.

Seeing her happily thinking, he felt good knowing he had the upper hand for a change.

Moving from his iPad to everyone in the room, Martin added, "Now, with that said, promptly meet at the front gates at eleven-fifteen. Please be on time," looking specifically at the engaged couple. "I also suggest you bring along a water bottle since there is a hike up the mountain. It is important to stay hydrated."

Everyone nodded when he mentioned that. Looking at the security team, he asked, "Gentlemen? Sara? Can I have you meet here at eleven to go over our plan of action in case we have some outside interference to contend with?"

Each one of them acknowledged his request.

"Very well. That concludes my update." Martin went about his business and spoke with Lorenzo.

Shane turned to Abi. "What kind of interference do you think he is referring to?"

Shrugging her shoulders, she said, "I don't want any more surprises aside from yours, of course."

"What if he knows something we don't?"

Out of the blue, Martin walked to Jade and Reggie's table. Under his breath, he asked, "May I have a quick word?"

"Sure," Reg replied, standing up respectfully. "What's up?"

Abi watched the man pull their friends aside. When he angled his iPad toward them, his expression changed. He was definitely concerned – all business.

Whatever they saw on the screen made Jade stiffen—then, without hesitation, she gripped Reggie's hand, her fingers tightening like a vice.

"She looks worried," Abi whispered, unease seeping in. "Something's wrong."

Now fully alert, Shane tracked the exchange, his eyes narrowing on Martin. "It could just be wedding plans—last-minute decisions they need to make," he speculated, though doubt laced his tone.

Then, abruptly, Jade's hand flew to her mouth.

Abi's pulse kicked up. "I don't think this is wedding-related," she said, catching the fleeting panic in Jade's expression.

The conversation ended as swiftly as it had begun.

Martin turned and strode off, his posture straight as a pin.

Frozen, Reggie's hands remained braced on his hips. Eyes fixed on the ground, it seemed he was struggling to process whatever was said.

Soon, the two headed in their direction. Notably disturbed.

Shane asked him, "Is everything okay, man? What did Martin say?"

Reg took two chairs from an adjacent table and sat with their friends. "Sounds like a guest at the Roku hotel might have posted a picture of Jade and me at the chapel."

Immediately interjecting, Jade added, "He believes it's just a matter of time before the post gains traction, given the headlines that have surfaced today."

"Headlines?" Abi repeated.

"Yeah, umm." His voice was tight, controlled—but barely. "Apparently, it's been reported that my father has literally run the company into the ground. Within a couple of weeks, possibly days, it will go bankrupt." A stroke of anger surfaced in his eyes. "Martin just showed us an article in the *Financial Times*." Tension coiled on his face. "The report claims my father was involved in some crooked business dealings. Fraud, offshore accounts—that kind of thing." He let out a bitter laugh, shaking his head. "Wilson Corp's stock price just plummeted. Now, we must race against the clock. The way it sounds, everything my grandfather built, all those years of work, will soon be gone. Like it never even existed."

"Unless..." Jade tugged on Reg's shirt. "We do something to save it."

Believing that was a tall order, Abi said, "How are you going to do that?"

He smirked. "I have a few ideas. Just need to think them through some more."

"You're sure you want to bail out your Father?" Shane knew the lengths the man had gone to in order to silence his son.

"No, I would never help save him. But my Granddad worked his entire life to build that company, and my father destroyed it piece by piece. I'll be damned if I just sit back and let it happen. I have too much respect for my Granddad. He's done a lot for me over the years."

His heartfelt speech resonated with Abi. "That's very commendable."

He nodded. "Now, we just have to figure out how to outsmart my father and save the business."

"Reg, we've discussed this. If you feel strongly about getting involved, you need to take the helm. Being emancipated does not change your status as heir. So, you can step in if you choose to."

"I realize, but I've gotta win the board's approval. The only way to do that is to bring something big to the table. Something that will save the company."

To lighten the mood, Shane said, "Piece of cake."

Reggie smirked as the burden of what he just said weighed on him.

Tapping his arm, Jade encouraged, "Don't worry. We will figure this out."

"So, how does this affect the wedding?" Anxious, Abi wondered where that left them.

"As of now, Martin is making a few calls. He intends to change the venue just to be on the safe side." Jade turned to her fiancé. "I'm scared that he won't be able to find another chapel."

Certain Martin would pull it off, Abi chuckled. "Don't count him out yet. That man can work miracles."

Tears developed in Jade's eyes.

Seeing this, Reg reached over and wrapped his arms around her. "Everything's gonna be okay. I promise. We are going to have a beautiful wedding. It'll be perfect."

Emotional, the girl nodded and dabbed her face with the napkin.

"As long as we are together, nothing else matters," he said.

"You're right." Stressed, she took a deep breath and rested her hand on top of his.

Hanging out a bit longer as their friends finished eating breakfast, the two couples soon bundled up and climbed the hillside to their pavilion once again.

Before parting ways, Abi suggested, "Want to meet back here and walk to the gate together."

"Sounds good. We'll see you shortly," Jade replied, giving Reggie a nod as he opened their door.

Leaving footprints in the thin layer of freshly fallen powder on the step, Shane reached out and passed the card key over the reader to unlock the room.

Abi headed inside and took her boots off before placing them on the tray. "I hope everything works out for them," she said quietly.

"For which? The wedding or saving the company?"

"Both. But I want them to have the wedding they were dreaming of. It will be hard if that doesn't happen."

He stopped and hugged her. "Like you said, don't count out Martin just yet. I'm sure the man has some tricks up his sleeve. He'll come through for them."

Cheeks flushed from the cold, she said, "Hope you're right." Heading straight to the bathroom, she called over her shoulder, "I'm just going to brush my teeth before we head out."

Shane followed behind her and grabbed his toothbrush. While standing side by side at their sinks, both focused on the simple chore. The bathroom was warm, the mirror fogged slightly from their showers earlier, and for a moment, the weight of that morning's anxiety seemed to lift. Abi kept glancing over at Shane, her eyes playfully narrowing as she tried to brush faster. Somehow, she had turned the mundane task into a secret competition.

Noticing, he grinned and quickened his pace, their quiet rivalry leading to shared laughter. The sound echoed lightly in the small space.

As they finished up, Shane wiped his mouth with a towel and looked at Abi, still smiling. Their lightheartedness gave him hope that maybe the rest of the day would follow suit—relaxed and carefree.

She smiled back, rinsing out her mouth. "You're ridiculous," she teased, but thankfully, there was warmth in her voice.

Shane shrugged, feeling confident. "You started it," he said, flashing a grin, thankful for the small twinkling of joy between them.

| 21 |

Torii Gates

Sunday, December 17

Fushimi Inari Shrine

Fueled for the day, Shane got dressed and grabbed his hat and mitts, along with a bottle of water for each of them, while Abi gathered her things. Putting on her coat, she slipped her cross-body bag over her head and stuffed her mittens inside with her phone.

"Good to go?" Shane asked, standing tall, his hand on the door handle as she approached.

She smiled. "Yes, ready."

They walked out to find their friends doing the same.

"Perfect timing!" Abi shouted to Jade.

The girl responded with a quick thumbs-up but didn't break her intense exchange with Reggie.

"I bet they will end up saving his Grandfather's company," she said positively.

"I wouldn't doubt it at all."

Abi and Shane followed their friends through Aman Kyoto's peaceful forest trails. The cold air tingled against their skin, and their boots crunched on the icy ground. Tall trees swayed gently, their bare branches forming a quiet, natural archway. The city's noise felt far away, leaving only the calm of the winter morning.

Spotting their group at the bottom end of the path, huddled near the sleek black coach bus waiting, they realized they were the last to arrive.

"Sorry, Martin," Abi said, believing they'd held them up.

Cordial, he replied, "No worries, Miss Abi. You are right on time."

Deep in conversation, Jade and Reggie's voices stayed low but animated while Martin scrolled through his iPad, likely making last-minute wedding arrangements.

Burton paced a few steps away. Upon spotting Abi and Shane, his gaze lingered thoughtfully on his friend, determined to steal a moment alone with her at some point.

As the doors to the coach bus opened, releasing a burst of warm air, Shane stood aside and had Abi board ahead of him.

"Thank you," she said, catching a glimpse of Burton outside through the glass, his eyes locked on her again as she walked down the aisle to have a seat. In true Burton fashion, she sensed that there was something he needed to say.

Pondering their thoughts, Jade collapsed in a spot behind them while Reg joined her to continue their brainstorming.

As Sara ventured toward the bus, she rudely passed by Burton and walked down the aisle to sit in the row directly in front of them.

That's unusual, Abi thought, assuming the girl intended to spy or listen in on their conversations.

Boarding the bus, Burton spotted his girlfriend and walked towards her. Having a seat, he suddenly turned around. "Excited to see the sights today, Abs?"

She smiled. "Absolutely. You?"

"When you visit cities like this, it is important to discover the culture and heritage within them."

"Well said."

Catching Sara's stare, Burton exhaled slowly, locking his frustration behind a calm exterior. Upon turning away, he made it very clear—she had no power over him.

With everyone on board, the luxury coach left the heavily guarded resort. Winding through the narrow roads of Kyoto, from the large, tinted windows, the group could see a patchwork of traditional Japanese homes with sloping roofs, surrounded by intricate gardens that even winter couldn't dull.

Shane reached for Abi's hand and held it tightly as they watched the city go by. Assuming they would see the outskirts of town at some point, strangely, they never left the densely packed streets behind.

As their driver slowed down, he carefully steered through the narrow lanes before turning into a parking lot. A bright red torii gate stood tall, standing out among the small shops and houses.

Soon, they arrived at another enormous torii arch vibrantly marking the main entrance. The first of many stretched beyond the buildings into the forested mountain path.

Martin addressed them one last time before their departure as everyone bundled up. "Just a few things before we embark on this adventure. If you get separated, please meet back here in three hours. We will then move on to our next destination. The bus will remain here in case you are cold and wish to warm up."

The driver nodded to acknowledge him.

"On that note, enjoy your visit." Martin immediately leaned over and spoke with Lorenzo and Andrew. Each man nodded at everything Martin was alluding to.

One by one, their security team exited and created a perimeter. It was definitely not a way to blend in with the crowd, as Abi noticed many eyes veering their way.

When they stepped off the bus and breathed in the cool, fresh air, she looked around at the shrine, bustling with handfuls of tourists moving through the iconic gates to the ornate red temple at the top of the stone steps. Entering the grounds, they found their translator, Hiro Matsumura, waiting for them.

Martin approached with an outstretched hand. "Kon'nichiwa, Hiro."

"Hello, my friend!" he replied. Dressed casually today, with hiking shoes on his feet and warm clothing from head to toe, he rested his hand on top of the canvas satchel, crossing his chest. "Are we ready for today's excursion?"

A few of them nodded while waiting to hear more.

"The Fushimi Inari Shrine is one of Japan's finest historical treasures. It is a stunning place of worship belonging to Shinto, Japan's indigenous religion. Known for its thousands of orange and black Torii gates, the arches literally cover Mount Inari. Let's proceed up the steps to the entrance. If at any time you have questions for me, please don't hesitate to ask."

Growing impatient, Burton wanted to get moving, so he reluctantly walked alongside Sara and moved onward, prompting the rest to follow suit. Passing the red buildings of Honden Hall, they headed toward the Torii Gates. Threading through the first section, cutting into the snowy forest, their group arrived at a fork in the path.

"Left or right?" he asked Hiro.

"Go to the right, Sir."

Turning, they proceeded in that direction. Venturing through the seemingly endless tunnel of vermillion arches, the forest around them grew dense as the world narrowed to just their footsteps and the low murmur of conversation.

Abi walked in quiet closeness to Shane, her hand occasionally securing her grip on him.

Behind them, the security team was sharp, ever-vigilant, while Martin and Hiro led the way, discussing the history of Japan.

"Wow," Abi whispered, taking in the scene. The grandeur of the place was breathtaking. She could feel the sacred energy all around her. "This is beautiful."

Shane nodded. "Yeah, pretty incredible."

Arriving at the first shrine, Hiro bowed before entering. He was calm and measured as he explained the history around them. "Fushimi

Inari," he began, "is dedicated to the kami Inari, the deity of rice, agriculture, and prosperity. But over time, Inari also became associated with industry and business, and so many people come here to pray for success in those fields."

Upon approaching the water basin, a thin layer of snow dusted its surface, giving the shrine an even more tranquil appearance.

Hiro completed the purification ceremony with smooth, practiced movements, dipping the ladle into the cold water to let some trickle through his fingers. Despite the chill, he maintained his composure. When this ritual was complete, he said, "Welcome to Okusha Hohaisho prayer building." Gesturing to the many structures surrounding them, he spread his hands outward and led the group toward a small area on the far side. "Over here," he continued, pointing to a smooth, rounded stone resting upon a pedestal, "You will find the Omokaru-Ishi, meaning light or heavy stone. It is said that if you make a wish and lift it with your bare hands, one of two things will occur. If you feel the stone is lighter than you expected, your wish will come true. If it's heavier," he gave a small shrug, "then perhaps your wish is not meant to be." Approaching it, the tall, young man stopped and took a moment to ponder his wish.

Everyone watched to see what would happen.

Stepping forward, he placed both hands on the round stone, lifted it off the pedestal, and smiled, somewhat surprised.

"So?" Abi asked, "Was it heavy or light?"

"Light as a feather," he replied contently.

"What did you wish?" Jade questioned.

"That must remain a secret."

The group gathered around, their curiosity piqued as they prepared to test it for themselves.

Abi went first, stepping forward with a mix of excitement and hesitation. She closed her eyes, her mind forming the wish as she placed her hands on the stone. It felt cold beneath her fingers. With a deep breath, she lifted it—and to her surprise, it felt lighter than she expected. A smile tugged at her lips as she placed the stone back down, a flicker of hope sparking in her chest.

Shane went next. He cast a reassuring look before stepping up. Pausing, he, too, made his wish, then reached down and lifted the stone. It was heavier than he had anticipated, but not unbearable. He chuckled under his breath, glancing at Abi as he set it down, his wish remaining a secret but his expression hinting at a deeper hope. As he stepped away for someone else to have a turn, he returned to Abi.

"Are you going to share your thoughts?" she asked.

Smiling sheepishly, he said, "You heard the man. It must remain a secret."

When he said that, Abi felt as though the answer he'd received may not have been what he wanted. A part of her wondered if it had anything to do with her.

Just then, Jade took a turn. Inhaling deeply, she cleared her mind and focused on her heart's desires. When she finally lifted the stone, her brow raised slightly. It was almost effortless. Smirking, she put it back down and glanced over at Reggie with a look that said, *I told you so.*

When Jade walked over to him, Sara decided to give it a try. Her demeanor was distant but determined. Almost skeptical of the whole ritual, she played along with an open mind. After thinking for a second, her fingers brushed the sides of the stone before she lifted it. But for her, it felt much heavier than she had imagined. A shadow crossed her face as she struggled to put it back down. When she stepped away, her arms folded across her chest defensively as she zeroed in on Abi.

Suddenly locking eyes with the girl, she knew right away. *If looks could kill, I'd be dead -* she thought as Sara's expression froze in place, almost contemplating a solution to her problem. It felt sinister. Elusive. Not knowing what else to do to improve things between them, Abi figured Sara felt more than threatened by her. Despite wanting Burton to be happy, she couldn't shake the gut feeling she had. A part of her hoped Burton wouldn't be with this girl much longer. There was just something about her. A strange vibe that left her unsettled.

Deliberately making a loop around the shrine with Shane, trying to avoid Sara, they rounded the corner and saw Reggie step up to give the stone a try. He seemed hesitant while glancing at Jade as if searching for some reassurance. His mind raced as he made his wish—a mixture of business concerns and complicated feelings about their future. He bent down and placed his hands on the cold ball, expecting it to be lighter. But when he lifted, his muscles tensed. A small frown formed on his lips as he struggled with it for a moment before setting it back down.

"What does that mean, again?" Reggie asked, slightly panicked.

Hiro offered a sympathetic smile. "If the stone feels heavier, it may mean your wish was not meant to come true."

Reggie exchanged glances with Jade. There was uncertainty in his eyes. He wanted to dismiss the stone's weight, but the result made sense—it matched the burden he'd been carrying.

Breaking from the group, wanting some space, Sara noticed the hanging fox heads similar to the wooden plaques from the Arashiyama bamboo forest shrine.

Hiro saw her curiosity and stood beside her. "In Japan, a fox, or *kitsune*, is a quite complicated character. Dedicated to Inari, their sculptures are the guardians of Shinto Shrines, the god of rice and good crops that represent a good life."

Somewhat interested in the explanation, Sara offered a flat smile.

"Would you like to write a message on one of the fox plaques?" he asked.

She nodded. "Sure."

Moving aside, he led her to the covered white tent. Hiro placed a five-yen coin in the box. "Most young Japanese people believe in an urban legend that states if you give a five-yen coin, it might increase your chances of finding a significant other."

When he said that, Abi spotted Andrew pulling several coins from his pocket.

Sifting through them in the palm of his hand, he tossed a few into the box. Catching Abi's eyes on him, he produced a slight smirk. "I'll give it a shot. I've got nothing to lose, right?" he said, shrugging his shoulders before going about his business.

"Right," Abi said in an upbeat tone. She felt for the guys. Their job made it hard to meet anyone, let alone maintain a relationship.

Watching Sara slip her offering into the red box, the girl picked up a marker and a wooden fox as Burton approached.

"What are you going to write?" he asked.

She quickly covered what she'd written thus far. "It's a secret."

Leaving her be, he spotted Abi examining the trail map before meandering around the buildings. Admiring her sweet appreciation for every aspect of the shrine, he quickly searched for Shane. Finding him taking another turn at the Omokaru-Ishi stone, Burton seized the opportunity and cautiously moved up behind Abi.

"Hey," he said, relieved to catch her alone finally.

"Hi." Taken by surprise, her eyes immediately drifted past him to take note of Shane and Sara's whereabouts.

When her attention returned, she found him with his hands buried in his pockets, exuding a strong presence that somehow instantly calmed her nerves.

Unshaken, he stood tall beside her. He had held back long enough. This wasn't the place to say it with the others so close, but he did anyway. "I'm done walking on eggshells around those two. Something needs to change."

"Yeah, it's hard," she admitted, frustration laced in her voice. "Feels like every time we talk, someone gets upset. It's exhausting."

He ran a hand through his hair, exhaling sharply. "We should've taken this trip without the entourage."

She tilted her head. "That wouldn't have gone over well either."

"Probably not." Standing in front of the map, he got his bearings and nodded toward the arched path. "Come on. We need to talk about what happened at Kifune Shrine."

As they moved further from the group, Abi glanced back to see Shane on one side and Sara on the other. Thirty feet inside the arches, she stopped.

Burton asked. "What's wrong?"

Her pulse quickened. "We should go back. I don't want to rock the boat."

In the middle of the path, Burton stopped. His expression shifted to a look of disappointment before flashing a small, bittersweet smile. "At some point, we need to figure this out," he said.

Grateful for his understanding, she nodded, still feeling the sting of unresolved conflict. Spotting their group through the trees while parting ways, she found Shane and walked over to him just as Burton emerged from the same place.

Concerned, Shane questioned, "What did he want?"

Knowing she couldn't hide what she did, Abi replied, "He wanted to talk about what happened last night at the shrine."

"Why? Does he know something? Is there a problem?"

"I don't know. We didn't get that far."

"Why not?"

Her frustration bubbled. "Because we are constantly worried about hurting your feelings."

"What does that mean?" he argued quietly.

Not wanting to fight, Abi said, "Nothing," and walked away.

Leaving him behind, she followed Martin and Hiro as they led the way through the winding paths of Fushimi Inari. As the air grew colder, their breath fogged in front of them. Abi watched as the snow lightly dusted the red torii gates, the bright color popping against the white backdrop.

Out of the blue, the banter from a pack of young teens infused their peaceful surroundings. With the path narrow, each of them brushed past, invading their space.

Shocked to see a couple of red tattoos hidden under their collars, Abi tried to get a better look.

Suddenly, one girl with long, black, straggly hair brushed past and turned around. One eye, blue, and the other brown, she smirked at Abi on the way by. The nape of her neck exposed dragon ink, also, but hers had a daisy next to it. Recalling the markings on their baggage handler at the airport, she thought, *Is it a gang? Or some sort of cult?*

Amidst it all, their security sprang into action.

Encircling the group, Lorenzo swiftly said, "Check your pockets. Bags. Was anything stolen?" His eyes stayed on the kids walking away. "Is anything missing? Passports? Wallets? Phones?"

Jade's hands instinctively flew to her waist as her face paled. "My bag—it's gone!" she cried, thick with panic.

Reggie's sharp eyes darted around, locking on the girl with straggly black hair and mismatched eyes. She was already several steps ahead, the glint of Jade's Louis Vuitton bag strap dangling from her hand.

"There!" he shouted, pointing at her. "She's got it!"

Not missing a beat, Reggie and Shane bolted, their long strides closing the gap. Burton and a few of the men quickly joined in, their heavy footsteps echoing through the winding torii gates.

The girl darted through the crowd, her movements agile and practiced as tourists stumbled aside, startled by the chaos. Her razor-sharp focus flicked back briefly, her lips curling into a smug smirk as she pushed forward.

"Don't let her get away!" Burton called out.

The chase intensified as the girl rounded a corner near a small Shinto shrine. For a moment, they thought she might escape, but the path narrowed ahead. With Shane cutting off her left, Reggie on her right, and Burton flanking them with the guys fanning out, they forced her to stop, her back inching closer to the shrine wall cut into the mountainside. There was no way out.

Despite her labored breathing, her defiance remained intact as her mismatched eyes burned with anger.

"End of the line," Shane said, low and threatening. He wasn't sure if she would understand.

Not responding, she sneered, her gaze darting between them before surveying the forest beyond the wall. Then, with a sudden, fluid motion, she shouted, "Totte kudasai!" and dropped the bag. Before anyone could react, she leaped onto the low stone wall beside the shrine and vaulted over it with startling parkour agility.

"Holy crap!" Reg yelled.

Watching as she scaled the rocky mountain face as if it were nothing, the girl suddenly disappeared into the dense forest high above them and did not look back.

Reggie grabbed the bag off the ground and quickly checked it.

"Is everything there?" Burton asked.

"Yeah, seems so," he confirmed, his relief evident.

Burton frowned, his eyes narrowing to the spot where the girl had vanished. "She knew exactly where to go," he muttered. "This wasn't her first time pulling this stunt here. I think they were testing the waters – seeing how we'd react."

The group stood in tense silence as Burton's mind reeled. "Come on!" he said, "We need to get back to the girls and make sure this wasn't a diversion to veer us away from them!"

With urgency, the guys ran up the path to where they'd left everyone behind. Seeing them gathered about fifty yards away, Burton was relieved to see they were fine.

As the guys breached the hill, Abi smiled as Reggie raised Jade's bag over his head, victorious. Her mind raced, replaying the details of what just happened—the dragon tattoo, the daisy beside it, and the smirk that seemed all too familiar. "I don't think this was random," she whispered.

Approaching his fiancée, clutching the bag tightly, Jade said to him, "I can't believe you got it! How?"

"We cornered her, and she handed it over," he replied.

"Just like that? Really?"

Hearing him, Abi asked, "Why would she risk it all and just drop it and run?"

"She didn't care about the bag," Burton said, stepping forward. "Real pickpockets are seasoned. They almost always get away because they have to. This was different. The girl didn't take anything. I think she was sending a message."

"What kind of message?" Shane questioned.

He analyzed what happened. "We took the bait and left the girls unattended."

"But Andrew stayed with them."

Finding Martin, Hiro, and Andrew looking his way, he pointed out, "Three against possibly fifteen is not the best odds."

"But nothing happened," Jade pointed out.

"Next time, we might not be so lucky."

"Three of them had that Red Dragon tattoo on their neck. The girl who took the bag had one, also," Abi informed as Burton looked on. "Our baggage handler at the airport had the same stamp."

Upon hearing this, they knew then that they'd been targeted from the moment they arrived in Osaka.

"Do you remember if the teens at the Consulate had these markings?" Burton questioned in an effort to gather more intel.

"I don't know for sure. It all happened so fast." She thought for a minute. "Two wore hoodies with a red dragon on them. That's all I remember from that. But, I did see a red dragon tattoo on one of the GTR guys getting arrested."

"We need to look into this gang and see what affiliations they have."

Martin agreed, about to call it in.

Stopping him, Sara interjected and said, "Leave that with me, Martin. I will reach out to a few of my contacts here."

The man nodded. "Very well."

"I'll let you know what I find out," she said, walking away and putting her phone to her ear.

"In the meantime, I think we need to cut our visit short." Burton noticed Abi lower her head disappointingly. Hating to see this, he turned to Martin and Lorenzo.

His right-hand man knew what he was silently asking. Without hesitation, he nodded at his boss with authority.

"Martin agrees that if we make this quick and stick together, we can continue."

Stealing Burton's attention, a brightness reappeared on her face. Seeing this, Sara got frustrated and walked away.

While taking the lead, Lorenzo changed his tone. "Let's move. Now. I don't like how this is shaping up. Make sure you keep your passports in an interior, zippered pocket. No exceptions."

Feeling violated to a degree, Abi was thankful nothing major came of it. Taking off her jacket, she threaded the bag across her body and quickly put her coat back on.

"Smart move, Miss," Andrew stated with a thumbs-up.

On edge, the guys stayed in close proximity to them. No one was going to come within twenty feet now.

Weaving in and out of many smaller shrines nestled in the forest, Abi noticed one had several fox statues.

"Foxes are the Inari's messengers. We call them the kitsune. Each fox holds something different in its mouth." Hiro pointed to one of the statues. "The key," he explained, "is said to be the key to the rice granary, symbolizing prosperity. People often come here to pray for abundance and good fortune."

Abi lingered by the statue, watching as a small wisp of snow blew across the fox's stone surface. There was something about the stillness of the place, a sense that the air itself carried the whispers of prayers made centuries ago.

Soon, they arrived at the Yotsutsuji intersection, also known as *The Crossroads*. A famous lookout point that offered a breathtaking view of Kyoto below. The city spread out in a patchwork of rooftops and temples framed by the distant, misty mountains.

The group paused to take in the view.

Burton stood quietly next to Abi, his breath puffing clouds in the cold air. "It feels like we're in another world," he murmured.

Given a moment to appreciate the vista before leading them onward, their guide added, "From here," he said, "we begin ascending the mountain. Fushimi Inari has over ten thousand torii gates, and the higher we go, the quieter it becomes. Few visitors make it this far."

The silence grew as they walked deeper into the forest, passing more shrines along the way. One shrine, small and almost hidden beneath the torii gates, caught Hiro's attention. He stopped before it, gesturing for the group to gather around.

"According to local folklore, Ganrikisha Shrine is home to a particularly powerful kitsune. It's said that this kitsune can shape-shift into a beautiful woman, using her powers to both help and deceive. Some believe that if you leave an offering here," he pointed to the ornate cloth garment around its neck, "the kitsune will protect you from betrayal, but others say she will test your honesty."

Reggie looked warily at the shrine, the fox statues guarding it appearing almost lifelike in the shadowy light. "And what happens if she doesn't like your offering?" he asked, half-joking but with a nervous edge.

Hiro smiled faintly. "If she does not approve, it's said misfortune will follow."

Ever curious, Abi stepped closer, her eyes scanning the offerings already left behind—small coins, folded paper, and the occasional sake bottle, all dusted lightly with snow. Something about the shrine's quiet, tucked-away presence made it feel more intimate than the larger, grander ones they had passed. Sadly, she did not have any coins to give. Thinking a moment, she took her Burch notebook from her bag and wrote something on a piece of paper before ripping the page out. Slowly recalling the steps to making an origami crane, she began folding the paper this way and that way with precision.

"What are you doing?" Shane asked curiously.

"I don't have any coins to offer, so I thought I'd do this instead."

Watching Abi from a fair distance, Burton could see what she was making and inched closer.

"I remember reading about a survivor of Hiroshima - a little girl who folded a thousand cranes while going through cancer five years after the bombing. While she was sick, she was very tolerant of the pain and suffering and didn't want anyone to worry. Not once did she complain to her friends or family. Her spirit encouraged others around her to speak of her bravery after she passed away. For some reason, that little girl came to mind just now. So, in honor of her, I will leave this crane and wish her a peaceful, eternal rest. Perhaps she will find my Mother amongst the clouds."

In awe of what Abi just said, Burton was speechless as he watched her put the finishing touches on her origami.

Bending the beak and the wings perfectly, she smiled. "There. Done." Approaching the Kifune, she bowed and held the tiny bird with both hands before placing it under the statue on the cloth, hoping her offering would be worthy.

Taken aback upon witnessing what Abi had done and said, Hiro walked up to her. "That has got to be the most beautiful offering I have ever witnessed. What a respectful act of kindness for a soul who has passed."

With tears in her eyes, she nodded and silently walked away.

Immediately, Shane and Burton looked at each other, realizing Abi was still very much dealing with the loss of her Mother.

Shane went after her as she continued walking down the path through the vermillion gates.

She felt his hand rest on the small of her back. Before he could speak, she said, "Don't say anything. I don't want to cry. Just want to enjoy the quiet. I like hearing the wind whistling through the trees. I feel like she's here."

"Who? The little girl?"

"No. My Mom."

Upon hearing that, he did as she asked while the two walked along in silence.

While threading through the arches, she caught a glimpse of a man emerging from behind the walls of a Shinto shrine. Dressed all in black with a hood over his head, she quickly veered away. Heart pumping, she tried to take a breath. When she glanced back to see if he'd followed them, she scanned left, then right, but the man was gone.

Having felt her hand grip his, Shane found her focused on something. It made him follow her line of sight.

"Did you see that?"

Not sure what she was referring to, he said, "Umm, see what?"

Afraid to bring it up, she replied, "Nothing," before glancing over her shoulder one last time to double-check. Thankfully, nobody was there.

| 22 |

The Summit

Sunday, December 17

Fushimi Inari Shrine

Midway up the mountain, they could hear Jade and Reggie locked in conversation despite hanging back and keeping to themselves. Their voices were hushed, but the intensity carried through the air.

Abi found Jade flashing a determined expression, her hands gesturing as she explained potential solutions to the family business dilemma now weighing on them. Slowing down and stepping aside, she waited for her friends to pass by before following behind them. Offering a distraction from her problems, she observed the two from afar.

"I still think you should speak to her," Jade said firmly, glancing at Reggie. "If your ex-fiancée is still open to the idea, maybe we can revisit the merger."

The guy's jaw went rigid. "Jade, I don't know about that..." he replied, shaking his head. "I believe that is a last resort."

Jade squinted, not in frustration, but in a calculating way, knowing she was right. Now, she had to convince him of it. "I get why you're hesitant," she said, her voice softening for a moment, "but if she's still on board, this could save everything. The merger could solve the cash flow issues, and I bet her family is still keen on expanding into that market."

With a heavy sigh, Reg ran a hand through his hair as they walked. He didn't want to go down that road for Jade's sake. He knew the emotional toll it had taken on her when things developed between him and the girl his father betrothed him to. But she had a point, and he couldn't deny that.

"If she says yes," Jade pressed strongly, "then I think we should fly there and talk to her in person. It's the right move."

Reggie hesitated reluctantly. He hated the idea of putting Jade in that position, forcing her to deal with his past, but he couldn't ignore the practicality of her suggestion. She was thinking with her head and didn't let her emotions get in the way. To her, it was just business.

"I don't want to do this," Reggie muttered under his breath, conflicted. "But...you do have a point." He seemed torn. "I'll think about it."

"Good," Jade replied with a small nod. "We'll figure it out. Together."

Up ahead, Burton slowed his pace, noticing the interactions between the happy couple, but soon, his focus gravitated to Abi. His expression shifted into something more serious as he tried to catch her attention. Despite Sara walking beside him, her arms clutching tightly around her body to stay warm, Burton glanced back at Shane. Giving the football player the eye, the guy knew he wanted to speak to Abi.

Silently agreeing, Shane suddenly stopped to tie his boot. "Go ahead. I'll catch up," he said.

Slowing his pace, Burton managed to fall back just enough to meet up with her.

"Hey. Noticed you were upset back there," Burton said quietly.

Thinking of the crane, the little girl, and her Mom, she turned to him. "It's nothing. I'm okay," she said, though it was clear she wasn't entirely fine. Checking on Shane's whereabouts, her eyes flitted toward the trail behind them and found him just raising himself off the ground from tying his laces.

"Don't worry about him. He did that on purpose."

"He did?" Surprised, she offered a small smile, appreciating his concern even if her mind was somewhere else. "So, you want the truth?"

"Always."

"I'm still processing the whole Mom thing and don't get me started on Dad," she admitted, quieter now. "But I'll be fine."

Before he could say anything more, Sara interrupted them, sharp and demanding. "Burton?" she said, waving him over. "Let's go!"

Unwavering, his gaze flicked between her and Abi while ignoring her rudeness. "One minute," he said, leaving no room for argument.

She didn't like that.

Glancing down at Abi, he could see a sense of fear develop as his girlfriend scowled. "Don't worry. I'll handle this."

"What are you going to say to her?"

"This jealousy thing is not working for me. At least Shane gets it."

"To a degree, I suppose." She checked to see how close her boyfriend was. "He, too, doesn't like us interacting."

"If it's alright, I want to talk to you without any interruptions later."

She nodded. "Okay. I'd like that."

Burton walked on ahead as Abi slowed her pace to wait for Shane. When he joined her, he asked, "What did he want?"

"He was just checking on me. He noticed I was upset earlier."

Taking her hand in his, he said, "If you need to talk, I'm here, too, you know."

Grateful to hear that, she smiled. Grabbing his hand with both of hers, she said, "Yes, I know. But I'm good. I promise."

While they walked along through the many shrines along the path, Shane could tell by her lack of conversation that Abi's mind was reeling. Immediately, he wondered what she wasn't telling him.

Catching up to Jade and Reggie ahead of them, the two were quieter now, with Reggie deep in thought, clearly considering Jade's many suggestions.

As the path narrowed between the closely packed torii gates, the light filtered through in thin golden beams. Despite how pretty it looked, Abi couldn't shake the lingering sense that something—or someone—was still watching them.

Hiro and Martin stopped at a small building.

"We are about halfway through the Inari hike now," their guide said. "Would anyone like some green tea to warm up? They also have coffee."

One by one, everyone agreed.

Gathering around, the man inside the building helped pour their drinks for them as they wrapped their fingers around the hot paper cups to warm their hands.

When everyone had theirs, Hiro said, "Just a bit of etiquette. It is frowned upon to walk and drink or eat at the same time. There is nothing worse than walking in a crowd and accidentally spilling something on someone. So, please finish your beverage here. Otherwise, you will also have to shlep your cup with you until we come across a proper receptacle to dispose of it."

"That is something I wasn't aware of," Abi said to Shane.

"Makes sense," he said while taking a sip of the tea.

Thankful for the chance to drink something warm, everyone disposed of their cups and got ready for the steep climb to Mitsurugisha Shrine at the top of the staircase after exploring the Yakunki-no Taki historical landmark.

Ascending the steps, under a series of torii gates, they reached the top, thankful to be on even ground. Upon threading through the two pagoda lanterns and another series of gates, their group continued on their way. Thick in the forest, they felt so far away from the sounds of the city. Abi took notice of the winds whistling through the trees as the branches swayed. Coming across another series of steps, Jade started to complain a bit.

Reggie tapped her on the shoulder to encourage the girl to keep going. "Think about how many calories you're burning, babe," he chuckled.

The girl smirked, then smiled, knowing he was right.

As the stairs got steeper, everyone began to slow their pace.

"Are we there yet?" Jade whined slightly.

"Almost at the summit, Miss!" Hiro bellowed from the steps ahead of her.

Arriving at the highest peak, Martin gathered everyone at the base of the sacred shrine as Hiro bowed before passing through the torii. Turning to the group, he said, Welcome to Ichinomine, on Mount Inari. We have reached the 233-meter summit. This is the home of Kamisha Shinseki. Wishes made here bring good luck in business."

This piqued Reggie's attention. He put up his hand. "And how do I go about doing that?"

"To offer up prayers?" the man asked.

"Yes, Sir," Reggie replied.

"Purchase an incense candle inside the store. Once you've done that, go through the purification ritual in the basin to the right," Hiro gestured with his hand. "Bow before the stone arch and ascend these steps."

The wealthy heir put up his hands. "Okay, wait. One step at a time." Quickly going into the shop, he bought an incense candle from the man inside. Handing it to Jade, he said, pointing to the basin, "Hold this while I do that."

Purifying his hands, he returned and bowed at the gate. Taking the incense candle from Jade, he joined Hiro at the top and mirrored the man as he bent at a slight angle with his hands together.

"I will leave you to your prayers," he said, stepping back from the young man.

The solemn atmosphere resonated as Reggie offered up his appeals in silence.

Overhead, the wind stirred the trees, adding an eerie yet peaceful whisper to the moment. Asking for guidance and the foresight to make the right decision, he knew he had to save Granddad's company from bankruptcy. Praying for the strength to go up against his father and take the helm, he felt a sense of desperation overwhelm him. Thinking of Jade and the promise they were about to make to one another, he hoped to be a supportive and loving husband. That is when it hit him. They were about to embark on adulthood sooner than later. It included starting a family with Jade in the future. The reality of it was both scary and exciting. "Family…" he whispered, thankful their friends were there to witness it. Turning, he found Jade a few feet behind him. She had gone through the rituals so she could join him. Reaching back to take hold of her, he said, "This will be something you and I will conquer together as husband and wife." His voice remained calm and certain.

Her eyes shimmered with unshed tears. "Yes, we will," she whispered. "I will never leave your side."

Stepping slowly toward the shrine, Reggie took the incense candle, lighting it with quiet reverence from a flame already burning. As he placed it among the others, the scent of sandalwood curled through the air. Together, they bowed, stepping back in unison. Reggie's arm slipped around Jade's shoulders—protective, steady as if shielding her from their unknown future.

"I love you," she whispered, her strength showing through despite the monumental task ahead.

Without hesitation, he peered into her eyes. "I love you more." To him, those words were a vow beyond the one they'd soon take.

Emotion swelled between them.

Witnessing it, Abi felt Shane's fingers brush against hers, a silent reassurance. She held on without thinking, finding comfort in the touch—a reminder she wasn't alone.

Across from them, Sara's guarded look diminished.

Even Burton, who was usually expressionless, watched the couple with quiet admiration.

The security team remained on high alert, their presence acknowledging what loomed ahead. But for this moment, even they seemed to recognize the gravity of what was happening.

Shane leaned closer. His comment was meant only for Abi. "This is what it's all about, isn't it?"

She didn't look away from the young couple, her heart full yet aching. "Standing together. Facing the world," she whispered. "No matter what life has in store."

| 23 |

#ReggieWilson

Leaving the summit, they started down the other side of the mountain toward the crossroads. Emerging on the right-hand side between the buildings, they took a moment to see the city lights of Kyoto amidst the snow falling lazily from the sky.

The paths, now quieter with fewer visitors, felt like a sacred retreat, the winter landscape adding a layer of tranquility to their journey. With each step, the stories of the shrines lingered in their minds, the ancient folklore weaving itself into the present as they returned to the world below.

More than ready to end their excursion, with numb cheeks and cold toes and fingers, they arrived back at the main shrine and took a few pictures with the torii gates before making their way back to the coach bus waiting for them in the parking lot.

Upon boarding, everyone collapsed in their seats, thankful to take a rest.

Martin stood at the front of the bus and did a head count. With their group present and accounted for, he gave the driver permission to get underway.

While leaving the shrine, they drove along a narrow waterway and crossed a bridge. Once on the other side, the driver entered a covered breezeway of a nice hotel.

When the vehicle came to a stop, Martin announced, "Welcome to the Ritz-Carlton. We are having dinner here at La Locanda Restaurant before making one last stop as per Mr. Coppersmith's request."

Shane smiled as Abi quickly turned to him, still wondering what he'd planned.

Knowing her all too well, he said, "Don't even ask," adding with a pleasant smile, "It's a surprise."

Excited to see where they'd go after dinner, everyone got off the bus and gathered around before following Hiro and Martin along the covered path to the main entrance. The glass doors slid open as they approached. Met by a feature wall of three-dimensional white flowers lining the lobby, everyone proceeded to the right and strolled down the contemporary hallway to the hostess podium at La Locanda.

Speaking to the woman, Hiro greeted her and gave her Martin's name.

She smiled graciously and led them to the middle of the restaurant. The group stepped into a beautifully recreated traditional Japanese room. Its timeless elegance was in stark contrast to the sleek, modern hotel surrounding it.

Hiro translated the woman's introduction to the space.

"Welcome to Ebisugawa-tei," he said while listening intently to her. "You have reserved the Goten and Chidori tables this evening. These rooms were once the townhouse of Denzaburo Fujita, the founder of the Fujita Industrial group. The 1907 structure was re-assembled as a private dining space and preserved for the ultimate culinary experience. The wood panels are extremely rare and are over 700 years old. Please have a seat and make yourselves comfortable. We will be with you shortly."

Thanking her with a respectful bow, Hiro clarified, "You have re-served both spaces."

When they gathered around the large circular table, their security took the rectangular one set for seven.

Burton moved closer to Abi. "Let me help you," he said, beating Shane to the punch.

"Thank you," she replied as he took her coat from her.

In his gentlemanly way, he pulled her chair out and waited for her to sit before gently sliding her forward and draping her jacket along the back.

Unfortunately, his strong presence did not go unnoticed by Sara and Shane. Before occupying the seat to her left, he did the same for Sara as she got settled beside him.

Admiring the Japanese screens with frosted panels, Abi scanned the room, remembering what the waitress had said about the history.

Not seeing any menus, Jade whispered, "How do we order?"

Overhearing the girl's comment to Reggie, Martin said, "We se-lected a prefixed fair this evening. It contains eight delicious courses. I am certain you will enjoy it."

Hearing this, Abi relaxed and placed her hands on her lap. Curious about their plans later, she leaned toward Shane and asked, "So, you won't even give me a hint?"

"About what?" he smiled mischievously.

"You know. After dinner."

"Oh, that." Getting settled, he replied, "Sorry, mum's the word."

Burton looked his way, aware that the guy had planned something special for his friend that night. Knowing what it was, happy he was going too, he waved their waitress down to order some red wine for the table.

Soon after, small amounts were poured into each glass, their plates arriving one by one amidst an abundance of conversation.

Jade and Reggie spoke with Martin about their wedding plans as the security team took turns eating and scanning the premises.

Indulging in a thoughtfully curated meal, they began with a delicate tartar made from fresh, local fish, served alongside a vibrant black rice and beets salad.

Unrolling her napkin and placing it on her lap as everyone did the same, Burton remarked, "Hard to believe we packed so much into just three days."

About to eat one of the beets, Abi said, "I feel like we've been gone a week already."

He sipped his wine. "This is just the beginning. There's so much more to see and do."

"But first things first," Jade intervened. "I need to marry this man."

Speaking of that, Martin decided to discuss the plan for the following day. "Tomorrow will be a busy one. We have dress and suit fittings. A floral and wedding ring appointment. Later in the day, we'll meet with the caterer."

Reggie took the hand of his bride-to-be just as his phone rang. Quickly slipping it from his pocket, he noticed the name on the screen. A grim look flashed across his face.

"Who is it?" Jade asked.

"Excuse me a moment." Not saying anymore, he got up and left the room as Bray and Andrew followed him.

Everyone turned to each other, concerned.

"It must be his dad," Jade said. "Only one person can have that effect on him." Worried, she got up and left.

Hoping to help the boy, Martin regally dabbed the corner of his mouth with his napkin and set it to the right of his plate. Calmly getting up, he grabbed his iPad. By the time he exited the restaurant, he found Reggie pacing the floor in the hallway, the cell phone melded to his ear. With his hand resting upon his head, Martin could tell the young man was frustrated. Their security team stayed at a distance but kept a keen eye on him.

"Is it his father?" Martin asked Andrew quietly.

"From what I gather, yes. I believe so, Sir."

Finding Jade with one arm wrapped around herself, biting her nails on the other, the gentleman stood beside them. When he opened his iPad and started recording, he prompted Reg to put the call on speaker.

Doing that, he noticed Burton, Shane, and Abi surface from the restaurant. Standing by in case Reg needed them, they silently listened in on the conversation.

His father's voice slithered through the speaker. "So, you thought you could get away with this? You do realize I have eyes everywhere. It didn't take much to find you."

Reg didn't respond.

"Haven't you learned? Everywhere you go, you always leave a trail. You can never outsmart me."

Hating the man more than ever, Reg didn't flinch. "Maybe, but at least I'm no longer pretending to be your son. I don't owe you any-thing."

His father interrupted. "Did you actually think I'd let you marry her?"

Jade looked up at Reggie. The guy hated that she heard his father say this.

"I own you," his father solidified. "Regardless of this ridiculous court order. You haven't won. Not yet."

Everyone was stunned by the manner in which he spoke to him. Reggie didn't deserve to be treated like that.

Shane could see the psychological damage inflicted on his friend from years of abuse. Until now, he didn't know the full extent of it.

Looking into Jade's eyes lovingly and gathering the courage to be the man she needed him to be, Reg said forcefully, "Are you done? It's my turn to speak now." Not hearing a rebuttal, he sternly revealed, "I am marrying Jade. I love her, and there is nothing you can do to stop me."

"Be careful what you wish for, boy," he scoffed.

Reggie knew a threat was coming.

"Wouldn't it be unfortunate if either of you had an accident?"

Everyone's eyes gravitated to the phone in Reggie's hand upon hearing what the man uttered.

"Typical. Here come the threats." He knew his father's ways all too well.

"No, count this as a warning. The last thing you want is to go to war with me. Those who do, do not walk away."

Deep in thought, listening intently, Martin crossed his arms in front of his chest. Resting his chin on his thumb as his pointer finger moved from left to right over his lips, he was mentally making a series of changes to their itinerary. Immediately, he motioned for Reggie to keep him talking.

"So, you'll take me out? Is that it?"

"You, like everyone else, are expendable. Don't think for a second that I won't waste an opportunity to crush you."

Reggie let out a slow exhale, his grip on Jade's hand tightening.

"I'll take that as a challenge... Dad."

The comment didn't go over well.

The man's voice darkened. "You will regret this decision, especially when I target the people you love in the process. Think long and hard." A sinister snicker followed. "I'll be watching your every move."

And with that, the line went dead.

Angry, Reg looked at the ceiling, almost shell-shocked.

Jade flashed a fearful look as she rubbed his back. "Are you alright?"

"I will be," is all he said.

"What does this mean?" The girl questioned. "Will he follow through on those threats?"

"Yes..." Turning to Martin, he asked, "How could he have possibly found out? I don't understand. We made all the reservations under Burton's name."

The clever man nodded as his mind analyzed every step they'd taken thus far. Opening his tablet again after ending the recording, he did a quick search on *#ReggieWilson*. Checking the images, he suddenly found countless pictures of them taken at the attractions they'd visited thus far.

Seeing them, Reggie was stunned. "We know that the guest at Roku took the one picture, but how did these people find me? I thought I'd be invisible here."

Circling back, Martin checked the headlines, assuming the news of the wedding had now leaked to the tabloids. Finding articles about the young couple rumored to be tying the knot, he said, "I knew it was just a matter of time." Not having a choice, he suggested, "I will put Plan B into action."

"Plan B?"

"We will have to do everything incognito. The venues associated with Plan B have VIP entrances, and I have NDAs ready for signing. We should be able to come and go without being detected. And the nondisclosures will guard us against anything getting out to the public."

"Are you sure? The last thing I want is my father showing up and ruining the wedding."

"Don't worry. Everything will be fine."

Trusting him and feeling reassured, Reggie took a breath.

Martin closed his iPad cover confidently. "We should return to the table."

Hesitant, Reg nodded and said, "Alright."

The group walked along together.

Placing his hand on his friend's shoulder, Shane said, "Don't worry, man. We've got your back."

The guy somehow managed a smile. "Appreciate that."

About to walk into the traditional Japanese VIP room, Burton pulled on Martin's arm, prompting him to stop. "I think this explains the craziness from the past couple of days. The teens. The man with the cane? It kinda makes sense now."

Martin exhaled sharply, looking away. "Perhaps," he muttered, thoughts racing. "We still need to confirm if Reggie's Father has connections to the Yakuza. If he does, this could complicate things for Nightfall."

Reggie, having pulled out Jade's chair for her to sit, caught the serious expressions on their faces and walked over.

Taking the lead, Burton quietly asked, point-blank, "Does your father have any connections to the Japanese mob?"

"The Yakuza?"

"You know of them?" Burton stated.

Reggie's eyes widened. "Honestly, I've heard him speak of the name before and wouldn't put it past him. He does business with shady people. That's why my granddad's company is in trouble—it's catching up to him."

Martin analyzed, "I believe the man is running scared. He's on the verge of ruin, and it seems he wants you to go down with the sinking ship."

"I will never let that happen." Reggie squared his shoulders. "I want to save the company. Can you help me do that?"

The two men exchanged a look. "We'll do what we can. Don't worry."

The young man exhaled, relieved to know he wasn't standing alone in this battle.

Noticing their main courses arriving, Martin motioned toward the table. "We should have a seat. Dinner is served."

A delicate rice pasta with tender squid and fresh arugula, a perfectly cooked local fish with sweet pepper and saffron sauce, and, for the meat lovers, a rich Wagyu beef sirloin served with pumpkin, chestnut, and truffle-infused potatoes got distributed around their tables.

As they ate, the group kept the conversation light. Reflecting on the past few days, they recalled the places they'd visited and the unexpected moments shared.

Burton nudged Abi playfully. "You're quiet. I can see you thinking a mile a minute."

One corner of her lips curled slightly. "Just taking it all in."

He caught the flicker of emotion beneath her words, a look he'd seen before. While everyone ate, he kept a watchful eye, knowing her thoughts were heavier than she let on.

Noticing he was fixated on Abi, Sara smirked while swirling her wine glass. "Well, I guess Japan's good at one thing—making food look fancy."

Knowing she meant the comment to sway him back to her, Burton did not reward it. Instead, his expression hardened with a hint of anger. "Well, some of us appreciate their great attention to detail." He could see that Sara was taken aback.

"Yes," Abi replied innocently, not aware of Sara's ill intentions. "Every dish is a work of art."

Burton smiled at her. "Couldn't agree more," he said as Sara sneered, and their hazelnut panna cotta from Pierre Hermé Paris got placed in front of them. An unforgettable dessert to end a nice meal.

When the staff cleared the dishes from the table, their waitress returned with the bill and hesitated before placing it beside Martin. About to reach for it, Burton extended his hand. Flipping open the folder, he glanced at the total and quickly calculated the tip. Lifting his hand to catch her attention, she brought over the card machine. When he slid his Amex Black into the slot, the thirty-five-hundred-dollar transaction got approved, and the receipt printed.

"Arigatō, sensei," she said before repeating in English, "Thank you. Sir."

He respectfully bowed when she handed him the slips of paper.

Gathering their things and putting on their coats and hats to greet the cold once more, Abi got excited. "Is it time for the surprise now, Martin?"

"Yes, Miss. But it is not my surprise to share." He looked over at Shane. "Mr. Coppersmith? Would you like to do the honors now or wait until we arrive at our destination?"

"What destination is that?" Abi asked with hands clutched together, her face brightening.

Seeing her almost vibrating, he said, "I think we should wait until we get there." Clearly not happy to hear that, Shane tried to diffuse her disappointment.

Their security led the way, with three of them in front and four bringing up the rear as the group proceeded towards the lobby.

Burton walked with the men, his posture straight. There was an air of quiet authority about him—calm and composed. He exuded confidence without needing to force it, his sharp gaze scanning their surroundings with calculated precision.

Abi noticed immediately—he hadn't spared Sara a glance, treating her like a shadow in his periphery.

Bothered by this, Sara kept to herself, knowing she'd have to make amends with the guy at some point and apologize for her actions rooted in jealousy.

Walking hand in hand through the doors and down the path leading to their coach bus parked in the breezeway, Abi and Shane inhaled some of the crisp night air.

Boarding, everyone took their seats. Not wasting time, they got underway.

Abi rubbed her palms together.

"Nervous?" Shane asked.

"No, just excited. I want to see what you planned."

"You're gonna love it," he said with a smile. "Trust me."

| 24 |

Lanterns of Light

Sunday, December 17

Heian Shrine

Eyes peeled, Abi watched as they crossed the bridge again and drove alongside the waterway. Veering right, they threaded through a questionable part of town.

Now dark, she said hesitantly, "This looks a bit sketchy."

"Don't worry. It's not far."

Slowing to maneuver a sharp right turn, their driver crossed over yet another bridge. The moment they did, the atmosphere changed. The area no longer looked scary. With uplit buildings and trees lining the center of the roadway, the man turned into a parking lot in front of the most incredible, red Japanese structure with a sloped green roof. Illuminated in red, blue, and purple floodlights, it gave it a fuchsia tinge.

When they disembarked from the vehicle, they caught sight of the various floral projections gracing the roofs of the buildings. It seemed the shrine had come alive for them this evening.

Led by Hiro through the Oten-mon gate into the courtyard inside, they marveled at the lights.

Before venturing to the ticket booth, Shane addressed everyone. "Today, I downloaded the app for this exhibit." Showing them his phone, their friends searched it up and did the same. Stepping toward a snow-white dandelion flower in the middle of the courtyard, Shane scanned the QR code on the black pedestal reader. Suddenly, an assortment of projected interactive flowers spread around their feet.

Abi's face brightened along with Jade's.

"Wow!" the girls said simultaneously. Their eyes filled with wonderment.

Proud that he arranged this for the ladies, Shane watched as they interacted with the art installation.

Giving others a chance to experience it, they followed Hiro to the building on the left-hand side to purchase their garden admission tickets at the booth.

Set to pay the bill, Burton pulled out a money clip of cash.

Immediately, Shane noticed and put out his hand to stop him. "No, I got it," he said, taking the Yen from his passport pouch.

"Are you sure?" the celebrity asked.

"Absolutely." Quickly taking a headcount, Shane noticed someone was missing. "Is Martin not joining us?"

Burton answered, "No, he wanted to stay back and make new arrangements for the wedding."

"I will be helping him with that, so please don't include me," Hiro added as Shane requested, "Can you tell her we need thirteen garden tickets and three lanterns?"

"Certainly." Relaying Shane's request to the young woman behind the counter, she smiled and slid the passes across the desk before placing three LED paper lanterns beside them. Hearing the cost of thirteen thousand Yen, Shane counted out the bills and passed them to her with two hands.

She accepted the money and bowed. "Arigatō," she said graciously.

Returning the gesture with respect, Shane took their tickets before handing Sara, Jade, and Abi the glowing spheres of light, each thanking him in the process.

"Which way do we go?" Jade asked, spotting others entering through the gates on the left. "I guess we head that way?"

Moving along to the entrance, Hiro said, "You go in here and end up wrapping around to the right and exiting on that side. We will be waiting for you out front."

Burton nodded. "Sounds good."

Seeing the stenciled pattern the lantern created on the ground by their feet, Abi said to Shane, "How cool is that?" In amazement, she was immersed in the tranquility of it.

Climbing the steps, they walked through the archway and into the garden beyond. The path, lined with small pillars of light, led to an uplit forest.

Stopping in her tracks, Abi admired the view.

Shane looked back, still holding her hand.

"This is absolutely magical," she gushed.

Sara and Burton passed them by while Lorenzo, Bray, and Ethan followed their boss through the darkness.

"Unbelievable..." Jade exhaled, clutching Reggie's hand.

Not knowing what to say, since words could never describe it, all Abi could add was, "I love it."

He wrapped his arms around her shoulders. "I'm glad."

"This was an amazing idea. Thank you for arranging it for us."

"You're welcome."

Able to overhear their conversation, Burton lowered his head and smiled, pleased to hear Abi was so happy.

While meandering along the path through the trees, following the string of lights, the scene reminded Abi of a fairy garden. In the air, they could hear sounds resembling that of pixie dust and calming tones creating this otherworldly atmosphere.

Rather mischievously, Shane pulled his girlfriend aside, a sly grin playing on his lips as he gently took her lantern from her hands. The light from it flickered across his face, making his blue eyes gleam. Handing the lantern over to Matt, he said, "Wait here. We'll be right back."

Before she could question him, he intertwined his fingers with hers and led her behind a patch of towering evergreens. The night was crisp, scented with pine and the distant hint of woodsmoke. A hush settled around them.

"What are you doing?" she giggled quietly, feeling the thrill of being stolen away into the dark. The moonlight barely touched them through the dense branches, making his features hazy, but his presence was unmistakable—strong, warm, and so very close.

Shane didn't answer. Instead, he wrapped his arms around her waist, pulling her against him with a quiet urgency, as if he needed to feel her, hold her, breathe her in. Her pulse quickened. He brushed a stray lock of hair from her cheek, his fingertips featherlight, sending a series of shivers through her.

Then, slowly, he leaned in.

His lips met hers in a kiss so tender yet so deep it stole the breath from her lungs. The world tilted, and for a moment, there was nothing but the steady strength of his hands and their hearts beating as one.

When he pulled away, his forehead rested against hers, his breath warm against her lips. "Sorry," he muttered huskily. "I've been wanting to do that all day. Couldn't wait any longer."

A laugh escaped, but faded when he hugged her—tightly, fiercely, as though letting go wasn't an option. "I love you," he said, pressing a lingering kiss to her temple.

Comforted, she could feel him whisper against her skin, melting through her defenses. "Love you, too," she expressed as her heart fluttered.

And at that moment, wrapped in his arms beneath the canopy of winter stars, she knew—this wasn't just a fleeting romance.

Each heard Matt clear his throat loudly, assuming they were no longer alone. Hearing people venturing towards them, they casually returned to the security guard and took the lantern back.

A pang of guilt hit her. "We probably shouldn't have done that. I hope we didn't defile a sacred place."

Shane tried to diffuse her anxiousness. "I'm sure it's fine." Squeezing her hand, they went to catch up to their friends.

Stopping alongside the pond, they found Burton deep in conversation with Sara. It seemed she was trying to talk things through while admiring the projections of a dragon flashing across the building.

Continuously keeping tabs on Abi, having briefly lost sight of her, Burton wondered where the two had disappeared moments ago.

Sara saw this. Not saying another word, she left and walked toward the exit.

Burton didn't stop her.

Unaware of what had happened, Abi watched the snowflakes fall through the air, adding to the whimsical evening as they admired the projections.

Looking for input, Shane got closer and whispered in her ear, "So? Good surprise?"

Without hesitation, she replied, "Are you kidding?"

He could see her eyes dancing with delight.

Despite being surrounded by darkness, Abi wasn't afraid.

When the presentation ended, they walked along the path to a covered bridge. To the left of the entrance, they discovered another QR code pedestal. Shane took out his phone and scanned the reader. When he did that, the lanterns hanging in a line down the center of the entire roof changed color and projected the stenciled patterns on the floor, adding mystic sounds as if it were a scene from Harry Potter.

Crossing the bridge with their security close by, they stopped midway to watch the next projection on the shrine windows. Abi and Shane leaned on the railing. She barely noticed the cold nipping at her cheeks. The scene before them was mesmerizing. Across the water, bathed in vivid colors from the art projections that shimmered on the surface, swirls of light transformed the ancient structure, casting another dragon-like figure that seemed to pulse with life.

Hues of purple, blue, red, and gold transformed the forest into something out of a fairy tale. Snow drifted down like glittering diamonds, catching the light and making everything shimmer.

Shane gently squeezed Abi's hand, drawing her from the trance of the display. His breath curled in the crisp air as he whispered, "I'm glad I came on this trip with you."

Lovingly looking up at him, she smiled. "I'm glad you did, too."

Across the way, Burton caught her eye and dipped his chin in his usual silent check-in manner.

Her face brightened to acknowledge she was fine, then she wrapped her arms around Shane's waist.

He pulled her closer as they stood quietly, taking it all in.

Even Reggie and Jade, usually so chatty, were speechless, their fingers intertwined as they watched.

The shifting colors deepened—blues and purples melting into fiery reds and oranges. A dragon emerged in the water's reflection, its body rippling as if ready to break free.

The snow thickened, casting a hushed stillness over the group, broken only by the occasional gasp of wonder.

Abi's heart pounded—not from fear, but from sheer awe. The lights, the snow, the ancient shrine—it felt like stepping into a dream.

She leaned into Shane and whispered, "This is just magical."

He turned to her, brushing his thumb gently over the back of her hand. "I hoped by bringing you here, the beauty of this place would lessen the grief of the holidays," he said sincerely. "I just wanted to give you a moment to breathe. A moment where you could feel happy, even just for a little while."

"Oh, Shane..." Her heart twisted at his thoughtfulness. Despite everything that had happened, he was still intent on shielding her—even from the things nobody could fix.

He reached up, tucking a strand of hair behind her ear, his touch lingering as he searched her face. "I know I can't take away everything that hurts," he admitted. "But I can be here with you. And I will be. Always."

Hearing that, she felt so loved.

Amidst the serene blend of blue and white, Abi barely noticed the sound of footsteps echoing across the wooden planks. At first, they seemed unremarkable, lost in the hush of the winter night. But then—another sound joined them. A sharp *tap*. A rhythmic strike that followed each step, distinct and measured.

It took her a moment to place it.

They weren't just footsteps. But a cane.

The realization sent a chill skittering down her spine. The steady *thud* grew louder, each impact like the ticking of a clock, counting down. With every beat, the sound drew closer and closer.

Abi exhaled fearfully. Whoever it belonged to was right behind them. Her body straightened as the breath left her lungs. "Do you hear that?" she whispered, grabbing Shane's arm.

"What is it?" he asked. Seeing the terror in her eyes sparked his protectiveness.

"It's him," she stammered, her head on a swivel, barely able to spew the words.

Shane tightened his grip on her and scoured their surroundings before spotting the eerie presence approaching. Immediately shielding Abi, he put himself between her and the tall man.

Wearing a black hooded jacket, the rhythmic thud of his cane against the planks continued slicing through the silence, piece by piece.

She tried to swallow the knot in her throat and ignore the gnawing dread in her gut. But when the man slowly passed, a shiver prickled her skin. Stealing a glance over her shoulder, she froze. Surprisingly, his focus wasn't on her. His gaze, piercing and calculated, was locked onto Jade and Reggie. Both were oblivious, quietly chatting as they admired the lights, unaware of the predator in their midst.

As if sensing her stare, the ominous figure suddenly snapped his head toward her.

Terrified, she couldn't bring herself to look away.

The lights from the display flickered across his face, exposing every unsettling detail—the deep-set wrinkles, the ghostly pale skin, the cold, soulless eyes that seemed to reach inside her and strip her bare. A bone-deep fear gripped her, primal and paralyzing, when he tapped the cane on the wood.

Her eyes dropped to his hand. Heavily tattooed fingers curled around its handle. After spying a bird etched into it, she caught sight of something horrific.

"His pinky finger..." she said under her breath, just enough for Shane to hear. "It's missing..."

Guarded, he bravely stared him down, unsure if it was the same guy from the Golden Temple. Soon, Shane veered to Burton.

They didn't speak. There was no need to.

The second his eyes gravitated to the sinister character, Abi heard Burton call out for his men.

"Guys! Three o'clock!"

It seemed their actions were muffled by the loud sound of her heart thumping in her chest. Amidst it all, she gasped and said, "Oh my god..." as the man bolted toward the end of the bridge and somehow slipped past them before disappearing into the thick, all-consuming darkness.

Andrew quickly approached.

"I'm pretty sure that was the same man from the Golden Pavilion," she said, "The one I saw watching us."

Burton joined them. "Was that him?"

Her hands shaking and voice vibrating, she replied, "Yes, but this time, I clearly saw him, and the tattoos on his hands. The tip of his baby finger was missing."

When she said that, Andrew shot Burton a look. They now knew exactly what they were dealing with.

Surprised by the detail she'd picked up on, Burton immediately motioned to Lorenzo, Bray, and Ethan. "Search the grounds!" he shouted. "Find him! Now!"

With their bright penlights turned on, hands resting on their holstered weapons, his men bolted toward the end of the bridge and fanned out in search of him.

Taking charge, Burton stood beside Shane. "Come on," he said in a commanding tone. "We gotta move."

Shane agreed.

Fearful of what was unfolding, Jade grabbed hold of Reg as she searched the shadows for any movement.

"You're okay, babe. I'm here. Stay close," he said to her.

Led off the bridge by Ted and Rob, the couples made their way down the path with Andrew and Matt following behind them.

Lanterns in hand, they passed the lights to a man collecting them at the exit.

Before emerging in the courtyard, Ted and Rob scanned the place from left to right. Opting to follow the buildings and stay away from the open areas, the guys corralled them to the far left side and swiftly kept them moving all the way to the front, sticking close to the tree line on the way out.

Thankfully, Andrew had already notified Martin they were on their way. Ready for them, Sara met the men and helped create a barrier as the group boarded the bus.

Within minutes, Lorenzo, Bray, and Ethan crossed the road to join them.

"Anything?" Martin asked as they got in.

"Nothing..."

Shane heard this.

As the vehicle started moving down the street, Burton spoke with Martin near the front. Stabilizing themselves as the Sprinter swayed from side to side, he told him, "Abi said she saw the same guy," while Sara listened in.

"How can she be sure? It's dark." His girlfriend was skeptical.

While Martin gave their driver instructions, Burton sternly stared the girl down. "If she says she saw him. I believe her."

Overhearing, his right-hand man faced his boss once again. "Even if we got camera footage, it would be hard to ID him at night."

"Exactly," the girl smirked.

Raising a hand for her to stop, Burton pointed out, "That's what? Three times now? It's not a coincidence. We need to find out who he is and what he wants."

Intent on joining their discussion, Shane said to Abi, "Give me a minute," before letting go of her hand and walking toward the men.

She watched her best friend eye up her boyfriend on the way over and hoped the conversation wouldn't start a fight.

In a low tone, he looked Burton in the eye and asked, "Who is that guy? Whatever you know, I want in."

With arms crossed over his chest, Burton was careful how he responded. "We are still trying to determine that."

Guiding their driver, Martin told him, "Please proceed to the extraction point."

"Extraction? For whom?" Shane questioned.

Zeroed in on him, Lorenzo stood tall. "Why don't you go and sit down and let us do our job?"

The guy's threatening manner set Shane off. Straightening up, puffing his chest, he said, "Let's talk about your job. How is it that Abi's spotted the guy more than once, and you, so-called professionals, haven't seen a thing?"

The men smirked angrily.

"Who says we haven't?" Lorenzo stated as the football player glared.

"So you know more than you're letting on?"

Burton stepped between them. "That's enough."

About to speak, hoping to bring things down a notch, Martin said, "If I may…"

Shane jumped on that. "No, Martin. Sorry. Save it. I need you to include me in whatever is happening here."

Backing his friend, Reggie stepped up. "I agree with Shane. If we're in danger, we need to know." He slipped his hands in his pockets.

Lowering his voice, Shane said under his breath, not wanting Abi to hear, "If there's a problem, you need to tell us."

Burton paused. "Fine. Once we know more, I will make sure you guys stay in the loop."

Happy with that, both turned around and went back to the girls.

When Shane sat down beside Abi, he could see she wasn't happy with how he'd dealt with things. "Don't be mad," he said, eyes focused straight ahead.

"I'm not. But that was a bit harsh. Don't you think?"

"No, I don't." He tapped his hand on her knee. "Look, if we are in danger, they shouldn't be keeping that from us."

She realized he was right.

Lifting his arm over her head, she inched closer to him. "I promise. As long as you're with me, I'll keep you safe."

After he said that, Abi watched Lorenzo take point behind the driver while Hiro translated for him.

"Tell the guy – we need to crisscross the city before going to the rendezvous point," the security guard instructed.

"Why aren't we going to the hotel?" Abi questioned quietly.

Giving them the benefit of the doubt, Shane said, "Let's wait and see how this plays out. If we don't like it, we can split up."

Not in favor of that, she replied, "I'm sure we will be back at Aman Kyoto soon."

Veering toward the downtown with the buildings getting taller and less residential, she heard Burton ask Lorenzo, "Anything?"

"Nothing. I believe it's safe to proceed."

Nodding to the driver, who was peering up into his rearview mirror, Burton nodded. "Let's get this done."

They made sure Hiro clarified their instructions. Relaying everything in Japanese, the translator turned to them when he had finished talking. "He understands what to do."

"Perfect. What's the ETA?" Burton asked.

Already calculating that, Lorenzo looked down at his GPS. "Fifteen minutes."

"Alright."

Martin stood up between the seats. "May I have your attention, please?" Looking at Shane, Abi, Jade, and Reggie, he said, "Little change of plans tonight. We are heading back to Aman Kyoto shortly. When we arrive, I need you to pack your belongings as quickly and efficiently as possible and hand off your suitcases to the staff when they come by to collect the bags. We will be moving hotels as a precaution."

Fussy about where they would be staying, Jade asked, "What hotel?"

Unable to answer that in the presence of the driver, he said, giving the girl the eye, "I will provide that information upon arrival." Reading their faces, he clarified, "Understood?"

Each of them either nodded or answered, "Got it."

Abi got up and scooched by Shane. "Where are you going?"

She raised her pointer finger. "One second."

Moving forward, she plopped down across the aisle from Burton.

He was surprised to see her there. "I assume you have something to say."

"There's one more detail I forgot to share." She leaned in and prompted him to do the same.

Whispering in his ear, she said, "When the man passed by, he wasn't looking at me and Shane or you. I saw his eyes locked on Jade and Reg," she revealed, hoping their friends hadn't heard her.

Burton straightened up. Signaling for Lorenzo to come over, the guy knelt in the aisle.

"What's up, Sir?"

Keeping a low tone, he said, "The target might not be Abi. Sounds like it may be Wilson and Webber."

Martin overheard him and took out his iPad to search for anything, making the rounds on the wire.

"Thanks for the info, Abs." Seeing the worry on her face, Burton reassured her, "Everything's gonna be fine. Trust me."

She nodded silently. "I do."

"Good."

Returning to Shane at the back of the bus, she smiled at her friends on the way by. Not wanting to ruin their wedding with bad news, she kept quiet - at least for now.

| 25 |

Security Breach

Sunday, December 17

Downtown Kyoto

Arriving in the downtown district, the driver looped around and doubled back between two large buildings before signaling and disappearing into an underground parking garage.

"What are we doing here?" Reg said aloud, turning to look at his friend.

Shane raised a hand to calm the guy down. "Just wait."

Standing, Martin once again announced, "We are changing vehicles as a precaution. Nothing more. We have three vans waiting to transport us to Aman. Shane and Reg go with the girls, Andrew, and Ted. Sir, you and Sara are with Lorenzo, Bray, and Ethan. Anton, you will be with me, Rob, and Matt." Turning to their young translator, he said, "I apologize, Hiro, but this is where we leave you."

Unsure exactly what was going on, he replied, "That is fine. I will catch the subway. It goes right past my place."

"Very good."

When they stopped beside three vans parked in a row, the driver slid open the door.

"Make sure you have everything," Martin warned. "We need to make this quick."

Assigned their vehicles, the group transferred when their security gave them the signal. Parting ways, Abi looked at Burton.

Before she got in the van with her friends, he stopped her and said, "I'll see you there."

"Okay," she nodded and found a seat as he raised a steady hand. While walking away, he peered over his shoulder and got in the other van.

The vehicles left in a hurry.

Following Burton, with Anton and Martin close behind, they all left the parking garage and approached the main street.

When one vehicle went left and the other right, Abi shouted, "Wait! Are we going the wrong way?"

Hearing that put Jade in a panic.

Intent on calming her down, Andrew turned and said, "This is standard, Miss. We do this tactical maneuver all the time. Just adhering to protocol. It's a textbook staggered departure. We will be heading in different directions."

Shane pulled Abi back and got her settled. "Abs, relax. They know what they're doing."

"Oh, now you think we're doing our job?" Andrew smirked. "Good to know."

"Look, man. I don't know you very well. We've barely spoken, but out of all you guys, I think I trust you the most. You've been there for Abs all this time and kept her safe. I respect that."

Not responding, he simply nodded once to acknowledge the compliment.

After taking the long way back to their hotel, the driver pulled through the gates. They were the only ones there.

"Where is everybody?" Abi got worried.

Checking his phone, he messaged Matt and Ethan. In seconds, he got a response. "Their ETAs are ten and twelve minutes, respectively."

Stopping outside the gate, Andrew slid the side door open.

"Remember what Martin said. Gather your things and pack up. Have your bags ready for the stuff to collect on the cart. I will stick with you as a precaution." Turning to Ted, he said, "You go ahead to the room and do the same. When you finish, we'll switch."

"Got it."

While they walked away, Abi saw their van leave. "Who will be driving us to the new location?"

Andrew smiled partially. "Fresh eyes," is all he said.

About to make their way to their pavilions on the hillside, Ted peeled off from the group. They went left while he went straight ahead and followed the path.

As the snow lightly fell, it dusted everything around them as they climbed the slope. Concerned about what was happening, Jade and Abi stayed quiet as they walked along. The weight of their situation, now very real.

Outside their pavilion, the man stood where he could keep an eye on both doors. "Be outside in fifteen minutes, tops. Make sure nothing is left behind."

Everyone nodded as Shane and Reggie opened their rooms simultaneously.

Dipping inside, Abi removed her boots at the door, put it in high gear, and started gathering her things from the bathroom while Shane moved their suitcases from the closet to the bed.

Still folding her clothes, Abi took the Red Dragon tote bag from the welcome basket and placed her toiletries in it. The last thing she wanted was the liquids leaking into her suitcase.

Watching Shane haphazardly toss his things together, she chuckled.

"What?" he laughed, knowing his was the opposite of hers. "The guy said not to be neat. I'm just following instructions."

Unable to go against the grain and do that herself, she continued packing. Amidst their conversation, she spotted the Red Dragon bookmark. It had moved from the waste paper basket to the inside page of her novel.

"I guess housekeeping thought it fell in there by mistake," she whispered.

"What was that?" Shane asked, not hearing her clearly.

She held up the bookmark. "The maid must have thought it fell into the trash. They put it back inside the pages."

Opening the book, she stared at it, contemplating what to do, recalling the words displayed on the front. Strangely not as fearful as she once was, she kept it, knowing it was evidence of something they still needed to solve. Despite being uneasy, she got down to business and slipped the book into her tote.

Soon, with everything packed and accounted for, Abi looked around the room. "I think that's it," she said before zipping the bag shut.

Shane did the same and lifted both suitcases off the bed to wheel them to the door.

Setting her bags beside them, she watched him grab his backpack from the closet.

With one final sweep, he said, "Think we're good to go," and carried their stuff outside.

She double-checked the bathroom and started turning off the lights. Slipping on her boots, not having any idea where they were going next, Abi hoped the place was just as nice as this one. Knowing Burton, she figured it would be.

Peeking outside, she found Shane loading their luggage on the trolley cart while speaking to Andrew.

Just then, Reggie emerged and did the same.

Out in the cold, Abi bundled up her neck and placed their carry-on bags on the step as the door closed behind her. Turning to her left, she found Burton and Sara climbing the hill. "Hey, you made it," she greeted, noticing his girlfriend scowling.

He smiled at her. "Looks like we are the last to arrive."

The luggage cart moved on toward his pavilion.

On their way past them, he said, "We will make it quick and meet you at the gate shortly."

"Alright," Abi replied while Sara suddenly took hold of Burton's hand.

Flinching, he looked down at it, almost contemplating what to do. Keeping the peace, he held on while they made their way to the next building.

With both backpacks hanging off his shoulder, Shane handed Abi the LV bag and took hold of her Red Dragon tote.

"Are you sure that's not too heavy?" she asked.

Positioning the straps, he chuckled, "Abs, I bench 225. I think I can handle it."

Easily seeing his muscles bulging under his feather-lite down jacket, she lightly giggled. "Guess you're right."

Lazy flakes continued to fall to the ground and caught the light here and there as they joined Reg and Jade to head down the path. Upon reaching the welcome pavilion, they found some of their group gathered inside. Martin and Anton were already there.

"Remain in the building. I will be right back," Andrew said to Abi. "I'm just going to go and pack my things."

"Okay. No problem," she said.

Reg opened the door for everyone. The girls walked inside first.

Curious as to the plan that evening, Jade asked, "So, Martin? We are we headed?"

He answered. "The Park Hyatt. A wall encapsulates the property. We will be safe there. It is more confined, not as open. They also have a VIP entrance that's hidden. Nobody will see us arriving."

Jade realized they were leaving this area of Kyoto. "I'm assuming this means no wedding?"

"Oh, there will be a wedding, Miss. I promise." Confident, Martin smiled. "You will love it."

Her face brightened as she clutched her hands under her chin. "Really?"

"One must always adapt, given any situation."

Eyes glistening, she said, "Thank you," while Reg stood to her left and gave her a side hug.

"You are very welcome," he nodded regally with a modest bow.

Just then, they saw three sets of headlights brightening the darkness. Finding black Escalades arriving, the concierge immediately began loading their luggage according to Martin's instructions as soon as they parked.

"Everybody good?" Burton asked, checking on Abi first as Sara glared. Met by a number of positive reactions and nods, he glanced at his watch. "We're making good time."

Andrew and Lorenzo flung their bags into the back of one SUV.

Listening to Martin's instructions, their security team discussed the transition and arrival procedures for their new destination.

When he returned inside, he advised everyone, "Stay in your assigned groups from the last transfer. When we arrive at the hotel, please remain in the vehicles until I give the signal." Ready to go, he said, "Alright. Let's move on then."

Sadly, leaving the picturesque resort behind, the driveway lightly dusted with snow, Abi and Shane got into the third row this time while Jade and Reg took a seat in the middle.

Snuggling up to Shane, he lifted his arm to hold her close. "Tired?" he asked.

"For whatever reason, since we got here, I feel exhausted all the time. Guess it's just a bit of jet lag, maybe. Perhaps it's the stress of everything going on."

Jade tapped Andrew on the shoulder.

The guy turned around.

"How long is the drive?" she asked.

"Twenty-three minutes from door to door, Miss."

Departing in the darkness, already missing the Aman Kyoto and the peacefulness it offered, Abi was sad to know she would never have another opportunity to experience such a wonderful place. She wished she had taken more photos. Promising herself to do a better job at documenting the trip and preserving their memories, she snapped a pic of Reggie's silhouette in front of them with Jade's head resting upon his shoulder.

Turning to Shane, he raised the phone and said, "Smile."

Obliging, she did just that. "This is my first trip abroad and our first trip together."

"What about Cabo?"

"That was a day trip. I feel this is a real vacation."

Clutching her tightly, he replied, "I don't know. I kinda liked that time away."

Fondly recalling the closeness that developed between them and their friends during that Baja adventure, she looked up at Shane.

Not giving it a second thought, he kissed her lips. "Love you," he whispered in her ear.

"Love you, too."

| 26 |

The Switch

Sunday, December 17

Park Hyatt, Kyoto

While weaving through the city, they passed by the National Gardens and crossed the bridge where the Takano and Kamo Rivers merge. The roads were quiet as they drifted south toward the Kyoto University campus. Bare trees and evergreen shrubbery lined the route. Somehow, the trip seemed to take more than half an hour.

When their driver slowed down, they passed through a large gray stone torii arch before continuing down the narrow road, unsure if they were heading the right way. Abi sat up and leaned forward to see where they were going.

Moving up a hill, they saw another torii gate coming into view in the distance.

Abi marveled at the Park Hyatt Kyoto as they drove into the roundabout. Warm lighting accented the hotel, illuminating it against the night sky as golden streams softened its sharp edges. The surrounding gardens, carefully manicured, shimmered with a hint of snow while shadows danced beneath the trees. Beyond the hotel, the faint silhouette of Kyoto's Hōkan-ji pagoda graced the serene backdrop, making the entire scene feel like a hidden oasis nestled in the heart of the city. It was a place that seemed both timeless and luxurious.

Passing the main entrance, the drivers moved into the parking garage and turned right. Stopping there, the concierge began unloading their baggage.

"Stay seated," Andrew said. "We need to wait until Martin gives the word."

Seeing the older gentleman leave the SUV in front of them, iPad in hand, he soon disappeared with Matt and Ted by his side.

"How can you be so calm?" Jade questioned. "Isn't this stressful?"

He glanced back at her. "No. This happens all the time."

"Good to know," she replied, leaning back against the seat. "Oh… I hope he makes this quick. I'm exhausted. Wouldn't mind a bath before bed," Jade whined.

"Yes, that sounds like a nice way to warm up," Abi agreed.

Receiving a text, Andrew looked down at his phone. Scanning the premises, he noticed Martin emerge and jump into the SUV. "Follow them," he said to the driver.

Upon rounding the corner, they moved toward the rear of the place. There, they found a set of double doors. Two men, dressed sharply in hotel-crested suits, greeted them.

"Right this way, please," the one said as they got out.

Shane grabbed their backpacks and Abi's Red Dragon bag while she slid her LV tote on her shoulder. Walking hand in hand with Shane amongst their friends, she noticed Burton glance over.

Inside the hallway, just past the entryway, the group gathered at a set of elevators.

"This will take you directly to your rooms on the highest floor," the other man informed as he held the lift for them.

Abi stayed back. "You and Sara go first with the guys. We will follow," she said.

About to state otherwise, Sara piped up. "Thanks, Abi," before stepping aboard. Seeing Burton wasn't moving, she added, "Come on, B."

Lorenzo, Ethan, and Rob waited for further instructions.

Martin prompted, "Go ahead, Sir. We will chat before you turn in for the night."

Hearing this, Burton conceded, not liking the fact that he was leaving Abi behind.

At the last second, Anton silently joined his boss.

When the doors closed, they waited for another elevator. Once it arrived, the men and Jade, Reg, Abi, and Shane packed in like sardines. Each chuckling bit to themselves, they soon arrived on the top floor to a flurry of activity.

The concierge had parked the baggage carts along the corridor. Smack dab in the middle of the action with his iPad in hand and a number of room keys, Martin instructed them as to where their bags got delivered.

"Miss Abi, you and Mr. Coppersmith are in room 701. Miss Webber? Mr. Wilson? You are in 702," he pointed at the opposite end of the hall. "Andrew and Ted, you are in room 704 to watch over them."

"Very well, Sir," the men said almost simultaneously.

"Are we all on the same level?" Abi asked, looking for Burton.

He knew what she was alluding to. "Master B is at the other end of the hall, Miss."

Shane turned to her, not at all surprised.

Uncomfortable, she tried to save face. "Just want to make sure we are all together. Not spread out."

"Before we call it a night, I will be ordering breakfast to your rooms in the morning. Listen for the delivery at nine o'clock. As mentioned, we have several wedding details to contend with tomorrow. Be sure to meet at the elevators promptly at ten thirty, dressed presentably for our outing."

Everyone acknowledged him.

Given their card key, Shane walked along to their room.

"Night, you guys," Jade said before disappearing into theirs.

Abi waved. "Night. Sweet dreams."

When they walked inside, they found a long corridor with storage closets and a black granite entryway table to their left. Hanging their jackets on the hooks, they took off their boots. Shane rolled their suitcases out of the way.

"Hey... It seems we have adjoining rooms with Reg and Jade," he pointed to the passageway.

"Don't open it. I'm tired and really need a break from everyone."

He moved toward her with open arms and asked, "Even me?"

Tilting her head, she said, "No. I'm not sick of you yet."

Thankful to hear that, he leaned in as his lips brushed hers lovingly. Parting ways, he added, "Let's see the rest."

About to pass the entrance to the bathroom, Abi stopped and couldn't help but walk in.

"Wow. Look at this. It's a wet room." She stepped inside the glass-enclosed shower with natural wood planks on the ceiling and marble on the walls and floor. Admiring the double sinks and the private water closet, she found another doorway connected to the bedroom. Beyond the king-sized bed was the most spectacular view. Under the sloped ceiling was a wall of glass that framed the five-story pagoda, shining brightly against the darkened sky. High above the rooftops, she rounded the bed and walked toward the view, speechless.

"That is something you don't see every day," Shane said.

"Now it feels like we are truly in Japan."

"I agree." He turned around. "So, what do you think of the place? Like it?"

"It's nice. It's not as secluded as Aman, but maybe that's a good thing. The security is much tighter. I like that we're higher up and all together."

"Definitely feels more secure." He went and sprawled out on his side of the bed. "Are you tired?" Shane asked, raising his arm to invite her in for a cuddle.

"A little. It's been a long day," Abi admitted, joining him. The closeness of the moment made her heart race, the simple gesture sending a flutter through her chest.

Clutching her tightly, he said, "Yes. It feels like we did a lot." His eyes locked on hers.

"My feet are killing me."

Reaching out, he said, "Give them here. I'll rub them for you."

She was surprised by his offer. "Really?"

"Absolutely."

Doing just that, propping it on top of his chest, he started with her toes and worked his hand to the heels and ankles. Abi felt like she was in heaven.

"Can you do this all the time?"

"If you'd like." He switched feet.

For a moment, neither of them spoke.

He could feel that Abi was still apprehensive, so he stayed mindful of that. Turning and finding her head resting peacefully on the pillow with eyes closed, he smiled. There was just something about how her hair cascaded over her shoulders. She looked so pretty. Almost angelic.

When he finished rubbing her feet, her eyes drifted open. "Thank you for that."

"Feel better?"

"Much."

When he rolled on his side, he inched closer and wrapped his arm around her waist. Pulling her in, his lips close to her ear, he whispered, "Being here with you...it's like everything else fades away."

The corner of Abi's mouth curled slightly as her eyes shimmered in the low light.

The world slowed to a standstill as he rested his forehead lightly against hers.

His breath felt warm against her skin.

"I love you," Shane whispered.

Her heart skipped a beat. About to close her eyes, she said quietly, "Love you, too."

Wanting to kiss her, he lifted her chin upward as her eyes drifted closed.

Amidst the peacefulness, Shane pressed his lips gently to hers. Tender and sweet, he could slowly feel her body stiffen, making him back off. "Want to go first?" Shane asked casually.

Distracted, Abi looked at him. "Sorry, what was that?"

He pointed toward the bathroom. "Do you want to use it first?"

"Oh, umm, sure. I'll be quick," she replied, anxiety surfacing.

"Take your time," Shane said, lying down on the bed and crossing his hands over his chest.

Getting up, Abi closed the bathroom door behind her. Leaning against it, she tried to gather her thoughts. With pulse thrumming, her body shook. It wasn't like this was the first time she and Shane had shared a room, but the quiet intimacy of the evening made it feel different. Taking a deep breath, she splashed her face with cool water before changing into her bamboo nightgown. Upon brushing her teeth, she ran her fingers through her hair, trying to calm the slight flutter of nerves.

When she finally opened the door, she saw Shane still lying on the bed, his eyes closed, seemingly relaxed. The sight of him made her smile, and for a moment, she felt more at ease. "All yours," she announced while stepping out of the bathroom.

Shane turned and swung his legs to the edge. "I won't be long."

As he disappeared, Abi slipped beneath the covers. The sheets were cool against her skin, but it was the nervous energy humming inside her that kept her from fully relaxing. Lying on her back, the bed felt so much bigger now, and the space between her and where Shane would lie seemed both comforting and intimidating at the same time.

Pulling the blankets up to her chin, she stared at the ceiling as her mind ran through their many conversations. The two of them had been through so much, and he'd stayed respectful and kept his distance all this time, but tonight, it felt like they were on the cusp of something more – like everything could change in an instant if she wanted it to. Not knowing how best to navigate it, she began to panic.

Right then, the bathroom door slid open, and Shane emerged wearing a T-shirt and pajama pants. Flicking off the lights, he casually pulled back the covers and got in beside her.

Feeling the mattress shift under his weight, she noticed he stayed a safe distance away, though she could still feel the warmth radiating from his body. With only the dim spotlights outside illuminating them, for a few moments, the room was quiet except for the rustling of the sheets as Shane settled in.

Immediately, he wondered what she was thinking. "Comfy?" he asked gently in the darkness.

She nodded and said, "Yes. You?"

"All good." His heartbeat thumped loudly in his ears.

Somehow, each sensed their connection seemed stronger tonight. It was like this electric charge, growing more intensely by the second.

Breathing lightly, instinctively sensing the tension mounting, Abi closed her eyes, trying to calm herself, unsure if she could relax enough to fall asleep. Lying there, she, too, shifted slightly and turned more onto her side.

Seeing this, he did the same.

Deciding to reach her hand out into the void between them bravely, she soon felt his hand clutch hers.

"So, what did you think of the Heian Shrine tonight?" he asked with a smile, "Aside from that man ruining everything."

She imagined still being there. "The uplit trees, the projections on the pavilions, and the falling snow, I just loved it. I was happy you were there to share it with me. It couldn't have been more perfect. Thank you for arranging everything," she beamed. "Makes me wonder what other treasures we will find here."

He peered out the window, the flakes falling lazily outside. "This place is pretty incredible."

"Isn't it? I never knew anything like this could even exist."

"Yeah, me either."

Tucking her arm under her pillow, she said, "From the moment we arrived in Japan, it feels like it's not real."

Hit by a lull in their conversation, their sights stayed locked as if contemplating their actions.

Desperate to read her mind, his gaze intensified.

About to second-guess herself, she inched a little closer, her head now resting on the edge of his pillow, before her lips faintly touched his.

Her innocence and tender kisses made him more mindful of not pushing beyond her boundaries. Reading her slow and timid movements, he proceeded with caution, unsure of her intentions.

His hand wandered and traced the curve of her waist before effortlessly pulling her closer until her body molded against his muscular frame. Having refrained from PDA all day, they soon got lost in the embrace they'd longed for.

Amidst the rush of emotions, his hand slid upward and weaved through her hair as he kissed her with controlled intensity. Propped just enough to hover over her, Shane searched her expression when their lips parted briefly, only to meet again. Legs intertwining, naturally shifting as if drawn by instinct, both felt their connection growing deeper.

Abi's hands created a possessive path along his back, each touch igniting a fire between them as they moved in sync.

The way she responded sent a wave through him. But it wasn't just about their physical connection—it was more. He wanted her, yes, but there was this desire to be close to her, to give in to the pull that had been simmering between them for months.

Their closeness, more comforting than scary, made her want to surrender fully.

But just as things intensified, Shane's conscience tugged at him, and this time, he was the one who hesitated. Loosening his grip on her, knowing she wasn't as relaxed as she claimed to be, he backed off. Breathing heavily, his cheek against hers, Abi could feel his chest rise and fall rapidly, and for a long moment, he stayed like that, eyes closed, as if trying to gather himself.

Catching her breath, with lips tingling, she could still feel the remnants of his touch. "Shane?" she whispered. "Is something wrong?"

He opened his eyes slowly, his breath uneven as he fought the pull of her. "Abs..." His voice was hushed, laced with both longing and restraint. She was still so close—her hand resting over his heartbeat, her lips softly parted, waiting. Every piece of him ached to close the distance again, to lose himself in her warmth. But there was something in the way she lingered and didn't press forward. It made him pause.

His fingers brushed a strand of hair from her forehead, an excuse to steady himself. "Being close to you like this, and... umm..." He swallowed, searching for the right words. "I don't know, but for whatever reason, all I can think about right now...is not crossing a line with you and being okay with that."

Her brows lifted slightly, but she didn't pull away.

He exhaled, pressing his forehead against hers. "I've spent so long wanting you," he admitted, his thumb tracing the edge of her jaw. "But now, all I want is to keep you like this a little longer—" He stopped himself, shaking his head, unsure if he was making any sense. "You know, protect you. Even from myself."

She searched for answers. "You won't hurt me," she whispered.

"I just..." There was a rawness in his tone. "I don't want to take that from you yet if that makes sense."

Her touch was light but grounding. As her lips parted, her breath caught while she cupped his face. "It's not wrong to want to give yourself to me."

Shane closed his eyes and slowly exhaled while processing what she meant. He kissed her forehead, lingering there, knowing it was enough. Because for now, it was. "I can wait," he said quietly.

A little relieved, she nodded and kissed him.

For the first time, he realized—it wasn't just about what he wanted. It was about how special she was. And that was worth protecting more than anything else.

Parting ways, he rolled onto his back. Searching for Abi's hand between them, his thumb brushed over her knuckles as he looked her way, the tension still there with their connection now more profound than ever. Returning to her briefly, he kissed her lips and said, "Goodnight, Abs."

"Goodnight."

"I love you," he said firmly.

"I love you too."

Pulling her in, he embraced her tightly, holding her head against his chest. When he kissed the top of her head, he added, "And I love the relationship we have."

"So do I."

| 27 |

Late Night Stroll

Monday, December 18

Park Hyatt, Kyoto

Cuddled together, Abi heard his breath slow while his heart settled into a steady, quiet rhythm. Soon, he fell asleep.

Left with her thoughts, listening to him breathe, she gradually started to get lost in her head as doubt crept in. Knowing what he'd done was selfless, she couldn't help but feel slightly rejected.

Thirty minutes passed. Then, an hour.

As Shane let out the odd snore here and there, Abi stared at the ceiling. Needing a moment, she very gingerly slipped from his arms and out of bed. Grabbing her tights and putting them on under her nightgown, she wrapped herself in a hotel white robe and slid on a pair of guest slippers before taking the card key off the table. Ever so quietly, she opened the door. Not hearing him stir, careful not to make a peep, she delicately stepped out into the hall. Cushioning the door as it closed behind her, she tied the belt around her waist, wondering which direction to go.

Knowing Burton was in the suite at the far end, she walked over to the elevators and descended two floors. When the doors parted, she peeked her head out and rounded the corner. The all-glass wall showcased a beautifully lit bonsai tree in the rooftop garden. Ahead of her, she saw the Yasaka Pagoda shining brightly in the distance. Shuffling along, Abi wrapped her arms around her body.

"Evening, Miss," a voice said lightly, making her jump.

"Oh, my gosh," she muttered, completely taken off guard.

Lorenzo chuckled. "Sorry about that. Didn't mean to scare you."

Both he and Bray were standing in the corner, speaking to one of the resort's security guards.

Slowly, the tension in her shoulders eased. "It's fine. Wasn't expecting to see anyone here."

"Everything okay?" Lorenzo asked, not sure what to make of her untimely stroll.

"Yes, it's a little late to be wandering around," Bray surmised.

Abi smiled sheepishly. "Yeah, just needed to clear my head," she replied. Their presence calmed her nerves. "Why are you guys not sleeping?"

"The boss is working." Lorenzo pointed to the Resident's Lounge.

Following his line of sight, she saw her friend sitting at a table in the far corner. The light from his laptop illuminated his silhouette with headphones over his ears.

She gave a small nod. "I'm just gonna say, Hi."

"When you're ready to head back to your room, one of us will escort you," Bray suggested.

"Thank you. I'd appreciate that."

"No problem at all."

When Abi walked into the room, Burton immediately spotted her while removing the headphones.

"Hey, Abs. You're up late," he said, concern flashing across his face.

"I could ask you the same thing."

He gestured for her to have a seat. "I'm working." Pointing to his computer, he leaned back in his chair. "What's your excuse? Why are you walking the halls alone? Shouldn't you be cuddled up with Coppersmith right about now?"

She looked out the window and didn't respond to that.

Seeing this, he closed his laptop. "Is everything okay?" Immediately thinking the worst, his protective instincts surfaced. "He didn't do anything to hurt you, did he?"

She shook her head. "No, nothing like that."

Contemplating whether to press further, he waited for her to elaborate.

Suddenly, in Abi Acardi fashion, she blurted out without thinking it through first – "Can I ask you something?" she said curiously.

"Sure. What is it?"

Leery, Abi stopped, careful as to how she'd phrase what she wanted to say. "Hypothetically speaking, how long would you be with a girl without, umm, you know, doing that before you broke up with her?"

He squinted his eyes, trying to decipher what she meant in a roundabout way. Reading between the lines, he rested his elbows on the table. "Wait... Are you saying you and Coppersmith haven't..."

Embarrassed, she shook her head.

Burton fell back against the chair again. "Wow, have to say, I'm impressed. And somehow, I find myself having a newfound respect for the guy. Imagine that."

"Burton..." she whispered, tilting her head disapprovingly.

He got serious. "I'm surprised that you guys waited this long."

"That doesn't answer my question."

"Why would he break up with you? Did he say he would if you didn't give in?" His blood boiled at the thought.

"No."

"Good, 'cause I would've set him straight."

"Burton, please..."

"Okay, so hypothetically speaking, if I were in his shoes, knowing the kind of girl you are, no, I would never break up with you, Abs, under any circumstances."

When he said that, she knew he meant it.

"After wanting me to do that for so long, now, all of a sudden, he wants to wait. He said he doesn't want to, you know, umm, take that from me yet."

Seeing her innocence shining through, he said, "Well, isn't it obvious?"

Unsure what he meant, she waved her hand, prompting him to spit it out.

"The guy's in love with you, and he understands how intimacy changes a relationship. There's no way he'll break it off. His heart is fully vested."

"How can you be so sure?"

Burton hesitated a second and told her the truth. "Because if you were mine, I wouldn't let you get away either."

An awkwardness erupted between them.

"Believe me, the guy is in it for the long haul."

"Really? How do you know that?" she asked, still wanting answers.

"It's the way he looks at you." He locked his eyes with hers as if searching her soul. "Bottom line is, if you are not fully ready for that type of relationship because it comes with its own set of rules, then wait. It's not a bad thing."

Noticeably absorbing what he said, she nodded and leaned forward to rest her arms on the table. Fidgeting with the cuff on her robe, she whispered, "Hmm..."

"Abs, I can't say I know the guy overly well, but from what I can see, I figure he would do anything for you. So, if he has to wait a bit longer, he will. Don't worry."

Thankful for his advice, she managed a partial smile. Having a few questions for him, she asked, "So, what's up with you and Sara? It seems things are okay one minute, maybe a little prickly the next."

"Like I said the other night, things are complicated. Jealousy is a bad thing. She assures me she's working on it, but I'm not convinced."

"I tried my best to set the record straight."

"I saw that."

Abi felt bad to hear her efforts may have been in vain.

"She's just insecure. You and I have this strong connection – a history. I'm sure it's the same for Shane. It's hard to compete with that." He paused for a second as his eyes found hers.

Seeing this, she muttered, "What..."

"Can I tell you something?"

"Sure. Anything."

He looked around the room to confirm they were alone. "There are times I feel like something is missing between her and me."

"Oh? Like what?"

"Not a hundred percent sure," he replied, unable to tell her the truth.

"Please don't hate me," she confessed, "but that's what I feel with you two also."

He rubbed his palms together. "So, you see it too?" About to let her in on a secret, he hesitated, then said, "When we get back to the States, I think I'm going to sever ties."

She felt bad that he had to go through this. "I feel like it's all my fault. I'm the one who told you to give her a chance when we were in Tahoe. I should have never interfered because now you're miserable."

"I'm not miserable. I'm just very busy," he said with a hint of humor. "Besides, I'm a big boy. I decided to move forward when I shouldn't have."

"Well, we need to find you a girl who's tailor-made for you. Someone who lights up when you enter the room. A woman whose smile melts your heart. The perfect partner to spend a lifetime with."

Not skipping a beat, he said, "You mean a girl like you?"

Hearing that took Abi's breath away.

"Sorry, I shouldn't have, umm..." he backtracked.

Not outwardly dismissing it, Abi sighed, "Yeah... But for how long?"

"I don't understand."

"Burton, I haven't told him that I'm going to Harvard."

"You haven't?"

She exhaled. "I'm afraid to. He has all these plans for us in Alabama. What do I say to that?"

"The truth."

"I know a long-distance relationship will never work. He's the QB and the player to watch. I'm sure he will have a million pretty girls vying for his attention."

"None of them can hold a candle to you, though."

She tilted her head. "Thank you for that."

He reached over and placed his hand on hers. "It's true."

"You always know the right thing to say."

He leaned forward and rested his hand on her shoulder. "Whatever happens, I'll always be here for you, no matter what, okay?"

"I'll hold you to that."

His feelings for her bubbled to the surface. Recalling the moments they shared together, each vivid, feeling like yesterday, he decided to change the subject. "So, enough of the heavy. Are you having a good time here so far?"

"This place is amazing. Thank you for bringing all of us."

"Don't take offense, but I didn't do it for them. I did it for you." He looked down at his feet.

She didn't know what to say.

"I couldn't leave you alone over Christmas with everything happening with your Dad, and it being the first without your Mom."

Abi swiftly wiped a tear as it drifted down her cheek. "You know I'm grateful, right?"

"Of course."

"I'm sure this is costing you a fortune. All the private cars, fancy hotels, food, and security, not to mention the plane."

"Yep. Almost two mill."

"Wait? What?" Abi choked.

"Relax. It's fine. Besides, it was worth every penny to get you out of LA and see you smile after all this time."

A level of guilt hit her.

"For the record, you haven't seen anything yet. There is so much more to come."

She smiled at how happy he was when he said it. "Well, then, I can hardly wait."

The snow began to fall heavier outside. It was so picturesque as it drifted past the glass.

"Being here has helped take my mind off my problems back home despite all the craziness."

"Speaking of that." He turned to her. "I need you to remain alert while we're here. We are still investigating who that mystery man with the cane is and how that card got placed in your gift basket." Suddenly, Burton saw a familiar face. "Incoming," he said.

Unsure what he meant, she followed his line of sight. It wasn't the guys.

Spotting Abi sitting with Burton, Shane stopped. "There you are? I've been looking all over for you. I woke up, and you were gone."

"Sorry. I went for a walk to clear my head and ended up here."

"Why...umm..." He stared down her famous friend. "Why did you feel the need to clear your head?"

"Just couldn't sleep. That's all. A lot on my mind," she paused. "When I ran into the guys, they said Burton was in here working, so I stopped to chat with him." Abi turned to B.

He nudged his head. "You go. I'll see you in the morning."

"Thanks for the talk," she said quietly.

"Anytime." When they were about to walk away, Burton said, "Night, you two."

"Night, man," Shane said as Abi waved to him.

As they moved towards the elevator, Shane glanced at Abi a few times. He pressed the up button. "Are you sure you're okay?"

"Yes, why wouldn't I be?" To send his thoughts in a different direction, she said, "Was thinking of my Mom tonight... It was nice to run into B. He helps me keep her memory alive."

Knowing that would never be the case for him, he said, "Anytime you want to share childhood memories of her, please do. I would never object to that, I hope you know."

She nodded. "I know."

"You just need to let me in. Don't ever think you can't confide in me, okay?"

Nodding again, she reached out.

Hugging her tightly, he kissed her and said, "Come on. It's late. We should get some sleep."

When they returned to their room, they got settled back in bed. Meeting in the middle, her back to him, he wrapped his arm around her waist and pulled her in close.

"Night, Abs. Love you."

Comfortable beyond, she whispered, "Love you too," as exhaustion set in. "Good night."

| 28 |

A Light-hearted Moment

Monday, December 18

Park Hyatt, Kyoto

A soft knock on the door echoed through the serene room at the Park Hyatt Kyoto. Exhausted, Shane stirred, his body still feeling heavy and severely fatigued. Abi was barely awake, her face buried in the pillows, wondering in her half-asleep state who could be at the door so early.

Groggily, Shane pushed the covers aside and made his way to the door, not expecting much. When he opened it, a smiling hotel attendant greeted him with a gleaming silver cart draped in white linen.

"Good morning, Sir. Breakfast for two, courtesy of Mr. Martin," the woman announced cheerfully, reading off a note card placed on top.

Shane blinked, surprised but grateful. "Uh, thanks," he muttered, stepping aside as she wheeled the cart inside the door.

"Enjoy," she said before departing.

The aroma of food began to fill the air, stirring Abi, still wrapped in the sheets.

"Who was that?" she mumbled, her voice muffled by the bedding.

Amusement surfacing in his tone, he replied, "Breakfast." With a smile, he added, "Martin hooked us up."

Abi's eyes fluttered open as she rolled onto her side while Shane expertly steered the cart over to the small table by the window. The morning sun peeked through the clouds, casting rays throughout the room.

Curious as to what Martin ordered for them, Shane removed the lids, revealing a spread of classic American breakfast dishes—crispy bacon, fluffy, veggie-filled omelets, golden fresh toast, and freshly cut fruit. His face lit up at the sight.

"Well, would you look at that," he grinned. "I think I may have died and gone to heaven."

Abi giggled from the bed, feeling a little more awake now. "I could get used to this." She sat up slowly, stretching, while Shane pulled out a chair for her with a playful bow.

"Your Highness," he emphasized as she laughed, feeling a warmth settle over the peaceful morning.

Sitting down to eat, the world outside felt far away—it was just the two of them and the quiet elegance of Kyoto.

Shane took the first bite of his eggs, savoring the flavors as he glanced at Abi. She was focused on her plate, slowly eating her French toast and enjoying the view. The morning hues made her hair shine, and her eyes sparkle.

The burden of his decision and their future hanging in the balance weighed heavily. What happened between them the night before added to it. The way they had connected was different. Not wanting to spoil the peaceful morning or the plans they had for the day, he chose not to bring up either subject.

Tonight, he decided. *I'll talk to her about it then.* With that said, he pushed the thought away and sat up in his chair. "So, do you think the wedding is still happening at that small chapel or somewhere else?"

Abi paused, her fork hovering over her plate. "I think it will happen elsewhere, given the fact that his Dad is aware they're here together." She lowered her fork and met Shane's eyes. "If his Father finds out where they are getting married, he'll definitely cause a scene. This will have to happen in private with the utmost secrecy."

"I agree. I've never even met the man after all this time, but from what Reg says, he's ruthless and usually gets what he wants."

She sighed. "Their wedding should be a joyful day. I can't imagine what they are feeling right now. His Dad's phone call yesterday added a layer of stress that they didn't need."

Despite this new development, Abi stayed positive. She couldn't help but feel excited about seeing Jade in her wedding dress today. Curious as to what she and Sara would be wearing also, the thought gave her goosebumps. "I can't believe our friends are getting married."

"I know. It's wild when you think of it. But, they are happy and so sure of themselves."

She looked on whimsically. "Yes, and they love each other so much. I hope nothing comes between them. Ever."

Shane reached over and took her hand, giving it a gentle squeeze. "Don't worry. Everything will go according to plan. Martin is at the helm. I have a sneaky suspicion the guy will have a few tricks up his sleeve to make sure the mission is successful."

Chuckling to herself, knowing very well that Shane was spot on in his observations, she stayed tight-lipped but replied, "You're right. Whatever happens, we've got their back too."

"Yes, we do. Without a doubt."

With empty plates sitting in front of them, Shane said, "You go ahead and shower first," knowing they needed to start getting ready for the day.

Abi stood up. "Are you sure?"

"Absolutely."

Moving toward the bathroom, she said, "I won't be long," before sliding both pocket doors shut.

Able to hear the faint sounds of the water turning on and gently trickling as it warmed up, Shane stayed where he was. With the sunlight spilling into the room through the large window, his gaze drifted to the view outside, but his mind was somewhere else entirely. The memory of last night still clung to him, but more than that, he found himself daydreaming about something bigger. The thought of one day marrying her crept in, catching him by surprise.

A smile tugged at the corners of his mouth as he propped his elbow on the armrest and rested his chin in the palm of his hand. The idea of spending his life with Abi filled him with a warmth he hadn't expected. He could picture it—the two of them together, just like this, waking up next to each other every morning.

But reality reared its ugly head, and with it came the weight of the conversation he needed to have with her later. His father and agent had been clear—they wanted him to leave Gilderson Prep and finish his senior year elsewhere. The pressure was mounting, but Abi didn't know about any of it. Believing he was protecting her by keeping it to himself for now, he recalled what Burton had said.

"You've gotta tell her," he whispered, wondering what she would think about moving with him. The idea of being away from her, even for six months, made his chest tighten.

Shane sighed and rubbed his hand across his face. Tonight, he'd have to share the news and hope she wouldn't be heartbroken. As a beam of light hit the Yasaka pagoda, he closed his eyes and let himself imagine the future he wanted with her, one that felt closer and more real with each passing day.

Suddenly, the door slid open, and Abi emerged in the hallway dressed in a white robe with her hair bundled in a towel. Light makeup enhancing her face, she opened her suitcase in the hallway and took a few clothes out to hang them in the closet.

Watching her, he smiled.

She noticed and asked sheepishly, "What..." while looking at him with a pleasant expression.

Her eyes were so blue in the morning light.

"Nothing," he said happily. "You just look really pretty."

Standing up, she walked towards him to place her clothes on the bed. Shyly lowering her chin, she replied, "Well, thank you," and pointed. "I'm finished in there for now. All yours."

"Alright." About to walk away, she suddenly stopped him. "Oh, wait!" She ducked inside and grabbed the blow dryer and her brush. "Sorry. I'll do this out here to save time."

Feeling the urge to kiss her, Shane opted to refrain, wanting to keep the morning stress-free as she waved slightly and slid the pocket door closed.

Abi stood in front of the mirror, worked the brush through her hair as the humming sound filled the room, but her mind was far from quiet. While Shane was just on the other side of the bathroom door, finishing up in the shower, Abi's thoughts kept drifting back to last night's conversation with Burton. What had started as a casual check-in turned into something that lingered, his voice echoing in her mind: *"If you were mine, I wouldn't let you get away."*

Lowering the blow-dryer for a moment, she stared at her reflection, recalling their time spent in Tahoe and what she felt then, despite how they left things in the end. Guilt settled in. Unsure what to make of it all, she knew Burton's protectiveness rivaled Shane's - maybe even surpassed it. She figured his age and their history made it so. Replaying last night in her mind, she couldn't believe she brought up the topic involving her intimacy fears. But for whatever reason, she felt comfortable enough to talk to him about almost anything.

Abi ran her fingers through her hair, setting the blow dryer aside. She didn't want to overthink it. *Maybe he didn't realize how he said it,* she thought, knowing Burton always spoke his mind. The truth was, his words somehow left her feeling uncertain. But it wasn't just about Burton. A lot was going on.

Every time she thought about telling Shane about Harvard, her stomach twisted into tighter knots. He'd made all these plans for them—plans that didn't include her being in another state, chasing her own dreams.

The sound of the shower shutting off broke her train of thought. She could hear him moving around, likely drying off and finishing his usual routine. She knew they needed to talk and have some real conversations about their future. But was she ready?

Sliding the door open, Shane stepped out with a towel wrapped around his waist, running his hand through his damp hair. He smiled at her the way he always did, like she was the only thing in the world that mattered. And instantly, thoughts of Burton vanished just like that.

"Are you almost ready? We gotta make sure we meet everyone on time," she stated, her tone light as she checked her phone.

He forced a smile, nodding. "Yes, almost done."

Dipping into the bathroom, Abi slipped on a pair of black pants and a lovely gray cashmere sweater. One by one, she put on her earrings and spotted Shane's promise ring on her finger, wondering what it would be like to have an engagement ring take its place one day.

When she walked out of the bathroom, she found Shane putting on his dress shirt. She couldn't help but stare at his washboard abs as he buttoned it and covered them up. Tucking it in, buttoning his pants, and adding a belt, he sat on the bed to slip on his shoes and tie them before going to the closet to grab his navy Norwegian cashmere jacket.

Suddenly seeing a more manly side of him as she slipped on her boots and took her coat off the hanger, Abi found it hard to veer away. Both sporting business-casual for their upscale appointments arranged today, she grabbed her small crossbody bag and carefully placed her passport and wallet inside.

Noticing this, Shane asked, "Can you take mine too?"

"Sure," she replied as he handed it to her. "Oh! I almost forgot my heels." Placing the dressy pumps in a tote bag, she zipped her crossbody shut and put on her white wool peacoat before adjusting the strap across her chest. Draping a warm scarf around her neck, she walked towards the door to check herself quickly in the full-length mirror.

Shane stopped behind her, his eyes tracing her silhouette as she wrapped her scarf stylishly. "You look great," he said with admiration, leaving no room for doubt.

She turned to him, a soft smile on her lips. "So do you," she whispered, rising on her tiptoes to casually kiss him. But when they parted, and she pulled away, he gently encircled his hand around her waist.

"Wait, wait. One more second," he murmured, his eyes darkening with a playful glint. Pulling her closer, his hand slid along her back, sending shivers down her spine. Before she could protest, he leaned in, brushing his lips across hers in a slow, lingering tease that made her heart race and her legs weaken. His body was warm against her, and the soft press of his mouth left her craving more.

Surprisingly frazzled, she tried to catch her breath. Biting her lip, she whispered, "No, no, we can't...we gotta go," but wavered, betraying the resolve she tried to hold onto.

He chuckled softly. His thumb brushed along her jawline. "You sure about that?" he asked, his lips ghosting over hers again, dangerously close but not quite touching, leaving her suspended in the moment.

Barely able to react, his kisses found her again. Soft but measured, each slowly melted away any intention of leaving despite hearing the voices in the hall.

"Shane..." Abi giggled against his lips, half-hearted in her protest, as her breath quickened. "We really gotta go..." Somehow, she managed to push back just enough to break the spell.

"Fine," he sighed humorously and fixed the collar on his coat.

They refocused before stepping out the door.

Taking a deep breath to compose herself, Abi offered one last flirty glance over her shoulder.

His grin widened when he saw that. "So that you know... I might not let you off so easy next time."

"Oh, my..." she said, tauntingly. "Is that right, Mr. Coppersmith?"

Eyebrows raised, clearly challenged by the comment, Abi could see it flickering in his eyes as she walked out the door.

Never having had banter between them like this, Shane got caught off guard by her sudden playfulness and didn't know how to react.

By the expression on his face, she knew she'd won that round.

Emerging, they found Jade and Reggie chatting with Martin in the foyer, while Burton and Sara moved down the hall to join the group. The guys, led by Lorenzo and Andrew, were scattered about, reviewing the plan for the day.

Anton stepped out of his room just as Abi glanced his way.

"Are you coming with us today?" she asked him.

"No, Miss Abi. I'm cooking with world-renowned Chef Yoshiro," he said, smiling.

"That sounds amazing."

"Yes. I'm excited," Anton said, his hands waving around expressively. "He wants to learn Italian cuisine, so he and I...we swap secret recipes."

Martin clapped his hands to get the group's attention. "Alright, everyone. Our first stop is Takami Bridal for dresses and suits. After that, we head to The Thousand Hotel to see the chapel there."

Jade couldn't contain her excitement. "He showed us the pictures, Abs! It's stunning. Wait until you see it!"

So happy to see her reaction, all of them could feel the contagious energy radiating from her friend. "I can't wait," she replied, her anticipation growing by the minute.

"Given last night's drama, please stick together and try to keep a low profile. Do not post anything on social media. No sending photos to friends, either." He looked at his iPad. "Our transportation has arrived. At each destination, we will be using the VIP entrance and exit points, so hopefully, everything will go smoothly."

29

Wedding Preparations

Monday, December 18

Takami Bridal

Thousand Hotel Chapel, Kyoto

With excitement in the air, they descended in the elevators to the private VIP exit. There, the group found their SUVs lined up, awaiting their arrival at the far side of the underground parking garage. Under the dimness of the lights, they quickly found their seats. Andrew got the engaged couple to join Abi and Shane in one vehicle while Martin, Burton, and Sara went in another with Lorenzo. The rest of the guys followed in the third truck.

Inching their way toward the bright sunshine at the exit, Abi and Jade squinted when they emerged.

The day ahead promised to be a whirlwind of wedding prep, and the anticipation seemed to have the happy couple buzzing.

"I can't believe I am trying on my wedding dress today," Jade said nervously, rubbing her palms together. "I'm so excited."

From the third row, Abi reached forward and placed her hand on her shoulder. "You will look beautiful."

"I can't believe it's finally happening." Filled with emotion, she sat next to Reggie. "I'm so nervous to see what Martin has planned."

"It won't be long now." Smiling, she glanced at her best friend. "The chapel. The gardens. It will all come together seamlessly."

Shane grinned and leaned against her. "And I'll make sure Reg and I look sharp in our tuxes." He nudged his friend's shoulder. "Right, man?"

"But nothing outshines the bride," Abi stated firmly.

"Our day belongs to you, hands down." Reg patted her arm.

With a tilt of her head, she grasped his hand and smiled. "That's so sweet. Thank you, Babe. I just want everything to be perfect."

As the car weaved through Kyoto's streets, the conversation shifted to their thoughts on the final touches, like flowers and the rings.

"I think I would prefer understated bouquets, mostly white. That's what Martin showed me. What do you think, Abs?"

"It sounds beautiful." With high expectations, Abi took a deep breath. All the decisions were a little overwhelming.

Crossing the bridge over the Kamo River, they drifted into the far left lane and slowed to a crawl in front of a modern building with greenery out front. With their hazard lights flashing, before they even stopped, the guys in the vehicle ahead of them got out to secure the area. Martin joined them and went ahead inside when Ted opened one of the natural-colored wood doors of the double entry into the place.

"Do we go in?" Jade asked Andrew.

"No. We must wait for further instructions," he said, keeping a keen eye on their surroundings.

In minutes, Martin appeared again and gave the men a nod.

Each got out of their vehicle and rounded to the back before opening the doors curb-side for their clients.

Offering his hand to Jade, Andrew said, "Right this way, Miss. Watch your step."

Jade stepped out with Reggie by his side while Andrew pulled the seat forward for Abi and Shane to exit.

Noticing Burton and Sara doing the same, the guys got them to file into the boutique quickly as they scanned the area.

When entering the airy modern space, the copper ceiling details immediately drew their eyes upward. A blend of textures on the walls, paired with the inviting, gray upholstered furniture, made the atmosphere more relaxing than the girls had anticipated. Given the stress Jade was under, this was a welcomed relief.

Martin was speaking to their wedding coordinators. One for the ladies and one for the gentlemen. Facing their group, he said, "Usually, the salon is closed today, but they've made an exception for us given our time constraints."

Bowing respectfully, Jade smiled and said, "Arigatō," her hands together in front of her body.

Graciously accepting her thanks, the one woman said, "Welcome to Takami Bridal. My name is Umeko, and these are my associates: Amasi, Rin, and Himari. We take great pride in serving you today. Follow me."

Moving towards the elevators, they ascended to the fifth floor. It was there that they parted ways. Abi and Sara went with Jade to the Vera Wang Haute area while Martin escorted Reggie, Shane, and Burton to the men's formalwear to try on the Tagliatore black tuxedos Martin had chosen for them.

"Guess I'll see you after?" Reggie said to his bride. "Have fun." Hugging her and kissing her cheek, he waved.

"Thank you. You too," she said nervously, "I'll see you soon."

Spotting Sara, visibly reluctant to leave Burton's side, the girl slowly joined Jade and Abi as they followed the woman down the hall. Able to feel her anxiety, Abi figured she'd try and make an effort to help the girl feel welcome. She'd been put in an awkward position, thrown into a wedding at the last minute, and Abi understood her apprehension.

Turning to her, she asked, "Are you excited to see Jade's dress?"

Taken off guard, Sara stammered. "Umm, yeah. I suppose."

With Andrew, Matt, and Ted tagging along, Abi included them in the conversation. "You guys got lucky. You get to see the dress before Reg does."

Strangely, each of them gave a subtle thumbs-up and didn't comment.

Abi assumed it was because Sara was there.

The woman opened a glass-paneled door as the girls watched Jade walk into the room, which had ebony walls and matching furniture in contrast to the white gowns hanging along the perimeter.

"Oh, my..." Jade bubbled.

"Here at Takami Bridal," Umeko stated, "We just celebrated our one-hundredth anniversary last year. The company began as a Kyoto kimono merchant in 1923, and the spirit of trust and hospitality has continued since then."

Jade noticed a dress on a mannequin in the middle of the room.

Noticing she was drawn to it, Umeko formally presented the gown. "Yes, Miss Jade. This is your dress. It is an iconic Vera Wang Gemma."

Shown a strapless vision with a sweetheart neckline, the asymmetrically draped bodice, and cut organza blossom hem with blizzard beading shimmered under the lights.

Approaching it, Jade held her breath as her eyes sparkled upon touching the delicate fabric. "It's even more exquisite than I remember," she whispered.

Abi raised her folded hands to her lips, beaming. Standing beside Sara, Jade suddenly turned to them.

"What do you think?" she asked, hanging on their every word.

"It's so lovely, Jade. Reggie will love it."

A happy tear drifted down her cheek. "I hope so," she said.

"Are we ready?" the woman asked pleasantly.

Daintily dabbing her face with her sleeves, Jade nodded. "Oh yes. I am. Very much so."

Following Umeko, the bride-to-be waved to the girls while an assistant removed the gown from the mannequin.

Left alone in the main salon, Sara had a seat.

Sitting across from her, Abi could feel the tension between them growing. They could hear a pin drop. It was so quiet.

Sara peered down at her phone, her face a mask of calm. With no choice but to make small talk and ignore the friction, Abi broke the silence.

"How have you enjoyed the trip so far?" Smiling, she tried to ease the mood.

The girl's expression stayed neutral. "It's been…nice. Busy, but nice." She hesitated for a moment, then continued, "There's a lot of planning surrounding the events coming up. Aside from the wedding, Burton has a full plate in the coming days." Their conversation dropped off there, but she added, "Jade seems happy."

"Yes, she is." Abi nodded. "She's been dreaming of this for so long. And it's going to be amazing. The wedding, the trip to Niseko…" She trailed off, then added, "Are you excited to spend Christmas there?"

Sara forced a small smile. "I guess. It'll be different. I've never done Christmas in the snow before."

Abi attempted to keep that conversation going. "From what I've read, it's a beautiful place. The mountains, the skiing, the hot springs—it'll be a great way to end the year."

There was a brief pause before Sara spoke again. "Yeah, I'm sure it'll be great." She fiddled with her hands, glancing toward the fitting room door. "Burton's looking forward to it, too."

"Do you ski, then?"

"Umm, no. Never have." Keeping things alive, she asked, "You?"

"Yes. Burton and I started skiing when I was six, and he was nine."

The girl nodded, seemingly disappointed to hear that. "How nice for you both."

A little put off by her tone, Abi replied, "He spent a lot of time with my parents and me. I'm an only child. He is, too."

"So I've heard."

Abi didn't miss the way Sara's voice tightened when she mentioned Burton. "Anyway, umm...after the wedding, I'm sure he'll enjoy the break. He's got a lot going on."

"Yeah, about that... I was hoping he and I'd get some time alone, but I hear you guys are staying in the house with us. Between Martin, Anton, and the guys, I doubt we will have a moment's peace."

Feeling that was far more than a guilt trip, Abi didn't know how to respond.

"That said, I don't think he's really interested in having one-on-one time with me anyway." Sara's lips pressed into a thin line.

"I'm sure that's not true," Abi said cautiously, trying not to tread on any sensitive ground. "Maybe things will be better once he gets there. It is Christmas after all."

"The way things are going, I doubt it." Sara seemed overly negative.

They both heard the soft rustling of fabric as Jade stepped out of the fitting room, guided by Umeko holding the train.

Abi was the first to spot her and gasped, her eyes widening. "Oh, my goodness, Jade! It's gorgeous," she exclaimed, full of awe.

The bride-to-be paused in front of the mirror, her hands trembling as she tucked them under her chin, eyes shimmering with emotion. Slowly, her hands rose to cover her face, and she began to sob, her shoulders shaking with overwhelming joy. "In two days, I'm marrying Reg," she whimpered through happy tears, staring at her reflection as though she could hardly believe it.

Abi stood and crossed the room, reaching out to her best friend. Jade immediately wrapped her arms around her and pulled her close as Sara watched.

Thick with gratitude, she added, "Thank you for making my dreams come true."

Hugging her tightly, Abi smiled. "Don't thank me," she said. "This was all Burton." Her friend's heart swelling with happiness, Abi clung to her, both sharing in the emotional weight of the moment.

From her seat on the sofa, Sara fiddled with the fabric of her sweater cuff as she tried to maintain a neutral expression. But it was impossible to ignore the pang of jealousy. Seeing them locked in a moment so pure and emotional reminded her that she had yet to find something similar. Not having any girlfriends to rely on, she felt alone and couldn't help but feel the sting. Her gaze flicked between them as she spotted Abi whispering something to Jade, their heads close, sharing a quiet laugh through the tears. And in an instant, paranoia set in.

"So, Jade? Are you saying yes to the dress?" Abi giggled.

"Yes!" Jade said loud and clear. "A million times, yes!" Seeing Sara hanging back from them, she reached out and said, "Come on, Sara. Join in!"

Uncomfortable, she slowly walked over.

Before she knew it, Jade had pulled her in tightly. "Now, it's your turn," she said to them.

Another attendant arrived with two stunning black gowns.

"These are for you. What do you think?"

Both Sara and Abi loved the formal dresses with a strikingly elegant design featuring a single shoulder strap, drawing attention to the neckline and leaving one arm beautifully bare. The bodice was intricately ruched, creating soft, flattering folds that would enhance the body's silhouette. Overall, it was timeless and sophisticated, perfect for a glamorous wedding.

The woman placed one gown in each of the fitting rooms.

The girls parted ways and went to try them on while Jade stood on the pedestal to see if she needed any alterations.

Inside her room, Abi slipped into the dress. Sliding her arm through the strap, she zipped it up on the side. Excited to show it off, she got out the pumps she brought along. Ready to step out, she pulled the curtain back. Eyes wide with excitement as she caught a glimpse of herself in the one-hundred-and-eighty-degree mirror, Abi admired how the design hugged her figure perfectly. Her heart raced as she watched the fabric flow around her legs, the side slit revealing just the right amount of skin.

"Oh my gosh, Abs! It's *incredible!*" Jade exclaimed, practically bouncing in place. She rushed over with eyes gleaming with excitement as she circled her friend, inspecting every detail. "This dress was made for you!"

Grinning, feeling a rush of confidence, Abi stared at their reflection, admiring the sharp contrast of her gown beside the bride's. She could see how happy Jade was with the wedding slowly coming together.

Seeing that Sara hadn't emerged, knowing she'd heard them gushing over the dress, Abi's heart sank a little, and she exchanged a knowing glance with Jade. They both sensed it—the subtle tension, the way Sara felt out of place, like a third wheel. Despite their differences, neither of them wanted her to feel slighted.

Jade leaned in close. "We need to make her feel more included. She's probably feeling awkward."

"Agreed," Abi nodded. "We need her to know she's a big part of this, too."

Hearing the drapery slide along the rod, the girls were ready to shower Sara with attention.

When she stepped out of the fitting room, still in her socks, holding the hem of the dress carefully, she shyly smiled. "Sorry, I didn't bring any shoes today. I left them at the hotel."

Quick to reassure her, Jade immediately waved it off with a warm smile. "No worries, we've all been there."

Umeko, who had been quietly observing, disappeared for a moment. When she returned, she was holding a pair of sleek, high-heeled shoes. "I think you're an American size eight if I'm right," she said gently. "These are a Japanese size 23. It's the equivalent."

Sara's eyes widened in surprise as she took the shoes with both hands and bowed slightly, a gesture of gratitude she had quickly picked up during their stay. "Thank you so much."

"So welcome, Miss," Umeko replied with a gracious smile.

As Sara slipped into the shoes, Abi and Jade wasted no time fawning over her. "You look amazing!" Abi gushed, her eyes lighting up as she watched Sara's expression soften in the mirror.

Smiling broadly, Jade stood beside the girl with a proud gleam in her eye and said, "If I haven't said it already, I wanted to thank you for standing with me. I know this must be weird for you."

"It is, truth be told, but it's fine. If it's important to Burton, then it's important to me."

Jade wrapped her arms around Sara, pulling her into a warm, heartfelt embrace. "Well, I appreciate it."

Caught off guard, the girl stiffened, her body instinctively tense. She wasn't used to this kind of affection, at least not from someone she barely knew. Slowly forcing herself to relax, she awkwardly placed her arms around Jade in return. Her movements seemed hesitant, and though she tried her best to accept the hug, the discomfort was evident in the slight tightness of her posture.

As Jade let go, Sara smiled weakly, hoping it would mask the unease bubbling beneath the surface. It wasn't that she didn't appreciate the gesture—it was just unfamiliar. Too close, too emotional. She hoped Jade hadn't noticed.

Finally, after all that, a small smile tugged at Sara's lips as she glanced at herself in the mirror. Her posture straightened, allowing some confidence to surface.

With both girls on either side of Jade, she sighed contentedly and said, "I think I'm ready to get married now."

The mood was light and cheerful as the sound of familiar voices echoed outside the room.

"Is it safe to come in?" Shane called out just as Reggie was about to make an appearance at the door.

"No!" Abi shouted at him.

"It's bad luck for you to see the bride in the dress," Sara said, joining the urgency.

Umeko shuffled Jade off to the dressing room.

With her safely out of sight, Abi said, "Okay. It's fine now!"

Sara shouted, "You can come in!"

The first to round the corner was Shane. His eyes soon landed on Abi in her black gown. He gave her a once-over, his smile growing. "Wow, you look..."

But before he could finish, Burton interrupted. "Stunning."

Abi's heart skipped for a brief second. She wasn't sure if Burton was talking about her or Sara, but either way, she felt the weight of it as the progress she'd made with the girl over the past two hours slowly crumbled.

Quickly walking over to Shane, her smile growing as she linked her arm with his, Abi tried to save face by keeping things light. But instantly, it felt like she and Sara had just taken ten steps back.

Not the only one to catch the comment, Shane raised an eyebrow at Abi, but she smiled, hoping he didn't notice the awkward undercurrent. "Ready to wrap this up and celebrate?" she asked, sending them in a more positive direction.

"Yes," Reggie said, more than ready to check off the next item on the list.

As soon as Sara disappeared into the dressing room to change, Abi seized the moment. She grabbed Burton by the arm, pulling him aside and lowering to a whisper, her frustration barely contained.

"What was that?" she hissed, eyes narrowing. "Why did you look at *me* and not *her* when you said that? We were just making progress, and now, *urgh*..." She ended with a huff under her breath. "I hate setbacks."

Confused to a degree, Burton blinked, clearly blindsided by the accusation. He raised his hands in defense, shaking his head as he tried to process what she was so upset about. "Before you bite my head off, I meant the compliment for *both* of you," he said calmly. "And for the record, I did look at her, too."

Her glare tempered slightly, but the tension still clung to her. "I should hope so," she muttered, still annoyed, not wanting to drag this out any longer. With a frustrated sigh, she left them standing there as she went to change.

Burton watched her go, bewildered by what had happened. This wasn't the first time he had seen Abi passionately fired up over something. Still, he made a mental note to tread carefully.

Within minutes, Jade returned. Seeing her man, she walked over to him.

"Hi," she said lovingly.

"How is the dress?" he asked, barely able to wait to see her in it.

"It's like a dream." Spotting Burton, she walked over to him. "Can I hug you?" she asked. "I just can't thank you enough for what you've done for us."

Accepting her friendly embrace, he replied, "No thanks necessary. Just glad I could help."

Standing with Reggie, his arm draped around her, she said, "Well, thank you all the same."

He put out a gentlemanly hand, and Reggie shook it.

Jade followed suit.

"Glad everything is working out."

Both girls finished changing at the same time.

Intent on showing she was with Shane, Abi b-lined it to him while Sara approached Burton as Martin and the guys joined everyone.

"The dresses will be delivered to the Thousand Hotel Bride's Room. Wednesday at one o'clock. Will you have someone there to receive them?" Umeko said to the older gentleman in charge, hoping to confirm that either way.

"Yes, we will have someone on-site for you."

"Very good," Umeko replied.

"Thank you so much for helping us today," Jade gushed. "I am grateful."

"Congratulations to you both," she said, hoping her English was correct. "All the best."

To keep the day moving on schedule, Martin announced, "We must be on our way. Next stop, the chapel and flowers."

The group descended to the main floor in the elevator and gathered inside the entrance while the guys went out to secure the area and ensure their transportation was ready.

Eight feet between Burton and Sara, Abi caught the girl's sight on her. Sadly, the happy girlfriend was no longer there. Not knowing what to do to fix it, it seemed like this would be an ever-growing battle as long as Burton was with her. She was beginning to see why he was frustrated. Like he'd said before, *jealousy is a bad thing.*

With the trucks prepared to depart, Lorenzo and Andrew swung open the doors.

"Let's go," Lorenzo instructed with his head on a swivel.

One by one, everyone found their seats in the SUVs.

Abi stared out the window. Thankful not to see anything suspicious, she leaned her back against the headrest and tried to relax.

Andrew peered in their rearview before they pulled away. After radioing the guys in the vehicles around them, the caravan suddenly broke apart and went in different directions.

Burton and Sara continued straight while they turned left at the next major intersection. Turning around, she noticed the men in the third truck had already disappeared.

With the Kyoto tower standing tall ahead of them, they passed an ornate shrine with a lotus flower fountain before threading through the city and making a quick left, then a quick right. Veering into a large hotel, they descended into the underground parking garage.

The driver brought them to a set of glass doors leading inside.

Not sure what was happening, Abi shifted in her seat so she could see what Andrew was doing.

Listening to someone through his earpiece, he nodded his head and said, "Got it," before getting out to open the passenger side. "Move along. No stopping, please."

While Jade and Reggie got out and did as he asked, Abi noticed a woman waiting just inside the entryway, which was decorated for Christmas. Four security guards flanked her.

Andrew pulled the seat back for Abi and Shane to exit. Walking with him, they saw one of the trucks appear.

The woman was speaking with Jade and Reggie when they joined them.

"Good afternoon, Miss Webber and Mr. Wilson."

Both of them bowed and said, "Hello," simultaneously.

"Welcome to The Thousand Kyoto. My name is Yasu. Right this way," she said. Dressed elegantly in black, with a sleek bob that framed her face, her light complexion was in soft contrast to her dark attire, enhancing her polished and professional demeanor. "You can wait in the studio until the rest of your party arrives."

Led into a pretty room dressed in calming white and light gray tones, they took a seat.

"The others are arriving now," Andrew confirmed.

A little out of sorts, Abi caught Jade whispering to Reggie.

Pulling Shane over to their friends, she asked, "Is something wrong?"

"I don't know, Abs. I really loved the quaintness of the chapel by Aman. It was so peaceful. This place is right in the heart of the city. It doesn't have the same vibe I saw in the pictures. I'm worried..."

Not telling her she felt the same, Abi could feel her disappointment. "Well, let's just see the chapel and decide after that. I'm sure you guys can voice your opinion."

Her friend nodded. "Maybe you're right."

In minutes, everyone joined them in the room. With hands buried in his pockets, Burton walked in with Sara clinging to his arm. She immediately watched his reaction to seeing Abi across from them while trying to ignore it.

The woman stood before the group. "Again, my name is Yasu. I will be escorting you to the wedding chapel we call KOMOREBIDO - a music hall of light and water among the trees," she smiled proudly. Before leaving, she remained calm. "Our chapel is unlike anything you'll find in a traditional hotel setting," she explained with a brightness appearing as she described the hidden sanctuary they were about to see. "Nestled within the heart of our inner garden, it changes with the seasons, blending with nature in a way that feels almost alive. When you step inside, you'll be greeted by the warmth of natural wood and light, with patterned waterfall glass that lets the sun pour in, painting the space in soft, golden hues. It's a place of peace, where the outside world feels distant, and all that matters is the serenity within." She paused for effect. Spotting some curiosity from Jade, she added, "You'll feel it the moment you step inside—the harmony of nature and design as if the space is breathing with you. It's more than a chapel."

Upon hearing that, Jade turned to Abi. She didn't seem as stressed all of a sudden.

"Follow me, please."

Making their way to the elevators, the group soon arrived on the lobby floor. When the doors parted, they found an enormous cathedral ceiling soaring at least six stories tall. Anchoring the space was a beautifully decorated Christmas tree situated partway up the black slate staircase that led from the ground level to the bamboo garden outside the tall glass atrium.

While they followed the woman up the steps, Abi and Jade looked around, amazed by the scale of the hotel.

Reaching the top, she said, "Right this way," before opening the exterior doors and moving up the staircase adjacent to the patch of bamboo. Amidst the trees, she said, "This is Okuniwa Garden." Pointing to the chapel behind her, Yasu explained, "A testament to modern elegance, its sleek design harmonizes effortlessly with the natural beauty surrounding it. Let's go inside."

The group quietly approached the building. Despite being in the thick of the city, it was strange not to hear it in the background. All they could hear was the swooshing sounds of water and the cool breeze moving through the trees.

For a grand entrance, the woman had Martin help her swing the double doors open for effect. Standing arm and arm with Reggie, Jade was in awe the moment she saw the inside. She clutched her heart. In seconds, the stressed expression on her face dissipated, and magically, all of her fears disappeared.

Their eyes lifted to the tall window, where waterfall glass softened the view of a winter garden. Sunlight filtered through the trees, casting shifting shadows inside. Above, the ceiling was a masterpiece—wood beams arranged like branches, blending nature and design in perfect harmony.

Abi admired how every detail reflected traditional Japanese craftsmanship.

Along the chapel's base, narrow peek-a-boo windows offer glimpses of the garden and trickling ponds beyond. Each set low to the ground, they framed the dry grasses swaying as if nature was quietly making its presence known. The effect, subtle yet immersive, deepened the chapel's tranquility, adding a seamless connection to the world outside.

In awe, Jade stood in the aisle, lost for words.

"So..." Reggie stated, waiting to hear her thoughts.

Able to exhale after holding her breath too long, she replied, "I absolutely love it. It's perfect."

Happy to see her friend's reaction, knowing they were back on track, Abi felt the weight of the moment suddenly lift.

Confirming the new venue with Martin, the happy couple thanked him for all his hard work. Both knew this was the beginning of something beautiful—something they'd hoped and dreamed of was finally coming to life.

| 30 |

New Arrangements

Monday, December 18

The Thousand Hotel, Kyoto

After taking a few minutes to sit in the serene space while Martin booked the chapel for Wednesday at 3:00 p.m., he and Yasu invited Jade and Reggie to the offices to discuss the wedding bouquets, as they needed to submit their order before 4:00 p.m. that day.

Returning inside, about to walk back down the enormous staircase, Burton turned to their right and spotted a restaurant.

"Anyone up for some lunch?" he asked Sara, Shane, Abi, and the guys.

Always hungry, Shane looked more than interested.

But as much as Reg wanted to join them, he knew he had to pass.

"We will go and decide on the flowers and return shortly," Martin divulged.

Knowing she was the maid of honor and couldn't abandon the bride, Abi asked, "Want me to come with you, Jade?"

She pulled up a picture on her phone. Showing the girl, she said, "Can we do something like this?"

"Certainly, Miss Webber. Very beautiful choice," Yasu stated.

Happy with that, she replied, "It's okay, Abs. You can stay with Shane if you like. We won't be long."

As the group descended the stairs, Abi watched her friends leave with Martin and Yasu before they reached the bottom and disappeared into the tunnel below them.

Burton and Sara walked towards the Tea & Bar. Met by a host, the gentleman slowly got their group seated along the back wall.

To Abi, the atmosphere felt calm yet sophisticated. Enhanced by the soft strains of traditional koto music playing in the background, the seamless window framed the bamboo inner garden outside, adding to the room's zen-like ambiance.

Not wasting a second, Burton glanced at the menu. Taking charge, he ordered an assortment of snacks, including cheese and fruits, cold meat platters, and a few orders of truffle fries for the table to share, along with cups of green tea. "Everyone okay with that?" he asked, looking around. When they all nodded, he set the menu aside, having confirmed everything with their server. Exhausted, he leaned back in his chair, his expression focused.

Abi sensed he had a lot on his mind. "So, tell us more about the events you've got coming up," she prompted, knowing that's where his thoughts had drifted.

Burton's gaze met hers, and after a brief pause, he began. "Well, Thursday night, I'll be with Red Dragon at a pop-up, standing-room-only gathering in the art space Yokaan, not far from the hotel. We're introducing Nightfall to some high-profile people. Then, on Friday, we're off to Osaka. The first event is at Nakka—the Nakanoshima Museum of Art—where a provocative Edokko artist requested Red Dragon and me to breathe some life into the place, hoping to attract a younger crowd. The same night, I might need to make an appearance at a private party."

He turned to Sara as she interjected. "Thankfully, you'll have the week to recover in Niseko before the Andaru event. That one's big."

"True," he nodded. "As of now, we've sold two thousand tickets for that and had to cut it off. It could've easily gone to six thousand if we hadn't."

The magnitude of his upcoming schedule hung in the air, and for a moment, the group sat in quiet acknowledgment of the energy and focus it would take to pull everything off smoothly.

"Can we do anything to help?" Shane asked, not wanting to sit idly by.

"Thanks, but I have a crew of eighty-three people here for set-ups and take-downs. I just show up when I need to. Martin converses with the project managers daily to make sure we execute the events according to plan."

"Sounds complicated," Shane surmised.

Having experienced quite a few over the past couple of months, Sara said, "Not really. Everything runs like a well-oiled machine."

The server returned with stacks of appetizer plates. Spreading them down the table, everyone took one along with the cutlery rolled inside the napkins.

Wondering if they'd get a chance to attend any of his events, especially with how immersive and unique they sounded, she asked, her curiosity laced with a hint of hesitation. "Do you think we'll be able to come to any of them?"

He considered her question for a moment. "I'm okay with you guys coming to the larger events," he replied, meeting her eyes. "You'll blend in more at those. But for the smaller ones, I'd rather you sit them out. I want to avoid any connections between us. You know how it goes. It's better to keep certain things separate."

Understanding the delicate balance Burton had to maintain, it wasn't just about the events—it was about staying under the radar.

Just as the food arrived at the table, Martin, Jade, and Reggie reappeared, approaching with bright smiles. The bride and groom-to-be seemed more relaxed than they had earlier today. Thankfully, they were clearly in high spirits.

After quick greetings, the group pulled up chairs, and Martin explained as he sat down, "We need to eat and run—we are to meet with the jeweler and caterer back at the Park Hyatt in less than an hour."

Not wanting the food to go to waste, he said, "No worries. You guys can head out when you need to." Turning to Abi and Shane, he suggested, "You two can come with us back to the hotel later. That way, we don't have to rush."

Abi and Shane exchanged glances, grateful for the extra time to relax despite the tight schedule.

"Very well. Please note that we are meeting for a special dinner at Forni this evening. We must meet in the hallway by six o'clock. Since the restaurant is upscale, I kindly ask that you dress accordingly. Until then, you have free time."

"Thank you, Martin."

Jade and Reggie took a few bites from the platters presented in front of them. Seeing this, Burton flagged down a waiter. "May we have a few to-go containers, if you don't mind?"

The man nodded, somewhat understanding what he wanted. Returning with folded cardboard cubes, Jade, Reggie, Martin, and the guys grabbed a few things to take with them.

"Remember not to eat and walk. They consider this rude. Wait until we return to the truck before you enjoy it," Martin advised.

When they left, the atmosphere around the table seemed to shift. Both Abi and Burton felt an invisible barrier form, preventing them from speaking freely. Keeping tabs on Shane's scrutinizing glimpses and Sara's glares, each read into every exchange between them.

Their conversation felt more forced than fluid as they touched upon the experiences at the Arashiyama bamboo forest, Tenryu-ji Temple, and Fushimi Inari, reminiscing about the beauty of the places they'd visited. However, the mood remained heavy as they discussed the strange encounter with the old man at Heian Shrine.

"So..." Abi said, her tone light but carrying an edge of concern. "Do we know anything more about the guy from the bridge? Do you know who he is?"

Hesitating for a moment, he glanced over at Sara, who quietly sipped her tea. At this point, Burton didn't want to say too much. "No word yet," he replied, keeping his voice steady. "Hopefully, we'll have him ID'd soon."

As the unease lingered, Abi could tell that he was holding back—just like she was. The conversation felt forced, not flowing the way it usually did between them. It was draining.

The air only thickened as the minutes dragged on.

Andrew, their security guard, sensed it too. He'd been watching the subtle shifts between the two couples, especially after the encounter at the bridal salon. Wanting to ease Abi's discomfort, he signaled for the rest of the men to join in and start a conversation, hoping to lighten the mood.

Uncomfortable, Sara knew what they were doing. Abruptly standing up, her expression tight, she muttered, "I'm just going to the washroom," before quickly excusing herself. As she walked away, Shane's phone buzzed on the table, pulling his attention. Rolling his eyes, he picked it up and sighed. "Excuse me a moment," he said, already standing. "My agent's calling."

As he, too, disappeared from the table, it finally left Abi and Burton alone to talk freely. The security team relaxed a little, their quiet conversations blending into the background. And for the first time all afternoon, they felt they could breathe.

"Do you feel that as much as I do?"

Burton nodded, his expression still calm but his eyes revealing a flicker of the strain he'd been holding in. "Unfortunately."

"What do we do about it?" Abi asked, her frustration slipping through.

"There's nothing we can do except be aware of their feelings," he said, his voice low but steady.

Running a hand through her hair, she sighed, "I feel like I'm walking on eggshells with her all the time. No matter what I do, I'm always making her feel awkward or angry, and that is not my intention."

"I know," he replied, his gaze not leaving hers. "At least with Shane, I can talk to him. We manage. With Sara, it's a different story."

She exhaled deeply, slumping back in her chair. "It's exhausting. I just want to talk to you without her getting upset."

He leaned forward. "We just need to get through the wedding tomorrow. After that, things will calm down. I promise. Sara and I will be busy, and you and Shane will have some space."

Abi nodded. "I just hate waiting for moments like this to be able to actually talk. Please don't think I'm avoiding you. But sometimes, the repercussions don't seem worth it at the time."

"I know."

"At least we got to touch base last night without interruption."

His hand moved to brush hers for the briefest moment, his touch grounding her. "Don't ever feel like you can't do that – that you can't come and talk to me anytime," he said firmly. "No matter what, you are still my priority - nobody else. We're just in a complicated spot right now."

Her heart strained upon hearing that. His strength was something she admired. "I wish I could be as calm as you are about all of this," she admitted quietly.

"You don't have to be." Burton's gaze relaxed. "If you feel the need to call Sara out on things, do it. Because, like I said, I feel she and I are somehow not meant to be. Maybe it's best to end things sooner rather than later…"

Hearing that created a knot in her chest. She could not respond.

"Don't worry. I'll give you a heads up if something is about to go down," he said, noticeably dreading it.

For a brief moment, the deep connection between them surfaced. But as the seconds ticked by, the security team's voices faded back in, reminding them of the world that would soon come crashing back around them.

The moment Sara returned from the washroom, she paused a short distance away, arms crossed, her gaze fixed on Abi and Burton, who were seated together, talking quietly. Abi spotted her from the corner of her eye and whispered to Burton, "Uh no, incoming."

Burton glanced over just as Shane ended his phone conversation and approached the table.

"They confirmed the Instagram live announcement needs to air on Thursday. I need to share the school I signed with." He then casually asked Abi, "Can you help me with that? Maybe record it for me?"

Without having to think twice, Abi answered, "Umm, yeah, sure. No problem."

As she responded to him, she happened to notice Sara brush away a tear with her pointer finger before quickly composing herself.

Glad Abi hadn't seen her in that vulnerable moment, the girl took a deep breath and straightened her posture before joining them at the table once again. She stopped beside Burton. Standing over him, she asked politely, "Is it okay if we go now?"

Glancing up at her, Burton nodded. "Sure." He waved down the waiter and settled the bill while the rest of them sat idly by.

When Burton stood up, he announced, "Okay. Let's move." Leading the way out of the tea room and into the corridor, they descended the stairs in a flood, surrounded by their security.

About partway down, Abi admired the Christmas tree. "Hey, Shane, let's take a selfie," she suggested, hoping to lighten the mood, if only for a moment.

Hearing her, Burton turned. "Give it here. I'll take it for you so you can get the whole atrium in the frame."

Reluctantly, Abi handed her phone to him while Sara glared. "Thanks. Appreciate that."

He moved a few steps below them, positioning himself to capture the whole scene, especially the grandeur of it—Abi and Shane framed by the elegant wall of glass with the Christmas tree sparkling in the background. Snapping a few pictures, soon, he soon walked back to them, taking a few close-ups as Shane wrapped his arm around Abi.

Handing the phone to her, Burton said, "Let me know if you like these. If not, we can take a few more."

The two scrolled through the pics.

Shane grinned, impressed. "Wow, these are really good."

Grateful, Abi smiled, happy to have the photos with Shane. But she wouldn't dare ask for a picture with Burton—even though she wanted one.

Leaving the lobby, they all moved toward the elevators, which descended to the lower level and the VIP parking exit. The security team spread out to guard the area. As Abi and Shane took a seat in the third row of Burton and Sara's vehicle, Sara stopped before getting in, turning to Burton.

"Why don't we give them this truck and split up the guys in both vehicles? We can go in the other one," Sara neutrally suggested, her eyes betraying something deeper.

Not wanting to let her dictate the situation, Burton's reply was firm. "No, they're driving with us."

Sara conceded. Nodding, she climbed into the middle seat without another word.

The ride from the Thousand Hotel back to the Park Hyatt was suffocating. No one spoke.

Abi stared out the window, her thoughts swirling, while Shane sat quietly beside her, his arm loosely draped over her shoulder.

When they arrived, the truck eased into the private garage, and they took the elevator to the top floor together. The awkwardness intensified in the confined space. Abi kept her composure, even as the silence gnawed at her nerves.

The moment the elevator doors parted on the top floor, she and Shane stepped forward, their room just a short distance away.

"We'll see you at dinner in a bit," Burton reminded them on his way past.

Given a tight smile, she replied, "Yes, see you then," and remained calm, though her emotions were anything but.

Shane waved the card over the reader and opened their door. As it shut behind them, Abi let out a quiet breath, thankful for the brief reprieve from the complications swirling. But she knew it wouldn't last long—not with the wedding tomorrow. There would be more to navigate, more to untangle, and more emotions simmering beneath the surface, waiting to break through.

| 31 |

A Reprieve

Monday, December 18

Park Hyatt, Kyoto

In the quiet of their room, away from the mounting tensions of the afternoon, Shane could sense Abi's stress as she paced back and forth, her arms crossed, clearly deep in thought.

"Why do you care?" he asked, breaking the silence.

Abi turned to him, her brows furrowed. "About what?"

"About what Sara thinks of you. Her apparent dislike of everyone is simply a reflection of her insecurities. You've done nothing to her," Shane clarified, his eyes never leaving hers.

"I don't get it. I felt this afternoon, we finally broke through her walls and made progress at the dress fitting. Then, everything fell apart when Burton made that comment."

"About that."

Knowing what Shane wanted to address, she quickly stopped him in his tracks. "Shane, please don't. He told me he'd directed the comment at both of us. It wasn't just me."

"Yeah, but he was looking straight at you when he said it."

She stood and walked over to the window. "Please don't rehash this because it will lead to a fight between us, and I can't take any more."

"Fine."

Tinged with frustration, Abi released a subtle sigh before returning to sit on the edge of the bed. "Bottom line is, what if she ruins the wedding with her antics? I mean, the way she acted today, I wouldn't put it past her to make a scene."

"Yeah, I noticed." Shane raised an eyebrow, nodding slowly. "She gets wound up, especially when you're around."

Leaning forward, Abi rubbed her temples. "I just want to keep the peace, you know? I don't want to make things worse for Burton. He's already got so much on his plate, and I'm worried that if Sara keeps spiraling, it's going to blow up."

Upon sitting beside her, he sounded more sympathetic. "You're not responsible for her behavior. If she's going to cause problems, that's on her, not you. But yeah... I can see what you mean. The last thing anyone needs is more drama. There's enough of that to go around already with Reggie's family."

About to divulge a secret told to her in confidence, she bit her lip, weighing the consequences of sharing what she knew. "Between you and me... And, for the record, I mean, you can't say anything to anyone..."

"I promise. What is it?"

"I think Burton's close to ending things with her. He's been different, more distant when they're together, and I get the feeling it's only a matter of time before he calls it quits."

Not surprised to hear that, Shane went quiet as his eyebrows shot up. "Honestly, that's probably for the best."

Abi let out a heavy sigh. "It's just so awkward being around them now. The tension is unbearable, and I feel like I'm constantly walking on eggshells. Everything I say, she reads into. And Burton... He barely talks to me when she's there because he's trying to keep her calm. The next few days could turn into a bloodbath when all is said and done."

Chuckling, he believed she was exaggerating and tried to diffuse the situation. "I don't think it will be that bad. Maybe she will be on her best behavior."

"I bet she pulls a Dr. Jekyll and Mr. Hyde."

"Perhaps," Shane said. "Let's see what happens. Maybe she'll surprise you."

"I hope so." Abi exhaled and flung herself back onto the bed. "I care about Burton, and I want him to be happy."

Shane flopped backward, also. Reaching over, he slid his arm around her. "You're not the reason. You and Burton have a history. It took me a while to understand that. Hopefully, she will too. In the end, if he's not truly happy with Sara, that's something he needs to figure out on his own."

She quieted. "I know. It just feels like I'm caught in the middle."

"Hey, let's focus on the positives. Wednesday's a big day. Our best friends are getting married. From what I gather, I think we'll get some free time on Thursday after my signing announcement. Maybe you and I can sneak away for a bit and see the city," Shane suggested.

Loving the idea, she replied, "Yes, I'd like that."

| 32 |

Forni

Monday, December 18

Mitsui Hotel, Kyoto

Within the hour, Abi and Shane stepped out into the hallway. The group was on time, which meant everyone was hungry. Martin had already started rounding up the troops and getting them in the elevators to keep them on schedule. Descending to the VIP exit, they found three sleek SUVs awaiting them.

As usual, Abi, Shane, Reggie, and Jade got in one together. About to take a seat, Abi caught a glimpse of Burton staring her way.

Smiling, he offered a subtle wave before getting into the vehicle in front of theirs.

Knowing that she and her friends had created this clique and kept separating from him and Sara made it hard. But given the circumstances, she didn't have a choice. Abi was certain Sara preferred it this way.

About to depart, with each settled in, they began their journey from the Park Hyatt Kyoto. The drive was serene as they cruised alongside the Kamo River, with the setting sun casting a gentle reflection off the water. The dusting of snow they'd gotten had seemingly melted in spots, making everything cold and lifeless.

Heading northwest, crossing a large bridge, and traversing the tree-lined city street of Oike-Dori Symbol Road, Abi stared out the window, watching the six lanes of traffic move slowly, wondering where their final destination would be.

Jade's voice cut through the silence. "Hey, this feels like we're back home."

Agreeing with her, Shane chimed in. "Yeah, it has a slight Rodeo Drive vibe."

"Minus the Ferraris and the palm trees," she quickly added.

Soon, the SUVs turned onto the main road. Maneuvering a narrow, one-way street winding through Kyoto's historic neighborhood, not far from Nijo Castle, Abi tried to see where they were going.

"Is this the right way? It's pretty tight," she said as they barely passed within inches of a few parked cars.

Their driver signaled. About to turn again, the man waved to the uniformed security officers standing guard. Stepping aside, they directed them into a meticulously kept courtyard before stopping in front of the main entrance.

A young concierge opened the door for them and bowed. "Yōkoso," he said, and in the same breath, "Welcome."

"Thank you," Shane replied, respectfully nodding as he got out and offered his hand to Abi.

Taking hold, she joined him and took in the sights while Shane flipped the seat forward for Jade and Reg to exit the third row.

Everyone's attention immediately gravitated to the traditional black structure with white accents and an intricately designed, arched roof.

While soaking in its grandeur, Martin took it upon himself to educate the group a little. "This is a three-hundred-year-old Kajiimiya gate. It is an impressive piece of history, welcoming us to this historic property."

Captivated by the craftsmanship, Abi smiled and did not notice Burton keenly observing her reaction to it all.

Comfortable in luxurious settings, Jade and Reggie strolled confidently ahead while Shane took hold of Abi's hand to follow them.

Walking under the white hotel-logoed valance hanging from its rafters, they felt like distinguished guests.

"Wow, this place is pretty nice," he said, also admiring the entryway before ducking under the fabric on the way in.

Always in tune with aesthetics, Jade commented, "The blend of the old with the new is seamless."

Proud of his fiancée's keen eye for design, Reggie grinned.

Entering the interior gardens just inside the gate, a sense of calm washed over them. To their right, slender bamboo trees stood tall, their narrow stalks swaying gently in the breeze, casting delicate shadows on the black cobblestone path leading them through the sanctuary. The fixed stones beneath their feet contrasted with the smooth, black modern slate, transitioning them toward the main doors ahead.

Abi marveled at the small bonsai trees, their branches precisely shaped into miniature, artful forms, while nearby Japanese maples had remnants of a few red leaves that had not yet fallen. Nestled in a few corners, stone pagoda lanterns cast a glow hue. Soaking up their surroundings, she felt as if she had stepped into a peaceful world far removed from the bustling city.

Stopping beside her, Burton said while passing by, "Beautiful, isn't it?"

She smiled. "Yes. It's so pretty." Just as she answered him, Sara shot her a disapproving look, making Abi recoil.

Noticing, Burton turned, causing his girlfriend to start damage control. He wasn't happy.

The natural wood doors slid open with a gentle hush, revealing an elegant and tranquil space beyond the second layer of glass. The modern lanterns inside immediately set a serene tone, their light creating shadows across the floor.

On their way inside, unbeknownst to Abi, Burton took note of her reaction to the lobby.

To her, the space felt intimate and calming as they explored. The walls, lined with warm sycamore wood, complemented the large, elegant shoji lantern hanging from the ceiling.

Reading the plaque on the sculpture below it, Jade admired the wing-like artwork that sat upon a bed of raked gravel. "Designer André Fu worked with Japanese artist Yukiya Izumita to add the ceramic sculpture," she said. "The earthy tones harmonize with the hotel's minimalist design, creating a serene space that bridges modernity and tradition."

In awe of it all, Abi stood alongside Shane and smiled.

Next to the lobby, the lounge was a natural gathering spot with rows of slender bamboo rods suspended from the ceiling, a dynamic visual texture reminiscent of a forest canopy or a traditional pagoda roof.

Immersing in the details, with so much to see, Sara noticed Abi's proximity to Burton again. Her jealousy simmered just beneath her somewhat calm exterior.

Looking up, Burton said to both her and Shane, "Do you like the place?"

"Have you been here before?" Abi asked.

"No, but I snooped and saw the pictures of it on the way here. So, really, I got a sneak peek at what to expect. Figured you guys would like it."

Martin led them down the hallway to their right. Peering upward, he remarked, "The architect created this hallway to resemble the Fushimi Inari Torii gates. Notice the precise spacing between each post." Embedded in the bottom were small LED accent lights, which he admired, along with the iron lanterns hanging here and there, adding to the elongated visual effect.

Threading through the corridor, they marveled at the full floor-to-ceiling glass wall to their left, showcasing a shallow pond of black water. Snow-dusted, spotlit trees in the zen garden created a forest within the confines of the hotel.

"This is just wonderful," the older man commented as they arrived at the end of the corridor.

Bubbling with quiet excitement, Anton followed him, anticipating the culinary journey they were about to embark on. His eyes gleamed as he spotted the hostess waiting for them.

"Good evening. Welcome." Bowing with a smile, she said, "Please follow me."

Surrounded by their security team, dressed impeccably but discreetly, Lorenzo, the lead, walked slightly ahead, checking to ensure everything was running smoothly. His right-hand man, Andrew, flanked him and scanned the area while the rest of the security entourage followed suit. Alert and ready, their presence never felt intrusive.

Guided out the glass door into the gardens, they crossed into a traditional-looking house.

Abi inhaled deeply, feeling the stress of the trip melt away as Shane gave her hand a reassuring squeeze, subtly letting her know he was still by her side.

"Welcome to SHIKI-NO-MA. It is the home of the Kitake, a branch of the Mitsui Family. This is where you will be dining this evening," their hostess revealed.

The quiet elegance of the space wrapped Abi like a blanket. The walls, crafted from pale, natural wood, were bare of ornament yet rich with warmth.

Instructed to remove their shoes and leave them at the door, each person did so and felt the comfort of the thick, soft, natural-looking rug, which grounded the long table set for fifteen, making it feel more like a home than a restaurant. Out of the public eye, it was the perfect escape after a busy day in the city.

Excited, Anton was more than happy to be the first to take a seat.

Easily radiating a sense of simplicity, the room spoke of a centuries-old tradition where every carefully thought-through detail added to the magic of it all.

Their hostess handed out two menus. "You will have the option of dining with either Forni or Toki this evening. Both in-house restaurants service the Shiki-No-Ma experience."

Shane pulled out a chair for Abi before he sat down beside her.

Admiring the view of the garden through the window, Jade and Reg sat across from them while Burton, on Abi's left and pulled out a chair for Sara.

When he did this, she got a quick glimpse of his girlfriend. She wasn't happy. Not knowing how to fix things with her, Abi was at a loss.

Jade admired the black-and-white screens on the back wall. Pointing at them, she said, "I wonder if those are hand-painted?"

The woman smiled and raised her hand to bring their attention to the screens. Everyone turned to her as she said, "The artwork on the fusuma sliding doors is the vision of modern nihonga artist Takafumi Asakura. He created these stunning motifs inspired by the garden at the hotel and shows how it changes across the four seasons."

Seeing his men standing strategically around the room, Burton said to them, "Guys? Please have a seat. You don't need to protect us from anything here. We're good. Take a break."

Lorenzo and Andrew exchanged glances, unsure what was happening.

"You guys need to eat. Please join us," their boss said.

With some hesitation, the men did as he asked but positioned themselves strategically around the table to keep a watchful eye over the group.

As the evening wore on, the conversation flowed easily, punctuated by soft laughter and the gentle clinking of glasses. The lanterns hanging above them added a warmth to the room, making the moment feel even more intimate, almost suspended in time.

Abi scanned the faces around her, noting how relaxed everyone seemed. Even their normally stoic security guards were enjoying the night. There, in that quiet, secluded space, the world outside felt distant and insignificant. All of her problems seemed to vanish, allowing her to lower her guard.

With the last course served—a delicate matcha dessert—the group leaned back in their seats, contentment settling in.

Shane caught Abi's eye, making her lean over and rest her head on his shoulder.

"This is the perfect ending to a perfect evening," she said happily.

| 33 |

Lurking

Monday, December 18

Mitsui Hotel, Kyoto

Ready to leave, one by one, they slipped on their shoes and grabbed their coats. Abi took a final look at the garden outside, the lanterns illuminating the night as a few snowflakes lazily fell. She exhaled slowly, realizing the memory of this quiet, peaceful dinner with friends would stay with her long after they left Kyoto.

After Burton settled the bill with their hostess, she presented his receipt to him and bowed. "Thank you for dining with us," she said.

"Thank you," he nodded while accepting the slip of paper with both hands.

The woman cordially replied, "Have a pleasant evening."

Before walking out the door, Martin bid the woman goodnight as well as the rest of the group. Venturing out in the cold, they soon returned inside and made their way down the artistically designed tunnel before rounding the corner to the right.

Moving past the entrance to the lounge, now filled with many guests, Abi was curious to see who was staying at this beautiful hotel. Catching a glimpse of someone sitting in the far corner, facing them, she briefly made eye contact with the man before he hid behind a newspaper. Concerned, she stared at him until her view became blocked by the corridor wall as they continued toward the lobby. Upon emerging into the open space once again, she turned in his direction but found no one there. Just the newspaper sitting on the table with a cup and saucer left behind.

"That's odd…" she mumbled.

"What's that? Sorry?" Shane questioned, not having fully heard her.

"Umm, nothing," she said, believing it wasn't a big deal. Sadly, her instincts were saying otherwise. Not wanting to bother Burton or Martin about it, she stayed back and pulled Andrew aside.

"Is there something wrong, Miss?" he asked, bending slightly to hear her amidst the hum of the lobby.

"There was a man – older, with round glasses, dressed in a black overcoat," she described, "He had a plaid scarf around his neck and was sitting at the table in the far corner. He looked straight at me, then hid behind a newspaper. When I took a second look, he'd, umm, vanished."

Taking note of it, Andrew scanned the room. "Do you see anyone who looks like him now?"

She stopped to zip her jacket. Checking every face, she said, "No."

"Okay. I'll watch for anything suspicious."

As Abi and Shane walked out the main doors following their friends, she could hear Andrew radioing to the guys quietly. In seconds, the men took up defensive positions.

Seeing this, Martin was beside Burton when he asked Lorenzo, "Is there a problem?"

He nodded and confirmed, "Miss Abi noticed a strange man sitting in the lounge. He mysteriously disappeared after making eye contact with her."

"Perhaps it was just a hotel guest," Martin assumed.

"He was wearing an overcoat and a scarf. The rest of the guests weren't."

Hearing this, Burton escorted Abi through the Kajiimiya gate. Resting his hand along the small of her back, he said, "Come on. Hurry."

Concerned by the guy's reaction, Shane intervened and took his place.

Upon seeing this, Burton backed off and told Jade and Reg, "Go with Andrew and Matt. We will meet you back at the hotel."

Confused, the two watched Abi and Shane move to Burton's vehicle.

Amidst the shift, about to get into the SUV, Burton's attention gravitated upward. There, hanging from the rafters of the ancient Kajimiya Gate, was a new valance with dark kanji letters. "Death to Her..." he said solemnly, not realizing Abi heard him.

"What? Where?" Frightened, she followed his line of sight.

The valance had changed from the stark white hotel-logoed fabric to one with blood-stained letters and a red dragon stamped near the bottom.

Angry, Burton grilled the valet. "Who did this!" Pointing to the fabric above them.

Startled, the innocent men exchanged glances.

"They change," the one man said in broken English.

The other added, "Yes. It change often. Not our job."

Unable to get the answers he needed, Burton prompted Martin, "Let's go," alarmingly.

The man scoured their surroundings before getting in the third SUV. Taking out his iPad, he quickly contacted the hotel to gather as much information as possible about the situation.

With Shane and Abi safely in the third row, Burton turned to them and said, "Tell me what you saw in the lobby."

Scared, she peered out the window at the valance blowing in the breeze as the vehicles moved out in unison. "When we were walking out, I saw a man sitting in the far corner of the lounge. He stood out because he was the only one wearing a coat and a scarf. Everyone else seemed normal."

"Any details?"

Shane intently listened as she said, "Just a black overcoat, plaid scarf." Pausing, she tried to recall what she'd witnessed. "White dress shirt underneath. Round black glasses. Harry Potter-like. Maybe in his late fifties or early sixties. He was holding a newspaper and hid behind it when I made eye contact with him."

Pondering the information, Burton turned to Lorenzo, sitting in the front seat, as the guy mumbled something into his comms. In seconds, the SUVs branched out and drove in different directions.

Both Shane and Abi looked at each other, knowing their friends would be freaking out.

In seconds, Abi got a text from Jade. Peering down at her phone, it read, *What's going on?* Finding Burton leaning forward, now speaking quietly with Lorenzo, Abi said, "Jade is asking what's wrong. What do I tell her?"

To keep everyone calm, he replied, "Tell her everything is fine."

When she sent that, Shane then got a text. "Now, Reg is messaging me."

The tension in the car thickened as he noticed Lorenzo glance in the rearview mirror past them.

"Is someone following us?" Shane asked firmly.

"No. Not that we can see," Burton replied. "We are just making sure."

Despite hearing there was no immediate threat, Shane wasn't satisfied. "Why is it that danger follows you wherever you go?" he accused, noticeably frustrated as Sara glared.

Angry, the woman stared him down. "What are you implying?"

Abi's pulse quickened. Sensing a fight could break out, she gently slipped her hand onto Shane's leg, patting it in a silent plea for him to relax.

Not flinching, he continued his line of questioning. "It just seems there's always one problem or another. Who are these people? Are we being targeted? Tell me the truth! Have you done something to piss them off?" His words came out like rapid-fire bullets. "Why the hell is Death to Her popping up all the time?"

"Shane!" Abi shouted, needing to de-escalate things, but the guy's gaze stayed fixed on Burton, waiting for an explanation.

The DJ held up his hand. "It's fine, Abs. He has a right to know."

"Know what?" The football player's protective instincts surged as he leaned forward. "What are you mixed up in?"

"That's none of your business," Sara snapped rudely.

"Like, hell, it isn't! If Abi is in danger because of you, you need to tell us!" he demanded, holding onto his girlfriend protectively.

With his life's complexities becoming visible, Burton said, "Despite all our efforts to maintain a low profile, we believe certain individuals are connecting the dots. Given my wealth, let's just say this type of thing is a common occurrence."

Abi could feel Shane's muscles tensing as his arm tightened around her. His brow furrowed upon hearing what Burton said. "So this is an ongoing threat?"

Unable to do much about it, he replied, "It's my life. We are always mitigating things on the daily."

Sitting back slightly, Shane tried to process it all.

Abi could see the flicker of understanding in his eyes, but there was still a fire burning there—a need to ensure she wasn't at risk because of someone else's world. His thumb absentmindedly rubbed her arm, comforting and grounding her, making her feel incredibly loved and protected.

"So this has nothing to do with you being..." Shane started, but Burton quickly interrupted, his expression clearly saying, *Not here, not now.*

Stopping him before he revealed any more, Burton tilted his head toward the driver, reminding Shane of the need for discretion. "Look, tonight's incident might be nothing, or..." He let the thought hang.

Abi finished his sentence, "Or, it might be something."

"Perhaps. Better to take precautions and be safe than sorry."

Nodding in agreement, Shane settled down while they took the long route back to the hotel. As he exhaled slowly, his gaze met Abi's. Gently cupping her cheek, he said quietly, "Don't worry. I'll keep you safe." His strong demeanor surfaced.

Overhearing him, Burton turned his back to them and smirked, believing the guy had no idea how to go about that if push came to shove.

As they rode in silence, Shane leaned in closer and pressed a soft kiss to her temple. His presence was like a shield, keeping her anchored amidst the uncertainty of the night. Not used to seeing this side of him—this fierce, protective part that was willing to challenge anyone who posed a threat to her, Abi found herself leaning into it, trusting him even more.

As Shane's hand slid into hers, Burton's voice broke through the quiet. "We need to stay under the radar from now until Friday morning."

Lorenzo looked back. "After that, we move on to Osaka for one night and then Tokyo before heading north. With your friends' wedding being what it is, there is a chance word will get out."

"And if it does?" Abi questioned.

Sara, who'd been mostly silent, faced Abi with unwavering confidence. "If it does, we'll be ready."

| 34 |

Safe and Sound

Monday, December 18

Park Hyatt, Kyoto

Close to ten o'clock, their SUV converged on the Park Hyatt and drove into the parking garage. Abi and Shane noticed a number of security guards on duty as they passed. It was more than usual—far more. Stopping at the VIP entrance and not seeing the other trucks, they got out of the vehicle. Just then, Bray, Ethan, and Rob appeared and opened their door.

With a sigh of relief, Abi asked, "Did Reggie and Jade make it back?"

Bray replied, "They are five minutes out."

Ushered inside, they were escorted to the elevator, which was held for them. The second they stepped in, the doors closed, and they were on their way to the top floor. Sara remained quiet, checking her phone. Nobody else said a thing.

When they arrived, Shane stayed by Abi's side as they walked to their room door. Hovering the card over the reader, he opened it, ready for her to enter first.

Sara kept walking while Burton stopped midway down the hall. "You gonna be okay?" he asked Abi quietly.

Back in familiar territory, she knew the drill. "Yes, all good."

With a reassuring nod, he said, "Okay, then. Night, Abs."

She flashed a partial smile and replied, "Night, B," as Shane stood by. About to go inside, she watched Burton glance back once and offer a low wave before slipping both hands into his pockets.

Upon closing the door when she walked in, Shane quickly locked up behind her. "Well, this was certainly an eye-opener. Guess you've been dealing with stuff like this for a while, huh?"

"What do you mean?" she asked, turning to him.

"You know, when he sends you away and puts you in hiding while he's gone somewhere. Like just before homecoming. Is this why?" Shane said with a mix of curiosity and concern.

Recalling those few days hidden in Newport Beach, unable to share the details, she divulged, "Yeah, something like that..."

Sensing that she was deep in thought, he opened his arms as she instinctively moved towards him. He pulled her close, his strong arms wrapping around her, offering her a sense of safety and comfort. "Hey," he whispered, brushing a kiss against her temple. "Everything's going to be okay. I'm here, and I will never let anything happen to you."

She nodded, believing him wholeheartedly as he tipped her chin upward. "I know things have been crazy, but as long as we're together, we're good."

Abi gave him a small smile, reassured by his steady presence. But before they could settle into the peaceful moment, a knock echoed through the room.

Reluctantly letting go of her, he went to answer it.

Peering through the peephole, he saw Jade and Reggie standing on the other side. The two were visibly shaken as Shane opened the door.

"Hey, man. Can we come in?" Reggie asked, his voice tense.

"Is everything okay?" Abi questioned, already knowing the answer by the look on their faces.

Wide-eyed and clearly rattled, Jade shook her head. "We just…we didn't know what was happening out there. Getting split up like that freaked me out."

Hugging the girl tightly, Jade clung to Abi. "Everything is fine. We are all safe," she whispered as she eyed up Shane.

The girl's breathing slowly steadied.

"We didn't know what to think." Reg rubbed his hand along Jade's back.

"It was just a precautionary thing," Abi smiled gently at both of them.

"Yeah, Abs saw a man sitting in the lounge. He was watching us and looked out of place, so the guys went on high alert, that's all."

Wishing Shane hadn't revealed that bit of information, Abi went into damage control. "It was nothing by the way. False alarm."

Somewhat relieved, Jade replied, "Well, that's good to hear."

Abi could see them slowly calm down. "Now, you two should try to get some rest."

A little hesitant, Jade nodded and said, "Alright," before the two bid them, "Goodnight," and walked out the door.

When it closed behind them, Abi exhaled while Shane wrapped his arms around her from behind and kissed her neck. "We should get some sleep, too. Are you going to shower first?"

"No, you go ahead," she said, wanting to change into something more comfortable.

"Are you sure? I can wait."

"It's fine. Really."

"Alright. I won't be long," he said before disappearing into the bathroom and closing the pocket doors.

Minutes later, Abi heard the sound of water pouring from the faucet.

While sitting in bed, her phone chimed. Receiving a message from Martin, she found their itinerary for the next day, outlining the bachelor and bachelorette events planned. Burton was CC'd on it. Disappointed, she noticed it outlined the Sumo event for the men and the shopping excursion for the women.

"I guess he didn't like my idea after all," she whispered under her breath.

In seconds, her phone buzzed. It was Burton texting.

Before you say anything, I'm sorry. I forgot to share your idea with Martin, and he ran with what we'd spoken about previously. This hasn't gone out to anyone else yet.

She smiled and texted back, *So does that mean this itinerary is subject to change?*

There was a long pause. His thinking bubbles appeared, then disappeared, then reappeared again. She could imagine his brain smoldering. Hearing the water still trickling against the tile, she kept close tabs on Shane, not wanting him to know that they were conversing. The last thing she needed was more conflict.

Suddenly, her phone rang. Fumbling to answer it, she said, "Hello?"

Burton cut to the chase. "What you had in mind is far more meaningful."

"I was hoping you'd say that..." she whispered, recalling the article about the forgotten children of Japan. "Does this mean we can do the charity thing instead tomorrow? Visit a children's home and give them a Christmas?" There was a brief silence on the other end. "Hello?" she prompted, wondering if he was still there.

"Yeah. It's a great idea," Burton finally responded. "I'm just sending Martin a message. The poor guy will be up for a few hours rearranging the schedule, but I believe it's worth the trouble."

Abi sighed thankfully.

"Leave it with me," he said. "I'll continue speaking with Martin, and I'll get back to you in the morning."

Hearing the faucet turn off, she said nervously, "Okay, umm, Burton. I've gotta go."

"Sure, no problem," he said, understanding that she wasn't alone. "Night, Abs."

"Night," she replied, just as Shane walked out of the bathroom with a towel around his waist.

"All yours when you're ready," he said, flashing a grin, not having heard her on the phone.

Putting her device face down on the side table, she muted the ringer. Walking past him with her nightgown in hand, he gave her a quick kiss on the way by.

"I'll only be a minute," she said before disappearing into the bathroom. Going through the motions while getting ready for bed, everything compounding upon her, she opted to have a bath at the last second. When she turned on the faucet, Abi inspected the spa products lining the tub and poured some lavender-scented liquid in as the water started to foam. Loving the heavenly smell of essential oils infusing the room, she slipped into the bath and closed her eyes, trying not to think too much. However, it was hard for her to shut off her brain. Aside from the Sara drama, her Dad haphazardly came to mind, making her blood boil, and thoughts of her Mom made her heart hurt. The family she once had felt like a lifetime ago, almost as if it never existed.

Suddenly, Shane knocked on the door. "Abs?" he said.

Turning off the faucet, she replied, "Yes."

"We have a situation. Jade and Reg need to speak to us again."

Sitting up in the tub, she said, "Umm, okay," and quickly got out and dried off. Fastening her hair in a messy bun and wrapping a white robe around her body, she tied the belt and slid the door open. At the same time, Shane was opening the adjoining room door between their suite and Jade's.

When the two walked in, they seemed noticeably bothered by something.

Gathering around the room, Jade sat on the sofa with Abi while Shane found a spot on the bed and Reg slouched in the chair.

Their friend leaned forward, resting his elbows on his knees. Phone in hand, he looked at the screen and said, "So, Page Six just posted this headline ~ Is Billionaire Heir Reggie Wilson about to tie the knot?"

"I've already heard from Allie and Laney," Jade revealed. "Both of them are upset that we didn't share our plans."

Seeing her noticeably distraught, Abi rubbed her arm sympathetically. "But you kept it quiet for a reason. I'm sure they will understand if you explain about his Dad."

"I wouldn't worry about any of that," Shane agreed. "When we get back, you can have an official reception for our friends. That way, everyone can celebrate with you."

"It's not just that. This post is likely to spark a major frenzy. Trust me." Glancing at Jade, Reggie knew their friends were the least of their worries. "Given this development, it makes me wonder if we shouldn't wait until Wednesday to get married."

When she heard this, Jade got nervous. "But we've already changed things once. We can't do it again. That's not fair to Martin and definitely not Burton. He's already incurred an enormous bill to help us, and Martin has put so much work into this, not to mention there's a hefty penalty for canceling..."

His eyes met hers. "Well, then, we will have to hide out until the ceremony and not be seen in public. I'm sure the city will soon be crawling with photographers. They will do anything for a picture."

"Then, that's what you do," Shane said. "Think of it as resting up before the big day versus hiding out."

"He's right," Abi interjected, "The next five days after the wedding will be pretty busy. So you should get some rest while you can."

Standing up from his chair, Reggie paced the floor next to the tall picture window. His arms crossed over his chest. "Guess I should talk to Martin about this."

Shane chuckled, assuming he knew more than what he was letting on. "The guy is probably already aware of it. He seems to be up on everything."

"Yeah, maybe." Turning to Jade, Reg said, "Guess we can't do much about it right now anyway." He paused. "It's late. We should let these two get some sleep."

"I'm sorry we interrupted your bath. We'll let you get back to it." Hugging Abi, Jade added, "We'll see you in the morning."

"Sounds good." Abi insisted, "Don't worry. Everything will be fine. You'll see."

Offering a hand to Reg, his best friend took hold, as he pulled Shane in for a manly pat on the back. "Thanks for listening, man."

"Anytime."

When the two left the room, both passageway doors closed and locked. Abi returned to the bathroom to run some more hot water in the tub. Slipping in again, she closed her eyes and tried to relax.

Noticing the pocket door opened a crack, Shane sat on the floor outside the room. "I hope his father doesn't ruin things for them."

"I was thinking the same thing," she said.

"The guy is ruthless. When he fixates on something, it seems he doesn't give up until he gets what he wants."

He heard Abi moving in the water. "Hey, maybe you want some company in there?" he joked.

Unsure of what to say, she froze.

Not hearing a response, he got worried. "Abs?"

"What?"

"Relax. I'm just kidding." Getting up off the floor, he said, "I'll leave you to it."

"Shane..."

He stopped. "Yeah?"

Wanting to share something with him, she said, "So that you know, I usually have a bath when I have a lot on my mind."

He leaned against the wall, his back to her. "Anything I can help with?"

Thinking about their trip thus far, she found it hard to turn off the negative thoughts rolling through her head. "Seeing that man sitting there tonight, the way he looked at me, I don't know. It wasn't random. Then, we mix in the red dragon-tattooed teens, the man with the cane, and the bookmark…" That is when she recalled, "The DJ who invited Burton here was also named Red Dragon. That can't be a coincidence? Can it?" she mumbled.

"All of this is a little out there, Abs. Surreal, really. It's hard to make sense of it."

"So, you feel that way too?"

"Absolutely." He turned to the crack in the door. "Listen to me, okay? From now on, you stick close to me when we're out."

She nodded. "I will."

"And if you see anything weird or out of sorts, you tell me right away. Don't hide it. Agreed?"

"Alright."

"Good," he said. "Now, finish your bath so you can come and cuddle with me."

She giggled. "I'll try and make it quick."

Having seen him walk away, she felt a sense of relief, knowing he would keep his distance and not pressure her. Somehow, she felt closer to him since he'd backed off and said what he did.

How do I tell him about Harvard? I hope he won't be upset, she thought. *Disappointed, maybe? Angry, perhaps?*

Deciding to get out, she pulled the plug and wrapped herself in a plush white towel to finish getting ready for bed as the water drained away. After washing her hair in the sink and positioning a towel atop her head, she took the blow dryer to it. Running a brush through to smooth the ends, she slipped on her nightgown. Surfacing, she walked around the corner.

"That was quick," he said, surprised to see her so soon. "I figured you'd be soaking for a while – not that I'm complaining."

She went to her side of the bed, pulled back the blankets, and got in. Covering herself up to her neck, she exhaled.

Noticing she was overly quiet, he said, "Want to talk about it?" While sliding over, offering that promised cuddle, he hoped he wasn't the cause of any heavy thoughts.

"Somehow, I assumed this trip would be carefree and enjoyable, not filled with worries, stress, and drama..."

"Guess when you have a big group like this, there's bound to be all of that."

Resting her head on his chest, hearing his heart beating, she replied, "Very true..."

"Hope I haven't contributed to it." Backing off a bit, he added, "If you need some space, just say. I know it can't be easy with me around twenty-four-seven right now."

"No, it's not you." Unsure how to explain herself, she sighed, "It's just..."

"Can I ask you something?"

Afraid of what he was about to divulge, she gave him her undivided attention.

"I hope our conversation last night helped things between us. I feel it did. You seem more relaxed. Not so tense. The last thing I want is for you to be scared of being alone with me..." he paused. "At night, I mean."

A little shocked by his comment, she raised herself up to see him more clearly. With sincerity in her eyes, she said, "I have never been scared to be with you - ever. Nervous, perhaps, but never scared. And our conversation did help. Somehow, it's made me feel even closer to you, if that's even possible. So, thank you for that." To prove it, she snuggled up against him again. "Truthfully, I was on edge sometimes before bed. I hated the thought of always saying no." She got a little anxious. "It made me think you'd eventually get tired of waiting and just walk away."

Hearing this, he tried to calm her fears. "I would never do that."

"Promise?"

He inched closer. "I promise."

Lying there in silence, Abi tried not to get stuck in her head.

Cuddling closer to him, he kissed her casually and said, "Umm..."

"What is it?"

Grabbing his phone, he asked, "Don't hate me, but do you mind if I watch some football?"

She laughed. "Of course not. Go ahead. I don't mind."

Putting in his earbuds, dimming the bright screen, he said, "Night, Abs. Love you."

"Love you too." Abi got comfortable as he reached over and held her hand as she fell asleep.

Between plays, he peered down at her. Appreciating Abi's beautiful hair cascading around her pretty face on the pillow and the peacefulness it offered, a million things flashed through his mind. His heart ached at the thought of leaving her behind once they got back to LA. Every time the reality of going to Alabama without her surfaced, it was like something inside him twisted painfully. He couldn't imagine a future without her by his side, cheering him on, grounding him when the world would become too much. As the days inched closer to his announcement, this feeling grew suffocatingly. He knew he had to go—it was the next step in his life.

"But what if she doesn't come with me?" he whispered, gently running his fingertips over her hand as she slept peacefully. "There's no way I can leave you."

| 35 |

Rise and Shine

Tuesday, December 19

Park Hyatt, Kyoto

The soft light of dawn slowly crept into the room as the sun attempted to break through the low-hanging clouds. As Shane's alarm broke the stillness, an annoying buzzing pulled them both from the last remnants of sleep. Turning it off as they stirred, Shane found himself tangled up with Abi, their legs entwined beneath the crisp white sheets.

"Morning," he muttered before kissing her cheek and rolling onto his back to stretch out.

"Morning," Abi mumbled, still lying on her side, her eyes barely open.

Propping himself up a bit, Shane grabbed the pillow behind his head to support his back. He glanced down at her. "Did you sleep well?"

"I did. I was pretty tired." She shifted to the view outside. "I feel rested now. How about you?"

"Yeah," he said, running a hand over his face. "I was up for a bit but managed to fall asleep eventually."

His tone was casual, but she could sense something beneath it.

Shane swung his legs over the side of the bed. Soon after, he walked into the bathroom, sliding the pocket door shut with a subtle thud.

Left alone in the quiet room, hearing the water running, Abi rolled onto her back and gazed out of the wide window. The Yasaka Pagoda, once so vibrant, now stood as a dark silhouette against the gradually brightening sky. The horizon blurred with shades of orange and pink, the early morning clouds casting patches over the city below. She sighed while taking in the view. It was so beautiful.

A knock echoed from the door, breaking the moment of solitude. Instantly, she heard the water turn off as the bathroom door opened.

Shane reappeared to greet the server.

"Good morning. You're breakfast, Sir," the man at the door said.

"Morning." Shane wheeled in the trolley. "Appreciate it."

As the door clicked shut, the clatter of the trolley wheels followed as he pushed the cart into the room.

Arranging their plates and utensils at the table, he caught sight of a cream-colored envelope nestled among the dishes. Curious, he opened it. His eyes scanned the note.

"We're supposed to meet in Burton's suite at ten o'clock this morning," Shane said, placing the card down on the small table beside the breakfast tray.

Abi sat up, smoothing the sheets around her.

"Wonder what we're doing today?" Shane added, glancing at the time on his phone. "That gives us about an hour."

Having an inkling of their schedule, Abi thought about what she'd wear while slipping out of bed, the coolness of the floor tingling against her bare feet as she made her way to the table.

The scent of fresh pastries and brewed coffee filled the air, mingling with the quiet rustle of napkins and cutlery. Sitting down beside Shane, he poured her a cup of coffee from the French press.

"Thank you," she said, as the warmth of it instantly comforted her as she cradled the cup in her hands.

"You're welcome." Shane took his orange juice and sipped it while leaning back in his chair.

While glancing out the window, her eyes lingered on the view. "Everything has been so perfect here. It will be hard to go home and not be waited on."

He nodded while eating his omelet. "At least you've got Anton making you breakfast. I'm always on my own."

She felt bad to hear that. "Well, we'll have to make a point of meeting at the coffee shop before school every morning, then."

A thoughtful silence hung between them, knowing that it may never materialize.

She noticed a question forming in his eyes.

"Sounds good," he replied, hoping not to continue that conversation. Opting to change the subject, he said, "So, what's been your favorite part of the trip so far? You know, besides the view."

"Honestly?" she paused before taking a bite of her eggs Benny. "Just being here is kind of surreal." Abi turned to him. "I suppose this will be our last vacation for a while. When we get back to LA, the world will know where you are going to school. I'm sure life will get busy after that."

"Yeah, I assume so."

"It's the last few months of our senior year," she whispered, tracing the edge of her cup with her finger, "Lots of changes are coming."

He looked down, pushing food around his plate. "Hopefully, we won't lose ourselves in it."

She reached over, placing her hand on his. "Don't worry. We won't."

His fingers wrapped around hers. "Let's try not to think about it, okay? We're still here for thirteen more days."

A small smile tugged at her lips. "Hopefully, it doesn't go by too fast."

Wanting to start their day a little more upbeat, he asked, "So, what do you think Burton has in store for us today? Knowing him, he's probably planned something crazy." A subtle snicker escaped him as he leaned back, eyes sparkling with amusement.

Abi chuckled, shaking her head. "I'm sure he did."

He pushed back his chair and stood. "Hey, are you okay if I go ahead and get showered?"

"Sure, no problem."

As he walked away and disappeared into the bathroom, she curled up on the sofa, gazing out at the view. The sun's rays streamed through the window, filling the room with warmth.

Deciding to make the bed first, she smoothed out the fabric and tucked in the corners with care before fluffing the duvet. After a moment, she walked toward the closet to gather the clothes she needed. Passing by the bathroom, her eyes got drawn to the pocket door that hadn't been fully closed. Slightly ajar, leaving a sliver of the room beyond visible, her gaze flickered toward the shower. Through the misty steam, she saw the faint silhouette of Shane behind the frosted glass, the water cascading over his bare shoulders. His outline was soft, blurred by the moisture clinging to the glass, and for a brief second, she couldn't look away. The sight was strangely intimate—his form was strong yet distant, almost like a figure caught in a dream.

Heat creeping into her cheeks, her pulse quickened with a mixture of embarrassment. Swiftly moving past the door, the moment was etched in her mind as she put an outfit together, hoping to shake the strange feeling before he finished. Yet, no matter how hard she tried to stay on task, the image of him lingered, stirring an unexpected desire that tugged at her, leaving her wanting him in a way she hadn't fully realized until now.

Thinking about the way he had confronted Burton and Sara the night before, his protective instincts surfacing as they left the Mitsui Hotel, the memory flooded her mind. Each detail was sharp and vivid. Abi felt both comforted and sheltered by his fierce determination to protect her. In that moment, she saw him not just as her boyfriend but as the man he truly was—strong, unwavering, and undeniably captivating.

| 36 |

A Day to Remember

Tuesday, December 19

Park Hyatt, Kyoto

About to walk past the bathroom, clothes in hand, the door suddenly slid open as Shane stepped out with a towel draped around his waist and another hanging loosely around his neck. The sight of him, droplets of water still clinging to his muscular physique, sparked a warmth in her cheeks once more.

"Hey," he greeted casually, noticing the way she quickly averted her sight elsewhere. A hint of confusion flickered across his features. "Everything okay?"

"Yeah, it's just—" she stammered, trying to steady her breathing. "You startled me. That's all."

A playful grin spread across his face. "Did I? Sorry about that."

She laughed nervously, feeling the heat rise in her cheeks. "You've gotta give a girl warning if you're gonna appear dressed like, umm, that…"

"Good to know," he shrugged while casting sexy sidelong glances her way. "I'll remember that for next time." Opening the closet, knowing she was changing just around the corner, he asked, "What are you wearing?"

"Just something casual," she replied, trying to focus on slipping into her yoga pants, t-shirt, and hoodie as fast as possible.

"Would joggers and a sweatshirt work?"

"Yep." Afraid to catch him half-naked, she sat on the bed and waited.

"Is it safe to come in now?" he asked shortly after.

She cleared her throat. "Yes, all done." Walking past him, she grabbed her sneakers.

"Something tells me you've received inside information from Martin on what we are doing today. Am I right?"

"Not entirely..."

"Can you give me a hint?"

Abi thought for a second. "No. I couldn't say because nothing was confirmed. Your guess is as good as mine."

Slipping on his running shoes, he wondered, "Do you think the bride and groom-to-be will join us, given our conversation last night?"

"I'm not sure. Guess we will meet everyone this morning and find out."

Giving her his passport to put in her crossbody bag, he grabbed his Featherlite down jacket and took hers from the hanger before handing it to her.

"Thank you," she said. "Got the key card?"

"Yes, right here." Zipping it in his pocket, they headed out the door and down the hall to arrive right on time.

When they turned the corner, they found Andrew, Matt, and Ted hanging around outside Burton's suite. With the door propped open, they could hear voices inside.

Walking into the foyer of the Pagoda House, Anton and the rest of the guys greeted them first. To the far left, they found Martin and Burton speaking with Reggie and Jade.

Seeing their friends' faces laced with concern, Shane and Abi joined them.

Reg offered a hand to the QB. "Morning, man," he said while Jade hugged Abi.

"What's happening?" Shane asked, knowing the two seemed tense.

"Martin agrees we should keep a low profile today and stay out of the public eye. It's better that way, given the circumstances. The last thing we want is anyone getting wind of the wedding at the Thousand Hotel Chapel."

"Don't worry," Martin intervened. "I have arranged for additional hotel security tomorrow. Only we will be given access to the rooftop gardens. I'm sure everything will go according to plan."

Reassured, the two thanked him.

"Guess we are stuck here today. Have fun today, you two," Jade said to Abi. "I'm gonna head back to our room."

"Okay. Rest up," Abi stated. "Big day tomorrow."

Anxious, Jade got giddy. "Yep! One more day."

"Soon, you will be Mrs. Reggie Wilson."

His fiancée smiled. "I love the sound of that."

Discussing what movies they were going to binge-watch, Reg allowed Jade to pick as long as he could order the food. The two went back and forth as they walked out the door of the presidential suite.

Saddened that their friends wouldn't be spending the afternoon with them, Abi turned to Burton. Not seeing Sara, she wondered where the girl was.

Almost as if reading her like a book, he said, "Sara will be out in a moment. She's just getting dressed."

Nodding, Abi was unsure what more to say to that. All she could do was muster a smile.

Amidst everyone's banter, Martin prepared to make his activity announcement just as Sara rounded the corner from the bedroom. Well-dressed, carrying her laptop bag, she slipped her three-quarter-length cashmere coat on, tied the belt around her waist, and grabbed her phone from the charger.

Burton made his way over to her as she headed towards the front door, not saying so much as Good Morning to anyone.

Curious, Abi watched as the two stood to the left of the foyer, seemingly having words before she walked out and disappeared, with Rob following close behind. When he returned, she asked, "Where is Sara off to?"

"She wants to check on the event space for tomorrow evening. There are a few security issues we need to iron out before I go there."

"It's too bad she won't be joining us today," Abi said.

"We're going into a few highly stressful events, and she's in charge of coordinating safety and security. That has to be her main focus."

Shane's phone rang. Looking at the screen, he paused and said, "Sorry, I gotta take this," before walking out into the hallway.

When he had gone, Burton offered Abi a seat across from Martin.

"Are you ready to hear what we are doing today?"

A little anxious, she inhaled. "Yes, I think so..."

Giving Martin the floor, the man revealed, "You will be shopping today for a group of children." Pausing to let that sink in, he watched Burton soak up Abi's reaction to the news.

Having quickly tucked her clutched hands under her chin, she closed her eyes. The look on her face was priceless.

Unable to hold back his smile, her excitement was everything he'd hoped for. "So? How does that sound?"

"Like a memorable day."

About to go over the agenda, Shane returned to them. "Excuse me, Abs? Can I talk to you for a second?"

Hesitant, she said, "Umm, sure," before adding, "Sorry, hold that thought. I'll be back."

"Take your time," Burton said while sipping his coffee.

Following Shane out into the corridor, he swiveled around. "Don't hate me."

Surprised, she replied, "Why would I hate you?"

"I've got to stay here today. There are some negotiations taking place, and I need access to the internet. Can't risk any interruptions."

"What is it about?"

"My agent doesn't want me sharing that just yet until everything gets finalized."

"So, you can't even tell me?"

He took hold of her hands in his. "Please don't be offended. Just trust me, okay?"

Not liking the secrecy, she sighed. "Fine."

"I've got a Teams call in five minutes. Can I borrow your laptop?"

"Sure."

"What's the pass key to get in?" he asked, overly preoccupied and in a hurry.

"My birthday. Twelve-eleven."

"Great. Thanks. Are you okay here, then?"

"Yes. You go ahead."

He kissed her and said, "If I finish early, maybe I can join you later."

"Alright. I'll keep you posted on where we are."

Giving her a thumbs-up, he turned and hurried down the hall.

Left alone, she gathered herself together and went back to Martin and Burton.

The minute she sat in the chair, her famous friend asked, "So, where's Shane?"

"Apparently, there's some kind of negotiation taking place. He needs to stay here. Guess it's just you and me today."

Secretly happy to hear this, he said, "We will have a good time. I promise."

Martin continued to explain the information about the children's home. "I received a modest list of things needed from the nuns there this morning, but I'm sure we can do far more for them."

Both excited and nervous, Abi got noticeably emotional. Eyes glistening at the thought of helping these children, she bowed her head.

"Hey, hey... What's wrong?" Burton got up and knelt before her.

"Nothing..." she replied, believing if she said anything more, the tears would flow. Composing herself, she looked into his eyes. "Thank you for doing this."

He tapped her knee with great sincerity. "Absolutely," he said.

Gathering the men around, Martin assigned their duties.

Ethan was tasked with keeping an eye on Reg, Jade, and now Shane, who had opted to stay behind. No one needed to watch Anton, as he'd be spending the afternoon cooking with the hotel chef. Meanwhile, the rest of them met in the hallway and prepared to escort Burton, Martin, and Abi on their charity drive.

Going to grab his coat from the closet, Burton returned. "Are you ready to head out, Abs?"

"Ready when you are."

The door locked behind them as the two moved down the corridor with Martin and the men leading the way. Passing by her room, she could hear Shane talking to someone inside. Knowing she was leaving him behind, she focused forward as they waited for the elevator doors to open. When they did, the two stepped in.

Glimpsing at her, he could tell something was wrong. He leaned over and brushed her shoulder with his. Giving her the eye, he didn't have to say a word.

Her expression switched from stoic to happy in an instant. "I'm fine. Really."

Not convinced, he got the feeling she was upset. "Are you sure you want to do this today?" he asked, giving her an out.

Shocked to hear him say that, she snapped out of her funk. "What? Yes, of course, I want to do this. It's very important."

With the old Abi shining through, he said, "Good. I think it's important, too."

She nodded as the elevator doors opened on the ground floor.

Two black SUVs were awaiting them.

Not giving it a second thought, Martin and most of the guys got in one, while Lorenzo got in the front seat of the other.

Burton opened the door on his own. "After you," he said, prompting her to get in first before he slipped in beside her. Settled in the middle, he took his laptop from his bag and showed Abi the children's home webpage and the nun's list.

"For obvious reasons, there were no pictures of the children, but they do show a few of the facility itself," he said while they left the hotel. "It gives you an idea of what it looks like."

Intently sifting through the site, she asked, "So, where's our first stop, then?"

"Martin said we are going to Toys' R' Us."

Surprised to hear that, she said, "They have one of those here?"

"Yes, apparently, it's a big one."

The more she thought about it, the more excited she got. Hoping to shock him a little, she questioned sinisterly. "So... What's our ceiling today?"

He laughed at her crazy expression. "Ceiling? What do you mean?"

"How much are we allowed to spend?"

Playing into her antics, the guy smiled from ear to ear. "Whatever it takes," he said without a hint of hesitation.

"No, seriously..."

Happily peering into her eyes, he replied, "We are going to outfit this place, and from what I understand, eleven more before we leave Japan."

Abi lifted her hand to cover her mouth. "Are you serious?"

Not flinching one iota, he said, "Yes."

Speechless, she reached out and wrapped her arms around Burton's neck. Hugging him tightly, she said, "Thank you for doing this."

"It's for a good cause." Right then, he received a notification on his phone.

She let go as he read the message. "Martin just got Uniqlo to help us outfit the children with winter gear and any other clothes they need throughout the year."

Stunned by that news, she said, "That's crazy." She tilted her head back to stop from crying. "Do you know how you will change these kids' lives today?"

"That's the plan," he paused. "Last night, I read the article you mentioned."

"You did?"

"It was tough to read about the thousands of kids ignored in the system, their isolation, lack of family placement, and the limited resources for those who make it out of the system at eighteen." He turned and looked out the window as they traversed the city. "I think I want to start a non-profit organization that supports these places. You know, promote fostering children as being a positive thing, versus the stigma the country attaches to it. Maybe that is something you want to do with me?"

Abi smiled with tearful eyes. "That would be so wonderful." Overwhelmed, she took a deep breath and exhaled. "What I envisioned for today was so much smaller in my head. How is it that you are able to take an idea and literally run with it so fast?"

"It's easy when you have unlimited resources." He closed his laptop. "In the great scheme of things, what do we leave behind that makes a difference? For most, nothing much. How many can say that they've changed someone's life for the better?" Sliding the computer in his satchel, he added, "You know, growing up, my life wasn't perfect, but at least I had a Mom and Dad. Can't imagine these kids not having anyone. It's heartbreaking." A silence fell upon them. "I will try my damnedest to find these kids loving homes, but in the meantime, I want to make sure they have the support, necessities, and the tools to survive in society despite their situation."

His brain kept mulling over more and more ideas.

Arriving south of Kyoto Station at Aeon Mall, the SUVs pulled up to the store entrance.

Lorenzo opened the passenger-side door and scanned the area while the others waited in the second vehicle.

"We will get out here and try and keep a low profile," Burton said to Abi, offering her his hand as she jumped out.

With Lorenzo following them at a distance, the two walked towards the storefront while the SUVs rounded the next corner and disappeared into the underground parking.

"Where is Martin going?" she asked.

"You'll see," Burton replied while swinging open the main door for her. As she walked into the store, he grabbed two carts. "One for you and one for me."

"Perfect."

"Ready to shop?"

Her hands gripping the handle, she said, "Yes. Put me to work. I'm ready."

Burton followed Abi. Both pushed the oversized shopping carts down the aisle, their wheels squeaking as he followed her through the towering shelves of the Babies R' Us section.

The store seemed to stretch on forever, with rows upon rows of essentials that they needed to gather for the children's home. From toys to bath items, feeding supplies, bedding, and tiny sleepers, it was an endless list, but as they started striking items off, both seemed to enjoy every minute of it.

Standing in front of a shelf full of pastel-colored blankets, Abi's brow furrowed as she gently ran her fingers over the soft fabric. "What do you think—cotton or fleece?" she asked, holding up two options.

Steering his cart closer, Burton chuckled. "Both. These little ones deserve the best." He took the fleece blanket from her hand, then grabbed armfuls of each without a second thought.

A smile spread across her face when she saw this. It wasn't the first time she'd seen Burton in a new light today. His usual tough, guarded demeanor had softened, and he seemed so at ease here.

Moving on to the toy section, Abi lit up at the sight of colorful plush animals, teethers, and interactive baby toys.

"This will be perfect for tummy time," she said, tossing a few squishy elephant, giraffe, and bunny plushies into the cart.

When she did that, Burton took hold of a white polar bear. "What about this guy?" he asked her, holding it up. The look he gave her was priceless.

"I love it," she said.

Taking ten more, he tossed them in his cart.

Conscientiously selecting a number of baby gyms and toddler toys, Burton paused and watched Abi read the labels. The way she smiled, the way she handled each tiny item with such care—it was impossible not to picture her with a family of her own. That was when the realization hit him – a very unexpected feeling.

"She will make an incredible mother someday," he mumbled under his breath.

Not having heard him, she called out, "Burton? Ohh! Look at this." Holding up a tiny onesie covered in duck prints, she laughed delicately. "Isn't it adorable?"

He grinned. "Yes, it is," but his focus stayed on her. The truth was, everything about this moment felt right. Seeing her so comfortable, so natural in this environment, stirred something deep inside him. Abi wasn't just someone he cared about—she had a nurturing side that made him realize how special she truly was.

As they continued to the feeding section, Abi picked out bottles and bibs while Burton grabbed sets of pacifiers, baby food bowls, spoons, liners, and sippy cups.

Overwhelmed by the amount they'd collected and the number of children who would benefit, Abi became emotional. While dabbing her tears with her sleeve, she spotted a staff member whizzing by with a full cart. One by one, she saw another. Then, another. "What on earth?" Counting between twenty and thirty full carts, maybe more, she scoured the store and found the men helping Martin at the checkout as the cashier rang through piles of items moving along the conveyor belt.

It was only then that she realized the magnitude of what Burton was doing.

Upon seeing the astonishment on her face, he walked over and placed his hand on her back. "You shouldn't be sad. We're doing a good thing," he said.

Choked up, unable to answer, she forced herself to stand up straight and blotted her eyes with her sleeve. Falling into his open arms, she wrapped hers around his waist and calmed her emotions. "Sorry, I don't know why I'm such a mess today."

He peered down at her. "You're not a mess. It just shows how much you care."

"Thank you for... well, all of this," she raised one hand in the air and scanned the store.

"These kids deserve a chance at a good life. And I will do whatever it takes." Wanting to address something, he added, "You're good at this, you know? Picking out what they need. I'm certain one day... You'll make a great mom."

Her heart skipped a beat upon hearing the compliment as her cheeks blushed, and a warmth spread through her. "Thank you. I think you'd make a pretty great dad, too."

His usual confident grin faded into something more tender as their gazes held for a moment. Hugging her casually, he said, "Come on. We only have ninety minutes left."

Drying her tears, she straightened her posture and gathered every ounce of her being. "Okay! I'm ready."

Within the hour, they finished their list. Both carts were heaping, so much so that Burton grabbed a third cart to hold the last of what they needed.

Trying to keep a low profile, they intentionally stayed away from Martin and the guys, and the two of them unloaded everything at a different cashier. Paying the bill, he inserted the Amex Black into the reader and placed all the bags in their carts while the other staff members rang through the mountains of toys, sports equipment, bedding, ride-a-longs, pack-and-plays, and more nearby.

On the way to the parking garage, Burton shot Martin a subtle look as they departed. A single nod was the only reply.

Having accomplished their mission, they went about their business. But something shifted in the air when Burton noticed a few people lurking. Their interest, more than a casual curiosity, made the hairs on the back of his neck prickle.

Clocking it, Lorenzo waved them off. It made Burton's grip tighten around Abi's waist. His touch was firm and urgent. "We gotta move," he murmured low, steering her toward the SUV.

His palm settled at the small of her back with a protective pressure that sent a jolt through her.

The moment they reached the truck, he said sharply, "Hurry. Get in."

Abi barely had time to process the change in his demeanor before he opened the door himself and practically lifted her inside, before slamming it shut.

Quickly helping Lorenzo load their shopping bags in the back, soon, they closed the tailgate and Burton slid into the seat beside her.

Through the tinted glass, she could see them now—a swarm gathering, drawn to something, but what?

Prepared to shield their boss, the men saw more closing in fast.

Ethan and Bray rushed over as shouts echoed in the underground garage - a clamor of confusion followed. In seconds, Andrew, Ted, and Matt took offensive positions.

And then, it happened.

A sudden impact. A hand slammed against the window.

Burton saw it immediately. The *Death to Her* card...

Before Abi caught sight of it, he moved like lightning as the SUV started to rock back and forth. She gasped when his body lunged to cover hers, a wall of heat and muscle caging her against the seat.

A pure command escaped his lips. "Stay down!"

Shaky and terrified, she inhaled.

The space between them was gone—obliterated by the weight of him. Dark and intoxicating, his scent enveloped her—a raw mix of adrenaline, expensive cologne, and something unmistakably him.

Her pulse stuttered. "Burton?" she said, trembling. "What's happening?"

He didn't answer. Tense, his body coiled like a predator ready to strike.

Outside, chaos erupted. Yelling followed a loud thud against the door as the vehicle shook again.

Even with Burton's heartbeat reverberating against her chest and her head tucked under his chin, she remained aware of everything—the sheer force of him, his control balancing on a razor's edge. The way his fingers curled against the leather seat beside her was like he was fighting the instinct to tear someone apart.

"Lorenz!" He barked lethally. The guy moved fast, slipping into the front seat as Burton snapped orders. "Get us out of here! Now!"

The SUV roared to life and began to move.

"Go, go, go!" his protection told the driver.

"Call Martin! Get him up to speed. Make sure he's covered at the store! Have him call this in!" His tone clipped with authority.

"Already on the line with Martin, Sir," Lorenzo updated. "He's safe. Andrew reported it to the authorities. Help is en route."

The driver floored it, yanking them into a sharp right out of the underground parking. Abi's stomach lurched, but it wasn't the car's movement that had her breath catching—it was the man still covering her, his body shielding hers like his own life meant nothing in comparison.

Burton gave another command. "Tag a truck that looks like ours. Stick to him. Weave and cruise."

Only then did he glance down—and *realize*.

Their eyes locked.

Everything else—the mayhem, the chase, the threat—fell away.

Her pulse pounded as she registered just how close they were. His breath was warm against her lips, his face a mere whisper away. Her fingers twitched against his chest. The muscle beneath his shirt was strangely rigid, solid.

"Sorry, Abs..." he mumbled, his voice rough and gravel-laced as if he wasn't used to apologizing.

Still hovering over her, his gaze flickered down to her parted lips, to the flutter of her pulse at her throat.

He swallowed. "I wasn't sure if it was a..." Hesitant to finish the sentence, he suddenly stopped himself.

"A...what?" she asked fearfully.

Jaw clenched, he scanned the city streets. Then, finally, he said it. "A shooter."

A shiver ran through her—not entirely from fear, but from the sheer force of *him* as he pushed back—too fast—like he needed distance before he did something reckless. His elbow clipped the door, and a rare, unfiltered curse slipped from his lips.

Heart hammering, Abi sat up. "Why would you think that?"

He didn't look at her when he answered. His sight was focused ahead like a man used to seeing death walk right up to his door. "Because we've dealt with it many times before." Somehow, he sounded too calm. "You know threats are not unusual."

Abi stared at him, her nerves twisting. *Not unusual?* She thought as if people hunting him down were just another day in his life.

The SUV picked up speed, the city blurring past. But all Abi could focus on was him. The way his fists clenched, his jaws tight, the storm raging behind his blue eyes – now darker than normal. And the way, despite the threat to his own life, his first instinct had been to protect *her*.

Not having experienced this firsthand, she sat stoically.

He felt terrible. "I didn't mean to frighten you. Just couldn't take a chance, so..."

She analyzed the series of events. "You were going to take a bullet for me? Is that what that was?"

With absolute certainty, he replied, "For the record, I wouldn't think twice. I told you I'd protect you, and I meant it." Seeing the shock on her face, he smirked, "It's not a big deal. I wear a ballistic Kevlar shell when I'm in public."

"What is that?"

"Bulletproof clothing."

When he said it, she understood why he was so protective of her all this time. "Why didn't you tell me about this?"

"I never wanted you to worry." Afraid the incident would ruin their afternoon, Burton hoped they could just move on as if nothing had happened.

Silence stretched between them, thick and loaded, as they drove along.

Burton repeatedly flexed his hands, trying to shake off the rush still pumping through his veins.

She could see it. "How did those people know we were there? Why would they want to harm us?"

Realizing she hadn't seen the Death to Her card, he wasn't sure how to answer. To keep her calm, he said, "I don't know. But we will soon find out." Keeping Abi in his peripheral, he knew he'd gotten too close and made it awkward. His body had reacted so quickly his brain couldn't catch up—and now, in the aftermath, he found it hard to *unfeel* it. To *unfeel...*her.

Staring out the side window, flashes of how she'd fit against him flickered in his eyes before he forced himself to free her from his clutches. Needing to break the silence, he said calmly, yet his pulse wasn't. "I didn't hurt you, did I?"

"No. I'm fine, B. Don't worry."

He nodded.

"Thank you for, umm..."

"Sure," is all he said in return. Focused straight ahead, he got Lorenzo's attention. "Drive to the children's home now. One of the delivery trucks will arrive shortly after us. Have the guys guard the main gate. Nobody else goes in or out."

"Roger that, Sir."

As they both calmed down, Abi didn't know how to get them back on track. They were having such a good morning until it all went downhill. Sitting quietly, proud of what they had accomplished prior to the craziness, Abi said, "We worked pretty well together, didn't we?"

The comment caught him off guard. "What do you mean?"

"The shopping. We got everything on the list and then some."

"We did okay."

Glancing at him, she reminded herself not to stare. "Shopping with you is always fun. I didn't know you knew so much about baby stuff."

"Honestly, I was winging it," he smirked. "Was mostly following your lead. You seemed more of an expert there than me."

She nodded with a smile.

Needing to say it, he added, "I meant what I said, you know."

"What's that?"

"One day, when you find the right person, I think you'll make a great Mom."

Lorenzo overheard him.

Abi could see the corner of the security guard's mouth curl slightly. "That is probably the nicest compliment I've ever received." What Burton said resonated. "I hope the same for you, too." She chuckled under her breath. "As a Dad, that is."

It was easy to tell that something was different in the way she looked at him and vice versa. He could sense it immediately. Somehow, once again, he felt a shift between them.

"Completely off-topic... How much did you spend?" she asked, recalling the endless items loaded before their departure.

"We budgeted for 45,000,000 ¥ today – roughly three hundred thousand in inventory." He was unbothered by the hefty bill and did not bat an eye at the number.

Speechless, Abi stared at him.

He chuckled at her reaction. "Hey, go big or go home, right?" Continuing to carry the conversation, he added, "The manager even offered to close the store for us for three hours, but we declined that to try and stay on the down-low. Guess that didn't help our situation."

She was taken aback.

Burton's phone rang. Answering it, he said, "Yeah. Martin. What's up?"

Abi listened and tried to make sense of the phone call, but she couldn't hear Martin on the other end.

"Are you sure? Is that confirmed?" Burton replied, nodding his head. "How many had the mark?"

She slid closer. As her pulse quickened upon hearing that, she could tell something wasn't quite right.

"A few of them had red dragon tattoos," he muttered. "Martin says the pictures are already online. It seems to be part of some kind of game or competition. He's trying to gather more intel and find out what we've gotten dragged into."

Fear spread through Abi like wildfire.

He hated exposing her to his complicated life and the shadows that followed him wherever he went. When he ended the call, he turned to her.

"So, what do we do now?"

"We move on to phase two of our secret operation." Pausing, he said, "And there's one more thing…"

"Oh, no… What…"

"Martin mentioned seeing pictures posted of you and me shopping for baby stuff."

"And that's a problem because…" She didn't fully know where he was going with that.

"No, you don't understand." Burton tread carefully. "What we were doing there could be, umm…misconstrued, if you know what I mean."

Putting two and two together, she lowered her head. "Oh…" It was then she realized people would think the two were shopping for their new arrival.

"I'll put one of my guys on it. I'm sure they can wipe it from social within the hour."

"You can do that?" she said, the gravity of the situation sinking in.

He started typing a message on his phone and offered a flat grin. "I can do anything."

As they moved northwest, the roads seemed oddly familiar. That is when they realized the children's home was a few miles from Aman Kyoto and the Golden Temple.

The closer they got to their destination, Abi's spirits started to fray. She began rubbing her palms together, unable to shake the tension building inside. "I don't know why I'm so nervous," she admitted. "This part scares me."

"Scares you? Why?" he asked, wanting to rest his hand on her arm. But he didn't.

"Because I am gonna get attached to them, and then we'll have to leave…" Her breath was uneven as Abi exhaled. "It's going to break my heart. I know it."

"Would it help to know that we can maybe stay in touch with them and check on their progress?"

"Like a Zoom call?"

"Yeah. We can arrange that and perhaps surprise them with a visit a few times a year. Or whenever you want to."

"I'd like that," she replied sincerely.

With a tilt of his head, he said, "Good."

Thankful to see her happy, Burton reached over the console, his hand finding hers between the seats. "Don't worry," he said gently, tapping her hand. "We'll get through this together today. We need to be strong for them. Deal?"

Her pulse steadied a little. "Happy and strong. I can do that," she whispered, trusting him as Lorenzo gave them the five-minute warning.

| 37 |

Children's Home

Tuesday, December 19

Undisclosed Location – Kyoto

Thankfully, Martin and the guys had arrived before they'd gotten there and had blocked the gate already. As their SUV pulled up to the Children's Home on the hillside, Abi felt anxious, not knowing what they would see. Bracing for the worse, hoping for the best, they arrived in front of a large white building, new and clean, in stark contrast to the smaller, older structure they had passed on their way up.

Outside, standing with Martin, was a group of people gathered, all bundled up, with bright smiles. Among them were Catholic nuns in black tunics, their crucifixes hanging from their necks.

Watching him exchange regal greetings, the women looked on with happy smiles. Despite the cold, their welcome was undeniably warm.

Abi glanced at Burton, feeling the moment settle in.

"Here we go," he said, giving her hand a reassuring squeeze as they stepped out together.

The translator's voice cut through, politely reminding the staff, "No pictures, please."

As they moved inside, the unloading of their donations had already begun. Abi couldn't believe her eyes as she saw the piles of new bedding—soft blankets, pillows, and sheets for every child. School supplies were unpacked: colorful backpacks, pencil cases, crayons, pencils, rulers, and more. Diapers, wipes, and other baby essentials followed, filling the entryway with bundles of gifts.

The reactions from the staff were deeply moving. Every few moments, one of the workers would hold up an item and raise their hands in prayer, thanking God for the blessings. The air was thick with emotion, and Abi found herself blinking back tears. The outpouring of gratitude was overwhelming.

After the warm welcome, Abi and Burton were introduced to some of the older children. Most were girls, standing shyly in a line as the nuns called out their names one by one. Little Emi, Sora, Etsuko, and Tenna stepped forward, linking their arms together bashfully, waving with sweet smiles. At the end of the line was a young boy named Aoto, who gazed up at them with wide eyes.

Instantly drawn to Abi, they noticed the little girls' curiosity shining through as they examined her French manicure and giggled.

"They like your nails," the translator said with a grin.

Kneeling to their level, she beamed. "Please tell them thank you," she replied, her heart swelling as they took hold of her hands joyfully.

Meanwhile, Aoto was staring at Burton.

"He's never seen anyone with such blue eyes before," the translator relayed.

"Oh, that explains it," Burton chuckled, watching as the little girls charmed Abi to bits. He was about to say something more when an idea struck him. "Hey, Abs, I'll be right back. You okay here?"

She nodded, happiness radiating from her. "Yes, I'm fine."

Slipping back to the foyer, Burton searched the supplies gathered. In seconds, he had what he was looking for: two hockey sticks and an orange ball. Smiling, he returned to where Aoto was sitting quietly by himself, staring at the floor.

When he approached, he gestured for the translator's attention. "Can you ask him if he likes to play hockey?"

After a short exchange in Japanese, the translator turned back to him. "He doesn't know what hockey is."

Kneeling beside Aoto, Burton handed him the stick and demonstrated how to hold it. Taking the ball from its packaging, he gently passed it on his blade toward the boy. Hesitant at first, Aoto stopped the ball with the stick and, after a moment's pause, hit it back toward Burton.

"That's it!" Burton clapped, giving him a thumbs-up. "Awesome job."

His praise sparked the little boy to expel an infectious laugh.

Glancing at Abi, now being led away by the giggling girls to explore the facility, Burton opted to stay behind with Aoto.

Suddenly, the boy ran off, leaving his hockey stick lying on the floor.

Burton's heart sank—had he done something wrong? He walked over to pick it up, but before he could, Aoto returned, this time with two friends in tow. The three of them stood in front of Burton, all eyes wide with excitement.

Raising his index finger, he said, "Wait here. One second," not knowing if they understood.

He hurried back to the front, grabbing as many hockey sticks as he could carry. Returning, he passed the sticks to each boy, and in no time, a makeshift hockey game broke out in the corridor. Laughter echoed through the halls, and though some of the nuns were initially uneasy, they soon relaxed when they saw the pure joy on the children's faces. One nun clutched her chest, a smile forming as she watched the boys laughing and playing.

As the last of the donations were distributed, the afternoon grew overwhelmingly emotional. It was like Christmas had come early. Every child wanted to express their gratitude, bowing respectfully, and some of the older ones tearfully thanked Abi and Burton for their generosity. The feeling of joy and humility filled every room.

The four little girls who had clung to Abi throughout the tour hugged her tightly as they said their goodbyes in broken English, wishing her a Merry Christmas. Abi smiled through her own tears and wished them the same.

Meanwhile, Burton was caught off guard as the little boys converged upon him simultaneously, playfully tackling him to the floor. Their rambunctious laughter stunned a few of the nuns, causing them to fling their arms up, believing they would have to rescue Burton from the children.

Finding him laughing hysterically at the unrestrained playfulness, their laughter joining his, the nuns seemingly scolded them, afraid the three were getting out of hand. Hearing the woman, each boy stopped what they were doing and froze.

Two of the boys disappeared, but Aoto remained and walked up to Burton quietly as he knelt to the little boy's level and held out a closed hand to knock knuckles. Smiling, he suddenly threw his arms around Burton, hugging him tightly. Frozen for a second, not knowing what to do, his eyes misted as he hugged the boy back. In his peripheral, he saw Abi watching, her expression soft and full of love. She had witnessed a side of him that touched her deeply, while Burton quickly wiped the tear away, hoping she hadn't noticed.

Witnessing this, Martin surveyed things between his boss and Miss Abi, knowing what today meant to both of them. With his eye on the time, he reminded them of the rehearsal dinner that evening and signaled that their visit had come to a close. As they prepared to leave, he spoke with the translator, explaining that a shipment of clothing would arrive in a few days if they sent over a list of sizes and quantities. He also presented the Children's Home with a cash donation and promised additional support to follow.

One of the nuns, hearing this, dropped to her knees. Crying, she gave thanks to God.

Abi knelt beside her, offering a side hug as each of them was immersed in a moment of prayer.

About to walk out the door, the last traces of daylight clinging to the horizon, deep blues and purples swallowed the sky as dusk settled over the quiet laneway. Their SUVs idled nearby, engines rumbling, each keeping warm.

Laughter and cheerful voices drifted through the open doorway, a final reminder of the joy they'd shared. The children, bundled in coats, waved excitedly from the steps, each alight with gratitude. Staff members stood alongside them, offering bows and heartfelt smiles.

With happiness ingrained in her soul, Abi knew it was now time to go. When she lifted a hand in farewell, a quiet ache settled in her chest.

Each step toward the waiting SUVs felt heavier than the last.

Burton noticed her apprehension.

Warmth brushed against her skin as a hand slipped into hers. Like a lifeline, steady and sure, Abi clung to it while the moment pulled at her heartstrings.

"You good?" His words were quiet, meant only for her.

Shaking her head, she opened her mouth to respond, but nothing came out. The knot in her throat tightened.

A deep breath, then a gentle squeeze of her fingers. No rush. No pressure. Just quiet understanding. His thumb brushed over the back of her hand, a slow, calming motion that sent reassurance straight to her heart.

"They'll remember today for a long time," he told her. "The stories you listened to, the way you made them laugh. That doesn't go away just because you leave."

A shaky breath left her lips. He made it sound so simple, as though he understood something she didn't.

An unexpected gust of wind sent a loose strand of her hair across her face. Without hesitation, he reached up and tucked it gently behind her ear. His touch lingered—just for a second—but it was enough to send a heightened affection through her. One she wasn't ready for.

"I know you want to go back," he said, reading her like an open book. "But if you do, you'll cry, and if you cry, they'll cry, and then...well... We'll just have to stay here forever." A small smirk tugged at his lips, an attempt to make her smile.

It worked.

A tearful laugh escaped her. "I don't know how you do that," she whispered.

"Do what?"

"Know exactly what to say when I don't even know what I need to hear."

For a moment, he didn't answer. He just looked at her with an intense expression. "Because I know you," he finally said, voice low and honest. "Sometimes even better than you know yourself."

When he draped an arm over her shoulders, guiding her toward the waiting car, she didn't resist.

He opened the passenger door.

She turned and bravely gave one final wave before getting in the truck. Helping her in, he stepped aboard before taking a seat beside her and closing the door behind him. The second it shut, she started to cry, unable to hold it in any longer.

Seeing this, he slid over with open arms. "Come here," he whispered as she wrapped her arms around his neck while the tears fell. Without hesitation, he held her tightly. "It's okay, Abs. Don't cry," as the driver moved down the laneway, honking the horn twice as they left.

It took a few minutes for the crying to stop and the heaves to calm down. But eventually, Abi took a deep, cleansing breath and let go of him.

Breaking their silence first, he looked into her eyes. "So...I take it you had a good day?"

Abi turned to him, her eyes shining with tears of joy. "No," she whimpered. "I had a great day." Her chest heaved. "How can I ever thank you?"

He left his arm wrapped across her shoulders. "I'm the one who should be thanking you. It was your idea, remember?" After a moment, he smiled mischievously. "I hope Martin told them about the bicycles."

Startled, she blinked. "What bikes?"

"I bought fifty bikes today, I think... Maybe it was two hundred. I can't remember exactly," he squinted. "They'll be delivered tomorrow. The staff at Toys R' Us are wrapping the remaining gifts. They'll deliver those on Christmas Eve."

She playfully smacked him as she started to cry again. "See what you did." Her heart swelled. Without thinking, she leaned over and kissed him on the cheek, her emotions spilling over. "Umm, sorry..." she mumbled, suddenly self-conscious.

Lorenzo glimpsed in the mirror as the air inside the car thickened with an awkward silence until both of them spoke at once. They laughed lightly, easing the tension.

"You go first," Burton offered, smoothing things over with his warm smile.

Fingers fidgeting in her lap, Abi wasn't sure where to begin. "I hope I wasn't out of line, you know, with...that..." Her words trailed off, unsure of his reaction.

Not giving it a second thought, he encouraged. "No. It's fine, really." He paused before adding, "This has been the most memorable day I've had in a long while."

"Thank you for being so supportive through it all," she said, smiling delicately. "Sorry again for crying so much. I don't know what came over me."

"You have a big heart, Abs. Those tears are genuine. Don't ever apologize for that."

She leaned closer and whispered in his ear. "Well, I noticed you shed one or two yourself, *Dark Demon.*"

His eyes widened. "You noticed that, huh?"

"I thought it was sweet," Abi added with a hint of seriousness. "It was a side of you I never get to see."

"What side's that?"

Abi's heart pounded in her chest while contemplating what to say. Fearfully holding back, she didn't want to risk making things awkward again, but he was waiting for an answer. Taking a deep breath, she peered into his eyes, only to find a hint of curiosity mixed with the guarded edge that always shadowed him. "Today, I didn't see the mysterious man behind the famous figure, nor did I see the one who commands the stage at every event," she began steadily. "I saw someone completely different."

Burton's gaze searched hers, the question still unanswered.

Continuing, she divulged, "I saw a man who is caring and thoughtful. Someone who wasn't just here to play a role or fulfill an obligation, but a man who was genuinely present. You gave your time. You laughed with those boys and played hockey with them like you were their friend, their protector, their guardian. And then, spending that much for supplies? That wasn't about showing off—that was you giving from your heart."

When she paused, Burton lowered his head humbly.

"You're someone who doesn't just provide but invests in the people he loves and the causes he believes in. A man who goes beyond his words and shows with actions. You're supportive, generous, and thoughtful, Burton. And today, I saw how deeply you care, how much you're willing to give of yourself to make others feel valued."

Hearing such kindness, he tilted his head and gave her an appreciative smile. "Thank you for that. Have to say... We did make a great team today, and I'd love for you to be involved in the foundation I'm starting here."

Her heart melted further, her voice genuine as she replied, "I would love to."

"Good," he said, his eyes sparkling. "Because that means we'll have to come back and visit these kids a lot."

With her smile brightening by the minute, the warmth between them was undeniable. For Burton, it was more than just a successful afternoon—it felt like the beginning of something important, something deeper than either of them had ever anticipated.

| 38 |

Aftermath

Tuesday, December 19

Park Hyatt, Kyoto

Feeling as though she was waking from a fairytale dream, Abi watched as they arrived back at the Park Hyatt. When the SUV entered the parking garage, their driver stopped at the VIP entrance. Prepared to escort them upstairs, the guys gathered around.

Burton got out first, slipping his satchel over his shoulder.

About to follow, Abi saw him reach out and offer a hand. Taking hold, she soon joined him.

Looking her way, hands in his pockets, he offered his elbow. Hooking her arm with his, she clung to it as he escorted her inside. They both seemed emotionally and physically drained, barely able to keep their eyes open as they waited for the elevator.

"I don't know why, but I am exhausted," Abi muttered, her body slumping slightly.

"Me too," Burton chuckled.

Behind them, Martin remained quiet as he lowered his head with a satisfied smile, thinking to himself, *Mission complete.*

When the elevator doors opened, Lorenzo joined them while the rest waited for another lift. On the way to the top floor, the big guy stood with his back to them, giving them some privacy. Abi rested her head on Burton's shoulder, her exhaustion catching up with her.

"Thank you for everything," she whispered.

Burton glanced down, grateful for the moment but equally overwhelmed. "Thank you," he replied, unsure how he would get through the next few hours.

The elevator dinged as they reached their floor. Lorenzo stepped out first. Burton and Abi followed, bypassing her room slightly.

Standing together, she hesitated a second but then stepped forward and hugged him. "I'll see you shortly," she said before having to knock on her door.

"Yes, it should be a busy evening." His eyes locked on hers as she let go.

Assuming Shane was in their room, she rapped her knuckles twice. Waiting, she heard nothing. When she knocked a second time, there was no answer. Pulling out her phone to call him, she realized her battery was dead since she'd forgotten to plug it in the night before.

Noticing, Burton put a plan in place. "Come wait in my suite until we track him down. I'll get one of the guys to find him."

She nodded. "Alright."

As they walked down the hall and into his room, Burton held the door open for her.

"Come on in," he said before instructing Lorenzo, "Please go and find Coppersmith and tell him Abi is back."

"Yes, Sir," the guys said simultaneously before radioing to the others to locate the football player.

Once inside, Abi settled on the sofa to the left, grateful for the chance to catch her breath. Burton poured them each a glass of water and took a seat beside her, his expression calming.

It wasn't long before they fell into a comfortable conversation, recounting their day.

Having unexpectedly connected with the children, Burton couldn't help but smile. "Aoto was such a little firecracker," he said with a fondness in his tone. "He had no problem challenging me once he got the hang of the game. That kid has skills. I don't know. There was just something about him. Like all he needed was someone to believe in him."

In agreement, she remembered the group of little girls who had clung to each other like sisters. Despite the circumstances they were in, she knew they'd formed their own little family within the walls of the home. "They were all so small," Abi divulged, voice wavering. "None of them knowing the love of a real family." Clutching her chest, she shook her head. "My heart goes out to them. How scary would it be for them to be alone in this world with no mom or dad to protect them?"

Moving closer, he reached over and placed his hand on her back. "Well, we did what we could for now. All the more reason to try and find ways to locate worthy couples willing to give them stability and support."

"Don't forget love."

His face brightened. "Of course. That most importantly."

Abi leaned into him, her emotions spilling over as silent tears slipped down her cheeks. Realizing how tight-knit the little girls were, she said, "But we can't split them up. That would destroy them. Wherever they go, they have to keep them together."

Seeing her so moved stirred something in Burton. It prompted him to gently wrap his arms around her and let her release her emotions freely as he whispered, "We'll make sure they are all safe and happy. I promise they'll be okay, Abs."

The strength of his embrace and the quiet understanding between them felt easy.

Parting ways, she needed to say her piece. "Can we talk about what happened at the store?"

"Which part?"

"You said they had red dragon tattoos?" About to calm her nerves, he turned to her, but she put up her hand to stop him. "Tell me the truth. Don't sugarcoat it."

He took a breath. "The team is working on it. Martin assumes we were targeted the moment we arrived in Osaka. You were right."

"So, the creepy man with the cane I saw across the street…"

"We believe that is where he made first contact. The fact that he resurfaced at the Golden Temple and Heian Shrine was not coincidental."

"Do you know who he is?" she asked, fidgeting with her sleeve.

"No." He shook his head. "We have yet to get a positive ID."

"If they've been watching us since the airport, do they know your identity? Is it because someone saw you meet up with DJ Red Dragon?"

"That's the assumption."

She stayed quiet while processing what he said.

"My guys are still trying to piece this together. From what we hear, a nefarious group is conducting some sort of recruiting exercise, and somehow, we've gotten caught in the crosshairs."

"Are we in danger?"

Before he could answer, the door opened, and Sara walked in. Her gaze narrowed as she took in the scene: Burton holding Abi tightly as she wiped away her tears.

"What's going on here?" Her tone was cold, and her eyes flashed with anger.

Shocked, Abi pulled away, her cheeks flushed, but Burton kept his arm around her protectively and said to Sara, "Abi and I were talking about the kids today."

The woman's lips pressed into a thin line as she stormed into the bedroom and then the closet. They could hear her yank her suitcase from the shelf and toss things into it.

Sighing heavily, Burton glanced at Abi with a look of silent apology as a text came through. "The guys found Shane. He's on his way back to your room."

Eyes still damp, she leaned close, needing to say her piece. "I think you need to let her go," she whispered. "She isn't good for you."

Not responding, he only nodded, eyes locked to hers. A sense of resolution settled over him. "You're probably right," he said under his breath.

Whispering goodbye before slipping out of the room, she left him to deal with Sara's anger as the door shut behind her. With a heavy heart, she felt a strange mix of sadness and a strong need to protect him. It was hard to walk away. Stopping only a few feet from his door, she turned slightly and listened a moment. All she could hear was Sara's voice growing louder, venom lacing every syllable.

"Oh, so that's what this is? Poor little Abi comes running to you with her sob story, and you can't help but fall all over her?" Sara was sharp and accusing.

"You and I both know this isn't about Abi. It's about you being jealous. She doesn't deserve to be treated like this—neither do I."

The scorned woman scoffed. "Of course, you'd defend her. She's got you wrapped around her finger, doesn't she? Playing the innocent little girl, pretending to care about those kids today, when really she's just a spoiled, manipulative—"

"Enough!" Burton firmly cut her off. "You don't know her, Sara. And you will not talk about her like that. Abi's done nothing wrong. She's kind-hearted and thoughtful, which is more than I can say for you."

"Oh, so I'm the problem?" Her voice shook. "I'm to blame for all of this?"

Abi froze upon hearing her anger. Torn, feeling the urge to return to him and set her straight, she stopped, knowing he could handle Sara on his own. But the pang of guilt stayed with her.

That is when she heard Burton say, "If you can't respect the people in my life, then you don't belong here. I want you to leave."

Unable to hear what Sara said, Abi continued down the hallway.

Seeing Shane about to walk into their room, he smiled and said, "Hey, you. How was your afternoon?"

She stepped inside as the door closed behind them. Her eyes were puffy, and her makeup needed a serious touch-up. "It was...a very emotional day," she admitted, hoping to share more with him.

But as she glanced at Shane, his phone rang. Holding up his pointer finger, he said, "Sorry. Give me one second," before answering it and pacing the floor by the windows.

"There is no point in trying to explain it to him," she whispered under her breath. "The only way he—or anyone—could truly understand what we felt was to be there themselves."

Deciding to let it go, Abi headed into the bathroom. About to close the second pocket door, she motioned to him that she was going to take a shower.

Upon seeing this, he gave her a thumbs-up and continued talking.

Alone, finally, she turned on the faucet and waited for the water to warm up. Staring at her reflection, a million thoughts rolled through her mind. While getting undressed, she slipped under the water as it cascaded over her head and shoulders. The mix of emotions, the exhaustion, the confusion of feelings—it was too much. And yet, amid the chaos, she felt a strange pull as her thoughts rested on Burton, a feeling she hadn't experienced since their time in Tahoe.

"Why do you do this to yourself?" With her feelings flip-flopping again, she heard Shane talking in the other room. "Maybe some time apart will be good," she whispered, thinking about the impending separation when she left for Harvard in September while he ventured to Alabama. Guilt crept in almost immediately. "No, Abs, stop it. Shane's a good guy. You just got pulled into B's world again, that's all."

Frustrated, she cut the shower short and stepped out before wrapping herself in a white robe. Reevaluating things, she did her best to decipher her feelings for B and Shane. But it was not easy.

After drying her hair and freshening up her makeup, there was a knock on the bathroom door.

"Is it okay if I shower now?" Shane asked. "I'm kinda running late."

"Yes. I'm done," she replied.

Abi left as Shane stepped into the bathroom. Her mind still clouded by the day's events, he sensed her quiet mood and followed her out. "Hey, are you doing okay?"

She wanted to tell him everything, to make him understand the gravity of what they'd accomplished, but she couldn't find the words. Instead, she smiled faintly and said, "It was really good."

Relieved, Shane hugged her tightly. "I'm glad to hear that," he said, kissing her forehead before going to get in the shower. "Wish I could've been there."

Finding her rehearsal dinner dress, she slipped it on while Shane was still occupied, then added a pair of heels and her mother's ivory cable knit cardigan before sitting down by the window to watch the sunset slowly sink below the horizon. The beauty of the moment did little to lift the strange heaviness inside her.

When Shane emerged with a towel around his waist and one wrapped closely around his neck, Abi remained stoic in her chair, with her back to him. Able to see his reflection changing in the open, behind the closet door, she tried not to look, but he didn't exactly hide from sight. Immersing in the quiet, taking time to reflect on the day, she didn't notice him walk over, dressed nicely in dark pants and a gray cashmere sweater. With a crisp white dress shirt underneath it, his brown belt matched his shoes.

Reading her distant expression while attaching his fancy watch to his wrist, he said, "Abs?" so as not to startle her.

Lost in thought, she didn't hear him.

"Abi?" he repeated, more urgent this time.

Jumping in her seat, she blinked. "Sorry. What was that?"

"Is everything all right?" Concern etched across his features. "Did something happen today?"

Breaking from her stare, she turned to him and said, "Umm, no. It was just a tough day. I'd rather not talk about it. I just fixed my makeup, and can't cry anymore."

He knelt beside her, searching her eyes for answers. "Is there anything I can do?" he asked sincerely.

She shook her head. "No, sadly not." Taking a deep breath, needing to change her perception of the world, she sat up straight and said, "Guess we should go and prep our friends for the wedding." Trying to perk up, she managed to smile.

He offered her his hand as she stood and steadied herself. But he unexpectedly wrapped his arms around her waist and pulled her close. "You look really pretty, by the way," he complimented, kissing her lips gently. "Missed you today."

"Missed you, too," she replied, with a nagging thought hovering in the back of her mind. "What was with all the phone calls, anyway?" she asked, still not knowing the full extent of what was happening.

Hearing their friends in the hallway, he glanced toward the door. "How about we talk about that later? We should get moving."

Abi nodded, a little uneasy but willing to let it go for now.

Walking out, she hoped tonight's rehearsal dinner would provide a welcomed distraction. Bravely putting on a happy face, determined to enjoy her friends' celebration, deep down, Abi wasn't sure if the storm developing in her heart would settle anytime soon.

| 39 |

Rehearsal Dinner

Tuesday, December 19

Park Hyatt, Kyoto

Joining everyone gathered at the elevators, Abi peered down the hall but did not see Burton coming. Neither was Sara. Following Martin's orders, they descended to the Komorebi banquet room on the lower level for the private rehearsal. Despite the warm celebration awaiting them, the air still felt thick to her.

Once on the ground floor, they walked into a dimly lit hallway lined with smooth, gray slate while Martin began to organize everyone. The atmosphere was charged with a blend of anticipation and nerves.

When Jade walked into the room, which was now partially set up for the event, her eyes lit up. "This feels even more real," she whispered to Reggie, hands clutched under her chin.

In a commanding tone, Martin directed the group to take their places. "I believe we are ready to get started," he called out, gesturing for Burton, Shane, and Reggie to take their places at the far end. When he said that, he realized Master B was not there.

As everyone waited, Burton suddenly walked off the elevator.

"Sorry, we're late," he apologized while Sara trailed behind him.

The two kept their distance from each other, maintaining a five- or six-foot buffer. Fairly cold, their expressions revealed a lot.

Easily noticing Sara's barely concealed scowl and Burton's stoic expression, it was clear they were on the rocks.

A flicker of concern sparked in Abi, but she decided to stay out of it. The last thing she wanted was for a confrontation to break out and spoil the night for their friends.

Catching Abi's eye, Burton offered a small nod before standing beside Shane and the Groom. His gaze never fell upon Sara again as she stood with her arms crossed at the opposite end, visibly uninterested in being there. Doing his best to keep his composure, he appeared frustrated and angry beneath his calm exterior.

The three men, shoulder to shoulder, clasped their hands together in front of them respectfully.

With everyone assembled and in their ready positions, Martin spoke over the quiet murmurs. "Let's walk through this carefully. We want everything to be seamless tomorrow. Jade, Reggie—are you ready?"

From afar, the happy couple shared a smile, breaking the tension in the air.

Exuding his unusually strong presence, Burton remained cool and collected. Both he and Shane could see the significance of this moment sinking in for Reggie.

With a strong pat on the back, the QB smiled at his best friend. "You've got this, man," he said.

Nervous, he nodded, barely able to speak a word. Rubbing his sweaty palms together, he whispered, "This is it. Can't believe it's actually happening. I'm marrying the girl of my dreams tomorrow."

His friend chuckled while Burton listened in. "And you're the luckiest guy on the planet," Shane said.

Meanwhile, outside the room, Jade was with Abi and Sara, her nerves evident in the way she fidgeted.

Trying to keep things light, Abi leaned over and whispered, "You're going to be an amazing wife, Jade."

"Oh my gosh." That thought suddenly sank in as her hand clutched her heart. "Still can't believe it. It's like a dream, and this is only the rehearsal. I can't imagine what tomorrow will bring." Flashing a small, jittery smile, her hands trembled slightly. "I feel like my heart is about to leap out of my chest."

Sara wasn't saying much but offered a few reassuring words. "Don't worry. You'll be fine," she said, surprising the girls. "You love Reggie, right?"

Her face brightened. "With all my heart," she divulged.

"Then, you will support each other, and before you know it, they will pronounce you husband and wife, and nothing else will matter."

Stunned by her comment, they teared up.

Seeing this, Sara said, "No need to get sappy."

Unable to help herself, Jade suddenly reached out and grabbed hold of the girl. "Thank you! I needed that."

Slightly taken aback, she smiled. "Glad it helped. Now, let's get this done."

Andrew and Lorenzo got the signal from Martin. Positioned by the doors, the men exchanged glances before opening them.

The moment had come.

Sara was the first to walk down the aisle.

Burton watched her briefly. But as soon as Abi stepped into view, his eyes instinctively veered in her direction.

Noticing where his gaze had gravitated, his girlfriend shot him a look on the way past.

Having smiled at both the men in her life, unaware of what had happened, Abi tried to keep her own emotions in check as she stood beside Martin.

Soon, the bride appeared.

Reggie's heart swelled at the sight of her as she glided toward him, his nerves fading the closer she got.

As she reached for his extended hands, his touch steadied hers. The strong connection between them was unmistakable.

Playing the role of the clergyman with surprising solemnity, Martin launched into an abbreviated version of the ceremony. "We are gathered here today to join Reggie and Jade in holy matrimony... After a short introduction," he said, "We will move on to the exchanging of vows and the giving of rings."

The room filled with quiet smiles as he continued, but the seriousness of the ceremony wasn't lost on anyone. Piece by piece, it gave them hope.

"And finally," Martin said, grinning as they reached the pinnacle of the rehearsal, "You may kiss your bride."

Eyes twinkling humorously, the Groom didn't miss a beat. "I thought you'd never ask."

The air lightened as the group chuckled.

Reggie leaned in, quite eager to steal a kiss. Before he could, though, Martin raised a hand, reminding him, "Just remember, no excessive PDA. Even tomorrow, the kiss must be rated PG. We've got rules, you know."

Shane interjected playfully, "But nobody is looking right now, so it's fine."

With a dramatic sigh of relief, Reggie kissed Jade. The sweetness of it caught everyone off guard.

Standing to the side, Sara glanced at Burton. To her surprise, she found him staring her way, prompting her to offer a partial smile despite what had happened between them hours earlier.

Joining together, Jade and Reggie walked back down the imaginary aisle with Abi and Shane beaming for their friends. But Burton and Sara kept their places before going their separate ways.

As the processional concluded, their group moved to the lobby in the back.

Abi bubbled over. "So, are you guys ready for this?" she asked, overly excited for the two of them.

Without hesitation, Reggie turned to his bride-to-be and locked eyes with her. "Without a doubt," he said with certainty. Taking her hands in his, he added, "I want nothing more than to be married to you for the rest of my life."

What he said melted the hearts of everyone around them.

Abi, moved by his sincerity, leaned against Shane, who gave her a small squeeze. "They're going to be so happy together," she whispered, her heart full.

Shane nodded. "Yeah. They're pretty lucky to have each other."

"Any questions before we go?" Martin asked while joining everyone as they gathered near the elevators.

Believing things would be fairly straightforward, Jade thought about walking down the aisle of the chapel in her dress. "I think it's going to be beautiful."

"I agree," Abi said excitedly.

"If there are no questions, we will move on to Yasaka for the rehearsal dinner. Master B arranged a private Teppanyaki experience."

Surprised by this, Jade and Reggie turned to him and Sara. "Thank you again for everything. You've been so generous to us," Jade said.

"Yes, thank you," Reg supported. "Once we get settled, I'll eventually pay you back."

Burton put up his hand between them. "No need, you two. Happy to do it."

"Well, thank you from the bottom of our hearts," Jade replied as Reggie gave her a side hug when she got emotional.

Standing tall, their famous friend gave a single nod.

The elevator doors opened. In groups of six, they departed from the banquet level to proceed to the restaurant. Emerging on the second floor, they bared the cold air for a few minutes while walking under the covered breezeway. Making it to Yasaka, Andrew swung open the door and allowed everyone to walk into the vestibule before letting it fall shut behind them.

Inside the traditional-looking space, the warm ambiance was so very inviting.

Their hostess greeted them happily. "Welcome to Yasaka."

Martin stepped forward and bowed slightly. "Good evening, Miss."

"Right this way," she said, turning and raising her arms to point to the rooms on either side of her. "Please be seated. The chefs will begin shortly."

Breaking everyone into two groups, Martin got their security to take a Teppanyaki table for themselves while they gathered at another."

Torn with that decision, not liking his staff segregated from them, Burton said, "Sara and I will sit with the guys. You go ahead and enjoy."

Splitting up, Burton looked at Abi, knowing that it was probably best, given the circumstances. He figured it would give everyone a cooling-off period.

Abi saw Burton conversing with his staff jovially as Sara took a seat at the far end of the table. Despite their problems, she seemed to enjoy talking with her coworkers.

Upon entering the room, Abi moved toward the picture window behind the Chef, awaiting them. Gazing at the famously picturesque Higashiyama townscape, with its overlapping tiled roofs and sloped winding streets, the Yasaka Pagoda towered above it all.

Chef Koyama greeted them with a warm smile and a sparkle in his eye as though he sensed just how special this evening was. Each course was crafted with precision, beginning with a creamy Hokkaido cheese topped with sea urchin and seaweed caviar. But the true highlight of the evening was the lively conversation around the table.

Jade leaned into Reggie playfully. "Any chance you can take over the cooking in our house?"

He chuckled and gave her hand a gentle squeeze. "Are you kidding? I don't even know how to turn on the oven." He winked, making everyone laugh.

"Oh, stop," Jade replied with a grin, shaking her head. "Guess I'll have to improve my cooking skills after we're married? Perhaps Anton will have some tips for me?"

"I am willing to help out," the Chef announced. "Just say the word, Miss Jade."

"Maybe we can both take lessons and learn together. How's that?" Reg said. About to kiss her lips, he suddenly stopped, reminded of the PDA rule.

Brushing Abi's shoulder with his, Shane revealed, "That's when you know the guy's in love."

"Would you cook with me?" she asked.

"If it means we're cooking together and not apart. I'm in."

Hearing that, she quickly got the gist of what he was saying.

Chef Koyama interrupted to announce the Kuruma shrimp and matsutake mushrooms subtly accented with yuzu as he served their plates.

Taking a bite, Shane leaned over to Abi. "Who knows, maybe we will be cooking together in another state other than Alabama."

She stopped dead. Terrified, she wondered if someone had told him about Harvard before she could.

He flashed an uncertain smile.

"What are you saying?" she asked.

He ate another shrimp. "I don't know... I'm just mulling over my options."

"But you signed with Alabama. It's a done deal. Isn't it?" She was so confused.

"Technically, yes, but players have the freedom to transfer schools if they enter the transfer portal. Once a player does that, other schools are free to recruit them."

She moved her food around with her fork. "But, by doing that, aren't you then giving up the number one school and possibly your ticket to the NFL?"

"There are no guarantees either way."

Able to see the level of commitment in his eyes, she said, "You can't give up your future."

Overhearing the heavy conversation, the culinary master, deeply focused on his work, suddenly made eye contact with them and delivered their perfectly seared grouper on saffron celeriac.

"Arigatou gozaimasū," Abi acknowledged, hoping to formally offer a higher level of respect, believing they were being rude by not paying attention.

"Dou Itashimashite," he bowed slightly.

Understanding Japanese culture, she knew a serious talk during dinner was usually deemed inappropriate, particularly in social settings. They view mealtime as an opportunity to relax, enjoy their food, and engage in pleasant discussions.

Embarrassed, she leaned over to Shane and said, "Can we talk about this later?"

He nodded willingly, knowing why.

At the same time, Jade turned to Abi. "So, how did it go today at the children's home? You and Burton went together, right?"

Having gone from the frying pan into the fire, Abi felt stressed. Bracing herself, she took a breath. "Honestly, it was a tough day." Gazing thoughtfully out the window, trying not to cry, she added, "The children were incredible, though. Strong. Resilient, even though they're so young." She grew a little quieter. "Burton...connected with a little boy named Aoto, who adored hockey. They played a game with a few of his friends. It was sweet to watch." Trying to put on a brave face, she leaned back and glanced over to where Burton was seated. Soon, their eyes met. Certain he hadn't heard their conversation, she found him deep in thought. Almost contemplative. His lips curled into a gentle smile as he raised his hand slightly off his lap to offer a subtle hello.

A lightness broke through the heavy air around her, offering an odd sense of peace. Seeing him happy despite all the issues they'd experienced that day somehow lifted her spirits.

Setting down a sizzling Ohmi beef tenderloin, Chef Koyama presented the aroma-rich dish with wasabi and crisp apple, drawing them all back into the moment.

"I can't imagine how hard it would have been." Jade reached over to squeeze her hand. "The kids were lucky to meet you both."

Desperately wanting to change the subject, Abi raised her glass and looked around the table with a warm smile, "Tomorrow's going to be unforgettable," she said to the bride-to-be. "Seeing both of you so happy means everything. You are our best friends. We love you and can hardly wait to share your special day."

"Aww, girl. You always know the right thing to say."

Jade hugged her while everyone clinked their glasses. Amidst it all, Abi happened to see Burton joining in on his side, too.

As the evening wound down with a light dessert of pear, cacao, and matcha, its flavors, sweet with a hint of bitterness, Chef Koyama's culinary mastery had woven seamlessly with the moments shared. As they laughed, talked, and grew quiet in thoughtful glances across the table, it felt as though they'd each leave a part of their hearts here in Japan, forever bound by the memories they'd created.

| 40 |

Overheard

Tuesday, December 19

Park Hyatt, Kyoto

Upon leaving the restaurant that evening, Jade walked alongside Abi with their arms linked together.

"So, are you going to stay with me in my room tonight?"

Abi said to her, "What do you mean?"

"Reg can't see me before the wedding. Remember? So, we need to be in separate rooms until we leave for the spa in the morning and move to The Thousand Hotel to get ready for the ceremony."

Hearing her, Reggie said, "Hold on, what did you just say?"

She stopped. "It's bad luck, Reg. We need to do it."

"Well, I don't believe in that. It's just a superstition."

"Too bad." She turned to Abi. "So, are you in?"

"I'm the Maid of Honor. Your wish is my command," she chuckled before checking on Reg's reaction.

The girl hugged her. "Thank you!"

"Absolutely."

"Oh, man. Then, if she's staying with you, where do I go?"

Shane rested his hand on his friend's shoulder. "Guess you're bunkin' in with me."

"Perfect," Jade replied. "Thanks, Shane."

"No problem."

Hoping to have some quiet time before bed, Abi wanted to read for a bit. She had so much on her mind after the day she and Burton had. "So, when are we doing this switcheroo?" she asked.

"How about ten o'clock? That way, we can get showered and changed, and we'll be ready to get some sleep."

"Sounds good."

Having taken the elevator to the Resident's Lounge, the group walked along to the second set of lifts that would take them to the top floor.

When they arrived moments later, Abi and Shane stood in the hall outside their room and said, "We will see you at ten, then?"

"Yep," Jade replied excitedly. "See you then."

Opening their door, Shane held it for Abi as she walked in. When it closed behind them, the football player took out his phone.

"I'm just gonna watch a bit of the game. Want to join me?"

She thought for a second. "Is it okay if I say no?"

Surprised, he sat on the bed. "Of course, it's fine."

"I just want to have some quiet time. Might read for a bit."

About to connect his device to the television, he stopped and turned to her. "If you want to stay here, I can go and just find a place to hang out and watch the game on my phone or your laptop. Haven't seen the lobby downstairs yet. Maybe I'll go there."

"No, don't be silly. You need a big screen. It's too hard to watch on your phone. I'll just go to the Residents' Lounge. I won't be far."

"Are you sure? Cause I don't mind going."

Fine with it, she said, "No. You stay here. I'll duck out for a little bit before returning to pack up and watch the end of the game with you."

"Okay, sounds good."

Clothes in hand, she retreated to the bathroom to change in private while Shane figured out how to mirror his phone on the television. Successfully doing so, she heard him take a seat on the bed as the distant sound of the game filled the air. Quickly pulling on a pair of tights and slipping on a t-shirt and a soft sweater, she wrapped it tightly around herself while walking around the room to collect her phone, book, and key card as the tassel from the Death to Her card caught her eye. Staring at it, Abi felt her heart drop. Determined not to pay it any mind, at the last second, she took her Burch Book to write down a few thoughts from the day. Not only did she want to research this so-called nefarious group, but she also had some ideas for Burton's nonprofit and wanted to ensure she recorded them. Grabbing the door, she announced, "I'll be back."

"Happy reading," he said before she left.

"Thank you!"

When she stepped on the elevator, she quietly descended to the Residents' Lounge level. Passing by the beautifully lit bonsai tree, the hallway was peaceful and serene as she walked to the far corner of the room. Happy the guys weren't hovering for once, she figured she was safe there for a while. Sitting with her back to the wall, Abi was able to see a full 180 degrees to survey her surroundings.

Pulling out a chair to put her feet up on, she walked over and grabbed a bottle of water and a glass. Setting it on her table, she got comfy and opened the book to the page held by the ominous marker where she'd left off. Slouching in the seat, with feet up, she started reading, but soon got distracted by the sound of Burton and Martin walking off the second set of elevators. Hidden around the corner, they didn't see her sitting there. Listening to their in-depth conversation, she saw Martin open the cover on his iPad.

Turning it toward Burton, he said, "This is the latest news coverage on *Nightfall*." He paused. "The exposure is helping build visibility, but there's some controversy, too. People love the music, but others are upset about the lottery for tickets not being equal. They're saying it creates a kind of caste system because the algorithm checks social media to decide who's *worthy* to attend."

Burton remained impassive as he scrolled through the articles. "I expected this," he said calmly. "For most, it's a new concept. You and I both know the reason behind it." Not having to spell it out for him, he added, "We must filter the clientele. There is no other way."

The gentleman nodded in agreement. "True, but you'll have to address it during your interviews tomorrow morning and again on Thursday before the Yokaan event. Someone will bring it up. I assure you."

"Then, I will explain that there are two types of events. Open and closed. The closed events must have vetted attendees for not only networking purposes but also for safety reasons. That is our prerogative."

"I understand. Just rehearse a very standard response and keep it as balanced as possible."

"I will. Don't worry, I...."

Abi heard Burton suddenly stop. Peeking out from behind her book, she could see him veer in the direction of the elevators down the hall.

Suddenly, Sara surfaced. Hearing a suitcase rolling along the carpet runner behind her, Abi saw the top of the woman's blonde hair behind the half wall. Immediately, she wondered where she was going.

As she got closer, he said, "You're leaving?"

"What does it look like?" she replied snarkily.

"Where are you going?"

"I'm heading to Osaka to help prep for your event there."

Able to feel the awkwardness of the conversation despite being on the opposite side of the room, Abi closed her book and eavesdropped.

Not shocked to hear this, Burton took his girlfriend aside while Martin stepped away to give them some privacy.

When he did, the gentleman spotted Abi sitting in the corner. He raised his eyebrows to indicate something was going down.

"Sara, listen..."

"Burton, please don't argue with me. I just need a little space."

He stared at her for a moment. Willing to do that, he nodded. "Fine. I will have Martin make the arrangements."

Unable to look him in the eye, she defied, "That's not necessary. I already have."

"Are you sure?"

"I'm more than capable of taking care of myself." With a noticeable awkwardness between them, she said before leaving, "I'll see you guys there."

"Alright," Burton said, standing straight and tall, keeping his strong façade.

Without another word, she walked down the ramp toward the elevators, close to Abi.

Quickly opening her book, scared to be seen, Abi tried to hide behind it, but with perfect timing, Martin blocked the girl's line of sight so she wouldn't spot her there.

In the aftermath, once Sara departed, Abi gravitated to Burton, who was left standing alone. Eyes following him as he walked toward the lifts leading to their floor, he suddenly turned around and paced back and forth.

Looking up, he found her at the far end of the room. Stopping dead in his tracks, hands resting on his waist, he hesitated before slowly making his way over as Martin hovered, then left.

"How much of that did you hear?"

Sad for him, she replied, "I'm sorry, I didn't mean to..."

"I know... Guess you just witnessed the extent of our problems." He silently gestured to ask permission. "Can I sit?"

She raised her hand and pointed at the empty chair.

"I suppose I should focus on the bright side. At least I won't be walking on eggshells for the next couple of days." Embarrassed, he ran his hand along the table, staring at it, moving from left to right. "This afternoon, when you left, things got heated."

"Because of me."

He quickly replied, "No. It's just..."

"Complicated?" she interjected.

"Yeah..."

"Does she know?"

"Know what?" he questioned.

"What happened today at the store and the Children's home?"

"I wanted to share the details, hoping it would buffer her reaction. Figured she'd understand what she walked in on, then. But in the end, she still wasn't interested in me justifying anything."

Abi ran her hand along her brow.

"Thankfully, I was able to convince her to attend the rehearsal."

"I was surprised to see her there."

"I figured as much," he replied, recalling the awkwardness. "Guess it was too overwhelming for her. Didn't think she'd leave, though."

"I'm sorry, Burton." She slipped the Death to Her card to mark where she'd left off and closed her book.

Seeing this, he said, "You still have that thing?"

"I thought I'd keep it as evidence."

He wondered if she'd seen it slammed against the window at the store that day. "Probably a good idea," he replied, not dredging anything else up.

"Speaking of which. Anything new to report?"

He understood what she was asking. "Umm, no. Still working on it."

"I'm a bit worried about tomorrow."

Eyes gravitating to hers, he said with certainty, "Don't be. Everything will be fine. I promise."

"Are you sure?"

Not wanting to instill any fear, he bypassed the question. "So, I should, ahh… let you return to your reading."

Realizing what he did, she placed the book on the table. "Nope. Think I'd rather talk to you." A warmth spread through her. Changing the subject to something more positive, she said, "I keep thinking about you teaching Aoto and his friends how to play hockey."

"Yeah. He was pretty enthusiastic." Burton smiled fondly. "Maybe the next Sydney Crosby."

"Did you see the hope in his eyes? He just lit up." A tear drifted down her face as she quickly wiped it away with the sleeve of her sweater.

Leaning forward, he reached for her arm across the table. "Hey, hey…" As he rubbed it gently, he said, "He's gonna be okay."

When he said that, she sobbed even more. "But, he's all alone. So are those little girls. It just breaks my heart. How could someone just give them up like that? I don't understand. Couldn't imagine the rejection they must feel," she whimpered.

"I don't know their stories specifically, but most get dropped off at such a young age. They don't know any different. It's sad, nonetheless, but they seemed pretty well-rounded despite it all."

"And smart." She peered up at the ceiling, hoping to hold back tears. "I just can't get the thought of them falling asleep in that place and not having a real home." Shoulders trembling, she wrapped her arms tightly around herself, trying to stay composed. But soon, tears streamed down her flushed cheeks as uneven gasps interrupted her breathing rhythm. Each inhale was shaky, her chest heaving as she choked back a sob. Lips quivering, with eyes red-rimmed and glossy, she stared ahead blankly. Lost in the vision that gripped her heart, she dabbed her face.

Though her tears continued to fall, Burton moved closer. With open arms, he said, "Come here a minute."

Obliging, she grasped hold of him.

Without hesitation, he tightened their embrace. "We'll set up regular video calls with the children to keep tabs on them and make sure they are doing well."

She nodded while resting her head on his chest. Hearing his heart beating brought back memories from Tahoe.

Suddenly, he asked, "Better?"

Able to manage a half-smile, she nodded. "Suppose so."

He rubbed the outer edges of her arms. "I promise. I will do everything I can for them."

Her chest heaved again.

Amidst the silence, he said, "Well, I'm heading to bed. Dark Demon has a few interviews in the morning. Want to walk back upstairs with me?"

Grabbing her book off the table, she placed the unused glass on the tray and took the bottle of water with her.

"I'll carry that for you," he said, reaching out for it.

"Thanks."

"Sure."

Burton pressed the elevator button. When the doors opened, he held them back for her to get in first. Joining his friend, he hit the number for their floor as the doors slid shut.

"You gonna be okay?" he asked.

"Hopefully. It's a big day tomorrow. I've got to stay focused. Being Maid of Honor is a huge deal," she giggled.

"Certainly is."

Arriving on the top floor, he prompted her to exit.

She moved past her room and a bit further down the hall.

Noticing this, he pointed silently.

About to say something, she interrupted, "Yes, I know. I, umm, just don't want Shane to see us. Sorry..."

He held up his hand. "No need to explain."

She reached for him and wrapped her arms around his waist. "If I haven't said this already, thank you for today."

Hugging her, he replied, "Sure." Handing her the glass bottle of water, he smiled. "Night, Abs."

"Night, B." Moving towards her door, she turned at the last second and waved to him before he rounded the corner, raising a steady hand at waist level while watching her disappear inside the room.

| **41** |

A Night Apart

Tuesday, December 19

Park Hyatt, Kyoto

Upon swinging open the door, Abi could hear the hum of football fans and the referee's whistle when she walked in. Composing herself, she took a deep breath before peeking in on Shane.

"Hey, you're back. Didn't expect you for another hour." He could see that her eyes were red. Sitting up in bed, as she took a seat beside him, he asked, "Have you been crying?"

Unable to hide it, she said, "Umm, yes. A little."

Immediately, he wrapped his arms around her. "What is it? What's wrong?"

His concern set her off, causing Abi to break down again. "I was just thinking of that little boy named Aoto. He was just the cutest."

"Oh yeah? How so?"

"It was his enthusiasm. He was just so animated. His eyes danced with excitement – literally."

"Wish I could've met him."

Silent for a second, she paused. "Yes, me too."

"I assume it was a rewarding day, but difficult?"

She snuggled up beside him. "That is an understatement."

His attention got diverted to the screen as the QB threw a long pass down the field. Abi could feel him hold his breath while it descended toward a receiver. When the guy caught the ball and entered the end zone, Shane whispered, "Touchdown," and raised a closed fist.

Realizing he could never fully understand what she was feeling at that moment, she sat up.

This caught him off guard. "Hey, where are you going?"

"I'm just gonna get ready for bed. Tomorrow will be a long day. I've gotta get to Jade's room. Reg is coming here, remember?"

"Are we really doin' that?"

"Of course. Whatever the bride wants, she gets." Taking a tote bag, she grabbed comfortable clothes for their morning spa appointments and packed all of her cosmetics, curling iron, and brushes. When she set it on the floor by the door, she got her crossbody and another tote to carry her wedding shoes and evening bag. Stuffing a nightgown in at the last second, she said, "Okay. Guess I'm ready to go."

He got up and walked over. Reaching out, he embraced her tightly. "I'll miss you." Kissing her lips, he then pressed them to her forehead.

"Enjoy your morning tomorrow, and I'll see you at the chapel."

Shane smiled. "I can hardly wait to see you in that beautiful dress."

She bashfully replied, "Is that right?"

"Will you dance with me?" he asked.

Squinting her eyes, she said, "I believe I can save a spot on my card for you."

"Card?" he asked, confused by the reference.

Realizing he wasn't familiar with the context, she explained, "A dance card is kind of old-fashioned," she began. "Back in the day, at fancy balls or formal dances, women would carry these little booklets or cards. Each guy who wanted to dance with her would sign up for a specific dance."

Getting the gist, he said, "Interesting."

"So, by the end of the night, each hoped her dance card would fill up—meaning, for every dance, she had a partner assigned," she chuckled. "Kind of a crazy concept, don't you think?"

"Obviously, those girls were single and ready to mingle," he laughed. "Unlike yourself, who has a steady man in her life."

She smacked his shoulder playfully. "That said, if someone asks me to dance, I'm dancing. There's no getting jealous and bent out of shape, deal?"

"Depends who it is." When she sternly tilted her head, he conceded, "Fine. I won't make a scene."

"I'll hold you to that."

He kissed her again.

"I'd better go."

A knock came to the door. Abi opened it and found Reggie looking fairly displaced.

"Hey, Jade's waiting for you."

Abi grabbed her bags.

"Want me to carry that?" Shane reached for them in her hand.

She shook her head, "No, it's all good. You go ahead and finish watching the game."

"See you tomorrow."

"I'll be the one in the black dress," she teased, waving at him. "Good luck, you guys."

Shane gave her a thumbs-up as Abi knocked on the door adjacent to theirs. Within seconds, Jade flung it open, her face lighting up with excitement. "Hey! Come on in, girl!" Jade practically bounced on her heels, grabbing one of Abi's bags.

Overwhelmed by her excitement, Abi stepped into the room, believing it would be a long night. With the wedding tomorrow, for some reason, she felt like it was the calm before the storm. Desperate to relax with her best friend, she hoped to simply watch movies and chat about the big day and everything that would follow.

"I can't believe it's your last night as a single woman." Abi set the rest of her things down.

"I know, right?" Jade beamed. "It's surreal. But I'm so happy you're here with me. It feels perfect. She tossed her a warm smile before settling down on the bed.

Abi joined her, already feeling tired.

Discussing some wedding details and Jade's vision for her life with Reggie, soon, the conversation took a more serious turn as her friend rolled over and asked, "So, have you and Shane…you know…" Her eyebrows raised and lowered insightfully.

Nervously looking her way, Abi turned and stared at the ceiling. "No…"

"What! Please tell me you're joking." Seeing her reaction, Jade knew she wasn't. "What is holding you back, Abs? You love him. He loves you. What more do you need?"

"I don't know…" At a loss, she wasn't sure what else to say.

Silence fell upon them. "I'm sorry, I didn't mean to pry."

"You're not prying. It's just a difficult subject for me. That's all," she nervously divulged. "It's not like he hasn't tried. I just…"

"Maybe the timing hasn't been right? Is that it?"

"Perhaps…"

Suspecting something, she said, "Don't get mad, but can I ask you a question?"

"I know what you are gonna say."

"Do you love him?"

She shook her head, trying to stop the feelings from creeping in. "Of course, I love Shane."

Her friend pounced. "Not Shane - Burton."

Shocked to hear her observation, she reacted quickly. "Burton? What do you mean…" and covered her eyes with her sleeves. Confused beyond measure, panic set in.

"So?" her friend prompted.

Abi realized she couldn't hide this from Jade. "Damn it!" she said. "What am I doing?"

Jade sat up as Abi started pacing the floor.

"Today, at the Children's home, I don't know what it was, but when he interacted with the kids, I felt something here." She clutched her chest. "I had never seen him like that."

"Because it was an emotional day, maybe you got caught up in it all."

"Maybe so..." Abi said wearily. "Besides, it's not possible to love two people."

"Are you kidding? Sure, you can. It happens all the time." The girl smirked. "Now, it's just a matter of deciding who you love more."

Her heart pounded in her chest as she continued to pace back and forth, hardly able to breathe. Hating the thought of hurting one or the other, she knew she was right. Sitting back down on the bed, Jade rested her hand on hers. "Everything is going to be okay."

Doubt flooded Abi's soul. She wanted to believe her so badly. "Can we talk about something else? Please, I'm begging you..."

Ready to help change the subject, she revealed, "So, Reggie and I have been working on something," Jade began, her expression shifting slightly. "In light of his father's failures, we discovered that those involved in the family business believe he is unfit to lead, so this opens the door for us to step in and save it."

Immediately upon hearing that, her attention shifted. "Really?" Abi raised her eyebrows. "That sounds intense. How are you planning to do that?"

Jade sighed, leaning back against the pillows. "We have to go see his ex-fiancée in Spain. Well, really, we will be meeting with both her and her new husband. Remember, she's the one with the Royal bloodline - if I'm not mistaken." Having veered off topic, she regrouped. "Anyway... Hopefully, we will strike a deal with them and keep both companies afloat, but there's a catch. The contract will only go through if Reggie takes the helm of the Wilson conglomerate and becomes President and CEO, replacing his father. The same goes for her. She plans to replace her father, also. Without this stipulation, the deal is dead."

Abi's eyes widened. "Wow, that's huge."

"Massive," Jade admitted, "but it's not a simple process. Reggie will first need to convince the board that this is a sound and financially viable decision. They will then vote to implement the change. If the deal's sweet enough, it could fall in our favor. Most of the board members hate Reggie's Dad for obvious reasons. He's not the easiest guy to work with."

Already picturing the kind of arrogance the man possessed based on what Jade had described, Abi said, "I'm sure."

"I've only met him once, and that was enough for me. Definitely not a people person."

"I can't believe Reg is his son. He's not like that at all."

"Exactly, he's completely the opposite of the man," Jade agreed. "But even if the board votes in Reggie's favor, it'll be a lot of pressure. We want full control of his grandfather's legacy—and we still have to face his father and hope the guy bows out willingly."

Understanding, Abi nodded. "That is a lot, but you and Reggie make a good team. I'm sure you'll figure it out."

Jade's eyes softened. "Thanks, Abs. We've been strategizing. Right after the wedding, it will be our main focus. I know we'll get through it."

Giving her friend's hand a squeeze, Abi encouraged, "You've got this, Jade. But let's not think about that right now. You need to focus on your special day. And tonight, you need to relax as much as possible and get a good sleep."

"You're right," Jade grinned, her eyes sparkling with excitement. "I'm so excited. Just want to be his. That's all I want."

When she said that, Abi felt a mix of emotions. Keeping them to herself, she said, "Before you know it, the ceremony will fly by, and everything will be set in stone. Remember to enjoy the moment."

The bride-to-be smiled at the thought. "I can't wait. Reggie and I have been planning every detail. It's surreal that it's finally happening." A flash of worry surfaced.

"What is it?" Abi asked.

"I don't know. I feel like his father is going to show up and ruin it."

"He won't. There's no way he will figure out where you are getting married. I'm sure Martin has hidden everything off the books," Abi said calmly. "Don't worry. The guys will be surrounding the church. They will make sure nothing happens."

"You're right. I think I'm just gun-shy after everything that's happened so far. Every plan we made, he infiltrated and ruined."

"Don't think of that now." Abi hugged her. "Just focus on tomorrow. Soon, you'll be Mr. and Mrs. Reggie Wilson. Forever."

She beamed upon hearing that. "On that note, I'm gonna jump in the shower. I need to wash my hair for the updo tomorrow."

"Sounds good."

When Jade disappeared into the bathroom, Abi thought about their conversation. Her mind was in a muddle. She was more confused than ever. Taking out her phone, wanting to text Burton, she stopped herself, knowing her loyalty had to stay with Shane. Guilt flowed through her. Nodding off, she whispered, "That's not fair to him."

Soon, Jade returned and climbed into the massive king-sized bed. Settling in under the covers, she lay there full of excitement but also exhaustion.

"Night, Abs," she said, closing her eyes with a contented sigh.

"Night, Jade. See you in the morning," she whispered, still heavy with sleep.

Her head sank into the pillow. "Sweet dreams, Jade."

| 42 |

Behind Closed Doors

Tuesday, December 19

Park Hyatt Kyoto

In the quiet of the room, Abi rolled on her back and stared at the ceiling for a while. Unable to turn off her thoughts, the softness of the bed finally lulled her into sleep. Hours later, the gentle buzz of her phone woke her.

Groggy, she squinted at the screen and found a text from Burton. Her heart skipped a beat. Reading it, she let the device flop onto her chest. He wanted her to come to his suite. Unsure what to do, she raised her head slightly off the pillow and found Jade snoring away. Texting back, she said, *I'll be right there.*

Putting the phone down, muting it, she gingerly pulled back the covers and wrapped herself in her robe. Tip-toeing towards the door, not knowing where Jade had stashed her key card, Abi quietly opened it and peeked out. Not seeing the guys in the hallway, she swung the security lock to prop it open and quickly hurried down the hall. Curious but cautious, she made her way to his room. To her surprise, he was already waiting for her.

Looking stressed, he whispered, "Hey. Come in."

"What's wrong? Are you okay? Did something happen?"

Ushering her inside, he offered her a seat on the living room couch.

"I was thinking, since Sara went ahead to Osaka, we forgot to tell Jade that she won't be standing in the wedding."

Still half asleep, Abi remained standing and replied, "That could have waited until morning, you know." Trying to formulate a response, she added, "Honestly, Jade would have been fine with it either way. No offense, but as long as Shane and I are there, that's all that matters."

"Right..."

Knowing that what she said came out wrong, she apologized. "I'm sorry. You know what I mean..."

"Yeah, I get it." Wanting to address something else, he said, "On a happier note, I've been thinking a lot about the Children's home."

"Oh? What about it?"

"When it comes to education, I've read that these kids are at a disadvantage most of the time, so I've decided to change that." He turned and walked over to the window.

"How?" she asked.

"I've decided to build a tutoring center, a library, and a computer lab – a place where they can have all the tools to succeed. I will put the proper people in place to manage it all and support the children."

For a moment, he stood silently before her.

She could see the commitment in his gaze. Surprised, she knew he was dead serious. "That's incredible, B," she said, full of admiration.

"I'm considering buying the plot of land next door. With that, we could add a gymnasium."

Staring at him, Abi's heart swelled.

Burton, meanwhile, continued thoughtfully, "It's frustrating that so few people here would even consider adoption because the child wouldn't be of their blood." He ran a hand through his hair. The weariness was undeniable. Slipping his hands in his pockets, he walked back toward her. "I've been racking my brain on how to change that perception."

Seeing him frustrated and his mind reeling, knowing he thought better on his feet, she said, "Burton?"

He suddenly stopped. "Hmm?" His expression was intense.

Her heart fluttered when he did.

Standing beside him, she brushed her shoulder against his. "Can we try to save the world on Thursday? We've got a wedding to prepare for and really need some sleep."

"Did you tell Shane what happened with the mob outside the store today?"

She hesitated, "Umm, no. I haven't gotten a chance yet."

"I believe it's best not to. At this point, it will set him off."

She knew he was right. "I kinda figured that," she said. Her sight gravitated out the window at the Yasaka Pagoda, uplit in the darkness. "Still can't get over that view."

He agreed. "Yes, it's pretty nice."

Linking her arm through his, she teased, "Promise me you'll actually get to bed."

He didn't answer.

"Burton, please?"

"Fine," he paused, "But I'm only doing it because you asked nicely."

She laughed. "Whatever works."

Moving towards the door, she wrapped her arms around his waist. "I've gotta get back to Jade. I'll see you in a few hours, I guess."

"Sounds good."

As she walked out, she gave him a little wave before he closed the door.

When she rounded the corner, her heart dropped. There, in the hallway, were Jade, Reggie, and Shane, their expressions a mix of curiosity and concern.

Noticeably upset, Shane headed back to their room in silence.

Jade turned to Abi, her brow furrowed. "Were you with him?"

Unable to deny it, Abi silently nodded.

The girl shook her head. "Oh, Abs, what are you doing?"

"He just needed someone to talk to about Sara. She left for Osaka."

Reggie was angered. "So, she bailed on our wedding?"

"Yes…"

"Honestly, it doesn't matter," Jade blurted. "As long as you and Shane are there for us, that's all we care about."

Staring at the door to their room, Abi exhaled. "I need to talk to him," she said wearily. "Can you give us a minute?"

After exchanging glances, the young couple both nodded and ducked inside their room, leaving Abi with Shane.

Slowly opening the door, she walked in and found him sitting on the bed, his fists clenched.

"I didn't do anything wrong."

He let out a humorless chuckle. "Abs, you always think that."

"What's that supposed to mean?" she shot back.

"If the roles got reversed and I went to Emile's room, how would you feel?"

"That's different—you two have a history," she countered, then softened.

"Right…"

Realizing she threw that in his face a little too quickly, she felt bad. "I'm sorry. I get it. What more do you want me to say?"

He looked at her, his frustration simmering. "I don't want to be the jealous boyfriend, Abs, but you make it hard."

Stepping closer, she explained, "He was upset. Sara left for Osaka tonight. She bailed on the wedding. On top of that, he's trying to fig-ure out how to help the children we met today. His mind was reeling, and he just needed someone to talk to. Please, don't be mad."

Still tense, Shane sighed and stood. Walking to the window as he gazed out at the darkened city, his arms crossed in front of his chest.

She placed a hand on his back. "Are we okay?"

Realizing that staying back that afternoon and not going with the two of them could have sparked this, he said, "Yeah, I guess so…"

Cautiously wrapping her arms around his waist from behind, she hugged him and whispered, "I love you," while tightening her embrace.

Unable to resist her, without saying a word, he turned and wrapped his arms around her, holding her close. Feeling her hands as they cupped his face, she kissed him tenderly to convey all her love and reassurance. Every time she did, he melted in her arms. "Sure, you can't stay?" he murmured, adding a bit of humor. "Don't make me room with Reggie."

"You're his best friend and best man," she reminded. "Tonight, you need to take one for the team."

Loving it when she used sports analogies, he said, "Fine," and chuckled. "But tomorrow night, you're all mine."

With a playful smile, she replied, "Deal."

As they walked to the door, hand in hand, he opened it for her and gave her one last kiss before heading over to Jade's room.

Reggie answered, giving her a searching look. "Everything okay?" he asked.

"Yes. We're fine," she reassured him.

Jade appeared, yawning. "Thank God. Can we sleep now? I'm getting married tomorrow."

Hugging his bride-to-be, Reg said, "Goodnight, babe. See you at the altar."

She sleepily replied, "I'll be the one in the white dress."

Closing the door behind him, Abi and Jade finally collapsed into bed, exhausted.

"Goodnight, girl," her friend mumbled, already drifting off.

"Goodnight, Jade. Dream of Reggie," Abi replied.

The girl mumbled faintly, "Already am. You'd better be dreaming of Shane."

Abi hesitated, a small smile creeping across her lips. "Don't worry. I will."

Spa Morning

Wednesday, December 20

Park Hyatt, Kyoto

A loud knock rattled the room as a man announced, "Room Service," just as Jade's alarm blared.

Eyes flying open, she realized it was her wedding day. A jolt of excitement followed. In an instant, she was out of bed and opening the door to greet the concierge, who wheeled in a breakfast cart overflowing with two entrees, pastries, fruit, and more than one steaming French press.

When the man left, Jade said, "Abi! Wake up! Come on—we need to eat and get going!"

Rolling over, groaning as she rubbed her eyes, Abi felt like she'd barely slept and wasn't ready to face the day yet. But seeing Jade's beaming face and smelling the aroma of breakfast waiting, she dragged herself out of bed, hoping a strong coffee would do the trick. Pouring a cup, she passed on the cream, believing it would wake her up faster.

Already halfway through a croissant, Jade started talking a mile a minute. "Martin will be here in an hour. Then we're off to the hotel this afternoon. Our dresses should be waiting for us in the bridal suite!"

Trying her best to decipher the girl's rambling, she simply nodded until her brain could keep up. Able to finally shake off the exhaustion, she glanced happily at her bubbly friend. Reaching for a slice of melon and cutting it into smaller cubes, Abi noticed Jade's face dim slightly.

"You know… My Mom used to talk about my wedding day all the time. How she'd be there, fussing over every detail, tearing up over nothing." She flashed a sad smile. "Now, I'm about to walk down the aisle without her. Without either of them."

Not expecting to hear this, Abi said, "Given the circumstances, you and Reggie didn't have a choice. It was the only way."

Her eyes got glassy. "I just can't help but feel this guilt."

"You've got nothing to feel guilty about. I'm sure she'll understand."

Jade's lips curved up, though her eyes still held a hint of sadness. "Hope so. She'd probably say the same thing. Just wish she were here."

Squeezing her hand gently, Abi understood more than words could convey. "She'll support you, Jade. Today and every single day after that. And I'll be right by your side, too."

The girl took a deep breath, nodding as her face brightened. "That means everything to me. Guess I'll just have to bring her with me, somehow." She brushed a stray tear away, looking at Abi with renewed determination. "Alright, no more tears. We've got a wedding to get ready for."

Giving her hand one last squeeze, Abi grinned. "That's the spirit. Today is yours, Jade. Let's make it amazing."

Quickly moving about the room, the two finished their breakfast, got dressed, and packed what they needed. Soon, they heard a knock at the door.

Martin arrived right on time. He looked more than ready to begin the day.

Each grabbed their bags and headed out, hoping Reg and Shane wouldn't see them. At the elevators, the men were already there waiting.

Standing aside when the doors parted, the gentleman said, "Andrew and Matt will be escorting you. I'm sorry. I have several commitments with Master B this morning. Afterward, I will meet you at the Thousand Hotel. If you have any questions or if there is a problem, please message me."

In an overly thankful mood, Jade hugged the man. "Okay. We will see you there. Thank you again for your help."

"Very well, Miss Jade. Enjoy your morning, ladies."

Quietly riding the elevator to the Residents' lounge, they transferred lifts and descended to the lower level. Reaching the spa entrance, Abi and Jade stepped into the lobby. It felt sacred.

A woman with warm eyes and perfectly styled hair approached, her spa uniform neat and polished.

"Ohayō gozaimasu. Good morning," she greeted in Japanese before smoothly transitioning to English with a slight bow. "I'm Michelle, your spa coordinator for today. Jade, Abi—welcome."

Jade's nervousness faded as she started to relax. "Thank you, Michelle."

"I hear you are getting married today. Congratulations, Miss."

"Thank you so much."

Michelle's expression was warm. Balancing professionalism with a touch of excitement, she announced, "Our goal is to ensure your day starts beautifully with a reflexology session, followed by manicures, pedicures, and a facial. We want you to feel pampered. So, follow me."

Walking along behind the woman, Abi said, "We are getting the VIP treatment, and it's not even noon."

Michelle nodded. "Exactly. We're here to keep you both refreshed and feeling your best, no matter how many butterflies you might be experiencing."

Taking a deep breath, Jade got a case of the jitters upon hearing that, as reality set in.

The hallway leading to the Spa was an enchanting path, dimly lit and lined with rice paper screens on the left side. Each was accented with delicate uplighting, giving the illusion of a modern shrine. Reminiscent of the iconic Fushimi Inari torii gates, the archways stretched out like an endless tunnel. As they walked, a sense of calm washed over them, deepening with each step.

At the end, Michelle opened a thick wooden door, revealing a reception area bathed in an orangey glow that felt instantly soothing. The warm hues enveloped them, adding to the tranquil atmosphere, while the scent of jasmine and lavender hung in the air.

"Here we are," Michelle said, checking their name off the list.

Signed in, the woman escorted them to the changing room. Given robes and slippers, they soon rejoined Michelle, ready for a couple of hours of relaxation.

Entering the first treatment area, the friends exchanged a look of gratitude as they settled into the reflexology chairs.

Reaching out, Abi squeezed Jade's hand. "This is it, Jade. Every minute is for you. Enjoy it all."

Content, the bride's earlier anxieties drifted away as Michelle's team began their treatments.

| 44 |

New, Borrowed & Blue

Wednesday, December 20

The Thousand Chapel, Kyoto

The three hours of pampering went by quickly. Before they knew it, they were on their way out to meet their driver.

In a daze, Abi stared at the ground. Having had time to relax and reflect on her thoughts, she felt a strong pull between Shane and Burton. Inevitably, she was somewhere in the middle, trying to make sense of it all.

Andrew's hand brushed her arm. "You okay, Miss?"

Caught off guard, she said, "Umm, yes. All good," despite her mind reeling. With a bit of fear surfacing, she suddenly turned to him and quietly whispered so Jade would not hear. "Burton told me about the Red Dragons at the store and the creepy man with the cane."

His face went stoic. "We're on it. Don't worry. Everything will be fine."

"Are you sure of that?"

With an air of confidence, he walked along, much straighter. "Between you and me, we have a number of people surrounding the hotel. You know, personnel hiding in the shadows," he winked, letting that sink in.

"So? We're safe?" she asked, needing confirmation.

"Trust me, Miss Abi. If anyone so much as breathes the wrong way, we will be on them."

She took a deep breath. "Okay. I trust you."

"Good, because you have bigger fish to fry today." He looked down at her and flashed a half-smile.

Following Jade out the main doors and into the courtyard, the guys helped them safely into the vehicle and got them on their way to The Thousand Hotel. Departing right on schedule, the driver headed south along the same route they'd taken before.

Upon arrival, they drove directly into the underground parking and over to the main doors, where four women were waiting for them just inside the glass. When they stopped, Andrew and Matt got out to secure the area before the two surfaced. The guys were happy to see extra hotel security hovering on the premises.

Met by their wedding coordinator, Yasu, she greeted them with a smile. "Kon'nichiwa." She bowed. "Hello, Miss Jade. Welcome! It is your big day! We are ready for you. Please follow me."

Doing just that, the woman led the group to the elevators that took them to the eighth floor. At the end of the long hallway, they turned right. There, Yasu passed the card over the reader and opened the door. Holding it for them, the girls walked in and saw hair and makeup people standing around, ready to make them look beautiful.

"Are we waiting for one other attendant?" Yasu asked, only seeing the two of them.

Glancing at Abi, Jade said, "Umm, sadly, she could not join us today. It will just be us."

Not asking questions, Yasu nodded. "Very well. I will be going. You are in good hands. Within the hour, I will return to prepare you for the ceremony. Takami Bridal has already arrived. They have your dresses upstairs, should you wish to see them."

Jade and Abi bowed slightly to the woman, who did the same in return.

Excited to see her gown, Jade addressed the glam squad and said, "One moment," before walking upstairs into the loft. Rounding the corner, she found her dress on a mannequin. It was just as she remembered it from Monday.

"Hello, Miss Weber," Umeko said while making a couple of last-minute adjustments.

Raising her hands to her lips, Jade turned to Abi and said, "It's perfect. I love it so much."

She offered the bride a side hug. "You are going to look beautiful." With her black bridesmaid dress hanging on a stand-alone hook, she could hardly wait to put it on. Today, her friend would be the Queen, but somehow Abi felt like a Princess too.

Descending the stairs to the lower floor, the girls settled into their chairs as the women started on their hair and makeup. With all of the products organized on the wooden table, they'd brought director's chairs for them to sit in. Reading the backs, one said BRIDE while the other said MAID OF HONOR.

A knock came to the door.

One of the women working on Abi's makeup went over to open it. Andrew and Matt stood by and said, "Delivery for the Bride."

"Please bring it in. It's okay," Jade instructed.

Yasu entered with the wedding bouquets and placed them on the counter inside the kitchenette as they heard another faint knock.

When Jade turned, she saw someone else standing in the doorway.

On alert, Andrew announced, "Miss, you have a visitor."

Eyes filling with a flood of emotion, Jade flew from her chair. "Oh my god! Mom!" Overwhelmed, she launched into her Mother's arms. "What are you doing here?"

"When I signed that paper, I didn't think it would be this soon." The woman tearfully smiled.

"I'm so sorry. Please don't hate me. I couldn't share the details. With everything going on, it's been so difficult. We needed to keep things under wraps."

"Well, a little birdie told me you were getting married today. He sent a plane, and I flew in from France last night."

"You did?" Guilt flooded her soul.

Knowing the situation, she said, "I understand, Sweetheart."

She clung to her Mother. "Ohh, I can't believe you're here."

"And, I can't believe my little girl is a bride today!" She shook with excitement. "Oh! Before I forget. I come bearing gifts."

Presenting her daughter with a red Cartier gift bag, she said, "This one is from my Son-in-Law-to-be."

"This is from Reg?"

"Yes."

Jade's heart leaped. "You've seen him this morning?"

"I have, briefly. He is very nervous but is confident in the love you both share."

She held the bag in her hand. "He said that?"

"He did." Her Mother choked up. "He loves you so much. That is all I ever wanted for you." Taking out her phone, she called him as planned and put him on speaker. "I have Jade with me here, my dear."

"Reg?"

"Hey, Babe. Did you like your surprise?"

She cried. "I can't believe you invited my Mom."

"I had to. You are her only daughter. She needed to share this day with you."

Breaking down, she said, "Thank you. You don't know what this means to me."

"I have a pretty good idea." Pausing a second, he said, "Did you receive your other gift?"

"Yes, I have it right here in my hands." About to ask if Shane gave him his, Reg suddenly said, "Thank you for the pen and my cufflinks. I love them. They match, too. I like that."

"I didn't know what to get you, but I thought since we have an important agreement to sign in the coming weeks, you would need a special pen to use. When I saw the cufflinks, I couldn't pass them up, knowing all your custom shirts need them."

"They're perfect. I am going to wear them today." He said on the other line. "Now open yours."

She took out the exquisitely wrapped white paper box adorned with a red Cartier wax seal on either end. Keeping it fairly intact, she removed the red box and flipped open the lid. Inside was a beautiful diamond tennis bracelet.

"Oh, my goodness..." Lost for words, Jade admired it while Abi helped clasp it to her wrist. "It's gorgeous. Thank you."

"From what I'm told, you needed something new, borrowed, and blue. Is that right?"

She giggled. "Yes, that's right."

"Well, this is your something new."

Abi stepped forward. "And, I have your something blue." Handing her a small box, Jade lifted the lid to find dainty blue sapphire earrings embedded in a halo of diamonds."

"Oh, Abs! They're so beautiful." Hugging her friend, she set them down to put on later.

Awaiting her turn, her Mother said, "And I have your something borrowed." Taking something from her bag, she flipped open the lid on the Tiffany blue box. Inside was her Victoria diamond necklace.

"You remembered..." she whimpered.

"Of course I did." Taking the necklace from the box, she took each end and clasped it around Jade's neck. "You've said for years you wanted to wear this for your wedding. Today, I wanted to make that dream come true."

Jade walked over to the mirror and admired the sparkling wreath. Resting her fingertips upon it, she was in disbelief. "This means so much to me."

Her Mother looked at the time. "On that note, we'd better focus, Sweetheart. The wedding is in two hours, and your hair isn't done yet."

Nodding her head, she sat down in the chair and allowed the woman to fix her makeup before sweeping her hair into an updo.

With anxious nerves making her body vibrate, she reached over and grasped her Mom's hand. "I can hardly wait to be Mrs. Reggie Wilson."

| 45 |

I Do

Wednesday, December 20

The Thousand Chapel, Kyoto

The air in the sun-filled bridal suite was electric as Abi, Jade, and Mrs. Webber prepared for the celebration ahead. Bubbling over with excitement, each felt a sense of anticipation just before Yasu returned to escort them to the chapel.

Abi looked sleek in her long black gown. Her hair was half-pinned back with a sparkling diamond brooch that shimmered against her loose waves, while Jade admired her reflection one last time as she gripped her bouquet a little too tightly, revealing the nerves creeping in as the minutes ticked down.

Standing nearby, graceful and poised in her silver Nicole Miller, Jade's Mother could sense her daughter's anxiety. Gently, placing a hand on her arm, she said, "You look so beautiful, Sweetheart."

Nodding nervously, the girl exhaled, almost unable to breathe. "Thank you, Mom." Hugging her, she added, "So do you."

"Are you ready, my dear?"

She nodded, tearfully.

A knock at the door startled them all.

Yasu peeked in with a kind smile. "It's time," she said.

Taking one last deep breath, the three women followed her down the hall to the elevator, with their black capes resting on their shoulders to guard against the cold. Asked to wait in a holding room just inside the hotel, Jade could see Reggie, Shane, and Burton walking through the doors of the chapel. Once serene, the gardens were now surrounded by security, and no one was allowed in until the ceremony concluded.

"This is it." Jade fidgeted, alternately shifting her weight from one foot to the other.

Not wanting to make the girl cry, Abi offered encouraging words. "Focus on Reg. Today, it's about you and him. Nobody else."

The bride silently agreed as she straightened her posture.

When Yasu returned, she said, "Follow me."

Walking outside in the cold, Lorenzo and Andrew were waiting by the doors as the other men circled the grounds on high alert.

Abi took her position in front of Jade, who had looped her arm with her Mother's.

Too overwhelmed to let her daughter go alone, the woman stood by her side, ready to walk her down the aisle. Despite their rocky relationship the past year, Jade found comfort in her presence.

Handing over their capes to the guys, the music spilled out as the chapel doors swung open, and all at once, time froze briefly. Flickering candles lined the aisle like stars guiding her path along the polished floor. Trembling, Abi stepped forward, the black taffeta of her maid of honor gown shimmering like midnight silk as she began her walk.

At the far end, in front of the waterfall glass window, the light illuminated Reggie, Shane, and Burton—all dressed handsomely in their tailored suits—lifting their eyes in unison.

Transferring his weight from left to right, the same way Jade did, the Groom clasped his hands in front of him and awaited the bride.

The moment Shane saw Abi making her way down the aisle, he smiled. *Wow, she looks beautiful*, he thought. *That's my girl.*

As the dark dress clung to her, he felt his chest tighten with the same rush he had when he first held and kissed her. *I don't need the crowd. I don't need the trophy. I just need her.* Nothing else mattered right then, and with absolute certainty, he knew: if he had Abi, his life was complete.

But beside him, Burton stood motionless and kept a sharp eye. Unbeknownst to those around him, a storm was brewing beneath the surface. *She's not the same girl who used to follow Shane around with stars in her eyes,* he thought. No, the woman walking toward him now carried herself with quiet power and grace. And something else—something he hadn't seen before. A future.

Hands trembling, her face brightened by the minute. Approaching the front, she glanced at Martin briefly before smiling at Reg.

Seeing Shane's eyes filled with love, hers soon drifted to Burton standing behind him.

In a heartbeat, something passed between them. It was a feeling he didn't recognize and couldn't ignore.

Noticing, Shane's fingers curled into fists at his sides while Abi took her place to await the bride, unaware of what had silently ignited at the altar. Peering down the aisle, the wedding march music soon filled the chapel as Jade appeared with her Mother.

Watching as Reggie saw her for the first time, he beamed with pride. Abi tried to hold back tears. From that moment onward, she could see every ounce of nervous energy melting away from them as they got closer to each other. His eyes never left hers. Every step Jade took reminded him how much he loved her.

Meeting them partway, Reggie embraced his Mother-in-law as the woman hugged him and kissed his cheek before taking a seat in the first pew.

The second Jade reached for him, he took hold of her hand and gripped it gently – never wanting to let go.

Approaching the Chaplain, knowing how much they had been through and how nothing—not even the looming threat of his Father—could keep them apart, they stood before him with confidence, ready to make this lifelong commitment to each other.

Smiling warmly upon them, the man began the ceremony. "Dearly beloved, we are gathered here today to join this man and this woman in holy matrimony. Jade Weber and Reginald Wilson the third have come before us to declare their love."

Jade's heart fluttered as she looked up at Reggie, his eyes filled with love and admiration.

She was the girl of his dreams. It had taken time, but with the help of Shane and Abi, their paths finally crossed. Despite the difficulties that plagued their relationship, none of it mattered now—because they were standing here, together, ready to start the next chapter of their lives.

The Chaplain continued, "Marriage is a sacred bond, a partnership that requires trust, patience, and above all, love. Today, Reggie and Jade are making these vows to each other, promising to stand by one another's side through every challenge and triumph."

Reggie's heart pounded in his chest. How true were those words, he thought.

The Chaplain turned to the Groom. "Reginald, please speak your vows," the man said.

His hands clasping hers, Reggie tried to recall what he'd rehearsed a hundred times. Taking a deep breath, he said, "Jade, from the second I saw you, I knew you were special. It took me two years to work up the courage to talk to you, but every single day of waiting was worth it. I've loved you since the very beginning, and I'll love you until my last breath. You're my heart, my other half, the person who makes me whole. Today, I promise to stand by you, protect you, cherish you, and be the man you deserve. Whatever comes next, we'll face it together."

Tears welled up in Jade's eyes when she smiled. Hearing him say that now made everything more real. He wasn't just her first love—he was her forever.

The Chaplain then turned to Jade. "And now, Jade, your vows."

She took a deep breath while trembling with emotion. "Reg, I watched you from afar, believing you never knew I existed. But then, you saw me. You gave me your heart, and in return, you became the missing piece of mine. You make me better and stronger, and every day I'm with you, I feel more alive. No matter what the future holds, I promise to be by your side through everything, to laugh with you, cry with you, and love you—always."

Reggie's grip tightened on her hands, his eyes shining with tears.

The Chaplain warmly requested, "May I have the rings?"

Without hesitation, Shane handed them to the man, who blessed them before giving one to Reggie.

He gently slid the ring onto Jade's finger, his hands calm despite the emotion coursing through him. Repeating what the man prompted, he said, "With this ring, I marry you, Jade. You are my heart, my soul, my everything."

About to watch Jade place the ring on Reggie's finger, Abi noticed a man walking along the outside edge of the chapel. Seeing only his lower body through the slender glass, it wasn't his presence that alarmed her, but the rhythmic tapping of the cane against the stone path and the unmistakable tattoo on his hand.

Abi pointed fearfully, barely able to contain herself.

Catching a glimpse of him, Martin got up and issued orders to intercept the man.

Witnessing this, everyone stopped.

Before the football player could even react, Burton's protective instincts surfaced. Having turned on a dime, he put himself between Abi and the door, shielding her with his body as he brought her to the floor.

Seeing this, Reggie did the same with Jade and had her duck in front of the first pew with her Mother. The three guys stood firm, unsure what was happening outside, as Martin moved to the back of the chapel, awaiting word.

"Status, Martin?" Burton shouted, seeing him listening in his earpiece.

"Mr. Wilson? Come with me, please." Having called it in, he closed his iPad.

Unsure what was going on, Reggie looked at Jade. They knew right away.

"Stay here. Don't move." Burton instructed Abi and the ladies before speaking with his team.

A number of bodies dressed in black emerged from hidden corners, each armed with heads on a swivel.

Surrounded by men positioned on the roofs nearby, Lorenzo opened the door when they secured the premises. "He's restrained, but he insists on speaking to a Reginald Wilson."

Hearing this on his way down the aisle, Jade called out to him and pleaded, "Please, be careful!" knowing this had his Father written all over it.

"It'll be okay, babe. Don't worry." Walking alongside Shane, thankful for his support, the two exited.

Outside, the cool air hit the guys before it drifted toward the women who had huddled together with Anton. Abi watched Burton scanning the area while they spoke with the man. Suddenly wanting answers, she got up and stomped away.

"Abi? Where are you going? Come back!"

"No, Jade! I want to know what this guy wants! He's giving me nightmares, and I want to know why!" Bursting through the door, she found Andrew and Lorenzo holding the man's arms and checking him for weapons. Matt was already holding the cane, and Reg had his arms crossed over his chest, with Shane and Burton flanking either side.

Not surprised Abi didn't listen, Burton said, "I thought I told you to stay back," while shielding her again.

"Who is he?" she demanded.

"I have a message from your Father," the man said calmly, his eyes locked onto Reggie.

Unafraid, the Groom blurted out, "So, let's have it! What does he want? This ends here!"

Leery of being in the open, realizing the seriousness of this, Martin interrupted and corralled everyone inside the chapel. The strange man included.

Sirens wailed in the distance and grew closer as the older gentleman tilted his head slightly and studied Reggie's facial expression. "You have dishonored your Father. This is a path of destruction, and now..." The man's eyes drifted past him to Jade. "Your Father knows of your betrayal, and that betrayal is not without cost." He zeroed in on Reggie's bride. "She will suffer the consequences of your actions."

Hearing this, Abi thought to herself, *Death to her.* Was this man and the plaque connected?

With his backup, Reggie yelled, "Is that a threat!"

"To you, she represents your future. But she is also a symbol of your defiance."

Martin heard the sirens getting closer.

The man's eyes flickered, acknowledging the authorities fast approaching. "I am not here to spill blood. I am here to offer a choice."

Reggie's heart pounded in his chest as he glanced at Jade, who froze with fear upon hearing that. "What choice?" he asked.

The man straightened, and for a moment, the tension felt thick enough to cut.

"Your Father wishes to see you fail. But he is giving you one final opportunity to fall back in line. Walk away from this union, leave her behind, and redeem your future. If you choose to stay with her, you are declaring war on your family."

Fists angrily clenched at his side, it took every ounce of his being not to attack. "I'm not leaving her!"

Respectfully offering a single nod, the man seemed to expect his answer. "Then your Father will have his war. I will relay the message." The old man bowed. His eyes glinted with sharp intent as he took in his surroundings in a single sweep. The faint scent of incense spread around them, and in seconds, he moved with an agility that defied his age, fluidly shifting his weight. Then, in one seamless motion, he performed a precise spin to dodge their reach, his feet barely skimming the ground.

"Get him!" Lorenzo shouted, knowing he was about to escape as the men converged all at once.

Not yielding a sound, with movements so smooth they seemed otherworldly, he swiftly ran alongside the chapel's glass window as the men chased the suspect. Then, as if the air itself swallowed him up, he grabbed hold of a rope and jumped from the roof.

The men reached the edge to find him swinging gracefully toward the street below before letting go and walking along the pavement in one failed swoop, only to vanish without a trace. All they were left with was the unsettling feeling of a shadow that had somehow slipped through their fingers.

"What the hell was that?" Andrew said, believing the guy possessed the skills of a Ninja.

The room went quiet, the energy tense as everyone saw the police flood the gardens. Instructed to search the area, the officers spread out but found nothing.

Reggie exhaled, his heart still racing.

Rushing to his side, Jade wrapped her arms around him. "What...What just happened?"

Squeezing her tightly, he knew this was his final warning. "This is it. The last straw. My Father will not stop until he wins."

Left puzzled, the group was in disbelief. The once serene chapel now felt heavy as the threat shifted the mood drastically.

Clinging to Reg, her face pale, Jade's hands trembled, her mind spinning with everything that had just transpired. The wedding she had envisioned felt distant, like a fragile dream that suddenly shattered before her eyes.

Reggie took a deep breath and tried to regroup as the security team gathered nearby. Looking to Martin and Burton for guidance, he asked, "What do we do?"

Strong and steady, Burton replied, "If it were me, I'd finish where you left off."

Finding Jade visibly shaken, he took her aside. Her eyes were glassy, and her body seemed stiff with fear. Speaking with quiet determination, knowing what this day meant to both of them, he whispered to her, "We came all this way to make a promise to each other, away from prying eyes and my Father's control. I'll be damned if I let him take that away from us now." Unsure what she was thinking, he reached out and gently took Jade's hands in his. Eyes softening, filled with love and resolve, he said, "Please, marry me today. Right now. No matter what happens next, I want you by my side in life. I can't promise what tomorrow will hold, but I will love and protect you always."

Jade blinked back tears, his words sinking in. She had always known Reggie's family was powerful, that he had fought his Father's influence in every way he could, but now the danger was real, present. Even so, she peered into his eyes, seeing the man she loved, the man she had always believed in. Her heart swelled with emotion. Giving a soft nod, tears spilling over her cheeks, Jade whispered, "Yes, I will." A small, shaky smile appeared. "I want to be with you—now and always."

Watching from a few steps away, Jade's Mother stood frozen. Her fear, evident. Upon witnessing Reggie's brave, unwavering determination to go up against his Father, she didn't know what kind of danger her daughter was truly stepping into until now. The man with the cane, the way the situation had escalated, was terrifying.

Quickly stepping forward, she voiced her concern. "I fear this will end badly, Jade. I'm sorry, Reggie, but I feel like you're putting my daughter in danger by going up against your family."

He squared his shoulders, his expression strong. "I understand. But I will do everything in my power to protect her. I promise. She's my life, and nothing will ever change that." Pausing for a moment, he stared her way. "I love your daughter—always have, always will."

Jade intervened, her heart pounding in her chest. She placed her hand on her Mother's arm. "Mom, I want this. I want to marry him. Please. Don't make me choose."

The woman's eyes searched her face, seeing the love reflected in her daughter's expression. She couldn't deny the strength of Jade's feelings. With fear still seeping through her veins, she nodded. "If this is what you want, I won't stand in your way." Giving them her blessing, she said, "I love you, Sweetheart," before stepping aside.

Jade smiled, tears still glistening in her eyes as Reg looked on reassuringly, ready to commit to the future they were about to claim—together.

Acknowledging her acceptance, they returned to the altar.

Reg said to the Chaplain, "I apologize for the interruption. Please continue."

In disbelief at what he just saw, the man fumbled through the pages of his book. "Umm, repeat after me," he said to Jade, her hands still trembling. "With this ring, I marry you…"

Saying the lines relayed to her, she ended with, "You are my home, my love, and my forever."

"With the exchanging of vows and the giving of rings, by the power vested in me, I now pronounce you husband and wife. You may kiss the bride."

Reg didn't hesitate. He pulled Jade into his arms, and their lips met in a tender kiss, sealing their vows, their love, and their future.

Amidst it, they heard Martin clear his throat, signaling that they'd crossed the PDA line.

While the world melted away briefly, feeling like it was just the two of them, they parted ways as Reggie whispered, "I love you."

She smiled with tears of joy on her cheeks. "I love you too."

The newlyweds walked down the aisle and stopped at the doors where the men had gathered.

Lorenzo stated, "We must leave. Now."

Unable to stick around for any additional pleasantries and congratulations, the guys prepared everyone for departure.

The women draped their black capes over their shoulders before covering their heads with the hoods. Moving efficiently, one by one, they entered the hotel and descended the massive staircase. Opting not to take the elevators to the parking level, they had the drivers pull the SUVs up close to the front doors. Swiftly scanning the trucks for trackers, the sweep came up clear. Given the go-ahead, they managed to get the bride, Groom, and Mrs. Webber into the first vehicle unscathed. Ready to move to the second vehicle, Abi noticed Burton and Martin secretly conversing. It made her wonder if they knew more than they were letting on.

Communicating to the guys, Martin instructed a staggered formation to ensure they weren't followed. He also told them to keep their eyes on the sky.

Instructed to exit the hotel, Andrew led Shane and Abi out to the truck as Burton followed and got in beside her. Before closing the door, he looked back at Martin and Anton before they ducked into the vehicle behind them.

Surrounded by security, a few unmarked trucks appeared along the curb, ready to escort them away.

Settled in, Shane on one side and Burton on the other, Abi rested her head back against the seat.

Lorenzo turned around and handed his boss his laptop.

"What are you doing?" Shane asked. He had a million more questions.

"Give me a minute," the mysterious DJ replied as his fingers flew across the keyboard, coding something on a black screen filled with varied keystrokes.

"Is that man connected to the Death to Her card?" Abi asked, haunted by it. "Was it meant for Jade, not me? Is that it?"

Upon hearing this, Burton said, "We have yet to confirm that, but we did discover the Death to Her threat is a mode of communication by Yakusa and, most recently, it's been adopted by the Tokuryū."

"What is that? Another version of the mob?" Shane asked.

"Our sources confirmed that Reggie's Father does not have Yakuza connections. He does, though, mingle with a few other crime families around the world. I'm going out on a limb, but I believe the man with the cane and these Red Dragons we keep running into are separate entities."

"So, what does that mean?"

Right then, Burton caught the man's face on the security camera outside the chapel. It was clear as day. "There you are... Gotcha." Burton mumbled and sent Martin the shot. In seconds, he ran a biometric scan.

Seeing this, Shane said, "Hey, how do you have access to that? Did you hack into a database or something?"

Burton didn't look at him. "Umm...Something like that."

A match appeared.

"It says here the guy's name is Tatsumi Kuro. He is a private investigator who works with international clients to gather intelligence within the country. He isn't connected to the crime syndicate." Burton thought for a minute. "I think he was a means of invoking fear in Reg. His Father used the guy to show him that he can run, but he can't hide."

"But why go through all that trouble?" Abi asked.

"Nobody knows their son like a father. I assume his dad knows his weaknesses. Perhaps Reg has a few irons in the fire, and his dad got wind of it."

"Jade said the other night that they need to go to Spain to meet Reggie's ex-fiancée and her new husband. They're hoping to strike a deal that will keep both family companies afloat. But there's a catch—the contract will only go through if Reggie takes over the Wilson conglomerate as President and CEO. His ex-fiancée is in a similar situation and plans to replace her Father as well. Before any of this can happen, Reggie has to convince the board that it's a sound financial move, and they have to vote in his favor to oust his Father. Luckily, most of the board dislikes the man, which could work in their favor. But even if they succeed, the real challenge will be getting his Father to step down without a fight."

"And by the sound of it, bloodshed," Burton added.

"You don't think he will kill his son, do you?"

"No, that would be too easy. The old way is to murder the woman he loves and make his son regret his decisions for the rest of his life. You know, make him live with the guilt and grief."

Shocked, Shane said, "Well, that's just twisted, but it sounds like something the man would do."

"If they go to Spain, they will be sitting ducks. His Father will suspect it, and he'll set them up. Reg and Jade need to meet his ex and her husband in an undisclosed location-somewhere with heightened security." Thinking, Burton sent a message to Martin. In seconds, he received a response. Aware he couldn't divulge intel with Shane there, he remained tight-lipped. "Leave this with me. We'll set something up for him to keep the two safe. I'll assign protective detail for them. Don't worry. They will be fine. I promise."

"So, when are you going to come clean and tell me straight up what you really do for a living?"

Not making eye contact with the QB, he said, "Dude, I work in the shadows. That's all you need to know."

About to ask another question, Burton stopped him. "Don't..." is all he said.

Abi figured it was a good thing she was sitting between them. At least a fight wouldn't break out.

Reading through Martin's follow-up message, he learned that the CIA was interested in bringing down Reg's father, too. It was an interesting piece of intel that would prove valuable in the coming days.

Crisscrossing the city, not picking up a tail on the streets or in the air, Burton's driver met another van in an obscure parking garage. Switching vehicles, they soon made their way back safely to the Park Hyatt.

| 46 |

Reception

Wednesday, December 20
Park Hyatt Hotel, Kyoto

Now dark, they pulled into the underground parking at the Hyatt. Unsure if the others had made it, they got out of the van and moved inside quickly, noticing an increase in security meandering around. Waiting for the elevator, Abi stood sandwiched between Shane and Burton before the doors parted. Soon, they were descending to the banquet level with Lorenzo standing guard.

As the doors slid open, the Komorebi ballroom welcomed them, setting a tone of elegance and anticipation for the evening.

Hotel security, discreetly keeping watch, eyed them up the moment they stepped out. Seeing Lorenzo, they backed off and gave the group some privacy.

Taking it all in, Abi walked through the threshold and smiled.

Twinkling lights shimmered amongst the uplit trees in the corners, adding a bit of magic to the festivities. Fragrant flower arrangements adorned each table, their sweet scent enhancing the ambiance, blending holiday warmth with sophistication—an atmosphere both breathtaking and intimate.

When Martin arrived with Anton in tow, the gentleman exchanged nods with their team, allowing the hardworking agents to enjoy part of the evening off to celebrate the bride and groom.

The last to arrive, Jade and Reggie stepped off the elevators to a round of heartfelt applause. Walking hand in hand, they took a bow and kissed.

Overflowing with emotion, Reggie pulled out a chair for Jade at the head of the table.

Her hand rested on his as she soaked up all the grandeur surrounding them. "The room looks incredible," she said, full of wonder.

He leaned closer. "The perfect end to our day."

The couple shared a loving glance, oblivious to the hum of conversations buzzing around them as laughter filled the air. Everyone seemed happy as they took their seats—everyone except for Burton.

Abi couldn't help but notice the strain in his expression as he sat apart from the others. Despite his efforts to hide it, the sadness in his eyes was unmistakable. Her heart ached as she realized how easily everyone, including herself, had overlooked him. After everything he'd done to make this wedding happen, he sat there alone, isolated in a room full of friends.

Having a seat next to Shane, Abi felt a wave of empathy and couldn't shake the sense of guilt tugging at her.

"You okay?" Shane asked quietly, squeezing her hand under the table.

She nodded with a somber expression, her thoughts still drifting to her friend, whose distant, unrelenting stare only deepened her concern. "Can he sit with us?" she asked, holding her breath.

Her boyfriend turned to the guy and saw him sitting with a glass of red wine in his hand. Feeling for him despite always being at odds, he said, "Sure. If you'd like."

Thankful to hear this, she tried to get Burton's attention and waved him over.

Catching him briefly, he raised his fingers an inch off the table to acknowledge her, but subtly declined.

Not willing to take no for an answer, she waltzed over with the quiet hum of the celebration all around her. With steady steps, her gown rustling, she approached to find his eyes distant and lost in thought.

The ballroom lights reflected off his red wine as he swirled it gently inside the tilted glass. His silence spoke volumes.

"You're not getting out of this that easily," came her gentle voice as she slipped into the seat beside him, breaking through the quiet barrier he'd built around himself.

A sigh escaped his lips as his expression betrayed the storm of emotions brewing. "I'm fine," he muttered, though the tension in his jaw told a different story.

A subtle shake of her head followed. "No, you're not," she said, refusing to be cast aside. "You shouldn't be sitting over here alone."

The sound of laughter from the nearby tables only seemed to deepen the gulf between him and everyone else. He leaned back in his chair. "Don't worry about me, Abs. I'm not sad. I'm just thinking."

Gentle fingers brushed against his arm, offering comfort where words might fall short. "You should have some fun tonight. Hell, if it weren't for you, there wouldn't have been a wedding in the first place."

Under his hard-as-nails exterior, the glass in his hand hovered for a moment before he took a sip and set it down. "Honestly, I'm good. Go back to Coppersmith." He could see the guy staring their way, wondering what was happening.

When she was about to get up and leave, he stated, "Any chance you will save me a dance?"

She replied, "Absolutely."

"Good. I look forward to that," he muttered.

"Me too, but on one condition," she teased, standing and gesturing back toward the larger table. "Come on. Sit with us. I'm not leaving you alone."

He hesitated and cast one last glance at the wine in front of him before pushing his chair back. A resigned sigh followed, but there was a change in the way he stood. Tall, confident, like he was ready to go into battle. "Fine. But I'm doing this for you," he grumbled.

Taking it as a win, a grin spread across her face as the two made their way back to the table. The tenderness of her concern drew him in as it normally did.

When they approached, Shane smirked. "Took you long enough, man," the QB playfully remarked to break the ice.

Burton chose to ignore his jab and remained silent.

Realizing this, Shane said, "I haven't gotten a chance to say it… Sorry to hear about Sara."

He fluffed it off as best he could. "It is what it is."

With everyone finally seated, dinner service began on time as a flood of people elegantly delivered a mouthwatering selection of appetizers. Everything on the menu reflected a nod to the Japanese philosophy of 24 Sekki, honoring nature's changing cycles.

As the night rolled on, the traditional clinking of glasses prompted the bride and groom to kiss each time while friends chatted away, savoring the next course.

Shane especially couldn't stop raving about the peppercorn-crusted beef tenderloin, paired with a smooth squash puree that added just the right hint of sweetness. But when the maple butternut squash soup followed, Abi thought it brought a homey warmth.

By the time dessert arrived, it felt like the perfect ending to a perfect meal. A tempting sweets table practically called out to them. Each treat seemed like a small indulgence that brought smiles to everyone's faces. The whole dinner wasn't just about food—it was about coming together, sharing a beautiful moment, and creating memories they'd carry with them long after the night was over.

Suddenly, Burton showed the faintest glimmer of excitement outside his composed exterior. Gently clinking his champagne flute with a knife, he called for everyone's attention, his voice sincere but commanding. "Sorry to interrupt this celebration." A touch of emotion crept in. "Watching these two today…" he paused with genuine affection before continuing. "Well, it made me realize just how special moments like this are."

A round of agreeable whispers rippled through the room, but Burton's eyes remained fixed on Reggie and Jade. "You both have something that most people search their whole lives for. The kind of love that withstands everything life throws at it and still comes out stronger on the other side. I couldn't let this night go by without adding something personal."

He nodded to Martin, who was standing near the back of the room, waiting for the cue. "You can't have a wedding reception without music. And, of course, that's where I come in. I hope this reminds you both of all the amazing moments you've had and all the ones still to come." His tone grew quieter but no less sincere. "To Reggie and Jade—here's to a lifetime of dancing together, no matter what song life plays."

The gentle strumming of a guitar began to fill the air—the unmistakable opening notes of *"Perfect"* by Ed Sheeran. The melody washed over the room, quieting conversations and drawing every eye to the center of the dance floor.

Reggie stood, his eyes lovingly locked on Jade. With a warm smile, he extended his hand toward her. His bride, radiant under the twinkling lights, rose from her chair and slipped her hand into his. Together, they walked hand-in-hand to the dance floor, moving as if the world had slowed just for them.

While the first notes of the song spilled into the ballroom, Reggie gently pulled Jade into his arms. They began to sway, their movements effortless and full of grace. The tenderness in their steps mirrored the depth of their love. Jade rested her head lightly on Reggie's chest, her fingers tracing the outline of his hand. Every twirl, every step, felt like a dance with destiny—two souls who had finally found their way to each other.

Abi watched, captivated by the romance unfolding before her. Around them, their friends sat in awe, but it was Jade's Mother who caught her attention. Alone, standing at the edge of the room, her tearful eyes never left the couple as they swayed to the music. She held a handkerchief delicately to her face, a smile playing across her features despite the emotion. The pride and love she felt for her daughter were evident, and her presence added a deeper layer of meaning to the day. But Abi saw a fear in her eyes. The woman knew that by marrying Reg, Jade would always be in danger.

Caught up in the uncertainty of it, Abi sighed. Not wanting to ruin the night with worry, her eyes drifted away from the happy couple. It was then she found Burton sitting quietly in the corner, focused on his laptop, notably prepping his playlist. But unlike the others, who seemed light-hearted and carefree, his aura was still heavy. She knew that look. He wasn't just queuing the music. It was more than that.

Her heart sensed something. About to move across the room, Maroon 5's "*Sugar*" pulsed through the speakers.

Shane wasted no time. "Hey, you," he warmly teased. "Let's go." With a confident grin, he took Abi's hand and twirled her onto the dance floor, his infectious energy propelling them forward.

Abi giggled as he uncharacteristically spun her. The melody matched the lightness between them, smooth and easy. With a few playful dips and twirls, their steps were in sync without even trying. Every move was effortless, sweet, and fun.

Burton leaned back in his chair. His jaw tightened as he watched them together. The easy laughter between them stirred something deep within him. Though he stayed where he was, quiet and still, there was an undeniable pull that kept him watching.

For a brief moment, as Abi moved across the room, their eyes met. A flicker of something passed between them. She gave him a small, reassuring smile, and despite the knot forming in his chest, he returned it with a subtle nod, composed.

When the song ended, Abi and Shane parted.

"I'll be back," she said before leaving the ballroom to visit the washroom.

He nodded. "No problem," and went to join Reg in conversation.

Returning not long after, smoothing the fabric of her dress, she was surprised to see some of the men had enlisted the waitresses to dance. Now, with multiple bodies moving to the music, she scanned the room and searched for Shane. But, instead, she found Burton.

Without hesitation, he buttoned his jacket and made his way toward her, confident, effortless, like he wasn't going to wait around for an invitation. Face to face, he didn't miss a beat.

"So, about that dance?" his voice was low yet filled with a playful challenge.

"Now?" she asked, through her excitement.

"Yes, if you would do me the honor."

Hearing this, she placed her hand in his.

On the way to the dance floor, he passed his laptop, and, with a smooth motion, he hit play.

When they made their way to the center of the room, Abi was aware of Shane watching from the bar. Raising an eyebrow, he didn't look away for a second.

The soft strums of Kina Grannis' cover of *"Can't Help Falling in Love"* filled the air - a gentle, romantic melody.

Abi's breath caught in her throat as she recognized the song instantly.

Reacting the way he knew she would, she clutched her chest and said, "Aww...Burton. How did you know?"

He replied boldly, "I have my ways," and wrapped his arm around her waist, then clasped her hand close to his chest. Moving together in sync, the world around them faded away while the lyrics wrapped them in a soft embrace.

Fingers intertwined, a warmth passed between them as Burton drew her close.

During the chorus, he pulled her in and gently rested his cheek against Abi's temple, causing her to close her eyes and surrender to the feeling it gave. Intimate and charming, neither dared to speak.

Memories of the movie's wedding scene flashed through her mind as they danced, sparking her mouth to curl slightly between quiet tears, just like she always did when this song played.

"Don't cry," he whispered, his breath warm against her ear. "It's okay."

Breaking from her emotions, she whispered, "I can't help it. This song. It gets me every time." Her eyes glistened as she spoke.

"I know. I was ready for it."

Filled with tenderness, his eyes searched hers, and for a moment, the space between them seemed to narrow.

Swaying effortlessly, Abi got lost in the smoothness of his movements. His hand, firm but gentle, rested around her waist, guiding her with a grace that unexpectedly left her breathless. Every note, every verse of the song, felt like it was enhancing their connection.

"I didn't get a chance to tell you earlier..." he paused. "You look beautiful tonight."

"That's sweet of you to say. You're pretty handsome yourself."

He nodded appreciatively. Feeling an awkwardness between them, he added, "The past couple of days have been..."

She finished his sentence. "A lot..."

Hoping she would elaborate, he asked, "Coppersmith giving you a hard time?"

Not wanting to start anything, she said, "No. I think it's the other way around."

"What do you mean?"

"Spending so much time with you...has caused a bit of strain."

"We haven't done anything wrong, Abs."

"I know..." Needing to change the course of their conversation, Abi looked at the newlyweds. "They are so happy," she said whimsically.

"Seeing them makes me realize I have so much yet so little," he admitted with raw honesty.

"Burton, don't dwell on what you don't have. Just be grateful for what you do." Her heart ached upon hearing that. "You have so much to offer, and one day, when the time is right, someone worthy enough will come into your life. And I'm certain that person will love and cherish you forever."

Focused on Abi, he saw her maturity once again shining through, always emphasizing the silver lining in every aspect of life.

"Opening your heart to someone is risky, but it's also the only way to find your happily ever after," she encouraged while her thumb gently brushed over the back of his hand. "You deserve someone who sees how incredible you really are."

"Is that right?" His eyes searched hers for more reassurance.

"Absolutely," she replied. "You're funny, beyond smart, and so talented. And that is what makes you extraordinary. I've seen how much you care for those around you. And I'll never be able to repay you for what you've done for me."

Hearing that caused a glimmer of emotion to shine through. "You never have to repay me, Abs. I'd do it all again in a second."

She felt his intensity. "See, that's what I mean," she said, her heart racing as the dance continued. "Someone else will come along and see that immediately. It might take time, but in the end, do you not think love is worth the wait?" She could see a flicker of hope in his eyes.

"You make it sound so easy."

"When it's right, everything will just fall effortlessly into place," she replied, tilting her head slightly.

"Does Coppersmith get these pep talks, too?"

She giggled. "Sometimes. His are mostly football-focused."

"Well, I appreciate the encouragement. Guess we will have to wait and see what the future holds."

With the final notes of the song fading into the air, the spell around them began to break, and reality slowly seeped in.

From the corner of the room, Jade and Reggie exchanged a knowing glance, noticing the undeniable chemistry brewing between the two. Finding Shane, they could see his brow furrow unhappily, knowing he hated seeing the guy embracing Abi so tightly in his arms.

Inching to the edge of the dance floor, Jade stood with tearful eyes, sensing their connection, validating her hunch all along.

The track changed as they parted ways.

Still close to her, gratitude filled the air as he said, "Thank you for the dance."

"Thank you," she replied, feeling something blossoming between them.

Letting go of Abi, he rested his hand along her lower back to escort her to their table. She smiled until she met Shane's stormy expression. It caused an icy dread to creep in.

Upon pulling out the chair for Abi beside the guy, Burton gestured for her to sit before leaving to speak with Martin and Andrew. He knew he needed to avoid Coppersmith for a while.

As the infamous guy walked away, for Shane, the chatter around them felt distant, drowned out by something brewing within him. Tired of the constant conflict erupting between him and Burton, his eyes darkened with a mix of hurt and frustration. It made it difficult to look Abi in the eye.

"Why are you mad?" she asked with concern.

"I'm not mad," he replied, fairly guarded. "It was just hard to watch."

Defending her actions, she retorted, "I think you're overreacting."

"Really? It's not how I see it." He raised an eyebrow, skepticism written across his features.

"I did nothing wrong. It was just a dance."

With a great deal of hesitation, he said, "After what happened to-day, I want you to keep your distance from him."

In disbelief, she stared him down. "I can't do that."

"He's dangerous, Abs."

Angry, as those words sank in, she turned and found Burton with his eyes on her. Needing to keep the peace, not wanting to cause a scene, she heard Michael Bublé's *The Way You Look Tonight* playing softly in the background. Wanting to bypass what he just said, forcing a smile to tug at her lips, she seized the moment and confidently leaned in. "I love this song. Will you dance with me? Please?" she pleaded.

Willing to go to battle for her heart, Shane turned to Burton, determined not to show defeat. *Two can play this game,* he thought upon seeing the anticipation in her eyes. It was hard to resist. Challenged, he knew he had to match her carefree spirit to keep control over what was happening that night. Silently standing, he obliged.

Relieved, she slipped her hand into his and walked to the middle of the floor.

Inching closer to his large frame, she clung to his hand as he wrapped his arm around her waist and pulled her in lovingly.

The lyrics of the song made him appreciate how beautiful she was in the evening gown, so much so that it took his breath away. "I'm sorry," he said. "When it comes to that guy, I get very protective."

"I understand," she replied reassuringly. "But you don't have to worry about him."

With a hint of disbelief, he said, "So, you say..."

"Well, it's true."

"You know he makes my guard go up. That isn't new."

Desperate to change the subject, Abi diverted their conversation. "You know what movie this song is from?"

Shane thought for a minute. "Is it recent or old school?"

"Umm, in between."

Not knowing what she was thinking of, he said, "Tell me."

She whispered in his ear. "It's from *First Daughter*, the movie where the President's daughter falls in love with her secret service agent."

Shane raised an eyebrow, still holding her close as they swayed to the music. "Secret service, huh? So, what are you saying? I'm the bodyguard?" He grinned, but there was a hint of seriousness.

Her eyes sparkled with affection. "Perhaps," she said, recalling her favorite part in the movie. "In the final scene, the girl is all dressed up at a Christmas ball, much like tonight, and they dance together so wonderfully to this song. Their eyes locked on one another like no one else exists. Sadly, they know they can't be together – yet – but hold out hope for the future."

When she smiled, he melted. "Sounds like a love story doomed to fail." Knowing their future seemed questionable with everything going on, he said, "It's not like that for us, though, is it?" Holding his breath, he waited to hear her answer.

Abi shook her head as her hand slid up to rest on his shoulder. "I hope not." Saying that made her think about their relationship and how their lives would get complicated in the coming months.

He got quiet as his hand loosened around her waist. "Are you having doubts… About us, I mean…"

"Umm, no. But we do need to discuss the future sooner rather than later," she whispered, her heart beating faster.

"I agree," he paused. "Remember, nothing is set in stone. We can always mold a future that benefits us both. I would never ask you to sacrifice anything for me. Understand?"

She nodded tearfully.

His lips met hers in a loving kiss despite the PDA rule. Filled with tenderness, it sent a surge through her entire body while her fingers traced the back of his neck.

Parting ways upon getting lude glances from the staff, Shane kept his forehead resting against hers. As his eyes opened slowly, there, across the room, was Burton—frozen in place. His expression was calm, but it said more than words ever could.

A smirk crept across Shane's face. Staring directly at the guy, he silently claimed his victory, showcasing the obvious - *Abi is still with me.*

It caused Burton to walk away.

Gently turning back to Abi, cheek to cheek, he whispered, "No matter what happens, we will be okay. I'll make sure of it."

Nodding as she looked up into his eyes, Abi couldn't help but feel hopeful, but as she caught Burton departing, her heart strangely felt torn.

Seeing this, Shane said, "I think I'm protective of you because you mean everything to me." Moving her chin to bring her back to him, he added, "And seeing you dancing with someone else was like a million stabs to the heart.

She blinked, surprised by his honesty. "You shouldn't feel that way. No matter who I dance with, I will always return to you."

His eyes flicked to hers. "I'll hold you to that."

Not sure what to make of his actions, she kissed his cheek.

Shane leaned down and pressed his forehead gently against hers again.

Her eyes closed. "I do love you."

"I love you, too, Abs," he whispered. "More than you'll ever know." Squeezing her tight, he whispered, "You really do look amazing. Like you belong in a fairy tale."

Her cheeks flushed. "Thank you. So that means you're my prince?" she teased, a playful glint in her eyes.

"Hopefully so."

Their gaze deepened as they swayed to the music. With one track ending and another beginning, it seemed nobody else existed, while the upbeat tune of *I've Had The Time Of My Life* filled the room.

Shane, with a mischievous grin, suddenly grabbed Abi's hand and twirled her twice with a playful spin.

A series of giggles escaped her as she stumbled slightly before catching her balance.

The energy in the room increased as their friends got drawn in by the infectious vibe of the iconic song.

Jade, always the life of the party, took it a step further and waved over some of the catering staff to join in. In no time, the security team and Anton were up dancing, creating a carefree whirlwind of laughter and joy. Even Martin and Mrs. Webber circled the floor regally.

Always in sync, the newlyweds playfully recreated the iconic moves from *Dirty Dancing*, their rhythm flawless and filled with undeniable chemistry.

The group cheered them on, clapping in time with the music as the room buzzed with excitement.

Burton approached the bar, his eyes locked on Abi more than Shane. A small, unamused smirk erupted as he watched the guy sweep her effortlessly across the dance floor. Despite knowing full well that he should look away, he couldn't. The rivalry between him and the QB had never truly faded—this only proved it.

But this wasn't about the past. It wasn't about old conflicts and run-ins with him. This was something else entirely.

His expression focused as a slow, quiet resolve settled in. For months, he'd kept his distance, convincing himself it was for the best. But watching her now, caught in the middle, not even realizing what was happening, he knew one thing for certain. Some battles were worth fighting, and this was one of them.

| 47 |

Midnight

Early Thursday, December 21

Park Hyatt Hotel, Kyoto

As the evening drew to a close, everyone retreated to their rooms on the top floor of the luxurious hotel while Martin made arrangements for Jade's Mother to stay with them.

The first to leave the reception, a hollow silence met Burton as he locked the door of his suite. The emptiness cloaked him like a heavy blanket. "It was inevitable," he murmured to the stillness, his heart feeling a mixture of regret and relief.

At the end of the hall, Abi heard his door close as the sound echoed toward them. She felt bad that she didn't get a chance to say good-night, but he'd slipped away unnoticed, and sadly, she hadn't realized.

Gathered with the newlyweds outside their rooms, they watched the security team begin their rounds.

"Congratulations again. We love you," Abi said, hugging her girl-friend.

"Thank you for everything, Abs. Love you guys, too," Jade replied, clinging to her tightly.

Shane offered his best friend a manly dap and pat on the back. "Yeah, congrats, man." Switching with Abi, he hugged the bride, and Abi did the same with the groom.

Parting ways, holding Shane's hand, Abi said, "Will we see you tomorrow?"

The two looked at each other.

"Maybe. Maybe not." Jade mischievously embraced her husband. "We might hide out for the day."

"No, we can't, Babe. Shane has his signing announcement," Reg reminded her.

"Yeah, big day tomorrow." Shane tapped their card on the reader while Reg carried his wife over the threshold.

"We will be there, Shane!" the girl giggled before disappearing into the room.

As they walked into their suite, the door slid closed with a click.

Shane began unbuttoning his shirt. His mood was in stark contrast to the festive energy that had filled the ballroom an hour earlier.

Sensing his frustration, Abi ducked into the bathroom. Shedding her elegant dress for a soft nightgown and robe, she washed her face as thoughts of Burton and his breakup with Sara swirled in her mind. Her feelings for Shane weren't far behind.

A soft knock interrupted her. "Can I come in and brush my teeth?" he asked, his voice strained.

"Sure," she replied, heart racing as he stood beside her, silent.

It was hard to fathom how one dance could change everything.

Going through the motions, neither of them said a peep. Taking turns using the water closet, Shane flipped off the lights while they walked into the bedroom and slipped under the covers. With his back turned to her, it was a physical symbol of the emotional distance that had grown between them over the past few hours.

Abi whispered, "Hey, umm…"

"What, Abs?" he replied, irritation creeping into his tone.

"Don't be mad. It was just a dance."

"No, it wasn't..." he countered, rolling onto his back. "Do you know how hard it was to watch you with him like that? That wasn't two friends dancing; that was two people in love."

A knot formed in Abi's stomach as each syllable landed like a stone.

"Do you have something to tell me? This seems to be an ongoing thing with us. There are times I feel like you are all mine, and then there are times I know you're not. I hate it," Shane admitted, bitterness weaving in. "What's worse is I can't compete with him. He's got enough money to fund a small country and genius-level smarts. I'm just a high school jock hoping to make the NFL."

"It's not like that," Abi protested, her heart aching.

"Yes, Abs, it is. That's the truth." He turned his back on her again, closing himself off completely. "I've gotta get some sleep. I have to be rested for tomorrow."

The finality of it hung heavily in the air, unyielding and cold.

"Goodnight," she said, as the space between them felt vast and insurmountable.

Each heartbeat echoed with unresolved emotions. Unable to bridge the gap and reassure him, Abi felt equally lost in her swirling thoughts. Taking a chance, she inched up behind him and wrapped her arms around his waist. To her surprise, he didn't turn her away. Cuddled up, she rested her head against his back. Able to hear his heartbeat, it increased the second she drew closer. Giving it time, she hoped all of this would blow over by morning.

| **48** |

The Big Announcement

Thursday, December 21

Park Hyatt Hotel, Kyoto

Shane woke early, long before the first light of dawn crept through the curtains. The room was still dark, filled only with the faint hum of the city beyond their window. Slipping out of bed, careful not to disturb Abi, his mind raced, still caught in the storm of their unresolved conversation from the night before. Quietly, he changed into his running clothes and headed for the door, glancing back at her one last time before sneaking out into the cool morning air.

Hearing the sound of the door closing behind him, Abi stirred. Her chest felt heavy, and the memory of their argument lingered, filling the room with an uncomfortable weight. Lying there alone, she stared at the ceiling, her thoughts a tangled mess of regret and confusion.

The minutes ticked by, the silence almost deafening. Abi tried to push away the anxious thoughts clawing at her mind, but they wouldn't let go. *Was there even a way to fix things?* she thought, rolling over onto her side, clutching the blanket close, wishing for some kind of clarity, for an answer that would make everything go back to the

437

way it was. Eyelids fluttering shut in the peacefulness, she drifted off slightly.

A little while later, the familiar sound of the door startled her. He was back. She intently listened as he moved through the room, his footsteps light. It wasn't long before the water turned on, and she heard the steady flow of the shower.

Sitting up in bed and leaning against the pillows, she watched the morning light begin to spill through the windows, but it did little to ease the tension that had settled deep in her heart.

He's dangerous. These words replayed over and over again. What was she supposed to say to that? Burton wasn't the problem. The circumstances of his work made things questionable, yes—but the man himself had nothing but good intentions. If anything, he was doing his best to keep her safe.

Still, she could see why Shane thought the way he did. He was on the outside, not part of the inner circle, not privy to the truths she had come to know. Part of her wanted to tell him, to clear the air so they could stand on level ground again. But that would mean betraying Burton's trust, and she couldn't do that—not now, not ever. Aware that she and Shane had managed to weather tough moments before, she felt this was different—like a breaking point.

The water shut off, and soon Shane emerged from the bathroom, already dressed and avoiding her gaze.

The knock at the door came just in time, the hotel staff delivering breakfast.

He dealt with the delivery and wheeled the cart over to the table, his movements almost robotic.

When their eyes finally met, she could feel the distance that had developed between them - something she hadn't felt before.

"How was your run?" Abi greeted nervously.

"Good. Peaceful." That was all he said before sitting down and focusing on his plate of eggs and orange juice.

Feeling the familiar knot in her stomach, she gingerly walked over and sat across from him. As she lifted the lid off her plate and set it on the table, her appetite just wasn't there.

The silence stretched on, thick and heavy. Finally, Shane spoke, pointing out the window. "I explored the town just over there," he said, noticeably detached.

Unsure of how to respond, Abi nodded at Shane.

"Want to go for a walk with me? There's a temple not far from here. I'm sure you'd like to see it." Not making eye contact with her, he took a sip of his juice. "And...I think we need to discuss a few things along the way."

Her heart sank, knowing this wasn't going to be an easy conversation. "Sure," she said. "We can do that."

When she finished the last bite of her breakfast, Abi couldn't shake the uneasy feeling. It was like this could end up being the beginning of the end if she weren't careful.

Slipping quietly into the bathroom to get ready, the warmth of the shower offered a brief reprieve from her swirling thoughts. Steam filled the small space as she mentally prepared for their impending talk.

"Harvard might end up being the least of our problems," she muttered quietly. "But I need to tell him everything. There's no holding back today."

After drying off, Abi applied a little makeup and pulled her hair into a low ponytail so she could comfortably wear her winter hat. As she got dressed, her mind returned to Shane.

How will he react? Will this push us further apart? She wasn't sure, but it was time for the whole truth.

Once ready, she grabbed her coat, stuffing her mitts and hat into her crossbody bag. Turning to him, she said, "Okay. I'm ready," nerves wavering beneath the surface.

Sitting on the bed with his jacket draped over a chair, Shane stood and put it on before zipping it closed.

As they opened the door to leave, they found Andrew and Matt standing in the hallway, blocking their path.

Andrew's sight bounced between the two, his eyes narrowing ever so slightly. "Where are you off to, Miss?" he questioned, though his attention remained fixated on Shane.

Abi kept it light despite the weight in the air. "Just going for a walk in the village."

Eyebrow raised, he replied, "Sorry, but we've got orders to escort you."

Frustration bubbling over, Shane exhaled. "Can't you give us a moment alone?"

"Not given the circumstances." Matt stepped forward, his stance firm.

"What circumstances?" the QB questioned.

Unable to elaborate, Andrew's reply was stern. "Look, take it or leave it."

Gently touching Shane's arm, Abi tried to diffuse the tension. "It's fine," she said quietly, turning to Matt. "Just...watch from a distance, okay?"

He gave a small nod. "We'll do our best, Miss." But there was little room for negotiation.

The elevator chimed.

Everyone turned and spotted Martin leading a group of people down the hall. Amongst them, several individuals lugged camera gear, padded tech cases, and collapsible lighting stands, their footsteps swift and silent despite the bulk they carried. Then, amidst a flood of security, she saw him.

Red Dragon, she thought as the unmistakable silhouette passed by.

Shrouded in a crimson hoodie, the infamous DJ moved fluidly with his head down, the hem of his hood masking his features. All she caught was the glint of a silver chain at his neck and the gleam of his watch under his sleeve.

He held the hand of the woman beside him. His wife, a vision of beauty. She wore a black trench with high leather boots, sleek dark hair cascading over her shoulders like silk. Her presence was as cool and calculated as his while they drifted past. Unlike her husband, she didn't hide her face. Turning ever so slightly, she locked eyes with Abi with startling precision, as if she already knew her. Her lips curled upward, not in a smile, but an unsettling expression, almost sinister, before she looked forward again.

Something about it felt off. The scene sent chills down Abi's spine as she watched them round the corner. Curiosity followed. "What's going on?" she asked Matt point-blank.

"Master B has a number of interviews with the DJ today," Matt replied. "They're promoting the upcoming events."

Concerned, Abi kept an eye on the entourage down the hall as the DJ's security guards took their positions. Most remained motionless, their eyes scanning, with heads on a swivel.

Suddenly, Shane's hand rested on her lower back, prompting her to move. "Come on," he muttered. "Let's go."

Hesitant, she walked with him as the men guided them to the elevator and pressed the button. Stepping inside when it arrived, they all rode together in the confined space. Filled only by instrumental music, nobody said a word. Descending to the Residents' Lounge floor first, they transferred to the main lifts. The quiet hum of guest conversations spilled into the lobby as the doors on the ground floor opened.

On their way outside, Shane stuffed both hands in his pockets, clearly unwilling to hold her hand. As much as this bothered her, she understood and gave him the space he needed.

Met by the crisp morning air, the sun's rays sparkled on the reflecting pond to their right. It seemed to provide a brief moment of calm amidst the awkwardness brewing between them.

The concierge stationed at the hotel gates greeted them warmly while their shadows followed at a respectful distance.

Finally, breaching the barriers of the hotel property, they mingled amongst the locals gathered on the historic streets of Ninenzaka.

As Shane walked beside her, she wondered who would speak first.

While wandering through the narrow pathways, the bricks seemed to stretch endlessly beneath their feet. A light mist hung in the air, clinging to the wooden façades of old shops, each selling hand-made trinkets and tea.

Shane's gaze remained fixed ahead. His posture was far from re-laxed. Opening up, he finally spoke. "I didn't come to the charity event on Tuesday because my agents were negotiating something for me."

Caught off guard, Abi turned to him. "Negotiating what?" she asked as the knot tightened in her stomach.

Without breaking stride, he continued. "I have to finish senior year in Huntington Beach. They arranged off-season training with a group of high-level coaches. I need to transfer to the High School there." He paused briefly as the news settled in. "That's where I'll be living for the next six months before I leave for Alabama."

She stopped in her tracks. "You're...leaving?" Her tone came out quieter than she intended, almost swallowed by the ambiance of a few tourists milling around them.

His pace slowed as his eyes flickered to the left to avoid her expres-sion. "It's an opportunity I can't pass up, Abs."

"When?"

"I move January 2nd."

A small breeze swept through the street, rustling the fabric of their jackets as Abi tried to process what he'd said. The future she'd envi-sioned with him now seemed to dissolve, the certainty replaced by a creeping sense of loss. "When were you going to tell me?"

A sigh escaped his lips with regret. "I wasn't sure how to break it to you with the drama surrounding your Dad's wedding and the grief of you missing your Mom."

For a moment, they walked in silence again, the sound of their footsteps merging with the soft hum of their surroundings while the walls of the ancient city closed in.

The men kept a keen eye and stopped every time they did.

Abi's heart raced as questions swirled in her mind, unsure of how to address them.

Finally, Shane stopped and turned to face her. "And, quite honestly, I'm contemplating whether I should stay here with you," he said, eyes searching hers for something—some kind of answer. "I mean, given what happened last night…is there even a point?"

Her heart dropped. "What? Of course, there's a point," Abi protested, her emotions teetering on the edge of desperation.

His eyes meeting hers, Shane's expression was a mix of disappointment and sadness. "I need to know something, Abi," he said, afraid of the answer. "Do you love him?" What he said next came out even softer. "Or do you love me?"

The gentle breeze stirred again, but Abi barely noticed as her world tilted. She searched for the right thing to say. "I've told you," she began, the ache in her heart reflected in her voice. "I love you both… just in different ways. He's family. You are more than that."

Fists hidden in his pockets, Shane had heard this before. "I'm not sure it's enough," he muttered. "I need to hear you say you're with me. I can't keep doing this."

She felt his infinity band on her finger.

Pausing, he said, "Abi, I want you to move to Huntington Beach. The place my Dad just bought is big enough for both of us. It's right across from the ocean. We can go to school together. Then, after graduation, we'll head to Alabama."

Unable to fathom what she was hearing, Abi couldn't believe he still hadn't asked. Angered, the thoughts she'd been holding in suddenly escaped her lips. "I can't do that."

He stared at her, almost suspicious. "Why? What's holding you back? Is it because he's in Bel Air? Is that why you want to stay?"

Forcing herself to look at him, seeing the guys over his shoulder, watching sharply, Abi swallowed the lump in her throat. "No, that's not it… There's something I haven't told you." She hesitated, nerves rattling. "I, umm… I applied to Harvard."

His expression shifted from confusion to something else—a look of shock. "And?" He held his breath.

Inhaling, Abi held onto his eyes. "And I got in. Pre-Med. I'll be attending there in September."

A groan escaped Shane's lips as he ran his hand through his hair. "Harvard..." His eyes closed for a second before he finally replied, "Wow... That's, umm, amazing news."

"Is it? Because I feel you don't think so."

When she said that, he stopped. "Please don't think that. I'm so proud of you. I just wasn't expecting it. That's all." He paused. "This changes everything, though."

She tried to decipher his reaction: "Yes, I guess it does."

"When did you find out?"

"On my birthday."

"And you waited this long to tell me?"

"For the same reason you kept your news from me," Abi whispered, her hands fidgeting nervously. "The way you talked about Alabama and our future there, I didn't want to ruin that for you."

He shook his head, realizing where he had gone wrong. "I'm sorry. I just assumed we'd be together." Analyzing it, he said, "I was so focused on succeeding, I didn't ask you what you wanted. Please know my intent was always to provide for us financially. I wanted to make sure you never had to worry."

"I get it. I do. But it felt like..."

He interrupted her. "Please don't think that." Inching closer, he offered open arms, which she willingly fell into. "Congratulations. This is a big deal. I can't say I'm surprised. You've worked so hard."

"So, you're not mad?"

They stood in the middle of the street.

"Why would I be mad?" He thought a moment. "I'm happy for you. It's your dream to become a doctor. Isn't it?"

"Yes. I hope so."

"Well, then, you need to go and make that a reality."

Her head rested on his chest.

At a crossroads, he asked, "So, where does that leave us?" With a raw understanding of what was happening, he added, "Where do we go from here?"

The once serene and beautiful backdrop now felt suffocating.

"I don't know..." Abi's heart ached, unsure how to move forward.

Shane stared at the ground and shuffled a stone between his feet before lifting his head. Feeling guilty for suggesting he leave her before the holidays, given everything going on, he tried to save face. "Maybe we just finish this vacation, then go back to L.A., and figure things out from there."

Despite sounding so final, at least there was no anger. Just this overwhelming sense of defeat. On the verge of tears, she kept herself in check long enough to respond. "Maybe that's best."

Continuing their walk, side by side, but not hand in hand, both felt the furthest apart than they'd ever been.

The path leading to Kiyomizu-dera was steep, winding through rows of ancient trees and traditional shops. The bright red buildings stood out amidst the muted winter day. Despite the beauty surrounding them, they walked in silence, their footsteps echoing softly against the stone steps as they began their ascent.

The climb felt heavy—each step pondering the conversation they'd had. The heartache wasn't far behind. Both carrying a level of guilt, they soon reached the top, where the majestic view of Kyoto, sprawling below in a blend of temples, gardens, and distant mountains, was bathed in a dull light.

Approaching the balcony of the Kiyomizu stage, Abi's fingers lightly gripped the wood railing as she marveled at the mountains in the distance. Finding it hard to breathe, a tear slipped down her cheek before she could stop it. Their questionable future suddenly hit her.

Inching to her right, he noticed it tracing its way down her face. Immediately, his heart twisted. Without a word, he instinctively pulled her into his arms and held her against his chest. "Please don't cry," he whispered.

Abi leaned in, her body slightly trembling as she sobbed, trying to stop the flood of emotions. His warmth contrasted with the chilly air, offering a brief moment of comfort.

"I'm sorry," she mumbled. "Please don't hate me..."

He tightened his grip, refusing to let her go. "I was going to say the same to you," he said sincerely. "I don't want you to hate me either."

"I don't..."

Pressing his lips to her forehead, he tried to mend their broken hearts.

Chest heaving lightly, she whispered, "Could we make this work? Stay together despite the distance, I mean."

Shane's head snapped her way. "You'd consider that?"

She silently nodded, desperation in her eyes. "At least we can try. Can't we?"

He kissed her forehead, breathing out relief. "If you're willing, then so am I."

Thankful for his loving response, his reassuring reaction helped settle her nerves. *Maybe we aren't over yet,* she thought.

Standing quietly, Shane knew he wasn't just holding her body; he was holding onto their shared dreams, their fears, their memories, and a love that was fragile but still there.

Her security team glanced away briefly to give the couple a moment alone.

Shane leaned back, his eyes locked on her. Ignoring the PDA rule, unable to deny the pull between them, he leaned in and kissed her gently. "I'm sorry," he whispered upon parting. "For everything."

"Me too," she said, seeing a few crude looks flashing around them.

Prepared to leave it at that for now, Shane checked the time. "We'd better head back." A reluctant sigh escaped. "I need to get ready for the announcement."

Abi nodded, her body calmer.

Extending his hand to her, he offered a fragile peace. "So, are we good?"

With a small smile tugging at the corners of her lips, her hand slipped into his.

Together, the two walked back toward the hotel, their pace in sync despite the morning they'd had. The familiar paths and buildings of the historic town faded behind them, giving way to the sleek interior of their luxury hotel. Once inside, they rode the elevator back to the top floor and returned to their room.

Shane checked the clock, calculating how much time he had left. As he paced back and forth, his eyes landed on the five hats sitting on the table, each symbolizing a different path for his future. In less than an hour, only one would remain.

"Guess today finally makes it official."

Abi could tell how nervous he was. "Everything you've done all these years has built up to this. You did it."

He smiled shyly. "If it weren't for you, I wouldn't have gotten this far."

"Sure, you would have. Without a doubt," she swiftly acknowledged.

"Appreciate that, but... What am I gonna do without you? Who will I study with? Get my pep talks from?"

Hearing him say that made her feel like she was abandoning him to a degree. "I'm sure they will secure a tutor for you. As for the pep talks? I'll only be a phone call away."

"But it won't be the same."

A knock came to the door.

Walking over to answer it, Abi found Martin standing in the hallway.

"Is our superstar ready?" he asked, having arrived thirty minutes before he had to make the post on Instagram.

Appearing from around the corner with the selection of hats in hand, he said, "I'm here. All ready. Let's do this."

"Very well. Let's get a move on then."

Nervous energy flowed through him as he nodded.

While they made their way to the banquet hall on the lower level, Martin offered a casual update. "We've got everything already set up for you," he said, referring to the room that hosted Jade and Reggie's reception.

Abi perked up. "Speaking of them, where are those two lovebirds?"

The older man chuckled. "They've got the 'do not disturb' sign on their door. Best to leave them alone until they decide to resurface."

Upon entering the banquet room, everything was in place.

"May I?" Martin asked, eyeing the hats.

Shane passed them to him.

He quickly set them up on the table. *Alabama, Georgia, Ohio State, Texas, and Miami.* Looking at each university vying for his commitment, Shane took a seat in the chair behind the skirted banquet table. Microphones set up in front of him, reality set in. *This is it*, he thought.

Taking Shane's cell phone, Martin installed it in the ring light on the tripod. With only a few minutes to go, he showed Shane the live feed and the pending teaser post on the laptop beside him. Opening a second tab, he pulled up the link for the questions posed by multiple news agencies, which were patiently waiting in the queue.

"Once you go live, you can use the prompt cards I prepared and fill in the blanks if you need," he showed him.

The QB acknowledged with a thumbs-up. Wearing their football team hoodie with a small school crest, he had a subtle but intense look on his face.

Counting down, everyone was ready and in their places. He'd imagined this moment for so long, but it felt surreal now that it was actually happening.

Martin pointed to Shane.

The camera started recording as he leaned forward, his nerves barely hidden beneath his calm expression, while speaking into the microphone with confidence.

"Hey, everyone," Shane began. "I'm Shane Coppersmith, currently playing at Gilderson Prep in California. Unfortunately, I couldn't make this announcement at home since I'm out of the country right now, but I still wanted to share this news with you all."

The room was quiet. The only sound was the soft buzz of the laptop as the live-stream audience grew. Glancing at the screen briefly, he noticed a multitude of comments flying by.

"I want to start by saying thank you to the coaches, my friends, my teammates, and everyone who's been there for me throughout this journey," he continued, as memories of the past few years rushed in. "This process has been incredible, and I'm grateful for every opportunity I've had."

He picked up the hat belonging to the Georgia Bulldogs. Looking at it, he suddenly set it aside when Jade and Reggie appeared.

"To my teammates at Gilderson Prep—you guys are like brothers to me. I wouldn't be sitting here without you. We've built something special over the years, and I'll always carry that with me no matter where I go."

Reaching over to select another hat, his hand hovered over the Texas Longhorns just as Burton surfaced in the doorway. As he teased the audience with his indecision, he tried to stay focused and ultimately set that team aside as well.

Shane paused for a beat. What he said next held more weight. "And to Abi... you've been my rock and strength these past few months. Your encouragement has gotten me through some tough games. I couldn't have done this without you. Having your support has made all the difference." He sounded so sincere. "Thank you for always being there for me and keeping me grounded."

Eyes shimmering with unshed tears, it took a second for it all to sink in. When one slipped down her cheek, she wiped it away quickly, trying to stay composed. But her heart ached. In that moment, torn between her love for him and the uncertainty of her future, everything seemed to shift as her decision to go to Harvard pressed on her more heavily than ever before.

Finally, with a grin, he moved those still in contention closer to the middle of the table. Reaching forward, he hovered his hand over each of them and picked up the red Alabama hat. While examining it, everyone watching thought he might put it aside. But to their surprise, he left it in line with the others.

Going back to the scripted cards Martin was holding, he read, "This decision wasn't easy. I've talked it over with those closest to me. All five of these schools are amazing, and they've treated me like family. But at the end of the day, I have to go where I feel is the best fit for me, both as a player and as a person." He paused. "After a lot of thought and consideration, I'm thrilled to announce that I will be playing for…." Shane hovered his hand over the hats one last time and chose one. "…the University of Alabama. Roll Tide!"

Upon placing the hat upon his head, the room erupted in applause, and the comments scrolled so quickly they were a blur.

"They are telling me to answer a few questions posted by the news outlets that have registered for comments. So, here it goes." He brought the laptop closer and said, *"What ultimately made you choose the University of Alabama over the other universities?"* Without skipping a beat, he took a deep breath and divulged, "Honestly, it came down to the culture and the brotherhood that Alabama has. When I visited, the environment felt different. The coaches believe in me, not just as a player but as a person. I know I'll be pushed to become the best version of myself on and off the field. Their commitment to winning, the intensity, and the standard they set—that's where I want to be. I want to be part of something great, and Alabama just felt like the right place to achieve my goals."

Moving on to the next question, it read, *"How do you see yourself fitting into Alabama's football program?"* Shane ran his hand along his jawline. "I've always been a guy who's willing to work hard and put in the effort, whether it's on the field or in the weight room. I know Alabama expects the best from its players, and that's the kind of challenge I'm ready for. I want to contribute in any way I can, and I know they'll develop me into the player I need to be to compete at the highest level. I'm ready for whatever the coaches need from me, and I'll give everything I have to make sure we succeed together."

On to the next, he said, *"What are your expectations heading into your freshman season?"* He peered down at the screen and thought for a moment. "I believe my main focus is earning my spot and showing that I deserve to be out there. I'm going to go in and work hard, learn from the veterans, and absorb the knowledge from the coaches. I know the transition from high school to college football is huge, but I'm ready to compete."

He smirked at the next question. *"How does it feel now that the decision is finally made?"* He smiled, a little relieved. "It feels like a weight just lifted off my shoulders. The recruitment process was amazing, but it was stressful at times—there were so many great programs to choose from. Now that it's official, I can focus on what's next and enjoy the moment. I'm excited to start this next chapter of my life."

Running out of time, Martin tapped his watch.

"Guess we only have time for one more," he said, perusing the list." Here's a good one." Scrolling down, he read, *"What advice would you give to younger athletes going through the recruitment process?"* Shane's face lit up. "My advice would be to take your time. It's easy to get caught up in the excitement, but be sure to choose the right school for you, not just the program with the biggest name. Get to know the coaches, the culture, and the environment. Make sure it feels like home because you'll be there for the next few years of your life. And don't be afraid to ask questions. This is your future—take control of it."

Looking at Martin, he held up the closing remarks card.

"Thank you all for joining me today. I'm beyond grateful for your support. I know this journey is just beginning, and I'm ready to put in the hard work. So, I'll see you soon, Alabama." With that, he waved to the camera as the announcement ended.

Watching from a few feet away, Abi felt a rush of relief. Shane had done it—made his choice, his next step in a future full of promise. She watched him leave the table with the red hat now sitting proudly on his head.

Soon, his eyes scoured the room. About to head in Abi's direction, his phone rang.

Martin took it from the light ring tripod and handed it to him.

Seeing it was his Agent, he walked away and said, "Hello?"

Concerned about who was on the phone and what they were saying to him, Abi remained close by as he paced back and forth, the phone pressed to his ear. Nodding his head, mostly with contentment on his face, she figured it was going well. But when he hung up, he froze for a split second as it all sank in. Wearing his new team's hat proudly, he suddenly walked over with open arms as she stepped into his embrace, feeling his warmth and strength.

"You did it," Abi whispered. "You achieved the next step towards your future."

Hearing her say that, he couldn't help but wish she'd said *their* future. But for now, he was just happy she was there to share it with him.

Reg and Jade sidled up, all smiles. "Congrats, man!" Reg said, pulling Shane in for a hug.

He, in turn, teased his friend. "Thanks for coming. Didn't think you newlyweds would come up for air and join us."

The comment made everyone laugh.

"We had to get up to say goodbye to my Mom. She left this morning," Jade announced, somewhat sad.

Hearing this, Abi tilted her head sympathetically. "Ohh..." and rubbed her friend's arm.

"It was hard to say goodbye, but I'm so thankful she was here to share in our special day."

Reg took hold of her hand and smiled. "Yes. Everything worked out really well."

Moving across the room, Martin offered his congratulations, proud of the decision Shane had made. But as the group conversed, Abi's eyes drifted toward the hallway, where Burton stood quietly. He kept his distance, watching from afar without interfering. Looking at her, he offered a silent nod before turning and respectfully walking away, knowing today belonged to Shane.

| 49 |

Distance

Thursday, December 21

Park Hyatt Hotel, Kyoto

In the aftermath of the day's events, the banquet hall gradually returned to its normal state, with the hotel staff working efficiently to restore it.

As Abi followed the others upstairs, her thoughts drifted, knowing Burton was likely alone in his suite, preparing for his upcoming Dark Demon schedule. She longed to check on him, but knew it would create tension between her and Shane. With a quiet sigh, she resigned herself to the fact that in just a few hours, the guy would be making his first appearance in Japan—and she hated that she couldn't be there to support him.

When they reached the top floor, they stood in the corridor outside their rooms. Martin stopped alongside them.

Cornering him, Jade asked, "I'm so excited about the NAKKA museum event tomorrow evening. I searched it up. It's a big deal. I was surprised to learn it's such a star-studded gala."

Upon hearing this, the gentleman's eyes reflected a bit of regret. "Initially," he said, "Master B was going to invite all of you, but has since changed his mind. Apologies."

"Did he say why?" Abi asked, knowing he probably had a good reason.

"If Red Dragon's team was seeking a younger crowd to elevate the venue's energy. Wouldn't that mean us?" the newlywed questioned. "It could have been me and Reggie's debut."

Put off, Martin stated firmly, "I'm sorry, Miss Jade. He has said no."

Exchanging looks, the girls both slouched and sighed in unison.

"Are we at least able to do our own thing, then?" Shane asked, secretly happy to hear the news.

The man hesitated. "We might have to reevaluate that upon arrival."

Immediately, Jade was disappointed. "Damn. I wanted to shop for a dress. I had the perfect one picked out, too. The new red Versace Medusa. Figured Laney would love to see that one on me."

Abi giggled. "It sounds a little evil."

"It would have been perfect for something as edgy and bold as a Red Dragon and Dark Demon gala. Don't you think?"

Knowing she was right, Abi grinned. "Guess we can scratch that off our to-do list then."

Always ready to mitigate problems, Martin cleared his throat. "If you wish to have a sophisticated night out," he said, "May I suggest the Osaka Symphony?" Ever resourceful, he pulled out his iPad and tapped the screen. "You can still dress – how do you say – *to the nines* – and enjoy a beautiful evening."

Knowing it wouldn't be as epic as the NAKKA event, the girls looked at each other.

Shrugging her shoulders, Jade replied, "Beggars can't be choosers."

"That sounds great, Martin. Thank you."

"Very well, Miss Abi. Let me call the Conrad Hotel concierge and arrange something for you. I can have a stylist from DAIMARU pull a selection from some of the finest boutiques in Osaka. We can have them brought to the hotel tomorrow afternoon—say, one o'clock? That should give you plenty of time to try on the dresses and prepare for the evening out."

"Can you see if they have the Versace Medusa in red?" Jade asked, hoping for the best. "Please…" she added.

"I will make a note, Miss Jade. What size?"

"Four," she said, certain the man would come through for her. "Thank you."

Acknowledging while jotting a few things down, he asked, "Any preferences, Miss Abi?"

"Just whatever they think is pretty." She thought for a second. "Or, I could just wear the black dress from the wedding. That way, we don't need to spend the extra money."

"Abs…really?" Jade seemed disappointed with her comment.

Agreeing with his girlfriend, Shane piped up. "Yeah, I don't mind wearing my wedding tux. It fit me pretty well. Just need it cleaned."

"I can arrange that, Mr Coppersmith. Just have it ready for the concierge upon arrival at the Conrad. We can have your dress freshened also, Miss."

Both she and Shane gave him a thumbs-up. "Will do, Sir."

"Well, if that is all, I must be on my way." Moving toward Burton's suite, he turned and said, "Remember to keep a low profile this evening. And make sure you are packed and ready by nine o'clock tomorrow morning."

Agreeing on all accounts, Reg asked, "Hey, you guys hungry?"

"Yeah," Shane said, never turning down a chance to eat.

"Maybe we should check out the restaurant downstairs or find a quiet place in the village?" Jade figured, liking the idea of a change of scenery.

Overhearing them, Andrew stepped in. "Sorry. No restaurant on or off the premises tonight."

Staring at the big guy, Jade joked, "Why are you always such a buzz kill?"

Clearly annoyed, he replied, "It's my job, Miss…"

Knowing Andrew thought of her friend as a royal pain in his behind, Abi chuckled, "It's fine, Jade." Making light of it, she said, "We can order in and hang out in our suite. Sound good?"

"Fine..." The teen conceded.

Seeing Andrew offer a subtle thumbs-up, Abi knew he appreciated the support.

"Come on, Babe." Reg tugged at her waist. "It'll be fun."

Shane passed the key card over the reader and entered their room while Reg did the same. Hearing a knock on the adjoining door, Shane propped it open, creating a pass-through between both spaces.

Mirroring a football game on their television, Shane plopped on the bed. In seconds, Reg did the same. It left the girls no choice but to move to Jade's side if they wanted to escape it.

About to place their room service order, the girls wondered what the guys would want. Mulling over the options, they selected the bistro's featured dish for them. Picking up the phone, Abi ordered everything while Shane and Reggie's voices drifted in from the next room, deep in a debate about offensive plays and defensive coverage.

While Abi spoke with the concierge, Jade watched the Nakka event advertisement on YouTube, then glanced over as her friend hung up the phone.

"Do you think there's any chance we could still go to the Nakka event? I mean... maybe if we stuck with security or just went for a little while?"

"Jade..." Abi's smile faltered. "If Burton and Martin are saying no, it's not just them being overprotective. It's for a reason. They see more than they're letting on. And they're not the type to make a call like that lightly."

Flopping back onto the bed, Jade replied, "Yeah, I figured. I just hate missing out, you know? This vacation was supposed to be fun. So far, it's been, well.."

"Look, I get it," Abi said gently. "But I'd rather miss a party than end up a headline."

They sat in silence for a moment, the weight of Abi's words settling over them.

To change the subject, Jade pulled up some YouTube Shorts—cute animals and a few blooper reels—making them laugh until their stomachs hurt.

"I wonder what the girls are doing right now," Abi said, suddenly thinking of Laney, Allie, Ming, and Mei.

Looking up from her phone, Jade pointed out, "Probably still sleeping. Isn't it early morning back home around this time?"

"You're right. It is."

Jade glanced down at her wedding ring and smiled. "I can hardly wait to tell them about the wedding."

"They're going to be so excited for you."

"It wouldn't have been possible if it weren't for you and Burton."

Abi nodded, her eyes thoughtful.

It wasn't long before the concierge arrived. Wheeling the cart into the room, the smell of steak, scallops, and truffle fries filled the air. The guys, still mid-discussion, paused as the scent drifted in from next door. In seconds, the two were peeking their heads around the corner.

"Hey, you ordered already?"

"Yes," Jade said as Reggie stole a fry from her plate.

"Did you order for me?" her husband asked.

"Of course I did, babe." She lifted another silver dome. "Will this do?"

Seeing his friend's endless Steak and Frites made famous by the hotel, Shane's mouth watered. "Please tell me you got me the same."

Abi gestured towards another silver dome. In seconds, his face brightened. Aside from their heavy conversation earlier in the day, he cast a loving smile. "Thanks for thinking of me."

Able to feel the air lighten, she replied, "Sure."

Taking the plate into the other room alongside his friend, he sat down at the table. The small gesture made him stop and reassess what was happening between him and Abi. Lost in his thoughts, he heard

Reg mention the significant point spread in the game. Both knew the match-up was pretty much over.

Shane turned to him. "Should we ask the girls to come in and watch a movie?"

Liking the opportunity to hang out, Reg hesitated before conceding. "I guess we could."

"Hey, Abs?" the QB shouted from their room.

"Yes!" she answered.

"Want to watch a movie with us?"

When they heard this, the girls exchanged glances.

"Do you want to?" Jade asked.

She shrugged and picked up her plate, then shouted, "We're coming!"

The suite buzzed with quiet energy as they settled in. A half hour into the newest Mission: Impossible, the boys' *Endless Steak and Frites* were almost gone.

Just then, a knock came to the door.

Shane got up quickly to answer it.

Wheeling another cart into the room, they saw matcha ice cream profiteroles arrive.

"Aww…" Abi said appreciatively, "You ordered us dessert?"

Holding up his phone, he said, "Yep. I discovered we can order room service on the fly?"

She was surprised.

"Thought after the day we've had, you'd enjoy a little treat." He handed her one of the clear containers with a spoon attached to it.

"Thank you," she smiled.

"Sure thing."

Conversations danced lightly, discussing their meal, the movie, and what the next day would hold in Osaka.

But beneath the surface, for Abi, heavier thoughts simmered. She wondered why Burton had decided against their attending his NAKKA Nightfall event. Had something gone wrong? Or was it not safe? She didn't know for sure.

Seeing Jade cuddled alongside Reggie on the bed, uncertain if he was welcome to do the same, Shane waited for the okay from Abi.

Noticing him, not giving it a second thought, she slid over to give him room.

The mood shifted into a more serious conversation. "Before we forget to mention," Reg announced, "Jade and I have decided to leave you a bit earlier than expected."

"Oh, why?" Abi asked casually, taking a bite of her dessert.

"We are heading for Spain on Christmas Day," Jade shared before Reg confirmed, "Yes, we've got some meetings lined up regarding the merger."

Brows raised, it caught Abi off guard. "With the ex-fiancée, then?"

A quiet laugh escaped Reggie as he ran a hand through his hair. "Yeah, believe it or not. If all goes according to plan, the merger will move forward, and the board of directors will make me president and CEO after ousting my Father. They were hoping a wedding between the families would seal the deal, but obviously, that's not happening - on either end."

Surprise flickered across Abi's face before she turned to Jade, who seemed remarkably calm.

"I don't feel threatened - if that's what you think," Jade replied confidently, sensing the unspoken question. "We found out she secretly got married a few days ago, too, so there's no weird tension. Honestly, I'm excited to meet her and her husband. It'll make the whole thing more bearable."

"Hey, you guys are forgetting a valuable piece of information here."

"What's that, Reg?" Shane prompted.

"Nothing happened between her and me. Barely met the girl. It was an arranged marriage. Remember?"

A smile of relief tugged at Abi's lips, though the idea of an ex-to-business partner dynamic still sounded complicated. "It's like you're joining forces to take revenge on your families for what they forced upon you."

Reggie's grin widened. "Pretty much. But we're saving the companies our grandparents fought so hard to build. My Father doesn't know I have it in me to run the business. He thinks I'm just a mindless kid."

"He's never spent any time with you, Reg," Jade defended. "No wonder."

Not wanting to ruin their night, he asked, "Can we change the subject?"

Jade could tell he was bothered by the conversation.

"A lot of changes are happening this year. Hard to believe. It feels like everything is coming to an end fast," the big QB said, hoping to steer them down a different path. But his comment was not exactly light-hearted.

The subject did not ease their stress.

Yet another shift came suddenly, with Shane clearing his throat and eyes darting briefly to Abi before facing the others. "Actually... Abi's got some news, too." He turned to her. "Are you gonna share?"

Put on the spot, she said, "I, umm, got into Harvard."

"No way! Harvard? Abi, that's amazing! Congrats!"

Witnessing Jade's genuine reaction, a modest smile tugged at Abi's lips. "Thanks. It's still, umm, sinking in."

Ever the realist, Reg eyed Shane with a thoughtful expression. "Harvard, huh?" He paused, studying their faces. "So, where does that leave you two? Long distance, then?"

The air got heavy as Abi's heart sank. "Yes, I suppose so. We will have lots of practice by then since Shane is finishing his last semester in Huntington Beach."

Everyone fell silent while looking at each other.

"What the hell, dude?" Reg was the first to question, "Why didn't you tell me?"

Abi's sight met Shane's as uncertainty flickered between them.

"You had a lot going on with the wedding. I didn't want to burden you with anything." Leaning forward, Shane let out a quiet sigh.

"Apart from that, we still need to figure some things out—there's a lot to decide."

Continuing to exchange glances, fully aware of what might be unfolding, Jade and Reggie had watched Abi and Shane navigate so much together. Now, the possibility of them going their separate ways was hard to accept.

Softening her tone, Jade said, "Whatever you two decide, we've got your backs. These next few months won't be easy, but I'm sure you'll figure it out."

A nod from Reggie followed. "Yeah, distance doesn't have to mean the end. People make it work all the time."

"Thanks, that means a lot." To Abi, the comment was bittersweet.

The pressure slightly lifted as Shane gave Abi's hand a gentle squeeze, though the uncertainty remained.

With food devoured, the soft, golden light from the setting sun cast shadows in the corners of the room.

Shane's NCAA signing earlier seemed like a lifetime ago. But Abi could feel it—the gravity of everything discussed today. While the movie drew to a close, it seemed both of them knew a moment was coming when they'd have to accept the inevitable.

With the credits rolling across the screen, the newlyweds slowly inched off the bed.

"Guess we should go. We've got packing to do," Jade stated sleepily.

Reaching out to her friend, Abi hugged her. "We will see you in the morning, then."

As Shane and Reg offered a manly handshake and a pat on the back, Jade replied, "For sure."

Closing the door between their rooms and locking it securely, Shane walked with Abi back to the bed. Cuddling with her, he stretched out, resting his head on the pillow with a sigh of contentment. "Today was insane," he murmured, still riding the high of his success. "I can't believe it's over. Now, it kinda feels real."

Pride swelled in Abi's chest as she smiled at him, her fingers brushing through his hair. "You've worked so hard for this. I'm proud of you."

His eyes searched hers, but his grin faded when a seriousness took over. "I meant what I said earlier, you know," he solidified. "You're my rock, Abs. Always have been."

Hearing that, she bit her lip as her mind swirled with everything unsaid. The excitement of his victory was undeniable, but so was the looming question of what came next for them.

Turning onto his side, Shane propped himself up on one elbow, studying her face in the dim light. "So," he said with a smile, "What about you, Harvard-bound Abi Acardi?"

"You know Harvard's in Massachusetts, right? That's... not exactly next door to Alabama."

"Yeah..." Shane said, sitting up straighter, his smile fading. "So how's this gonna work?"

The question hung in the air, heavier than either of them wanted to admit.

"I don't know," Abi whispered, eyes locked on the ceiling. "You leave the moment we return home. I wish we had more time."

Rolling on his back, Shane rested his hands on his chest. "So, are we still talking long-distance? Or...something else?"

Abi turned to him, her voice trembling. "I don't want to lose you, but I know what it'll be like for you there. You're the starting QB. Girls will be all over you, and I—" She swallowed hard. "I don't know if I'm strong enough to watch that from the sidelines, hundreds of miles away."

"Wait..." He sat up. "Do you actually think I'll cheat on you?" His voice was firm. "Is that what you think?"

"No, but..."

"Really, Abs? I figured you'd know me better than that." He raised her left hand. "I gave you this promise ring for a reason."

"I know. But, you'll be under an enormous amount of stress, and..."

"And, you'll be there to help me through it despite the distance between us. Besides, being dedicated to you in my mind makes it easier That way, I don't have to worry about any social pressures."

"That is just it. What if you resent me for taking you away from all that?"

"I won't." He shook his head slowly while processing what she said. "So, what are you saying?"

"I think maybe we try. We give it everything we've got. We text, we FaceTime, we visit when we can. But if it starts to fall apart, if we're just hurting each other, we agree to hit pause."

Shane's jaw clenched. "And then what? That's it?"

"No," she said firmly. "Then we live our lives. We chase what we were meant to do. And if, after four years, we still feel the same, then we find our way back."

For a long moment, he didn't say anything. Then he leaned against the headboard and scrubbed a hand over his face. "That sounds like it would be hell."

She reached out and took his hand in hers. "It won't be forever. Just long enough for us to become the people we're meant to be."

He looked at her, his expression torn between heartbreak and hope – the scope of it so final. "Okay," he said at last. "We give it our all. And, if it gets too hard, we pause. But for me, so that you know—there's no one else I see in my future but you."

Tears blurred her vision as she leaned into him. "Same."

Happy she agreed, he wrapped his arms around her and pulled her close, anchoring her in that moment. "Let's just deal with this later. We have ten days left on this trip. We should make the most of it."

Both knew this was a turning point. Their futures were calling them, and for now, the decision was made. Thankfully, it wasn't the end for them yet.

A knock came to the door.

"Room service," the person on the other side announced.

Shane got up from the bed and went to open it as Abi wheeled the carts over to the man waiting.

"Thank you, Miss," he said before diverting to a commotion coming down the hallway, making him quickly move aside.

In seconds, Abi soon saw Burton surrounded by his security.

Dressed head to toe in his Dark Demon attire, her friend moved with precision. The black hoodie draped over his face cast a shadow that obscured his features, making him look like an entirely different person. His satchel, sleek and black, hung over his shoulder, the weight of his laptops and gear secured inside. Even his posture seemed different. His usual casual demeanor was replaced with something far more intense while the men's silent, efficient movements flanked him, reminding her of a choreographed routine.

Suddenly, in a split second, he peered past Shane. Boldly winking at Abi and raising a subtle, steady hand at waist level, he bid her good-bye on the way past.

Afraid to respond, she lifted her hand to wave just before he disappeared in the elevator, his security detail tight to him.

Standing there, Shane turned and watched Abi walk back into the room.

She found herself gravitating toward the large window. Standing stoically, she waited. Soon, amongst the city lights glittering below, she spotted the convoy of vehicles pulling away from the hotel. Disappearing into the night, Burton, inside one of them, was heading to his first major appearance on this whirlwind trip. A mix of pride and worry settled in her chest, twisting her emotions. She wanted to be there and see him on the stage, but knew it wasn't safe. Spotting Shane's reflection, she watched him walk up behind her, figuring he wasn't happy with what had just transpired.

Not speaking, he just quietly stood behind her. "He's going to be fine," Shane said, despite a faint edge of jealousy in his tone that didn't go unnoticed.

"Yeah, I know." Abi forced a small nod and wrapped her arms around her body.

To offer a distraction, he stated, "We should pack so we are ready to leave in the morning."

She acknowledged him, quieter this time, and crossed the room to begin folding her clothes. The only sounds were the soft rustle of fabric and Shane occasionally clearing his throat. They moved around each other, their usual warmth now absent.

When catching him glimpse her way from time to time, each was brief and never lingered long enough to be questioned. To her, thankfully, he didn't seem angry. Just...off. The same kind of quiet he'd fallen into after the reception.

He didn't ask, and she didn't explain.

But he'd seen the way she'd watched Burton leave—how her gaze had followed him, how the moment had occurred between the two. That silent connection. That parting glance. Sadly, despite the day belonging to him, he knew her heart was, once again, elsewhere.

While Abi packed, she couldn't help but fear for Burton's safety. Offering silent prayers, she asked God to guide him through whatever danger lay ahead. The image of him disappearing into the night, masked and unrecognizable, stayed with her. A phantom worry clawed at her chest, stirring memories of Newport Beach—waiting at the house, fearing the worst. The unknown. The danger. It all felt the same. And somewhere, amidst it all, questions surfaced: would the Red Dragon teens return? And if they did...what would they do this time?

With suitcases lined up at the door, their travel clothes ready to slip into the next morning, the two of them moved through their bedtime routines, not having said a word.

Shane changed into a T-shirt and shorts before scrolling through his phone in bed while Abi slipped beneath the covers, her body exhausted but her mind still restless.

Barely paying attention, he remained engrossed in the flood of comments on his ESPN announcement video—praise, excitement, and speculation filling his screen. Face bathed in the glow, his mind was clearly elsewhere, carried away by the possibilities awaiting him back home.

A few feet away, Abi lay on her back, eyes tracing the shadows on the ceiling, wishing for sleep but instead feeling the quiet distance settling between them.

At some unmarked hour, her eyes finally slipped closed, only to flutter open again when the soft chime of the elevator broke the silence. Shane snored steadily beside her as she lifted her head from the pillow, heart quickening while holding her breath, listening. Footsteps echoed down the hall—slowing, then stopping, before moving on and fading toward the far end. She exhaled softly. For a fleeting moment, unease knotted her stomach until relief washed over her. A quiet sigh escaped her lips. Burton was back. He was safe.

Her body loosened as though some invisible weight had lifted. Settling onto her side, she let the tension drain from her shoulders as her eyelids grew heavier. Nestling into the blankets, the faint glow of city lights slipped past the drapes. Despite the beauty of Kyoto, she welcomed the thought of Osaka tomorrow, whispering a prayer that everything would be better once they disappeared into the endless sea of faces.

The Story Continues In...

VISIT MY WEBSITE AT

FOR MORE

YOUNG ADULT AND WOMEN'S FICTION.